Fatal Deadline

by Stephen Michael Berberich

Dedicated to Barbara Kriesler, former Sunday Journal editor
Washington, D.C.

Table of Contents

Chapter 1: Fateful Phone Call

Friday evening, May 11, 2007

He couldn't take it anymore.

Young reporter Christopher Gilley grabbed the phone on the tenth ring, setting aside his weekly pile of Wall Street Journals. At the same time, he instinctively checked the huge clock on the far wall. The monster clock ruled when reporters filled the newsroom. But it was 8:15 p.m. and Chris was alone.

Before he could say hello, Chris was captivated by the sultry voice on the phone.

"Hello Dickie, it's Vick," she said in a quiet, breathy voice.

He heard a slight girlish giggle and faint sigh. Chris was stunned, speechless. The voice sounded delicious.

Who was it? A news tip? No. No one ever called in a news tip this late to the die-hard Maryland Inquirer. *God, it's Friday night, way after deadlines,* he thought.

He noticed the words "Radisson entertai..." on the phone id screen... *Oh wow, the new hotel.* Curiosity runs thick in the DNA of cats and newspaper reporters, even rookies like Christopher Gilley.

"It's Vickie, Dickie? (The voice paused) You knooow sweetie. At the Radisson." The sultry voice became a whisper. It was the most exciting voice Chris had ever heard. No woman ever spoke to the shy, lonely boy that way.

He looked around the newsroom for someone to pass along the call to. No one was around.

Reporters and editors at the Inquirer were always out the door by five o'clock p.m., many by three, content to finish copy at home, and then email it in before their deadline. On Fridays, many didn't come into the paper at all. Copy editors, most of them barely 25 years old, were already home by six o'clock p.m. most days, perhaps, cramming for that MBA course that might ticket a new career path for their superior command of the language. And the Inquirer's editors? If there was a murder after 7 p.m., or the Governor again caught with a high-priced escort, let the Washington Post and TV cover it, they'd say.

Young Chris, only 19, was different. He often stayed late. He coveted his new job. He knew he was lucky to have it.

On such a late hour on a slow Friday, he was puzzled by the voice on the phone. That voice. He listened, silently, his ears drinking in the purring tones of the mysterious woman. She was so friendly, so seductive, Christopher couldn't believe she was whispering to him.

And then, he remembered. Perhaps she was mistaking Chris's voice for that of her lover. That lover might be the alleged reporter and full-time playboy, Richard "Dickie" Randim. He used to sit at Chris's desk. Until Randim got into serious trouble six weeks earlier, Dickie had been the statewide real estate reporter on the business section, now assigned to fledgling Chris Gilley. The editors had to take a chance transferring such a thorny beat to the inexperienced Chris, who had joined the Inquirer only two months earlier.

"Well, Dickie, can you at least say hello?" the voice said, noticeably perturbed now.

Chris managed a half grunt, "Yeah," enough to assure the voice that she had indeed reached her arrogant, yet charming Dickie. Chris hoped she'd just keep talking sweetly. Now it was fun.

The voice was indeed none other than Dickie's lover, Victoria "Peeps" Martin. She was the concierge at the brand-new Radisson Hotel in Largo Maryland, just across the Capital Beltway from the new Washington Redskins football stadium. Peeps was known for her inviting cleavage and skin-tight outfits. Male co-workers joked among themselves that Victoria was a walking peep show. They wagered on what and how much skin she'd show each day in her always sexy office attire in the hotel lobby.

Vickie kept titillating Chris's ear, pausing for a momentary tender sigh, "Guess what Dickie, the hotel is finished and I ... I mean we would love you to come by for a pre-opening tour tonight. The opening is tomorrow night, but everything is set up now. Free drinks, pre-opening raw bar. You still love oysters on the half shell? Yeah you, ... you do, I know."

She ran on, getting more and more excited… "the lobby and bar and rooftop restaurant, … well the view isn't much, just the Capital Beltway really, sorry, and of course … the rooms are beautiful, and we could test the mattress for bounce, as you always say. You are a real comedian, Dickeee boy...Well, you… well, you haven't said a word. Still there, I hope?"

Chris opened his mouth to talk but could not utter one intelligible word. He was getting aroused, and slightly embarrassed. He had no girlfriend; knew virtually no one in his new town of Rhodesville, Maryland.

Irritated, Vickie resorted to street slang, cranking up the volume, "Well, ya comin' or not, man? Ain't chu there, or what? Somebody's with you there, I guess, huh? Who you with, you damned .... Hey, put her on."

Chris stuttered, "De ... Dickie doesn't work here any…mm ... more." He stammered. "Any more in news, that is."

Vickie went silent, then, "Oh, this is Victoria Martin, concierge at the new Radisson. I beg your pardon, sir."

"That's okay, ma'am."

"Where is Mr. Randim? He's supposed to be back from the Caribbean this week."

"Well ma'am, I don't for sure know because he left the pa ... ap paper, the reporting side of things here ma'am to take that vaca ... cation. Don't know why or where he mi ... ma ... might be. He's supposed to be back Monday … in a job upstairs, I think."

"You must be the cleaning staff. Yes, of course, it's late. I'm so sorry to bother you." There was a long pause.

"Ma'am, I'm not housekeeping, I'm a reporter named…" Chris tried but failed to identify himself. She just kept talking rapidly, almost as if on Mylar tape that got stretched in a tape player.

She said, "Okay, will you tell Mr. Randim that the Radisson's pre-grand opening is this evening, with a reception on Saturday night in the Senator Ballroom and a Sunday lunch with Joe Theisman, the former quarterback with Redsk ...? Well, you know who he is. Well, goodbye." She hung up abruptly with a loud click. And she was gone that quickly.

Chris took a long, deep breath as he softly hung up the receiver as if it had been a tender kiss at the doorstep after a nervous first date. He imagined Victoria Martin as a curvy blonde in a tight red dress, cross-legged at a glass table, somewhere off to the side of the hotel lobby next to a brass-plated sign "Radisson Entertainment" or "Events" or something, he didn't care. It was the mental staging that was important. Chris was very lonely.

He glanced again at the monster clock.

8:50 p.m.

The telephone call awakened a boy's romantic notion of love, unfulfilled, on another empty Friday night. There he was again alone in the cavernous and silent newsroom with nothing to do except daydream—usually about winning a Pulitzer Prize for investigative reporting.

He knew that would take time. Chris was so green that the boy didn't even own a home computer, yet. Chris was a prodigy writer and a bookworm from a small town in West Virginia. He'd graduated with a scholarship from Northwestern University's famed journalism school in three years. He was too young to know about former Washington Redskin Joe Theisman, whom Vickie mentioned, or that Joe once played in a Super Bowl and now does hotel and car dealership openings. Besides, everybody in the Gilley family was a Pittsburgh Steelers fan.

"I'll see if I can ..." he said out loud to himself.

Quick fingers at his keyboard brought the lobby of the new Radisson Hotel up on his screen, and then photographs of a guest room, and then that "bouncy" bed the sexy voice mentioned. He slumped and clicked air from his cheek, cocking his head in resignation as he failed to bring up a photo of his ... or rather... Dickie's Victoria Martin, indeed listed as the hotel concierge.

If his old, dull blue Mazda hadn't been in the shop again, he'd cruise by the Radisson, he thought. It would be a nice evening drive, clear skies, spring sweet air on May 11.

* * *

He dreamed that night as he laid on a futon with only a couch, bookshelf and piles of newspapers in a drab room he shared with the cockroaches and mice over Don Quantos's Puerto Rican Restuarante, across the tracks in East Rhodesville.

As he dozed off, Chris tried to remember what Vickie said to tell Randim. But he couldn't. He did remember that voice clearly though, and imagined her lips close to the phone, nipping at his ear.

And then came the dream—the one he always dreamed:

Famous Watergate reporter Bob Woodward is speaking at the podium amid a banquet hall festooned with shimmering crystal chandeliers, "The winner of the Pulitzer Prize for the year's best investigative series for a daily newspaper is Chris Gilley of the Chicago Tribune." "… Gilley of the Wall Street Journal." "… of the San Francisco Chronicle." The dream always changed according to what he'd been reading that day. But on this night, in this dream, his date at the awards dinner was that Victoria woman, the one with the voice.

Chris had no way of knowing that Vickie's voice would haunt him, change him and greatly impact his new job. How could he yet know that her mistaken phone call was a sure sign of serious trouble ahead, trouble for such an untested, novice reporter, who was ill-prepared for his fate? For Chris, Vickie's fascinating, lovely voice foretold of a difficult deadline ahead, perhaps a fatal deadline.

Chapter 2: Dickie's Return

The following Monday morning, early, May 14, 2007

Richard "Dickie" Randim returned from his trip to the tropics as expected to start his new job in public relations upstairs at the Maryland Inquirer, a weekly newspaper chain near Washington, D.C.

Dickie drove recklessly fast into the parking garage, top down on his new sports car. He was tanned and cocky as usual, with his styled curly blonde hair approaching his shoulders. But on that day, he wore saucer-like sunglasses and a stern, determined expression. It was an unusual look for normally happy-go-lucky Dickie.

Also, Dickie's mind seemed to be focused; very unusual. The normally freewheeling fellow was dead set on serious damage control to salvage his employment with the Inquirer. Dickie figured to first smooth things out with the editorial department where he was fired before starting his new job upstairs. Maybe they'd let him return to reporting, though he doubted that possibility. Dickie had messed up royally. Let's just say, his departure from the news staff had been less than gracious.

Dickie Randim was a decade older than Christopher Gilley, yet he was less mature than youthful Chris. Dickie was a total jerk on the job and a notorious womanizer on and off the job.

Perhaps three maybe four people working for the Inquirer newspaper chain had money. Dickie was one. He was filthy rich. Dickie was raised in affluent Potomac, Maryland by Belle and Jimmy Bob Randim. They invested in cell phone startups in the 1980s. Dickies dad, Jimmy Bob, advertised his businesses in the Inquirer and played golf with the newspaper executives regularly. Dickie was not only wealthy. He was charming, handsome and self-centered. Newspapering, as he called it, was a gas, just fun and quite easy when he set his mind to it.

By contrast, Chris Gilley, the reporter replacing Dickie in the newsroom, was poor, shy and naive. He wore hand-me-downs from older brothers. Newspaper reporting was serious stuff for

Chris. It was also rather easy for him to turn in copy, but a challenge to turn in the best news reporting he possibly could.

Chris heard about Dickie's carefree attitude from women reporters who sat nearby and had to put up with Randim's toxic behavior, they said. But, Chris didn't yet know why management had fired Dickie.

Richard Dice "Dickie" Randim, 31, had to leave the newspaper's editorial staff quietly in disgrace. He was forced by the suits upstairs to take an involuntary six-week "vacation." Punishment? Sure. But everyone knew Dickie would spend the time off having fun on his daddy's yacht somewhere in the Caribbean.

The car Dickie drove in that Monday was a new, baby blue Porsche Boxter S convertible. He wore designer clothes. Each morning he doused himself with cologne specially made for him by a former lover, an ex-model at Max Factor he'd met at the annual beauty and cosmetic show at the Washington Convention Center. Dickie never missed an opportunity to be surrounded by gorgeous models, eager for publicity.

Dickie didn't need his salary at the Inquirer. Daddy's trust covered everything. He simply loved acting out the role of a newspaper reporter and voraciously devouring his special kind of perks that came with it: the women, the bribes in exchange for good copy, the gifts, the tickets for the latest shows, sports tickets, and invitations to private parties.

He cultivated sources with ease for all the wrong reasons. He ignored the rules and would do anything to file his stories quickly and get back to playing in his sandbox—his business/real estate beat. Management had their suspicions about Dickie's unethical methods. But the charmer had his way, sort of an understanding among his sources: don't tell, get good coverage.

Dickie Randim was rarely in a newsroom where good reporters and editors work hard and stick to their newspaper ethics, research stories, and write fair, balanced copy. Dickie didn't care about that side of reporting. He'd always compose quickly on his laptop and send in stories with little interaction with editors. Copy editors cleaned them up. He got by with plenty of sources, most of which the other reporters never heard of.

The newsroom veterans were convinced he took favors in exchange for putting opinions of shady characters in print. Dickie was clever enough to hide such deals.

* * *

When the impressionable young Chris Gilley arrived in the newsroom that Monday, Dickie was due back, and the first thing Chris saw was Dickie sitting at Chris's desk and computer. Chris's desk had been Dickie's six weeks ago before management banished him from the newsroom.

What's going on? Chris thought. He glanced at the monster clock and did a double take.

8:38 a.m.

Chris thought, *Dickie's in early. And, he's in my seat! Oh God.*

He didn't know that Dickie had planted himself there to manipulate him. Sitting at Chris's computer guaranteed he'd get the kid's undivided attention. Dickie planned to show the kid the ropes, how to cover the statewide real estate beat with a minimum of effort, while having a good time to boot. Helping train Chris would put Dickie back in good standing with management, he was figuring.

Chris approached cautiously. He walked slowly across the newsroom and stood a little distance behind Randim's back. He was suspicious of Dickie's motives, but without malice or resentment of the strange fellow, whom everyone had an opinion of. He didn't yet personally know the notorious Dickie Randim.

As he walked closer, he noticed that Dickie was surfing the Internet on Chris's PC for photographs of women flight attendants, flashing across the screen in their button-down airline suits.

Chris's long reflection in the computer monitor caught Dickie's eye. Chris came closer to him. Chris's image on the screen stopped between the Air Jamaica logo and the airline online site's search function, yet Dickie continued to ignore the approaching young man. Dickie typed 'Regina Hernandez' over and over.

Without turning in Chris's direction, Dickie said, "She's got a really fine ass." He'd later learn that Miss Hernandez had given the handsome, yet pesky newspaper man a fake telephone number after serving him five bourbons on his flight back to Reagan National Airport in Washington, D.C.

"Hi, Mr. Randim. You're back." Chris's voice hit a high-pitch and cracked.

"Call me Dickie," he replied, motionless, transfixed on the computer's monitor, still facing the monitor. "Hey, check her out. The little vixen gave me a phony number. Imagine that?"

Chris was apprehensive and took several steps back as Randim caught him in the corner of his left eye.

Dickie bent back to greet the boy with a pleasant smile. "Sorry about that Christopher, my man. Little late today, huh? Buses running late?" Randim said sarcastically.

Chris quickly ticked through annoying possibilities for Dickie's obviously deliberate encounter with him: *Darn it, maybe Randim's back on covering news. Does he want to replace me already?* he thought.

"Management asked me to show you the ropes, my man, tell you all my best sources," Dickie lied without hesitation. "What's your day like Christopher? It's just barely Monday—can't be all that bad, right? Bet nothing is going on in your head 'cept gettin' some action from the chickies sittin' here in your group. Where are they anyway?"

"I don't keep their schedules, Dick," Chris said, slightly bolder, having trouble calling a man-size person 'Dickie.' Chris noticed a large cut and a black eye on the right side of Randim's face." Are you hurt?" he asked.

"Surfing accident. I'll be fine," dismissed Dickie. "So, let's go out to my car; show you my side of the beat, the good side. You wouldn't want my best stories to go to waste would ya, now that I've been promoted out of this hell hole? I'm your new PR director. Scary huh? Chris, you ever been in a Porch Boxster rag top?"

Chris felt his body relax some. His only assignment that day was to report on bids for the new physics building construction at the University of Maryland in Prince George's County. Eager to make an impression, Chris was not excited by such a simple story assignment, but he realized it was only part of his editor, Robert "Benny" Bradley's plan of easing the kid gradually into the rough and tumble real estate beat. He was intrigued with Dickie's idea and could bang out Benny's assignment easily when they got back to the newsroom.

In a few minutes and after a dash to the garage led by a hustling Randim, Chris was squeezing his lanky frame into the Porsche while Dickie stood, waiting for Chris to notice him. He posed by his picture-perfect sports car, and then slowly slipping on a suede Ralph Lauren bomber jacket and his Flavio Briatore Formula One driving gloves. While flipping his blond, curly hair back, he slid into the driver seat—the entire performance wasted on a nearly empty, dimly lit garage.

Dickie pursed his lips and turned the ignition key. He revved the 310-horsepower engine, the roar reverberating through the empty concrete stacks—his performance lost and alone in cold concrete.

He turned to Chris, "Here, you'll need this for the real estate beat." He tossed a little notebook from his shirt pocket into Chris's lap. "You'll find the private numbers and email addresses of the people who really run things on my, I mean your, beat. Those are my best sources, my network of informants." He laughed. "I mean insiders, for development deals, politics, and who's bonkin' who. Or is it whom?" he said, mocking Chris. Even Randim knew the new kid was a stickler for good grammar.

But Chris was looking at the source notebook and didn't hear the question. The little book contained only bleach-white pages full of names and numbers, all written in the same ink, all neat and alphabetized by raised alphabet letters on page tabs. It appeared to be a female's handwriting. And the notebook felt new, not a typically weathered and tattered reporter's notebook.

If Dickie had such a book for his reporting, why not just Xerox the pages for the next reporter on the real estate beat? Chris wondered. *Why does he want to help me at all?* He had just a second to ponder before his body was pushed back violently into the bucket seat. He was startled by a burst of speed.

Dickie zoomed off with the top down. "Summer air today, Chris. I brought it back. What's today? May 11?"

"It's the 14th, Dickie. Friday was the 11th." *There, I said his crazy name,* Chris thought.

The main offices of the Maryland Inquirer Inc. were in the new Rhodesville Town Center, a multifunctional downtown redevelopment that was a beautiful mixture of commercial ventures in an already high-density urban setting that regularly paralyzed daytime traffic on Rhodesville Pike.

The Inquirer Company had lobbied the county to include a large parking garage next door to the newspaper's Rhodesville headquarters. The company owned the public garage, while it charged Inquirer employees to park in it on a five percent discount.

Dickie booked his Porsche out of the garage. He blindly raced it onto busy Rhodesville Pike, ignoring a red light. He zig-zagged the car at high speed. He drove manically through old, tree-lined residential streets.

The once quiet homes, now next to commercial clutter, were remnants of old residences of mostly retired Jewish, Italian and Greek retail merchants, who used to run a more homie mercantile Rhodesville. The high volume of traffic within the confines of the pretzel-like layout of the commercial redevelopment permanently trapped original Rhodesville shop owners in the very homes they'd built decades ago, and which used to be an easy walk from their shops. Theirs were the only residences left within the vice grip of steel and glass office towers and twisting one-way streets.

Whizzing out onto I-270 South, Dickie yelled with delight, "That so-called modern Town Center is a joke, huh?" as he began his tour for the kid reporter.

Chris was terrified by Randim's reckless driving and braced himself in the passenger seat of the open convertible. He swallowed hard and checked the tightness of his seatbelt, again.

Dickie continued, "Things look pretty in Rhodesville with the new architecture, but who can get in there and back out without a migraine? ... or a zippy blue sports car? Some mighty good deals from Chicago investors got this pretty little puzzle passed by a rotten county council. Those folks, you will learn, now reside amid million-dollar homes in rural Olney, Germantown, and one near to one of my daddy's homes in Potomac."

Homes? Plural? Chris thought.

"Another councilman lives in a nice horse farm in Middleburg, Virginia," Dickie asserted. "Doesn't even live in Maryland anymore. Illegal? Of course. Elected officials, like council members, are required to live in the state, but official business is rarely done in person. Nobody knows about the Middleburg alien member of this county but me, I guess. Gives me an edge. Got it? They all have something to hide. This kind of stuff is gold for stories kid, great scandals, and great chips to play. I hear you're pretty good."

Chris thought, *Well, I guess Dickie does know some stuff. Better pay attention. Maybe I'll survive this reckless ride.* He then realized that he had forgotten to tell Benny Bradley, assistant business editor, where he was going. His broken voice barely breached the surface, "Where am I going, Dick?"

Dickie seemed puzzled over Chris's annoyed tone, but said, "A real gold mine of insider stories: Loweville, the King's County seat, which is 30 miles around the Capital Beltway in what I call McMansion country."

Dickie continued, "You will find whole neighborhoods filled with half-empty, three- and four-story brick and shingle mini-mansion homes so big some of them hide 3- and 4-car garages. King's County led the nation's suburban counties in $1 million-plus foreclosure homes for three straight years and counting. Great stuff for your paranoid debt-reddened readers, Chris."

"Oh right, Dickie. I'm sure that's great stuff for my readers," Chris replied, feeling bolder and annoyed by all the negativity. He questioned his judgment in going with Dickie, vaguely remembering someone saying that Randim is a "toxic" person to avoid. *Maybe Benny said that*, he pondered.

Cruising south at 95 mph on the Washington Beltway, Dickie's face took on a disturbing expression for a second, perhaps reflecting on a hint of sarcasm in Chris.

Maybe the fledgling reporter wasn't buying what Dickie was pitching. Perhaps his plan to make Chris an ally for his return to the Inquirer wouldn't work, no matter how thick he laid it on, how much he tried to suspend the young crackerjack reporter's state of disbelief. Maybe he was losing Chris fast. Dickie changed the conversation to his favorite subject, maybe to perk up the boy, hot looking women. "Chris, by the way, don't believe all you might hear about me and some of the girls around the paper. One percent of it is not true," laughed Dickie as he adjusted the rear-view mirror to check himself out.

"Oh," Chris replied looking the other way as if he didn't hear.

"You've seen Cushions, Chris?"

"Seen her? I have to sit right across the desk from her every day looking right at her." The conversation had drifted to Melissa

Cushen, the attractive reporter on the paper's county desk. Melissa Cushen, 27, was aptly nicknamed "Cushions" because she always seemed lean forward walking around the newsroom with her huge breasts pointing the way, especially in tight sweaters even in summer.

In his new beat, the shy and often horny, young Gilley found himself sitting every day directly across the desk from the pretty sandy-haired blonde, green-eyed Melissa who was eight years his senior and still single, a miraculous attribute he didn't get. He often let his eyes drift back to her ample breasts involuntarily.

Dickie said, "Man, let me be the first to tell you, first hand, he said as he held both hands off the wheel chest high squeezing his fingers together, "They're real!" He tossed his curly blond hair from his face. He struck a pompous expression and checked his movie-star good looks in the rear-view mirror once again.

"You've...?" Chris began asking.

"Well, you didn't hear it from me. Why that girl is still at the Inquirer all this time and not in entertainment I'll never know," said Randim.

"She's actually a very good reporter covering the town beat, Dickie. Don't you like her stuff? Her profiles of the movers and shakers around Rhodesville are good every week. How she gets so much out of those guys is beyond me."

"Exactly," Dickie said, glancing at Chris with raised brows. "I like her stuff, yes I do." Dickie trailed off into a laughing fit so hard he let the car drift left over the warning perforations cut into the edge of the road and then he jerked the car back onto the road.

Chris felt queasy, wished he was back in the newsroom.

Randim's voice pierced into Chris's head, then perhaps daydreaming briefly about Cushion's figure, "Yea, I like the ladies, sure," Dickie said, "but, I certainly don't get tangled up with the wrong kind when I'm working. Women are just good sources. Remember that. But I do love 'em."

Chris could not help watching Dickie Randim driving and bragging continuously. He found himself shaking his head. Never had he encountered someone so self-absorbed. As he tried to fathom the reckless beast next to him in the speeding Porsche, Chris watched with wonder as Randim's incredibly thick wavy hair blew in the wind, feathering back into a perfect haircut again and again.

He felt overwhelmed and tried to gain some control. “Hey Dickie, do you know Victoria Martin at the Radisson Hotel in Largo, the new one? She called my phone Friday night trying to reach you, I think.”

Chris noticed Dickie swallow hard as he stiffened his back and said, “I’ve heard of her, yea. A waitress or something? What did she want with me?”

Chris was pleased. He had struck a nerve. *Why though?* he thought.

As the newest beat reporter on the staff, Chris didn’t yet know that Vickie was married, though separated, to Johnny “Boss” Martin who was the shadiest developer in Maryland and very dangerous.

Boss Martin was also one of Dickie’s real estate sources. It was a thrilling challenge, Dickie Randim was currently savoring. It made Vickie all the more exciting.

Chris said, “Victoria wanted to invite you to a party at the hotel Friday or Saturday. I didn’t know how to get a hold of you. I thought you were still on vacation. Sorry.”

“Me, a party? Why me?” Dickie was visibly nervous.

Chris was beginning to have fun. “She seemed to be a manager or something. She said she’d give you a personal tour of the hotel. She made a big deal about the guest rooms ... ah ... Mmmm, yeah, (He put his index finger to his jaw and his eyes skyward as if contemplating.) that’s right, said you’d like the bed, I think, or something, she said. This Ms. Martin seemed pretty friendly, Dick.”

Chris sensed he’d finally gotten an edge on the cavalier Mr. Hotshot. He smiled devilishly at Randim and waited in ambush.

“Oh, that Vickie Martin,” said Dickie with a big painful glance to his understudy. “That’s the concierge, I believe. Oh, a real looker, that Vickie, redhead. Stay clear, my man. A real vixen there.”

Chris realized he hadn’t mentioned the name ‘Vickie,’ just Victoria. He realized he was sniffing up a pretty juicy little bit of gossip for the women near him in the newsroom, the Vickie and Dickie story, if they didn’t know about it already. He noticed sweat beads on Dickie’s brow and upper lip, even in the wind.

Dickie tightened his grip on the steering wheel and changed the subject again. “Do you know why they call this winding part of the Beltway the spur? Old, rich neighborhoods wouldn't sell out. And because of that, they couldn't move that big brick structure. That's Walter Reed Medical Center." (He was mistaken.) "That's where all the paraplegic soldiers go. The place is a mess, total disrepair. I wondered for a long time why they never tore it down or turned it into something else. Hell, of a story there, Chris, but you'll never crack the Army's silence kid."

"Oh?" asked Chris, realizing Dickie hadn't followed the Washington Post's coverage of the poor conditions at the famous, and sometimes, infamous Walter Reed recovery wards for wounded warriors. But he stayed quiet and let the Vickie Martin conversation keep sinking into Randim's thick head.

Dickie continued as Chris's tour guide, "If we got off this ramp at Wisconsin Avenue, you'd hit the National Institutes of Health," he said. "Too serious for me. Yuk, medicine. You've probably been seeing stories on smart people who work there and live out in Montgomery, Prince George's, and King's Counties. They bring vaccines and stuff out of NIH to launch worthless little biotech startups, soak up government grants and incentives. But that's about all they do, startup. Never market the shit. Talk with Jean Spicer, cute PR girl at the Maryland Bioscience Tech Council. Make sure to call her Jean Splicer. She hates it. A little tag I gave her at my place over dinner."

Further east on the beltway, Dickie offered, "Over there's the National Agricultural Library, fourteen floors of farm books with a lunchroom at the top. Great place to take a chick, Chris. Nobody knows ya there. The place is crawling with college girls from the University of Maryland." he said. Another lie.

"I don't think Benny considers the ag library part of my beat, Dickie. It's federal government," said Chris.

"You mean Benny 'pain-in-the-ass' Bradley? He's not your editor, is he? Damn, I'm sorry Chris. I worked for the business editor Steve Mothershart on this beat and not Bradley. Steve was cool. Hi let me alone."

In truth, Randim drove Mothershart crazy by missing deadlines after Bradley begged off trying to supervise Randim. His habits were intolerable in newspaper work. And, Mothershart often could not verify Dickie's news tips.

Chris said, "They promoted Benny to assistant business page editor while you were away. They say he's the best. Hey, Dick, by the way, where'd you go on vacation anyway?"

Dickie let it pass. "Yeah, Bradley is a hardass; I think he must have been hatched from an old rusty printing press in the '60s. Big time liberal, too. It's a shame, Chris. Bradley needs to get a life, or maybe a new wife. He's had four."

Chris checked his watch. 10:45 a.m.

Editor Benny Bradley was a fair editor but was a royal pain in the ass to slackers like Randim.

So far, Chris was lucky. Bradley recognized raw genius in the tall, skinny, slouching boy, who only lacked assertiveness to make it in the Fourth Estate.

"Hey Dick, do you have a phone in this car," he asked. "I need to let Benny know what I'm doing."

"Here, I have a Vertu Signature phone," Randim said, whipping out a pink and silver mobile device from an inside pocket of his bomber jacket. He tossed it toward Chris, while the car motored at breakneck speed toward the right-hand lane.

Chris reached his hand out but missed catching the device. It popped up above windshield level. The wind sailed it out of the car. But Dickie stretched his right arm back to snatch the tiny pink projectile from the air.

As he stretched out for the phone, with his left hand still on the steering wheel, the car took on its own path and jerked sharply to the right. It crossed lanes to the right, miraculously missing other cars. It took Dickie and Chris off the highway entirely.

"Whoa! Dickie ... What are you doing?" Chris screamed.

Randim, to himself, said, "Oh damn, not again."

The Porsche skidded sharply into high grass, digging deep into the soft spring mud as Dickie braked hard. The front tire caught on a half-buried old cement curb. The powder blue chariot with the two reporters flipped in the air several times over thick Euonymus hedges and somehow crash-landed upright.

They found themselves on a dirt farm road, 90 feet from the beltway, the two men still strapped in with seat belts, unharmed.

Rush hour continued on the busy road as if nothing had happened. The upright Porsche rested in a cloud of dust, its muscles in idle, and with Dickie and Chris immobilized like scared rabbits.

No one stopped to help. As far as the two shaken reporters could tell, not one car even slowed to look.

Dickie turned to a severely shaken Chris Gilley and continued in denial that anything extraordinary just happened, "Yea, that little phone was a gift from Vi..., that is, was a gift. ... the phone, Chris, the phone? Hey, you okay buddy? Hey, you look like you've never flipped through the air in a Porsche with the top down before?" He forced a chuckle and took a deep breath, perhaps to hide his own terror.

Chapter 3: Down in "The Hole"

Nothing seemed to bother Randim, not his 'punishment and demotion,' not the crash. not the damaged car. He'd likely get another Porsche from his daddy.

Meanwhile, Chris's pale complexion had flushed crimson. He wanted to say, *You damned idiot, of course, I'm not all right. You scared me shitless.* Instead, he thought better and said, "Yea. I think I'm okay. You okay, Dickie?"

"Sure. Lucky, ain't we?" Dickie said with a confident tone, as always. He slouched down into his seat to rest. "I'm fine. Need a nap."

Chris struggled with the car's door but finally sprung it open. He walked back toward the highway, his head spinning. He wanted to vomit but didn't. He had nothing in his stomach. Dickie had stolen those early morning donut moments at the paper before they left. He fell to the grass and tried to compose himself.

Dickie turned off the engine and leaned back in the leather bucket seat with the steering wheel pinching his crotch.

The crazy fool is sleeping, Chris thought when he looked back at the mangled car. He got on his feet and decided to look for the flying phone. The pink thing left Dickie's hand on the second flip of the car.

Chris gave Dickie time. He started to relax near roaring beltway traffic by looking for familiar signs of mid-spring emerging in the grassy edge along the highway—a botany study habit he'd practiced in open fields since childhood.

He spotted deep blue-green field cress, ground ivy sprigs, second leaves of smartweed and feather-like Achillea. After 20 minutes of combing through the weeds, he found the phone, almost a letdown after his brief escape in Nature, the best part of his day so far.

He jumped again into Dickie's deathtrap where Randim was sleeping like a baby. "Hey, Mario Andretti. Wake up. Pit stops over."

"Let's get the hell out of here," Randim said. He put the beat-up car in first gear and slowly made his way down the narrow dirt road. It turned out to be a long homestead driveway lined with mature red and white cedars. They had landed on the last working farm in north King's County, the Claggett farm. Dickie wheeled around in a circle at the farmhouse. "Mmm, I think I know this place," he said.

"How do you work this thing?" Chris asked, holding the pink cell phone, "I wanna call Benny."

"Oh, it's easier if I dial. Don't want to damage it. This baby's got a sapphire crystal screen and ruby bearings beneath the keypad."

"What?" Chris could not fathom such ridiculous bragging continuing from his companion after what just happened to them.

Dickie continued, "But I don't want to talk with Mr. H. L. latter-day Mencken. Here, take it."

Chris, confused, took the phone.

"Hello Benny, this is Chris. Hey, I forgot to tell you I'm on my way to Loweville to cover a story at the courthouse. ... Oh, ah ... it's an anonymous tip about vacant developments." Chris watched Dickie give him a cross look. "Oh, my car? Yeah, well, not yet. ... I got a ride ... Oh, ... ah, with Dickie, he's back. What's that? Yeah, Richard Randim."

He put his hand over the phone and offered the phone to Dickie. "He wants to talk with you."

Dickie ignored him. He was about to greet a farmer who had climbed down from his front porch and was walking toward the beat-up convertible, which had trespassed on his property. He wore dusty overalls and was eating a juicy red apple, wet spots on his clothes.

Instead of greeting the man, Dickie turned away from the farmer rudely and grabbed the phone from Chris, keeping the suspicious property owner standing idly by. "Hello, Bradley. This is Dickie. Hey man, don't tell the suits upstairs that I'm back yet, okay? I wanna surprise them. ... Chris? Yes. I know he's new. I was worried about you guys. Didn't want the latest on the stories I left dangling, sources hanging loose, you know, so I grabbed your boy for a little real estate tour. Okay?"

He knew Bradley would report him to management a nanosecond after their conversation. Just to irritate the fussy New Englander Benny Bradley, Dickie continued in his best fake Virginian hill-country accent he could conjure up. He was from Northern Virginia, not the Virginia mountains, and was practically a Yankee himself.

"Bradley, you know that human stem cell science deal with Governor Guy Scruppels? I know who caved on the legislation. Let me tell you, buddy, it wasn't Bishop O'Toole. You want the story? ... Okie dokie, bye bye."

He gave the phone back to Chris, "He wants to talk to you again."

Bradley was upset, but contained and said, "Chris, what the hell? I don't know how Randim talked you into a joy ride, but…."

"No, no, Benny. I am getting a lift to my story. Dickie's just chauffeuring me," Chris answered. He had not lied to Benny before and it stung.

Dickie's irreverent attitude was contagious. The lie stuck deep into Chris's conscience. Bradley would know that absolutely nothing was happening at the courthouse on a beautiful Monday morning in spring except for the tee times attorneys scheduled to kiss up to judges on the links.

But, Bradley conceded, "Whatever. Just be careful. I can show you the beat anytime, Chris. Just get back here in one piece. We need you, kid."

Chris was elated. In his embryonic journalism career, no one had yet said they needed him. Some people at the Inquirer considered him a bad hire, a loser, too young. Now, he knew for sure that Benny Bradley thought he was worthy and was on his side.

They drove off in a cloud of dust, leaving the farmer's face contorted from the dry earth dug up by the racing tires and Dickie's disrespectful send-off, "We're with the Inquirer, Pops. We're on deadline. Bye."

Chris glanced back to see the farmer toss his apple core angrily and a wave of disgusted good riddance.

* * *

The King's County seat of Loweville had always been a town without a modern government office building because of its colonial tradition, which was historically secure until Boss Martin arrived.

Colonials built it on a country trade road that ran from the hills of Piedmont to the lower end of the 110-mile Patuxent River, more than 100 miles west of its origins northwest of Baltimore. The road served agrarian colonials' land, to the Chesapeake Bay and early shipping piers. The state's founding fathers picked the exact center of King George's grant to establish a governing town on the trading road. They chose a fertile valley near the river and called it Loweville, named for their surveyor and a distant cousin of the colonial governor. The surveyor, Thomas Lowe, was a fraud. He was later convicted of robbing and killing a real land surveyor and stealing his credentials as he held up a carriage on the very road he suggested to his cousin, the governor.

At the time of the siting, the location seemed like a good decision, but it must have been conceived in a colonial tavern during a sweltering summer drought.

As it turned out, the topography of the valley at Loweville often acts as a cauldron of fast-running streams that flood the town every third spring. County offices and the District Courthouse share Main Street with 250-year-old structures holding retail stores and attorney's offices. Those are mostly empty, sort of ceremonial, until the state legislature or county council convenes.

Driving the damaged Porsche to the edge of Loweville, Dickie Randim and an exasperated Christopher Gilley pulled in to Dunkin' Donuts for free pastries and coffee from the drive through window, courtesy of another of Dickie's "sources."

As Dickie had hoped, there was pretty Kizzy Washington at the Donkin' Donuts drive-through window, a young divorced mom of five. Her parents loved Leslie Uggams, the actor who played Kizzy in Alex Haley's *Roots*.

Kizzy leaned out and kissed Dickie as he in turn leaned out to take the free coffees and donuts. "Dickie, there is a party tonight at the office tower here," Kizzy suggested, "Love to see you there, handsome. It's Monday, free drinks for the judges and court lawyers, you know."

He promised to meet her that night at the tower.

Boss Martin's tower was the first and only modern building ever allowed in town, only because it was Boss Martin's and he wanted it.

Dickie zoomed off in his scratched and dented Porsche in a more pensive mood.

"I don't think she noticed what happened to your ride, Dickie," Chris said.

"Of course not. But, Kizzy hears things around here and I'm good to her."

He let the car drift down the hill on Main Street and into downtown Loweville. They reached the county seat center at precisely 11:49 a.m.

* * *

Chris studied the old historic King's County Courthouse with its buckteeth of giant marble pillars and expansive steps. But, Dickie surprised Chris by driving right past the old courthouse without pausing or saying a word. Chris had been expecting the courthouse to be a deep well of story leads. He asked Dickie to stop at the big brick Georgian structure; he'd not been inside yet.

Dickie explained, "It's Monday Chris, nobody's workin' today in the legal eagle nest, not really. Besides, the best information in the courthouse is always from the cute receptionists and secretaries who are already out for a two-hour lunch. I know that for a fact."

He waved at two young women on the sidewalk who waved back and smiled. "See the courthouse clock? Mid-lunchtime," he said. It was 11:56 a.m.

"Talk with them long enough, they're ready to suck you right into their bosses' confidential drawers," said Dickie. "I've had the pleasure, success with that technique, that is. On the other hand, the politicians and lawyers give you nothing but grief just to rattle your nerves. How are your nerves now kid?"

Chris wanted to say, *Rattled, you fool. Are we done yet?* Instead, he said, "Be...tter, Dickie, thanks. If not the courthouse, where are we going?"

"Over there," Randim nodded toward Martin's tower, a glimmering blue, 13-story First Union Credit & Mortgage tower.

Chris pondered the acronym, FUC&M, and begun to laugh; he had heard the name somewhere before. As he chuckled, his gaze caught hold of the wondrous tower and the contrast it struck in the old town. He was transfixed on the dreamlike image in mid-day sunny splendor, reflecting puffy clouds and blue sky. He was very impressed and wondered, "Hey, this big glass tower is gorgeous, but it does not belong in the town's colonial setting. "How the heck did this…"

Dickie cut him off, "At its 1998 ribbon cutting ceremony, then Maryland. Governor Marvin Randell hailed the structure as a great symbol of King's County progress and the supreme triumph of the county's favorite son."

"Who's that?"

"The builder of this magnificent tower was JDR Company's Johnny Martin. And lucky you, we are going to see him today, I hope."

He failed to mention that the locals still seethed from the financial scorching they were inflected from financial sharks inside the stark, steel and blue glass office building.

In the minds of traditionalists, like shop keepers, cops and school teachers, not to mention a spattering of architects venturing to Loweville to pitch for their new projects, the tower was a monstrosity, ill-fitted to the historic Georgian colonial lines of old Loweville architecture.

Dickie said no one ever seemed to know how Boss Martin got zoning approval for the big blue thing. Remarkably, it stood tall on the hill directly across from the historic courthouse, circa 1798. Long before Martin constructed the blue tower, the county banned all buildings that would dwarf the five-story courthouse at the center of town. He got it zoned anyway.

Locals nicknamed the FUC&M structure the FUC'M tower. It housed the worst predatory lenders in Maryland. They were infamous for screwing over home buyers, especially minorities.

Still, by offering great lending rates and with enticing advertisements, the affable and cunning lenders in the impressive FUC&M tower easily lured first-time homebuyers, who got sucked into the showy edifice like mindless drones, drugged more with emotion to secure their dream home, than by sound finances.

Dickie, of course, was at home in the glittering nest of crooks, "You'll find as many corrupt money predators you'd ever want here for coloring a story," Dickie laughed mockingly. "They're all in my little book. Today, I want you to meet the interesting people who work in this glass entrapment where they snare and rip off the good citizens. First, though, we'll meet Boss Martin himself, whose company is on the first floor," he said. "I called in an appointment for noon."

The time was 11:58 and 15 seconds.

He drove around to the back entrance of the office tower, as was his habit to hide his car as well as he could everywhere, everywhere the Inquirer staffers would not see it.

Occupying the entire first floor was the headquarters of the JDR Builders Inc. the development company owned by Johnny

"Boss" Martin and his separated wife Victoria Martin, who was still part of his business, but not more than Johnny's trophy wife for parties and chamber of commerce events.

One of Dickie's sick reasons for the tour for Christopher Gilley, kid reporter, was to have him meet the infamous Martin. Dickie intended Chris to meet others, but Martin was key to Dickie's devious devices.

Johnny "Boss" Martin and Dickie Randim were "good friends," said Dickie, unconvincingly with a deep exhale.

Chris was flabbergasted. *This is nuts*, he thought. *Dickie's sleeping with Martin's wife.*

Dickie's plan was to leave Chris to chat with Martin, while "I have further business up in the tower," he said.

"Why? And why are you hiding the car back here anyway?" Chris wanted to call the whole thing off. It was too bizarre, with Dickie's lies, the miraculous survival from the flipping car, then flipping off the farmer, free donuts, no stop at the courthouse, and now leaving him with a notorious sleaze bag named "Boss"? *That is enough*, he thought, *Dickie wants me dead.*

"I like parking back here in the shade," Dickie said, laughing, as he maneuvered his mangled sports car under a scrawny honey locust tree, crunching through a cheap, weedy gravel parking lot. They finally came to a skidding stop, gray dust enveloping them. Dickie eased back the tight torqued muscles of the motor and let it hum. He then just sat admiring the big blue phallic intrusion to the charming old town of Loweville. He checked his Rolex. "Perfect, thirty seconds past 11:59 a.m."

"Whew, get me out of this thing," Chris said while springing from the car as if he were finally free of a frightening theme park ride. He slammed shut his battered car door and took a step toward the tower while hoping there was a bus stop in front of it.

But Randim stayed in the car and was struggling to open the driver side door. "God damn it. Chris, would you come back here? Please pull on this damn door as I push. It's jammed."

"What?" asked Chris, already halfway to the tower on foot. "Okay, wait, let me pull."

Dickie was frantically pile-driving his shoulder into the jammed driver-side door. Chris came around to tug. But the smashed door would not open.

"It's 10 seconds before noon. We will miss him. Hurry up, kid!" Randim banged his shoulder on the door harder and harder, cursing louder and louder, pounding against and cutting into the soft, calf-skin leather on the inside of the door with the buttons of his bomber jacket over and over, harder and harder.

Chris pulled and pulled.

As the car door gave way, tumbling both men flat onto the asphalt, all hell broke loose at 12 o'clock high with an ear-splitting explosion. The blast blew out all the bottom windows of the FUC&M tower with a burst of debris and black smoke that reached Dickie and Chris about 60 feet away.

Seconds later, another, stronger blast hurled fire and debris above their heads. The heat was searing, the smoke suffocating. Luckily, Chris and Dickie were not burned because they landed face down in the gravel with the driver's side door blanketing both of them from the waist up.

Smoke billowed from the lower windows of the building, blown out by the blast. Glass, bricks and shrapnel of wood and plastic rained from above them and shot past their bodies as they were sprawled on the parking lot, both then curling into a ball like sleeping lovers spooned there.

As Chris recounted later, there was then a full 15 seconds of eerie silence.

Chris heard people screaming. He opened his eyes and saw people running from smoky tunnels of the building's back and side fire exits.

He looked up and saw the tower listing to the left. *All that glass couldn't hold*, he thought.

"We better get away from here, fast!" said Randim, pulling young Chris to his feet and jumping into the driver's seat, leaving the car door in the debris.

"Come on, get in, get in quick," said Randim in a panic. Glass crunched under the tires as Dickie drove his car across the scattered rubble covering the gravel toward the back parking lot exit.

Witnesses later told the police that they saw a badly damaged, "getaway car" and a mangled convertible door left behind. Some said it was a sports car. One witness said a blue Porsche.

When Dickie and Chris reached the back of the parking lot, Randim braked and slowed the Porsche.

They looked back, each resting an arm on the leather seats, and facing each other. Dickie spoke first, "It must be terrorists."

"Terrorists? What? Here? Why?" asked Chris, still groggy. "It is only a local shithouse for money grubbing bastards, you said."

"Oh. my God, look," Randim interrupted. They watched in horror as the building tilted more to the left, then gaining momentum, collapsed and fell to the ground, spewing glass in all directions. Bits of silver and gray rubble blanketed the ground and pavement, a jagged blanket of glass, all pushing a huge cloud of gray construction dust away, in a circle.

They sat silent, too stunned to speak further.

At that extraordinary moment, the odd companions, Chris and Dickie, each hoped that would be the last time they would ever have to work together. They shared roughly the same thought, *This guy is bad luck.*

Chapter 4: The Gilleys

Christopher Stanton Gilley was raised in Glasgow, West Virginia, near the Kentucky line, population 92. Glasgow is 234 miles from the Inquirer newsroom in Rhodesville. It was far enough to make a real newspaper man out of Chris and too far for a lonely country boy to drive his laundry home in his crippled old Mazda.

Chris was blessed with natural writing abilities; a gift not equally sewn into the genomes of Ma Gilley's other eight children. He was destined to do great things, everyone in Glasgow figured. He was just that smart, all agreed.

His Ma, especially, never let Chris forget his amazing gift for crafting the written word.

When he was four years old, Chris could read adult books, thanks to his grandfather, who was a Scottish immigrant coal miner, who was held back in school and labeled an illiterate in his new country. The elder Gilley's illiteracy ended when, still as a young man, he met a school teacher from Charleston, West Virginia while shopping in a drug store. He asked the pretty customer to read a prescription label. She agreed to marry him three days later.

That kind of grit and resolve carried right on through the Gilley clan including his youngest grandson Christopher.

Inspired by his educated wife, Chris's grandfather took on a singular mission: he made sure all the Gilley children would learn how to read as soon as they could say 'Da Da.'

Chris's mother had six boys and three girls. Chris was the youngest. She doted mostly on baby Chris. She made him behave and to be polite always. And he did, nearly to a fault. He appeared to be incorruptible to his friends in grade school.

Before college, Chris worked as a gopher at a mountaintop radio station called WSNT, or as the locals called the uninspiring "good music" station, "Wasn't Radio." The Dee Jays nicknamed Chris 'Silly Gilley,' on and off the air, for his extremely good manners and eagerness to please. Chris didn't mind being the goat of on-air jokes about his shyness, his stutter, and his gawky looks clothed in pass-me-downs from brother to brother—threadbare remnants of forgotten styles.

After earning a Bachelor of Science degree from the prestigious journalism program at Northwestern University at age 19, Chris's only other pseudo-journalism job before the Inquirer was writing news copy for the Congressional Roll Call in Washington, D.C. for two months. It followed a career misstep that at least got him into D.C.

On Ma's suggestion, he accepted a political public relations internship on Capitol Hill with West Virginia Senator Robert Byrd. The Gilley family was flattered that the Senator recognized the boy's talents from his college record. But Chris didn't fit in a political office. He was not assertively partisan; had no political will whatsoever and even less interest in the infectious personal power of working on The Hill.

The next step was the Inquirer. Chris found himself at the Inquirer in suburban Maryland at the tender age of 19 because of his friend Liza Leah Lopez. The pretty dark-haired Puerto Rican American woman of about 30 also worked on Capitol Hill, for New York Senator Charles Schumer. They met when they tried to ladle some Senator Kennedy Bean Soup, a specialty at the Senate Cafeteria, at the same time and spilled some on each other. The friendship at the legislature would only last two weeks before Liza landed a job at the Maryland Inquirer. She immediately remembered promising to help her friend Chris if she heard of a job at a newspaper or at the bureaus in the National Press Building on 13th Street.

Chris would never knew how she did it. But the energetic and engaging Liza got Chris an interview with the Inquirer almost immediately upon her arrival at the paper in Rhodesville. It was not the Press Club, but it was a real newspaper, she said to Chris.

Perhaps Liza recognized that the boy from West Virginia needed such a break to get started in the big city. She told the Inquirer editors, "Gilley was that shy hillbilly boy I met on The Hill, a wonderful writer who doesn't belong in a political office, but a newspaper." She didn't say he was still just 19, but offered, "He might be young, but he is passionate about doing some serious reporting one day. He told me that when I saw him in the Senate lunchroom. Maybe he can copyread or something."

Christopher Gilley would be forever grateful, though, curious as to why Liza was so very kind to him, since he still thought of himself as a kid and she, well ... he thought she was just super.

What counted to Chris was that he now thought he had a best friend at the paper and he would do anything to help her in her new job as well, not as payback, but just to have a friend there.

* * *

Chris Gilley was all country and not fit for life on The Hill. He loved Reba, the Seldom Scene, motorcycle races though he couldn't afford a bike of his own, NASCAR, and fishing. Shy and accepting of life as it came to him, not as he took it, Chris was fun loving, but followed the crowd, watched people, and drank quietly when at bars. After a beer or two, he was a wiz at billiards, darts, any other individual game or sport.

His favorite recreation by far though was the TV cable channel Nick at Nite, the retro-programming cable channel of mostly black and white sitcoms from the 50s and 60s. He was that old-fashioned. He liked things simple.

After he joined Liza at the Inquirer, he soon thought that he was out of place again, although not to the extreme as on The Hill.

The other young reporters sharing Chris's low-rung, entry-level status came from affluent families. They all seemed satisfied with just putting in time at the stupid little newspaper chain before moving up to the Washington Post, New York Times or CNN. Some got their jobs at the Inquirer through family connections, landing in the D.C. area from Ivy League schools.

Those other young newcomers annoyed the hell out of the older reporters, many of whom had begun their careers with less education but survived through good hard reporting of sometimes uninspiring local news and sports.

Soon after Chris arrived, however, those same veteran reporters, who may have resented the other new kids, accepted Chris without as much as a word of brownnosing from him. They knew Chris was the real deal. Some were even secretly inspired by the kid. He rekindled a spark long-extinguished in their reporting.

He was almost a mystic presence at the paper. He possessed mature journalistic instincts, which were recognized clearly by the veterans, but never spoken of in the newsroom. They'd say, "That kid's got a knack," after Chris would turn a puzzling trial proceeding or complex political scandal into a lucid and succinct news story within an hour.

Good reporters can call up phrases and modifying clauses unconsciously to color stories better and better with each new source, each new story, each edition, year after year. That sort of quality was already hovering somewhere over the boy like a halo. Everyone he encountered at the paper recognized his potential.

Despite such encouragement from other staffers, Chris's priorities were to remove himself from a lifetime of poverty, write good copy, and make his mother proud. His Pulitzer dream could wait.

His mother's words always nagged him, however, that he was wasting the best brain in the family on a worthless newspaper job, when everybody, even in Glasgow, knew, sadly, that newspapers were dying all across America, replaced by cable news and the Internet. "Why Christopher? It's a dying profession," he often heard his Ma saying in his mind. It would only inspire Chris to work harder, write better copy and show her he'd made the right career choice.

Once settled into his first real reporting job, Chris still struggled with his meager salary to pay off repair bills on his 1987 Mazda, a hand-me-down junker that had already managed to survive several of his big brothers before they escaped Glasgow.

The jalopy was hell bent on falling apart as if the aging heap of metal resented Chris driving her in snarling urban traffic instead of getting to retire to rust away with her compatriots at the Glasgow's only junkyard, Mike's Hilltop Junk Heaven.

Yes, Chris hailed from a poor family and was the youngest of nine children, the oldest 32 years old, all raised in a shotgun cabin in the Appalachian Mountains. But, he was simply a whip.

Soon after he arrived, everyone at the Inquirer knew he could quickly translate his thoughts into newspaper copy that sang. The country boy had found his way.

Chapter 5: Gift Wrapped Story

Moments after the tower was destroyed

From the far edge of the parking lot away from the fallen tower, Chris and Dickie watched in horror as survivors and spectators circled the destruction and stared in disbelief.

Chris finally said to Dickie Randim, "I know this sounds weird. It's just awful to say, but I can't believe our luck in a way." Chris glanced across and saw fright on the face of the normally unflappable Dickie Randim.

Dickie nodded but kept staring at the destruction.

Chris said, "We are not just the first reporters at a major crime scene, but are actual eyewitnesses as it happened. Do you know how rare this must be Dickie?"

Randim still did not reply; didn't even look at Chris; just stared at the awful scene with his mouth open.

* * *

Chris called Benny to tell him what he's witnessed.

When Chris told Dickie that Benny was on his way, Dickie turned the ignition on and said, "I'm leaving. I'll leave you here to go back with Benny."

Chris stepped out of the car. His parting words were useless, "Don't go. We can do this together. Bennie said to gather as much from witnesses as possible before he gets here."

"No thanks."

Bradley and Inquirer executive editor Lloyd Sollem would need about an hour driving to Loweville. Still Dickie was leaving the scene and leaving Benny's orders entirely with Chris.

Before he zoomed off, Dickie watched his kid companion for a few minutes wading among the survivors near the rubble to get quotes and background. Chris swung into a bare-knuckles reporter mode, like nothing Dickie had ever done. Chris ran from person to person with a notebook in hand. Dickie was truly impressed with Chris, even a little saddened. Chris seemed to be possessed.

Dickie's admiration of the kid faded fast, once he figured that when Bradley got there he would surely want a better explanation why he had driven his boy wonder to the FUC'M tower in the first place.

He had to split fast. Before leaving the scene, he left his car and tracked down Chris on foot at the courthouse steps. Dickie lent Chris his Nikon 6000 and MacBook Pro laptop after he had crowbarred them out of the smashed trunk. He only made Gilley promise to return his phone and laptop, because, "It's got all the good numbers on it. Don't lose it kid, hear?"

Bradley and Sollem arrived at 1:10 p.m. pale and nervous. Normally the two editors never got out of the newsroom it seemed. They worked as editing opossums, never leaving the newsroom in daylight. Local police in Loweville knew all the regular reporters but didn't recognize those two. The cops demanded press credentials and triple IDs just to let Bradley and Sollem get to a 7-Eleven store, two blocks from the disaster scene.

When the police then escorted them to the courthouse, Bradley and Sollem found the paper's wonder boy on the courthouse steps writing on a laptop. He was well into reporting the story and working on a second update.

"I got the story," is all Chris said as he stood for a second, then hunched back down, Dickie's laptop opened on his knees.

Christopher Gilley, potentially their best reporter, but still an unknown, was finally into his element. The small-town boy didn't have to dream any longer of reporting a big story, after honing his skills in college and around Capitol Hill for a couple of months before the Inquirer hired him.

Using Dickie's laptop and cell phone, plus the courthouse Wi-Fi hotspot, Chris had already written and filed a story for the Inquirer's website before his bosses had even entered the county. Eager young copy editors back at the paper, recognizing an amazing scoop, already had Chris' first story online on the Maryland Inquirer's home page. It helped that the young copy desk loved Chris. They ran the story on the authority that the editors couldn't be reached on such fast-breaking news. Instead, they got the sports editor to okay it.

The story ran online at 1:35 p.m., just an hour and a half after the disaster:

Glass Office Tower Destroyed; Terrorism "Not Likely"

by Christopher Gilley, staff reporter

LOWEVILLE, Md. (May 14)--The monolithic, glass-encased First Union Credit & Mortgage, FUC&M, office building crashed to earth this morning at 12:17 and 12 seconds p.m. following a massive explosion, likely triggered on or near the first-floor offices of JDR Builders, Inc. development company.

The tower, which is best known locally as an architectural misfit at the center of historic Loweville, was still standing after an initial explosion but was listing at 20 degrees while people inside, screaming and shouting, ran from exits seconds before the structure collapsed on its side.

It fell after a second explosion caused a horrific roar--the concussion of tons of heavy walls and floors smashing to earth, the whole of it then overtaken by the ear ringing, reverberating sound as tons of glass and steel hit the ground with rubble strewn across the parking lot and parked vehicles.

Dozens of spectators had collectively gasped out loud when the structure, still intact, seemed to groan and crackle with its first movement. Human voices were then drowned out by a thunderous landing of the tower as it broke into smithereens of glass, drywall, and what were once office desks, chairs, file cabinets and their contents in smoldering tangles of steel I-beams and concrete reinforcing bars.

The number of people killed or injured has not yet been determined. Witnesses said more than 100 people ran from the building, surviving the blast before it fell on its side. Police have not ruled out foul play or terrorism, but say the latter is "not likely."

County Fire Marshall William W. Windfild said the first explosion occurred only 12 minutes before resulting fire and weakened girders caused the decade old office tower to fall with the second explosion. He reported that three workers at the building are still unaccounted for.

Windfild said preliminary information indicates that a bomb had been deliberately planted on the ground floor of the building, but offered "No comment" when asked about the juxtaposition under the office of Johnny "Boss" Martin, also known as John Martini, CEO of JDR Builders, Inc.

Martini could not be reached for comment.

Firemen first on the scene from the Largo Volunteer Company, unaware of Windfild's assessment, stated unofficially, that the blast was likely a result of a gas leak.

Witnesses said the Largo firemen were seen arriving first, yet their firehouse is some 40 miles west of Loweville. The Largo firemen told the Inquirer they couldn't explain their promptness.

Local officials downplayed the likelihood of terrorism but confirmed rumors at the nearby 4th District Courthouse that federal officials from the U.S. Homeland Security Department were on their way to the scene.

The FUC&M tower management leased offices to regional offices of two federal agencies. Other tenants were finance and real estate development companies, and consumer service companies, including a KINKO copy center and a United Parcel Service packing and mailing store.

According to sources at the courthouse, people living in or near Loweville considered the modern glass tower an unwelcome addition to the historic buildings at the town center. The Board of Zoning Appeals in 1996 passed the petition of John Martini of JDR with a minimum quorum on hand for the vote on Christmas Eve for the County Council to build it as planned. Martin's original name is Martini.

The contrast of the ultra-modern glass tower to the dozens of colonial style buildings had been a sore spot among locals and subject of frequent negative columns in the King's County Current.

Martin was not in his office today and his whereabouts were unknown at the time of the blast, according to JDR Chief Operating Officer and longtime Martin associate Col. Humphrey Isaac Hurt, who told the Inquirer that he scrambled from the building moments before it collapsed.

Several former workers of companies in the tower, who were eyewitnesses, said another bone of contention over the building was its two largest occupants, Best Opportunity Mortgage, Corp. (BOM) and Lifetime Deal Financing, Corp. (LDF).

The two firms have been targeted by hundreds of lawsuits from homeowners and builders, according to Melma Smith, manager of the copy center desk at the destroyed Kinko's. "These people are no good and now I've lost my job I guess, but this is not about me. I hope no one was hurt too awful bad," said Smith.

Bernard Madinoff, CEO of BOM, and Samuel Johnson, chair and president of LFD, could not be reached for comment. According to American Home Mortgage Association records, the companies issued the most adjustable, no-interest loans in the United States each year from 2002 through 2006. King's County is among the nation's leading counties in foreclosed homes.

Foreclosed homes from loans originating from BOM and LDF have resulted in several pockets of vacant neighborhoods now occupied by gangs and drug dealers, according to police records in the courthouse.

Alvin Spiveowak, the county court clerk, said that "almost every day" someone files a complaint against one or both of the two companies. Martin's JDR Builders maintain a partnership with at least one of the companies, BOM.

Sheriff Barney Standard said he does not anticipate that the incident involved crimes against the mortgage firms, which he said are "law-abiding, long-term citizens of the state."

Chris showed the story to Lloyd when he and Benny found their young reporter still wandering among the witnesses. "The sports desk ran it through copy when you were not there. Hope that's okay."

"Sure Chris. Take a look Lloyd," Benny said proudly.

After a quick scan, Lloyd was not pleased, "Benny, there is no way he got all this in an hour?" Yet he was astounded. Lloyd never liked the kid and three months earlier was against hiring someone so young and green.

"Yep, that's our boy wonder. Amazing kid. This is a bit rough Lloyd. He can do better" said Benny, hoping Lloyd wouldn't complain that Benny didn't clear the copy, an essential step in preparing the story for print on the business desk.

Chris filed an update at 4:12 p.m. alerting the copy desk with RBB, Benny's initials over the copy this time.

Bomb Fragments, Two Bodies Found in FUC&M Rubble

by Christopher Gilley, staff reporter

LOWEVILLE, Md. (May 14)--King's County police say they have recovered fragments of a bomb that likely destroyed most of the first floor of the 13-floor First Union Credit & Mortgage office tower in Loweville this morning seconds before the entire tower collapsed.

Two unidentified bodies have been recovered from the outer edges of a massive pile of rubble where the FUC&M tower fell. Other deaths are feared, say local authorities.

The bomb fragments were taken to an undisclosed forensic laboratory in Washington, D.C. to determine if they are of foreign or domestic origin, a first step in pinpointing the bomb's placement in the building, said King's County Fire Marshall William W. Windfild.

In an unusual twist for a county crime, agents of the U.S. Homeland Security Department (HSD), instead of local police, roped off and quarantined the disaster site, according to King's County Fire Marshall's office.

The building housed regional offices of two federal agencies, the FBI and the Internal Revenue Service. Homeland Security agent Michael I. Brauni denied rumors of possible terrorist motives for the blast, but he conceded that the explosions that brought down the tower seemed to be a deliberate act.

Nothing was left standing from the former glittering blue iconic tower that had dominated the skyline of the historic King's County seat. Many eyewitnesses expressed relief that it would no longer mar the colonial architecture of Loweville. There was nothing left but an enormous pile of smoking rubble of sprawling glass shards, furniture, pipes, toilets and other interior building materials as far as across Gov. Scruppels Parkway on one side and Main Street on the other. Some debris projectiles had ricocheted off the marble facade of the 4th District Courthouse and landed on its steps.

Damage to the tower is estimated at more than $300 million, by an official of JDR Builders Inc. of College Park, who asked to not be named. The company built the tower in 1998 and is owned by John Martini, known in the building trade as Johnny "Boss" Martin.

Horrified workers lined the periphery of their previous place of employment, expressing sadness and concern for others who are still missing and may be trapped below the rubble.

"I was walking to my car to get my lunch when the explosion knocked me to the ground about 100 feet from the explosion," said Harriet Baldus, an assistant at Baden and Baden, Attorneys at

Law who occupied the 13th floor of the tower. "I just ran as fast as I could. Lucky I'm not one of those big shots who park under the building. Their cars have got to be toast." Baldus said she screamed for her four coworkers when the explosion occurred. They couldn't hear her, but she said that in another five minutes the four escaped with dozens of other people from the side exits moments before the tower fell.

King's County police are following leads of a possible local motive. Court records reveal that the destroyed building had been a place for frequent disturbances in recent months, even fistfights between residents of foreclosed homes in the county and their mortgage agents in the building.

The two leading mortgage lenders in the state, which rack up millions of dollars for foreclosures in King's County and beyond, housed their headquarters in the FUC&M building. The companies are Best Opportunity Mortgage, Corp. and Lifetime Deal Financing, Corp.

Last September, reports of the extremely high numbers of foreclosed homes in King's County splashed across national news media. The stories stemmed from a wave of associated crimes in neighborhoods filled with vacant large single-family houses in Bowie Heights, Loweville, Charmington and Kingston.

"Those people won't help us with refinancing or even keep appointments to get federal help," said Janet Boone of Charmington, wife of a laid-off state government employee and mother of four. Johnson had driven into the FUC&M parking lot just as the first blast occurred.

Another witness to the tower collapse, court clerk Horace Bowling, said the building was always filled with angry people, but that he couldn't imagine anyone wanting to destroy it because of their financial predicament.

Copies of any records lost in the destroyed building of final deals on residential and commercial real estate conducted there were likely on file at the courthouse, said Baldus.

"Whoever did this is just plain sick," said fireman Judd O'Toole of Kingston. "But, I still can't believe a bomb down here [the first-floor entrance] would bring this big building down."

Police spokesman Denny deFrockt said more details on the investigation into the cause and motive and casualties will be released at 6 p.m.

deFrockt said he looked forward to a quick conclusion to the investigation, "So we can get this mess cleaned up fast and these God-fearing folks can feel safe and secure in their jobs elsewhere or with legitimate companies again." Mr. deFrockt is also a minister at My Lady's Holy Grace Church in Loweville, circa 1744, a national registered historic site.

* * *

After listening to an impromptu police press conference at the courthouse, which revealed nothing new, Chris caught a ride back to the paper with Benny Bradley and Lloyd Sollem.

Back at the paper, Bradley said loud enough for the few evening stragglers to hear, but mostly for Sollem's ears, "Our new reporter Gilley uncovered more in one afternoon than the police will reveal or admit to all week. I'd bet on it." Bradley had seen Chris's full potential for the first time and no doubt wanted the entire newsroom to know about it, especially Lloyd Sollem, one of his bosses.

Short, slight and with a touch of gray at his temples, Bradley was a seasoned veteran who knew his stuff, although one would barely guess how much of an accomplished editor he was by the tight intensity he always wore on the surface. He was the consummate fussbudget, frugal, feisty and a sharp-tongued New Englander through and through. He came to the Inquirer from a small newspaper in New Hampshire. It was there where Bradley first relished the role of the high priest of the newsroom. At the Maryland Inquirer, Bradley's final word in news copy was never questioned.

He was fastidious and methodical with his daily routine: Ate an apple at 10:25 a.m., took lunch at 12:45 sharp while reading the Washington Post style and business sections, searched hard news story ideas until 3 p.m., except on Wednesdays and Thursdays. On those afternoons, he edited and rewrote copy from the staff up to deadline at 5 p.m. on Thursday to get the edition on the streets on Friday. He always displayed his quick, competitive intelligence, yet in a cooperative manner. As a senior editor, he had a scrupulous eye for mistakes and inconsistencies in the copy that crossed his desk.

Bradley and Chris watched the 6 to 7 o'clock news broadcasts from their desks for anything they had missed, but there was little more than statements by the county executive and sheriff that the explosion was not a terrorist attack and that their hearts and thoughts when out to the families of the three victims killed in the blast. Their identifications would be held until family members could identify them, said the sheriff.

Chris then dug in for more than an hour on the phone collecting more news from emergency first responders he met at the site earlier. Bradley was pleased that Chris flipped open his notebook to show him a long list of those numbers. Bradley copied some, which were new to him.

The long day ended after all the newsroom staff had gone home, except for Chris and Benny. Chris filed his next story at 9:19 p.m.

Boss Martin Dead, Entombed in Rubble of "Prized" Tower
by Christopher Gilley, staff reporter

LOWEVILLE, Md. (May 14)--Federal detectives this evening found the body of John Martini, better known in the construction industry as Johnny "Boss" Martin of College Park, in the rubble of the First Union Credit and Mortgage (FUC&M) building in Loweville, which collapsed following a massive dual explosion this morning.

Martin was founder and president of JDR Builders Inc., the contractor for the 13-story office tower which was built in *1998, in partnership with two mortgage investors from New York.*

JDR was incorporated in Delaware in 1983 as JobsDoneRight Inc.

The building was destroyed. Damage is estimated by unnamed JDR officials at $285 million, according to county police.

Martin's firm was based in Loweville in the destroyed FUC&M building. It was Martin's most prized project, according to employees, though its construction was fought by locals who opined that it was inappropriate for the historic district of the county seat.

Martin's body was found in the mangled frame of his new $55,000 Ford-450 crew cab pickup truck beneath piles of lumber and masonry of the collapsed building. His truck had been parked in the basement garage in Martini's reserved space just below his company's first floor headquarters, said officials. The heavily *damaged garage was exposed after the building leaned and fell to the west southwest. Police inspected some of the vehicles that were exposed by the fallen structure, leading to the discovery of Martin's remains.*

Martin's was the fourth body recovered from the rubble so far, said police spokesperson Denny deFrockt. The others, believed to be Latino men of the building's cleaning crew, are yet to be claimed and identified, said deFrockt.

Martin is survived by his wife Victoria Martin and a 5-year-old daughter, Gigi.

Several witnesses at the crime scene today implied a possible motive from escalating anger expressed publicly by foreclosed homeowners financed by Best Opportunity Mortgage, Corp. and Lifetime Deal Financing, Corp., two tenant companies in the tower.

"I don't think this is a coincidence, what happened here today and the trouble those predators were causing," said Sam O'Neill, owner of nearby Sam's Wine and Spirits Shop. County records obtained by the Inquirer revealed that the two companies offered financing to thousands of new would-be homeowners with no interest, no down payment adjustable loans that may have contributed to massive numbers of foreclosures, which are among the highest in the nation.

Just before the tragedy, Brickhouse Security Company guard Lester Patience arrived for his noon to 8 p.m. shift at the building. "I park in the back, not in the building. I sat watching this. Man! There was nothing but smoke and fire, yea, big fire, but not at once. After a bit, then it sent the whole damn thing over just after lots of folks got out. Praise the Lord," said Patience.

A personal video shot by Patience last Friday afternoon, and provided to the Inquirer today, captured a chaotic demonstration of about 150 disgruntled former owners of foreclosed homes, all of which were financed by BOM or LFD, as the former owners marched on the FUC&M building and often shouted obscenities. The video of the demonstration last week showed, protesters carrying signs aimed at the mortgage firms. One read "Down with the FUC'M Tower" and another "My House was from LFD, Left for Dead!!"

The signs alleged insensitivity and lack of concern for minorities and underemployed residents, who tried in vain to work new deals to save their homes, according to eyewitness Melma Smith, an employee of a Kinko's Copy store destroyed in the tower.

Although talk from eyewitnesses about the mortgage company problems outnumbered comments on the horror of the building collapse and the four deaths, police officials have no information tying disgruntled former clients with the incident.

Martin's firm was also the primary contractor for homes in Charmington and Kingston costing more than $1 million each, most of which are now vacant. The housing foreclosure crisis has had police nationwide on their toes.

According to the Maryland Real Estate Board, high numbers of foreclosures in King's County are impacting suburban, middle income families. Many of those are African Americans who moved out of cities to the county with less crime and congestion, said King's County Executive Joseph Collins. "Our citizens here are building strong communities and successful black businesses."

Bradley was still at the paper with Chris until 10 p.m. to approve the online copy for the next day, he said. His real reason to stay late was to have a man-to-man. "It's your slant," he said with some trepidation, not wanting to discourage Chris at the height of the young man's triumph that afternoon.

"Slant? What slant?" Chris was crestfallen.

"Well, call it then your choice of an angle," said Benny. He told the young reporter that it was likely that managing editor Michele LaProbe won't like Chris's heavy emphasis on referencing predatory mortgage groups in his story on the disaster. "Don't be surprised when she says the story should cover more on the human tragedy side of the building collapse, not on possible prior crimes of the occupants. Don't say I didn't warn you. She's tough. You have not seen that side of Michele, my boy! I think you did a great job and I have no major issues."

"Is this a major?"

"Your harping on the lenders? Well, it may be with Michele."

"Well okay, Benny, but I couldn't get any more information on Martin yet," Chris said. As Benny lectured, Chris didn't look up from his notes for his next story on the FUC'M tower, which he hoped to file in the morning. He didn't hear most of what Benny said about the Queen of the newsroom Michele. He did hear that Benny wanted more on Martin himself, not his company. Chris knew the error of his copy and didn't have to look up at his editor. Benny also knew it too.

Benny just chuckled at his prodigy. "I'm going home. But I'll say again, it is amazing how much you were able to get into the paper in just an afternoon. I am so impressed. It's like there were five of the regular mugs around here covering it. Don't say I said that or you might be covering the Girl Scouts cookie drive," said Bradley, who turned and walked out.

Chris looked up this time and replied sharply, "I just did what you always tell me. I talked with everybody I could find. They wrote the story, not me."

"Don't worry about Michele, Chris. I'll take the heat," Bradley answered warmly.

Again, Chris was only half listening, half organizing thoughts for the next day on the story. While covering the event all afternoon, Chris was most impressed with the rage he heard against the mortgage companies by everyone at the disaster site, in the courthouse, and on the street. It was consistent disdain, which he couldn't have ignored. He wished Lloyd and Benny had heard it firsthand. He was prepared to present his case to Michele the next day.

* * *

Back at his apartment, the paper's whiz kid crashed on his couch with a Yuengling beer and a slice of day-old, cold pizza. The plastered grin on his face spoke both satisfaction and readiness to do even better tomorrow and the next day and the next. He was pumped.

"I have already made it into investigative journalism in my first few weeks with the first friggin' paper. Good job, eh?" he said to his empty green beer bottle. He got two more out of the frig to celebrate. "I can't WAIT to pick up the story tomorrow," he said to the next bottle, already half empty. He'd show his mother back in Glasgow that he was not wasting his abilities by pursuing a career in news reporting, even if it was a dying industry, as she had warned.

When his phone rang, he was grateful to be out of beer. No need to go out for more as the calls were intoxicating enough for one evening.

Two of his brothers called to congratulate Chris after reading his stories online. He asked them to send copies to Ma because she no longer needed internet service with all her children out of the house.

Liza Lopez reached him next, "Chris, I've been trying to call you for a half-hour. Great job, my boy wonder. I am so proud of you."

She rang off after a brief exchange.

Wow, Liza is my one-person fan club, he thought. Chris was thrilled to hear from his buddy Liza even if he did see her every day at the newsroom. Her call was special. He admired her reporting of consumer issues and valued her friendship more than anything.

Meanwhile, Chris didn't know that Benny had held back on another issue. With the paper's ultra-thin profit margin, editors at the Inquirer hadn't assigned any real investigative reporting for the past ten years and would not likely follow through with much vigor for this gift-wrapped sensation either.

Chapter 6: Carrie and Martha

The staid, conservative Inquirer management was a sucker for a clever, opportunistic slob the likes of Richard "Dickie" Randim.

The sad truth was that if Dickie ever put out the effort, he could have been a pretty good reporter. His professional resume was decent. He was educated at New York's Columbia University, but he nearly flunked out twice because of his heavy partying. He managed to get his degree after seven years in the big apple on his trust money. There was also a rumor that daddy's half million-dollar grant for a library extension helped get Dickie through.

Again, with his daddy's influence and foundation money, he slid into a slower pace, earning an MBA at the University of Maryland in College Park.

But everyone knew Dickie's best skill was romancing, especially after he pulled off a bold chauvinistic play right in the newsroom late one day on a returning employee.

New hire, op-ed editor Carrie Amora was the latest of Dickie's femquests. The pretty blonde mother of five was returning after a two-year absence with the birth of twin daughters and a runaway husband. Carrie was a sensuous creature at heart, loved sex and was perhaps a nymphomaniac, so the Inquirer's maintenance men liked to believe at least. She was "just damned sexy," they agreed.

In truth, no one knew if Carrie was sex crazy. It was apparent, however, that she used the inherent power of her catchy looks to flirt and reject males with a lilting eye or inviting half smile just enough to get what she wanted in life without lasting damage to herself.

But, that was before she had the misfortune of encountering Dickie Randim.

At home, Carrie was a virtual baby machine, always getting pregnant and requesting maternity leave from work. Each time her family swelled with another child, Carrie came back to the Inquirer looking hot as ever—the perfect figure, face of a fashion model, flicking and stroking her long flaxen curls. Carrie, who had once been abandoned as a child by her mother, could never stand to be alone or unloved and or unappreciated.

On that fateful day, she came back once again to interview at the Inquirer after she had been gone for many months on maternity leave with her twins and an abusive husband.

This time, however, Carrie would be unfamiliar with the new personnel and was entering the new Rhodesville headquarters.

She had worked previously at old rat-infested Inquirer building in nearby Gaithersburg. She was also aging more than she knew and came in a bit too confident of her feminine powers with the new group of male bosses including new executive editor Lloyd Sollem, whom some called a cold fish.

Admirers who knew Carrie when she worked in the old building told Dickie about "smoking hot" former employee Carrie Amora. Someone even innocently told Dickie "it will be good to see the girl again." With some additional pumping of her male admirers at the paper, Dickie learned of Carrie's insecurities.

On her interview day, Dickie was all set and positioned to make her believe he was the last word, the last interview, the final approval to get hired. It was a long shot, but exactly the kind of thing Dickie loved.

He was clever. After her final real interview, that with Lloyd Sollem, Dickie approached Carrie immediately outside Lloyd's office, pouncing from a nearby chair like a tom cat. The charming Dickie told her "this part of the hiring interviews will be over coffee in the building's café across the hall. Have you had lunch? You should see what they have done with the new set up. … Me? Yes, I am fairly new. After coffee, Lloyd said I am to give you a tour of the paper."

Indeed, Carrie believed Dickie was a senior editor and was to be her final interview and deciding factor. Too bad her old 'girlfriends' at the paper hadn't warned her.

He managed to seduce her after two hours of mutually enjoyable conversation about his reporting, his family's wealth, and his love of "the finer things in life." He admitted being "stunned" by her "abilities" as he risked touching from time to time.

And then, he showed her the Inquirer's new fitness center in the new Rhodesville location. He knew she had never worked in that building. He found her to be indeed vulnerable, desperate to rejoin the Inquirer as a line editor, after a two-year absence because her babies were in dire need of more income at home.

She had come back to the paper to apply for another editor's position once she felt that her new twin daughters were safely away from a jealous and abusive husband. He bolted when he learned he was not the biological father of Carrie's twins. With her sister then living with her, Carrie felt secure to go back to the Inquirer.

She had never been an actual reporter, except on her high school newspaper's sports pages, but she had good story instincts. Management remembered and gave her an interview with no questions asked. Unfortunately, Carrie's good story instincts did not include judging character.

A week later, after she was hired, Carrie learned the truth about Richard Randim, that he was nothing but a flake and a rake, not an editor, and that he had completely duped her. Worse, Dickie leaked word of his "great sex with the new girl in the gym" to a few envious older guys in maintenance."

From that point on, she hated Dickie with a burning passion. She got the job. But, Carrie futilely and vehemently denied having a tryst with the notorious Dickie. She was ashamed, mostly that her ambitious, mid-career insecurities led to a one-timer with the Dickster.

It was the worst day she could remember. For her interviews, she had arrived in a state of super confidence until she muddled through the Lloyd Sollem interview. She found Lloyd's demeanor to be vague and detached. She believed she had lost her chance. Dickie was waiting for her and gave her hope again.

To make matters worse, Carrie learned that her interview with Lloyd was a formality only. He had already called the Personnel Department and hired Carrie before she arrived at his office door, based on her hardnosed reputation among the editors who knew her previous work at the Inquirer. While Carrie was ill prepared for Lloyd and was simply counting on her looks and self-assuredness, Lloyd had done his homework on Carrie. He learned that Carrie brought needed abilities to sharply judge and assert opinions in story meetings, with remarkable insight into the meat of a story, questioning the motives and methods of reporters. She had been a terror to young reporters, much to the delight of deadpan Lloyd "bottom-line" Sollem, who was always the senior editor in any story meeting he attended.

Brooding yet handsome Lloyd, true to his nickname, was dead serious about the newspaper. He dressed in suits of blues and black, white shirts, polished wingtips and woolen blend slacks, always gray. He looked like an undertaker, according to managing editor Michele LaProbe, who hid her affection for Lloyd and his outstanding manners and abilities as an old-school journalist. He redefined dull and it was not surprising that pretty, gregarious Carrie had misread him.

And then there was Michele, always Michele to consider by everyone and every situation.

Despite Lloyd's senior position, Michele was the dominant force in the newsroom, simply because of her intellect and nose for news, though she technically worked under Lloyd. She was enormous and wore bigXgirl tent dresses with no style at all. She thus had no room to criticize Lloyd's dress code, but it was all in fun to the staff. Besides her size, Michele was easily recognized around the Inquirer with tightly curled reddish brown hair and deep-set piercing sky blue eyes.

Michele had faith that Lloyd could manage such wild seeds as Carrie and had also approved her hiring before she had arrived.

And, when she learned of Carrie's simmering hatred of Dickie, Michele considered it a real plus.

By the time of her latest arrival, Carrie distrusted most males, except perhaps for mild mannered Lloyd, whom she would become endeared to and trust.

She vowed to get back at Dickie somehow, she told her delighted female companions.

For Dickie, the notorious womanizer, Carrie was the best kind of gratifying challenge. The handsome charmer expected little resistance from the ladies because he was such a shrewd player. Dickie's other conquests included Inquirer Inc. publisher Martha Gray Read, 54, the Radisson hostess Ginger Bedford, 18, (well before Vickie), and 21-year-old bikini-clad lifeguard Goldie Lust, in the equipment shed twice a week at the Jewish community pool cabana across Rhodesville Pike, near the Maryland Inquirer. Those were the women on Dickie's dessert menu. But mostly, Dickie preferred the naive and simple, seductive charms of more dim-witted working-class girls. He loved them maybe because they liked him, unlike some professional women who grew to hate the man for his phony charms.

Occasionally, Dickie was frightened by his charm when he'd bed down a professional married woman he'd picked up at some bar or business reception, an influential woman directly connected to his beat perhaps. He'd be nervous the next day wondering whether his conquest would get back to management. But that wouldn't stop Dickie from constantly using his sex appeal for favors and tips from such women to find dirt on corrupt legislators and especially real estate developers and predatory lenders.

It was all good sport to Dickie. He was never mean or hurtful to his women in sex, just persistent, charming, and eager to satisfy his ego and please them too. Love and commitment? Forget it. He thought he loved them all, but only briefly.

For the most part, Dickie protected his hobby. He was liked by some of the men at the newspaper—office, maintenance, and press workers mostly. And, he'd share tales of his female exploits with the older, perennially frustrated newspaper reporters who were stuck in modest salaried jobs, yet addicted to the strong drug of news gathering. They loved the Carrie story since she had always been a dick tease.

Dickie tactfully shared such stories with only one guy at a time in a whisper tone and manner of Watergate's Deep Throat, as if sharing an exclusive story that will be told to only one reporter sworn to not reveal the source.

Just three years after he joined the company, employees across the Inquirer's 88 weekly editions covering the entire state of Maryland and extending to northern Virginia and Delaware knew of Dickie's reputation with the ladies. The rumors reached management. The suits upstairs at the main Rhodesville office grew tired of distressing over whether Randim's compromising sexual adventures would eventually compromise the integrity of the paper.

And then, his misbehavior did affect the paper one day. Management sent him away for a while.

* * *

Dickie's banishment from the newsroom resulted from pushing his raking habit too far. He 'felt' all the talk and figured that maybe he needed some cover. He decided to try to score with the paper's publisher, 54-year-old Mrs. Martha Read, the most powerful woman at the newspaper. She occupied the spacious and comfortable corner office on the third-floor business offices opposite CEO Chuck Bear's large office down the hall at the far corner of the building. Martha Read was in the habit of having her coffee in the café across the hall adjacent to the newsroom where bagels and donuts were fresh each morning. Dickie timed her appearances and discovered that Mrs. Read had her coffee reading a newspaper at 9:35 a.m.

Dickie had no real desire to bang Martha Read. But it might help him. He hoped to charm her into liking him as rumors continued about Dickie's questionable reporting habits. And he guessed correctly she knew nothing about him as a playboy. Perfect.

It was odd to see Dickie sharing coffee many mornings with Martha Read; even Chuck Bear noticed them sharing a table for a couple of weeks. She laughed at his jokes and they discussed story tips for his real estate beat. Martha was married for 26 years to condo developer and millionaire Lester Peter Read, the Inquirer's biggest advertiser.

People noticed Dickie calling her Martha, and to Bear's memory, people in editorial always referred to her as Mrs. Read, and with great respect.

On a Thursday evening, deadline night, Bear believed that Martha had already gone home for the evening when he innocently walked into her office to retrieve a mockup of the new Friday layout. He saw a layout but not the newspaper's layout.

Bear opened her unlocked office door and saw Dickie's bare behind aimed directly at him. Dickie Randim was blanketed over half-dressed Read, who was sprawled out on top of her Zairian teak desk, in full view of her office window and the 10-story condominium building behind the Inquirer offices, condos built by her husband.

The copulating couple was surrounded by the weekly layout pages scattered about when they shoved them off her massive hand-carved desk and onto the floor.

Back in his own office, the usually fearless business tycoon Chuck Bear dreaded calling Jimmy Bob Randim, Dickie's father, even though they were old fraternity chums from the University of Virginia.

But, he had to do something fast. He made a person-to-person call to Jimmy Bob at his yacht club in Florida. He'd shared drinks with Jimmy Bob many evenings there. He got lucky His old buddy was in. "Jim Bob, thank goodness you are there."

"What's up Chuckster? My boy in trouble again? Don't worry, I trust he does his job well, right?"

"Well, ... yeah."

"So, what is it? You don't sound too good, Chuck."

Bear told Dickie's father that his son did something he could not excuse and "if he was anyone but your son, I'd want to fire him?"

"My, my. Can't be that bad."

Bear came right out with it, that Dickie had a recent tryst with his publisher, a woman married to another of the Inquirer's big advertisers. He gently added, "She is very well respected and my friend, Jim. I cannot let a word of this out. Dickie needs to disappear."

He hoped the senior Randim would offer to reprimand his no-good son.

Instead, Jimmy Bob blurted, "Well Chuckster, that's my boy all right! Sure, I'll ship him off in my boat, go for some yellowfin and swords for a while down here. Why, he's nothing but a clown. That beats all." Daddy Randim burst into a belly laugh and kept on laughing.

Bear, a devoted family man, then hung up abruptly on Jimmy Bob Randim, all shaken and confused. After his disgusting discovery and shocking call to his old chum, Bear closed the door of his spacious office and spent hours staring at waves of starlings dancing in the sky outside of his window.

He was greatly disturbed because since he founded newspapers years ago, Bear held true to a pledge to himself that there was no place in such community work for indecency and wickedness that was becoming common in society.

For Chuck Bear, Dickie Randim had become the epitome of wickedness he feared. Randim was the last straw. Bear contemplated resigning soon and closing his upstanding Inquirer chain, his life's achievement. He was a very proud man.

He also felt the fool.

No one really faced what they were seeing in the cafe for two weeks before Martha Read was overcome with the excitement of doing it on her desk with handsome Dickie. She had been enjoying his company.

Dickie had made a game with his time with Martha, reading her mind over morning coffee in the cafe. She had delighted with the attention and looked forward to their morning chats. He had discovered that she was a lonely woman who was at an age when she felt a loss of her feminine wiles.

He would make ever-so-slight flattering advances. "Martha, you look ravaging this morning." "New hairdo? Very attractive, I'd say." And then, he'd walk by flashing his irritable charming smile. He rationalized his goal by conjuring up in his mind images of humping a voluptuous and desirous Martha.

She was no Hollywood cougar. Martha was a wiry, graying, nice woman with a stern and unforgiving expression she wore at work.

Dickie felt that he needed her power and influence in the company. He feared that his "reporting" was threatening his job, his health and maybe his life if the dangerous Johnny Martin ever learned of his affair with his wife Vickie.

After Chuck Bear saw what he saw, his passion for his newspaper chain revived, and instead of succumbing to what he saw as an increasingly immoral world, he relieved himself of Dickie, sending him off to the tropics to play for a while and let things calm down. Word of the scandal never left the building.

Chapter 7: Snatched Away

Tuesday morning, May 15, 2007

On the morning after the FUC'M tower bombing, Dickie Randim went missing. He didn't show for his belated start at his public relations job at the Inquirer. Management's calls to his apartment went unanswered.

Benny Bradley arrived at the paper early and anxiously waited for Chris, who arrived at 9:45 a.m. Chris was still without his Mazda. He had to take the No. 9 bus in a soft spring rain.

"Don't sit down, Chris," Bradley shouted out when he saw him. Bradley walked briskly from his desk to intercept Chris, who had just sat at his computer and punched in his password 'Yuengling.' "We are going to get some background … together this time. Come," Benny said. He patted Chris on the back in a fatherly manner.

Benny piled him into his Buick Lucerne for a drive back to the Loweville crime scene.

"Could have caught a cab, Benny, or something. You don't have to …"

Bradley cut him off, "Here, borrow this laptop now. Oh hell, just keep it, Chris, you'll need one. I'll talk Michele into a new one for me. Just save my files. We'll download them to my PC later."

Bradley had rushed the kid off before the sharp-tongued group of four women reporters, including the distracting Melissa, could smother their cute boy pet with leading questions. These were Melissa's 'girls' who sat in a cluster of desks with Chris.

They were already annoying Bradley with: "Hey Bennie, why did Chris and Randim just happen to be right next to the FUC'M building when it exploded?" "Why did witnesses quoted in the Washington Post see the two fleeing in a beat-up pale blue Porsche?" "Someone snapped a photo of them, or what? "What the hell happened to Dickie's car anyway?"

Once Benny was motoring out of the garage, he said to Chris, "You would not believe those women at your business desk. They were waiting to ambush you with questions about yesterday. I thought instead we could take a ride together."

"Okay, but I can handle them."

"Oh, you can, eh? I've seen you cower to all their attention, young man. Melissa's not that cute, you know. You need to ignore them, but on the other hand, I understand."

* * *

Halfway down to Loweville in the Buick, Bradley's cell phone rang.

"Benny? Randim's been arrested." It was his boss, business editor Steve Mothershart. "The police want Chris too. Look into it when you get there, okay? Act like you don't know anything."

"That's easy. I don't," said Bradley. "What else you got, Steve?" After a minute, he hung up.

"What's easy?" Chris asked.

"Steve said you're off the story. Conflicting interests," Bradley lied. Mothershart said nothing of the kind. Bradley was always a step ahead. Mothershart had conveyed to Bradley on the phone that managing editor Michele was in a rage. She'd learned that people at the scene suspected that Dickie and Chris were involved in the bombing. Mothershart told Benny that he argued with Michele, said her argument was absurd, which pissed her off more. Despite Steve's best effort, Michele had canceled Chris's ticket to continue covering the story, Mothershart conveyed.

Chris was confused, "Interests? I have no interests in anything. This is my story, Benny. I was there; saw everything; talked with everybody."

"Exactly. Michele took you off the story because you were seen with Randim at the crime scene as it happened, and then seen running," said Bradley. "It's a cardinal sin in journalism for a reporter to be any part of the story, even by perception alone. You know that."

"It was a coincidence, Benny. And, a great break for us."

"Not for you Chris, not at this time. There will be other big stories for you. I'll talk with Michele." Bradley said.

The reality was that the local news oriented Inquirer did not have the resources to follow up on such a once in a century, eye witness story.

"Listen Chris, she's smart, smarter in this business than us. Trust me. Michele brings no BS editing to this paper. She's a manager, but not of management if you know what I mean. She'll look out for you in the long run. Michele had to do this. Don't be fooled by her angry act. Eccentric behavior is the way she deals with pressure.

"What you haven't seen yet is the touch she can give to improve stories, just a word here, a phrase there; she immediately enhances what you wrote. She is a tremendous editor and, like I say, this will pass and you'll learn to appreciate these kinds of decisions.

"Here's the deal, Chris. A lesser journalist than Michele would have put the paper at risk and let you hang with it, supporting the hardworking reporter. Not Michele. Steve said she got calls and emails from people who saw you there and they suspect you and Dickie. She earned her bread on this approach. She is old school journalism, tough and fair, and that pays off in the end. You'll see," he said.

"I don't understand. She didn't like my stories yesterday?" Chris said.

"Well, she actually liked what you wrote, especially the threads through the homeowners and mortgage jerks in that building. I guessed wrong on that."

Chris felt like responding in anger but kept his mouth shut. He loved his job too much to risk it. Instead, he thought, *This is totally unfair. It's darn stupid of Michele not to use me. I was there!* He settled for saying, "What's easy then?"

"Excuse me?"

"You told Steve that's easy."

"Oh, nothing. The thing is, Dickie Randim was arrested late last night. Pulled right out of his condo by the cops with a warrant."

"What the hell?"

"Chris, come on? Think. Dickie's hanky-panky with Vickie Martin? Boss Martin probably hated Randim. Witnesses placed Randim at the scene, running from the bombing. Want more? Oh, yea, when the cops arrived at Dickie's place, guess who was already with him wearing his slippers, you know, those Deputy Dog ones, management gave us last Christmas? Oh, yes, I forgot. You weren't yet at the paper. Point is, Martin's wife was with him when Dickie was arrested too."

Chris tried to lighten up the conversation, “I’ll bet she is hot,” he said meekly. He was getting scared.

“Yea, Chris, she’s hot alright. She may be a suspect in her husband’s death. Oh, and the police want to talk with you. Guess why? You’re a suspect too, along with Dickie. [He couldn’t help a little uncomfortable mock laughing.] People said you were there in a beat-up powder blue sports car that fled the scene. Seen any of those in our garage lately?” he asked.

“Oh God, Benny. I am so sorry. We were just there by accident. Dickie said he liked Johnny Martin. He wanted me to meet him…because of my real estate beat and all.”

“Wow, he’s cleverer than he looks,” said Bradley.

“What do you mean?”

“Randim was probably setting you up, buddy boy.”

“For what? Suspicion of bombing the FUC’M tower? That’s ridiculo...”

“No, no. Of course not. But, something. I know that creep. Stay away from him. Why did you agree to go with him anyway?”

Silence.

“I know you were there by circumstances, Chris,” Bradley continued, “Unless Randim wanted you there. For now, I need to take you to the state police barracks on Route 301. They consider you a suspected accomplice. This shouldn’t take long. I’ll stay with you. Steve borrowed Fayme to go to the tower site now instead of us.”

“Fayme!” Chris was outraged and insulted that the paper was sending a flighty writer like Fayme to replace Chris on the best story imaginable. He was afraid to express what he thought of about cute, young Fayme Lovelace. She was a newly hired reporter who was a lightweight in both body and mind. Instead, Chris stared out into the rain, now a driving, windy downpour that masked details of new May foliage into a Monet-like impression of the green tones the trees, lawns and gardens passing by. He daydreamed of Glasgow, his West Virginia home.

Chapter 8: Facing the Feds

Noon, Tuesday. May 15

Benny Bradley had never seen so many vehicles on the parking lot at the King's County Sheriff's Office. Every space was filled with county patrol or state trooper cars, and black SUVs with D.C. tags and tinted windows all around. As he parked with others on the roadside, he said, "You believe this?"

Silence still from Chris. Then, after a moment, "Huh, yeah sure."

Inside the double glass doors of the station, there was hardly room to move. The lobby and open rooms on either side were buzzing with chatter like a strategic war room.

Sheriff Barney Standard and two men in dark suits were crossing the lobby as Benny and Chris entered. The Sheriff nodded and pointed at Benny, but spoke to the tallest of the men in suits. "I thought I told you not to bring in that boy. He is the reporter who was all over the site yesterday and covered the story in the paper."

The man replied, "We know, Sheriff."

Benny approached them, "Sheriff, I hope this won't take long. My reporter is not implicated, is he?"

"Of course not, Mr. Bradley. These fellows from Washington said …"

Stepping partially in front of the sheriff, the man in the suit said, "We want to ask Mr. Gilley a few questions, sir. That's all. If he was to be held we would have arrested him along with Mr. Randim, who is here you may know. And, you are?"

Sheriff Standard stepped forward, "I'm sorry. This is Benny Bradley a local newspaperman who works with Mr. Gilley; I suppose his editor, right Benny?" Bradley nodded. "And Benny, this is Mr. Smith who works with the federal government."

"Saw the D.C. tags outside," said Benny. "FBI?"

Mr. Smith ignored the probe and requested instead, "If you will follow me, Christopher? It is Christopher Gilley, correct? I did read the stories. Very good reporting, son."

"Yes sir. Thank you, sir."

Benny piped in, "I'll say it was good reporting and very thorough too," he said raising his voice as Chris, Smith and

Standard picked up their pace to leave Chris's editor behind and ignoring his comment.

"We won't need you to come back, Mr. Bradley," said Smith as they entered another room. "You can wait. Or we can bring Chris back to Rhodesville if you wish." Smith's friendly face took on a frown. He seemed to sense some irritation on Benny's face. "Say, maybe you would like to talk with Mr. Randim in his cell meanwhile."

"No thanks."

* * *

After 25 long minutes, Chris immerged smiling from an interview room. The law enforcement officers told Benny Bradley, still waiting in the lobby, that they were satisfied that he corroborated Richard Randim's version of the ill-timed reporting trip to Loweville.

Benny asked Chris, "What's got your tickle bug. You went in there with a sour puss attitude."

"Outside, come on," Chris shook his head and waved his hand toward the double doors, snickering. Once he was in Benny's car, he continued, "I saw Dickie."

"And?"

"After I told them what we were doing at the tower when it blew, they wanted me to ask Dickie a few questions."

"That's not normal procedure, Chris."

"I figured that."

"What did they want you to ask the fool?"

"Just stupid stuff we had already discussed. But I don't think that was why they took me to his cell at all."

"Why did they?"

"They wanted me to see him, I think. That's all."

"Again, why?

"Dickie had an Elvis suit on. I asked him why he was sitting there on the cot wearing it. He was just super pissed off; didn't say anything, while the cops just laughed their asses off. They said they had to pound loudly on Dickie's door to get him to hear them knocking because of the music inside."

"What kind of music. Oh, don't tell me."

"Yeah, Elvis. Hunka Hunka Burning Love, they said."

"For Mrs. Martin, no doubt."

"No doubt. But, you should have seen that beautiful outfit in a stark jail cell, Benny. Very theatrical. You know, white sequined jumpsuit open at the chest, big collar turned up, medallions, bell bottoms, the whole bit. Oh, I asked him one more thing, with a straight face too, Benny. You'd be proud of me."

"What was that?"

"Lose your Elvis wig, Dickie?"

"I'm going to try not to laugh, but … Bah! (laughter) … I love it."

The police lacked evidence of Dickie's involvement in Martin's death. Also, they believed young Chris's story. At Dickie's request, the police also confirmed their story with the farmer who saw Randim and Chris intrude on his farm that Monday, just a little time before the thunderous blast at the FUC'M tower. That would place them on the road with no time to plant a bomb; and why go there if they'd known, one detective had told Chris.

The police held Dickie overnight and released him. They put a tail on his trip home in a cab and overnight.

Benny and Chris agreed it would be too distractive to tell anyone at the paper about the Elvis suit. They wished they could, they both said.

Chapter 9: Girl Shy

The previous day, Chris had been a real investigative reporter for the first time. But, that quickly, one day after feeling his calling as an exceptional reporter, Chris's promising career seemed likely no more than a few hours of hanging out with crazy Dickie against his better judgment.

Worse than that, he was under suspicion. Despite being cleared by the police of any involvement in the disaster at Loweville, he was angry with himself. He had been naïve to get involved with sleazy Mr. Randim. He had wanted so badly to make a good start at the Maryland Inquirer. Now, he believed he was stained and had cast some doubt on Christopher Gilley's judgment at the paper.

The newspaper staff, the editors and management, had to feel it, he reasoned. They had ripped from him the best story of the year, the decade for all he knew.

The truth was that management didn't know Christopher Gilley existed and would probably not think he was a newspaper reporter at his age.

Once again lonely as a boy with no home, he coped with having no car, no girlfriend, no friends in Rhodesville except Liza at the paper and perhaps Benny.

Chris got back to work. He wondered what Liza would think of him blowing his big chance. Perhaps his judgment would reflect on Liza too, he thought. She brought him to the paper.

While trying to concentrate on his PC screen, his eyes ping-ponged lazily between the screen and the sweet face of Melissa seated across the abutted desks. Mel's face gushed with an expression of *Oh, you poor dear*. He adored Melissa as a colleague but hated how she doted on him. He wished she didn't look so sexy.

As a habit, Melissa would tell people she likened Chris to her "adorable" pizza delivery boy in Montgomery Village apartments where she lived by herself.

"What's wrong, Chris?" she said, her words pawing out with affection. She was worried. Chris's face carried a spacey and innocent expression.

Chris tried to wear a deadpan expression while sitting at his desk, facing his kind female companions.

When landing his job, Chris had vowed to himself to stay clear of dating or close relationships in his first year at the paper. Girls in school and women he'd met in his brief career always seemed to get the upper hand on naive Chris. He had been determined to focus all his energy on his big break, the Maryland Inquirer.

It wasn't easy for an innocent kid from the sticks to remain uninterested while rubbing elbows with urbane, beautiful females every day at the paper. He found himself quivering when Melissa came close and stood over him with hug-me eyes. Her firm jugs only inches at times from his face were a major distraction when she'd come around the desks to help him with copy or a photo on his computer screen,

He composed his best copy when away from his desk, away from Melissa's girls. He'd compose copy on location or even in the paper's lunchroom, so he wouldn't miss deadlines by losing himself in Melissa's allure as she inadvertently tossed her torso to-and-fro. The close-up 'show,' could at times kill Chris's creative juices.

He knew he was being ridiculous, but, again, the kid was lonely, and after his setback, unhappy and suppressing horny thoughts.

At 6' 3" tall, 178 pounds, Chris didn't consider himself attractive. However, he was far more appealing to females than he knew. He was humble and genuinely more impressed with others than with himself. He brought out nurturing instincts in females and was no threat to them when they roped him into their clever bantering.

The women in the newsroom, in addition to Melissa, thought he was adorable, with his large brown mop hair hanging loose, close over his PC screen.

He stuck to himself socially and was puzzled by the motherly attention he got from the women around his news desk cluster, without trying, especially from Melissa Cushen. After Michele took him off the FUC'M tower story, he hated the pity Melissa and the others showed him. He was nobody's little mascot or cute boy.

He knew he was a fine reporter, but after the fateful ride with Randim, he just wanted to crawl into a hole under his desk and disappear. He was embarrassed and hurt, not as a man, but as a serious journalist.

Chapter 10: The (Un)Inquirer

The Maryland Inquirer had five newsrooms around the state it called bureaus, with the largest at its corporate headquarters in Rhodesville and four smaller operations.

The newsrooms were filled with reporters' desks arranged in clusters assigned to different regional beats. For the most part, the reporters and beat editors sat transfixed to their computers, writing their copy with an innate capability to drown out everything else. The newsroom was flanked by a few small rooms for managing editors.

The large Rhodesville newsroom was typical of a modern newspaper operation—quiet and efficient by all appearances. Very little paper would be seen strewn across the reporters' desks.

Forget those Hollywood images from the great Cary Grant-Rosalind Russell screwball comedy *His Girl Friday*, or the riveting Nixon-Era *All the President's Men*. Long gone was the familiar scene of constant movement of reporters in and out of the newsroom, while burned-out editors would shout "stop the presses" for a new headline, such as "Earl Williams Arrested." Gone were the days of the chain-smoking scribblers and stale coffee in the wee small hours. No more police scanners squawking and news wire services chattering.

Drama was at a minimum. Typically, there were long, tiresome lulls between deadlines or rare, fast-breaking stories, such as stabbing, a local celebrity scandal or a real estate development deal threatening to destroy wildlife habitats. But most of the time, the vacuous newsroom was about as animated as a giant tortoise at the zoo.

The Inquirer's Rhodesville newsroom was especially quiet. The dominant sounds were the murmurs of reporters doing their fact gathering by phone and clicking of keyboards. The Inquirer reporters did most of their research online and during basic work hours.

Chris was different. He liked the off hours to gather facts for the next week's edition, both in the same manner as the others, online and by phone, and by car when his Mazda was running. He preferred to talk to sources in person if the newsroom monster clock permitted.

Unlike in the old days of the clamor of typewriters keys as they struck paper and busy ratatat wire service machines, Chris and his colleagues could gather up-to-date facts and figures on their desktop PCs: tax records of corporations and non-profits, real estate deals, commercial and residential real estate records, court records just entered two days earlier, rap sheets, arrest records, marriage and driver's licenses, medical publications, trade and association columns and opinions and news clips of newspapers and web sites of broadcast stations around the world.

News clippings for only the past 15 years were online.

Because news can be depressing, older reporters at a small paper, those at the ripe old age of 40 and burned out, would often escape to less demanding public relations jobs at a university or large corporation. And some would sell out their newspaper skills and stale ambitions to take a job as a flack at a small startup company. That could be career suicide in high-turnover-biotech Maryland, but necessary if you wanted to support your family, alimony and earn a decent wage, for a while at least.

In the beginning, the Maryland Inquirer was a trendsetter, emphasizing community news and interests. The Inquirer squeezed out profits by filling in local news, sports, classified and ads in communities of the Washington-Baltimore suburbs, while the major newspapers, Washington Post, Washington Times and Baltimore Sun, shrunk their budgets, reporter pool, news hole, as readership continued to free fall with the rise of on-line news outlets.

The Inquirer's simple business plan was to minimize space for the news reporting, thus skimping on reporters' salaries, and rewarding the advertising staff for every dollar they brought in for selling ad space. The Inquirer had the best crossword puzzles, comics, and kid's pages of games and educational quizzes of any publication in the East.

With the Maryland Inquirer then, Chris's could put little hope of uncovering who killed Boss Martin and blew up his FUC&M tower. The Inquirer did not encourage investigative reporting.

Chapter 11: The Prodigy

Despite all the negative trends in newspapers, Christopher Gilley never lost sight of pursuing journalism as he grew up. He loved the idea of being the conscience of the people.

He was the most intelligent of the nine Gilley children and probably the most creative thinker among them. But few people other than his mother gave Chris that kind of credit. His gangly frame, shy manner and slouch defined him on first impression as otherwise a rather dull boy for most people who just met him.

When Chris considered colleges, his mother pleaded with him not to enroll at a journalism school. He loved editing his high school newspaper. Yet, Ma kept repeating her little joke, "A mind is a terrible thing to waste," hoping to steer him in another more intellectual direction. As time passed, she considered her opinion less of a joke. She took on a didactic bite in her voice, then a desperation pleading, as he enjoyed more and more success with his high school and college newspapers. Yet, she watched and admired her son's reporting skills getting better and better.

When Chris was 16, he interned without pay at a local newspaper in West Virginia where he found himself in love for the first time with commercial newspaper work: Getting the story, checking two or more sources on every detail, covering both sides of every public issue, exposing the bad guys who sometimes were his neighbors or his father's business associates at Peterson's Coal Company, where his Pa worked as a tool machinist.

Chris was hooked for life to reporting, despite Ma's pleas. He sensed that he was good and was determined NOT to be that 40-year-old, chain smoking, burned-out alcoholic reporter, trying to explain his journalistic idealism to his kids when he was retired without much savings and leaning on a measly Social Security check every month. Chris just promised his Ma to do his best.

Though he embodied all the best of journalism, lived by all the rules, all the ethical boundaries of reporting, and abided by principles of writing a balanced, original story, Chris had no delusions of making it to his goal of being a top national reporter soon.

At the Inquirer, his launching pad, he just wanted to fit in, at least for a while, and climb out of being poor.

On the other hand, certain realities of the industry were working against him. The shrinking news hole, that is, the amount of actual news copy appeared in each successive edition, was a concern for new employees at the paper who worried about last-in-first-out layoffs.

Chris and his fellow young reporters were acutely aware that the Maryland Inquirer was in a serious budget crunch. At any time, the paper could reduce its labor force again as it had several times in the previous three years. Chris for one, could not fathom that newspapers in America would die out completely as some of his media professors had said.

On the plus side of the page, Chris was a true paradox at the Maryland Inquirer. It was soon clear to everyone that his skills and instincts as a beat reporter were superb. Yet, he lacked the stuff of a true newspaperman, the cynicism, the dark humor, the emotional detachment to horrible events affecting innocent people. With the reporting limitations at the Inquirer, he was unwittingly vulnerable to possibly succumbing to a frustrating future unless he could continue to brighten his copy with the best of himself.

So far, at the time when ill winds of American media blew hard against dailies, the Maryland Inquirer and other innovative weeklies remained in the black. Chris and his pal Liza could benefit from the experience by giving readers in communities what they wanted most—the local stuff.

This was the special genius of CEO Chuck Bear and his investors--to figure out the only formula left for a profitable paper, years before anyone else saw the light of going local and remaining local.

The Inquirer shaped local editions of news, classified, advertising, and sports for specific individual communities. Those editions were folded into each region in Maryland and Virginia. In less than a decade, the paper grew from a single edition in Rhodesville to more than 80 editions from Cumberland in the western Maryland Appalachians to Cambridge on Maryland's Eastern Shore. New editions cropped up in nearby Delaware and northern Virginia counties.

Supporting headquarters in Rhodesville, the four smaller, satellite Inquirer newsrooms were spokes of its news wheel 30 to 100 miles out. Therefore, the few jobs at the little local desks were coveted by those young folks like Christopher Gilley who read the foreboding tea leaves of journalism and wanted to start out on a safe track regardless.

In the spacious, main newsroom in Rhodesville, with its clusters of desks pulled together to staff the various beats for towns and regions, there were also special beats, like Chris Gilley's statewide real estate beat, part of the business section, managed by Steve Mothershart and Benny Bradley. There were others, like Melissa Cushen's wide-reaching Rhodesville beat, rich in profiles of movers and shakers, statewide sports, entertainment, and G & P (government and politics).

* * *

Considering its all-local-all-the-time business model, The Maryland Inquirer and its editors faced a dilemma with their freak eye-witness advantage to cover the story of the First Union Credit & Mortgage tower bombing at the King's County seat.

Their reporters were first on the scene, led the story with a crackerjack young reporter who lit up the readership statewide in print and online. Readers wanted more.

However, the resources were limited. It could not compete with the Washington Post, Baltimore Sun, and even Washington Times, not to mention "out of town" papers such as the New York Times and Richmond Post-Dispatch.

None of this mattered to Christopher Gilley. His career expectations were suddenly within his grasp because he had witnessed and reported a fabulous story.

And then, just as quickly, his momentum and confidence were gone.

Still, Chris considered himself lucky to be assigned to the real estate beat, along with his companions reporting business stories in their cluster. There was another, small positive. After losing his big story to Michele's better judgment, Chris found it easier to ignore the sexy, loving smiles from Melissa. He didn't know why, but he felt stronger and more focused. He had to still prove himself.

Meanwhile, Benny Bradley became concerned about Chris's feelings after Michele cut him out of the big story. Benny was fond of the kid. He gave Chris easy assignments for a while, to work him toward developing a weekly real estate column of opinions and projections. Chris faked being grateful.

Those assignments were published in the newspaper almost word for word, with little editing from Benny or Steve Mothershart, as Chris cranked them out effortlessly: 'Teamsters Strike to Slow Port America,' 'Poolesville $1 Million Homes Still Selling,' 'Scruppels Opens Rhodesville Complex.' He could knock out background filler articles effortlessly, while his colleagues were constantly behind on their deadlines.

He was annoyed when Benny started giving him little pep talks, much out of character for his matter-of-fact boss. "Good story, Chris." "Liked that a lot." "Steve, check this out. Chris nailed it."

Gosh, I wish he'd stop patronizing me. I'd rather get screamed at, Chris thought, but buttoned his lip, waiting for better days.

Still, Chris was confounded. He had seen and heard far too much about the FUC'M tower incident to let it go entirely. He still wanted to cover it. It possessed him day and night. He read everything his colleagues and other papers wrote on the developing story. He read all the coverage of the incident in the Washington Post, Baltimore Sun, and, when his liberal-leaning editors weren't looking, he pulled up the conservative Washington Times coverage online.

Chapter 12: Knife

Quiet Wednesday until 5 p.m., May 16

In a flash, the newsroom was buzzing with chatter as the entire staff learned that their Richard Randim had been arrested again, this time as a likely suspect in the death of Boss Martin.

The only evidence--besides his not-so-secret affair with Martin's wife--was from comments by Johnny Martin's personal aid, a 22-year-old Latino named Juan 'Knife' Garcia. Knife said he heard Dickie threaten to kill Martin in full view of Vickie and others.

Garcia was an odd choice of a personal aid and protector of Boss, but understandable. Martin had been like a father to Garcia who previously was a juvenile delinquent. The developer adopted the short, stocky Juan when the boy was a teenager. Martin arranged a deal with a county judge to release the kid on good behavior.

Garcia had been sentenced to serving six months for stabbing a fellow gang member in Charmington Village, one of Martin's "upscale" housing developments, which was filled with foreclosures.

When Garcia learned of Boss Martin's death on Monday, he was paralyzed with grief.

By Wednesday morning Garcia managed to compose himself enough to tell police that he heard a drunken Dickie Randim threaten to kill Boss Martin at a meeting at the Radisson on Saturday evening, May 12, before the FUC'M tower "fell down in da hole, officer," Garcia said.

Garcia knew that Dickie liked Johnny Martin. However, Garcia was overwhelmed with emotion over what he thought he heard in the meeting room at the hotel. He told the police that he thought Dickie was the murderer of Johnny Martin.

The police took additional interest in Garcia because of his past record. They took his deposition of descriptions of real estate developers who were in that same meeting with Martin at the Radisson on Saturday night.

Later, police records would reveal that two employees of lender Samuel Johnson's Lifetime Deal Financing, Corp., (LDF) were in the Radisson meeting with Martin and that they confirmed

Garcia's account in separate police interviews, nearly word for word. Dickie had threatened Martin in that meeting room exactly as Garcia said.

The police also interviewed Vickie Martin. She confirmed that Dickie was at the Radisson that night.

Still, the police considered Dickie to be a coward, not likely a killer

She told them, "Unless the fool was drunk out of his mind." She later regretted her statement.

Dickie surrendered easily to officers camped outside of his condo when arrested again, without an Elvis impersonating outfit.

On the evening after Dickie's second arrest, Chris was still at the paper. He was not one to be resting idly. He recalled Vickie's sexy phone call on Friday, May 11. She had invited Dickie to attend the hotel's opening the following day. It was the same Saturday of Martin's Radisson meeting, according to police.

Chris wondered why Michele sent Fayme out to focus on the "suspected terrorist attack" in Loweville that other newspapers keyed on. Instead, Chris was intrigued with Garcia's statements.

Chris thought through what was known and still unknown about Martin's odd meeting at the Radisson. Staring into space, elbows on either side of his keyboard with his hands holding his head, he spaced out for several minutes.

He instinctively believed that Martin's death was tied directly to the bombing at the FUC'M tower. *But how?* he thought. *That meeting was the real key to Johnny Martin's death and the bombing of FUC'M tower and no one has quoted any sources to tie them together.* He was fascinated with how, when, and why did Boss Martin die? *Yes, that is the key to who destroyed Martin's building,* he thought.

Ever since Michele removed him from the story, Chris was driven by finding any way to replace the inept Fayme and hitch a ride again onto the story. He considered the prospects of investigating it on the sly, behind the backs of the very people who had given him a good career start. Weighing that temptation against his loyalties was the most difficult decision of his young life.

He began to quietly conduct some independent research. Could he uncover anything completely by himself? And, with virtually no resources other than his instincts? He believed that he could. But, a private detective he was not.

He was more like just a scared kid with a wish.

<u>Chapter 13: Showdown</u>

6 p.m. the previous Saturday night, May 12, at the Radisson

Johnny "Boss" Martin instructed Knife Garcia, "Juan, I want you to just listen from behind that folding wall that divides the conference rooms."

They surveyed the meeting room together half an hour before Martin's meeting with developer Johnson and others from LDF.

"And, take this," he added.

Martin surprised his young Latino protector by handing Garcia his revolver. "Look son, don't plan on using this. It's insurance, get it? If things get out of hand with these guys tonight, I want you to come through that door and point the gun at these guys but please don't shoot anybody. I don't want a murder wrap. The safety is off, see?"

"Okay, Boss." Garcia knew how to handle a gun and took it from Martin confidently, barrel down.

Martin explained, "This is just a shakedown tonight. I need to keep these fellows in line. I think I should take the bullets out."

"No, Boss, please. That won't be too necessary, sir. I want to shoot when some guy, he tryin' to shoot you. Maybe they bring guns too. You think of that?"

"Nobody is going to bring guns, Juan. But just in case there's trouble, stay back there in the next room and listen," Martin warned.

The meeting had been proposed by Martin's corporate officers. They were worried over rumors of racial profiling by Martin's current and former collaborators in the FUC&M tower: BOM Corp. and LDF, Corp.

Martin's men failed to tell him that Sam Johnson of LDF had also requested a meeting. They preferred to let their boss think he was in control.

Chapter: 14 Johnson's Dirty Game

Johnny 'Boss' Martin knew for a long time that Sam Johnson hated blacks with passion. The hatred was rooted in insecurities during his upbringing. His racism was only matched in degree by his ability to mask his prejudices in his business for many years.

Inside his company, however, Johnson was known to enjoy "ruining as many of them darkie invaders as I can" in King's County, which he considered his personal kingdom. But he was shrewd and didn't flaunt his bias outside of a tight inner circle.

Johnson was a throwback to old-time Southern racists with a powerbase of money or politics. He used money and power to hide discrimination practices at LDF.

Boss Martin considered Johnson's racism unacceptable, but he also saw it as Johnson's Achilles heel that he could one day exploit. He knew Johnson's whole story.

Johnson was raised to believe whole heartedly in the superiority of the Caucasian race. Despite the changing times and the national acceptance of the growing awareness of the humanity of embracing civil rights in all aspects of our society, Johnson's racial prejudice was ingrained—planted and nourished by his daddy and reinforced by his granddaddy and other relatives. He longed for living in the legend of his family's glory days when their farm was prosperous and maintained by hard-working, fearful black slaves. Resident slave families on the farm dated back to Africans purchased by Johnson's ancestors on the auction block in Annapolis, Maryland.

Throughout the late 19th and early 20th centuries, the farm profits had begun to slip following emancipation and steadily declined.

Sam Johnson lamented that only a generation ago, his family profited from the rich, sandy loam of lower eastern King's County.

Now in his 60's, Johnson deeply resented that his county was mostly occupied by blacks. As a result, Sam Johnson's cruel heart and his duplicitous business were largely energized by his racial anger.

In 1965, Sam Johnson threw up his hands on keeping the family farm and put for sale the 395 prime acres on the riverside, rolling hills of southern Maryland. He chose the very day that President Lyndon Johnson signed the federal voting rights bill.

Sam Johnson cleverly subdivided the 395 acres into very small parcels and leveraged them to builders to put up hundreds of cheaply built track single family houses and townhomes. He was anticipating that black families moving into the county could be tricked by his unfair lending schemes just to grab the low-end priced homes.

As months passed, he realized many of his black prospective buyers had more expensive tastes. He ordered his builders to plant larger homes on the small lots, still cheaply built, and high-end bait gave him even more profit margins.

This would-be Sam Johnson's revenge. He made a fortune, but never anticipated his county becoming a haven for middle class blacks migrating from deeper in the South than D.C., seeking well-paid jobs in the metro Washington area. He grew more and more bitter and more predatory with every sale to African Americans.

* * *

Because of rumors of Johnson's strong bias against African Americans, developer Boss Martin decided to investigate racial profiling in mortgage lending in the King's County. The association between Martin's construction business and the prejudicial practices at Johnson's finance company and possibly at the Best Opportunity Mortgaging Corp. did not sit well with Martin nor with his managers, most of whom were African-Americans themselves.

Martin was no angel. He was an unscrupulous builder himself, perhaps even criminal in cheating on codes, zoning, and building materials. But he was not a racist and the whole idea of working with racist financers worked on his conscience. In the spring when housing construction normally picks up, Martin's business was stalled that spring of 2006 and he decided to do something about the racist lenders he did business with.

He hired reporter Dickie Randim to investigate his collaborating lenders, Johnson's LDF and Best Opportunity Mortgage, Corp. in the First Union Credit & Mortgage tower in Loweville.

The insane collaboration of Johnny Martin, Vickie's husband, and Dickie Randim, her lover, was nothing short of ingenious from a business sense. Martin needed a snoop and why not a reporter? he thought.

For Dickie's part, he had no conscience as a reporter and figured he could conceal his extracurricular snooping for Martin from his regular employer, the Inquirer. Being unethical never entered Dickie's mind. It was yet another risky challenge.

Martin shared with Dickie his suspicions that somehow, Johnson and CEO Bernie Madinoff of Best Opportunity Mortgage, Corp. might be violating the law by targeting blacks for fraudulent home loans, "and I want you to find out about it before it takes us all down. I don't want you to report it in the paper. I want you to report it to me, personally," he said to Richard "Dickie" Randim.

Johnny Boss Martin was an attorney and thus didn't want his fingerprints on any requests for legal documents. He needed to appear ignorant that mortgage companies in his own office tower were discriminating against African-American home buyers with unfair terms on their mortgages.

To get around his dilemma, Martin recruited Dickie to find out if rumors were true. It was a match of two scoundrels made for each other.

He came upon Randim as his choice serendipitously. Martin read Dickie's story in the Inquirer about mounting foreclosures on Martin's housing developments, including hundreds of them financed by BOM and LFD. It was a simple story for Randim to tease from court records and innocent enough. He didn't know Martin at the time or have any news reporting desire to expose him.

But, in the story Randim wrote before he knew Marten, he had singled out Charmington Village, Martin's pet project in King's County which had been financed by BOM out of the FUC'M tower. Dickie filed his stories because other newspapers had already mentioned Charmington Village in their stories on financing fraud. Most of his copy was just that, a mix of sentences and paragraphs from other papers, backed by court records.

Johnny Martin fumed over Randim's Charmington story. He ordered his secretary to, "Get that damn reporter into my office, NOW!"

But when they met, Randim's charm melted any friction between the two men. They hit it off. They shared common interests in sailing the Caribbean and picking up local girls for sport. They even had a former girlfriend in common, the Baldur Real Estate Agent of the Year, Addie "Happy" Handwerker. Over whiskey in Martin's office, the two discovered that each of them had had sex with Happy on the balcony of her eighth-floor pad at The Plaza condominiums in Ocean City, Md. in broad daylight. "Oh, yeah Randim, she was wicked," Martin bragged. "Another? Help yourself to another Old Grandad, my boy. Here's to happy days."

Martin told the reporter that he needed some private investigating from "a pro, like a newspaperman." He offered to pay Dickie handsomely to use his reporting skills to get the dirt on mortgage predators, which, rumors held, discriminated especially against blacks and Latinos, maybe Catholics too.

* * *

As his clandestine assignment panned out, Dickie wasn't disciplined enough to focus well on Martin's instructions. Martin told Dickie that he mostly suspected shady dealings of Sam Johnson's LDF, but Dickie was leery of Johnson. Like nearly every businessman and woman in the county, Dickie Random feared Sam Johnson.

Instead of focusing first on Johnson, Dickie started his investigation on perhaps a safer path, investigating Madinoff's BOM, the lending company more often associated with Martin's development firm. Besides being afraid of Johnson's reputation as a hardnosed thug in gray pinstripes, Dickie was finding it hard to get anyone to talk much about Johnson.

As time went on, Boss Martin counted more and more on Dickie, to the degree that the reputation and future of his JDR business depended on information from Dickie for Martin to stay free of the problems of the predatory lenders, especially as mortgage money grew thin in the housing bust of 2006-7. Boss Martin promised Dickie a luxury McMansion on the Potomac River if he indeed helped Martin nail Johnson and or Madinoff, based on Randim's info.

For a couple of months, the arrangement seemed to work for both men. Dickie was getting dirt on the financiers, his down payments for a dream house.

By May 12, the day of his meeting at the Radisson Hotel with Johnson and cronies, Martin believed that he was in a position to use Dickie's information to apply leverage on the suspect lenders.

Chapter 15: Vickie's Passion

In late March, two months before the FUC'M tower disaster, Victoria "Peeps" Martin first set eyes on the handsome and vigorous 6'5" Richard Randim of the Inquirer as he sauntered into a Baltimore/Washington Corridor Chamber of Commerce holiday mixer. It was held at the new Chili's Restaurant, which was to be part of the Radisson. As the official hostess, Vickie was dressed as a very sexy Easter Bunny, not the dough-boy, fir-ball version of children's stories, but showing her figure and lots of cleavage.

Her radar locked in on Dickie's long, blond curly mane in the crowded restaurant, his stature and confident air.

Ironically, Dickie was not there to check out women but to watch and learn about Bernie Madinoff and Sam Johnson, who would likely be attending. In no time, Dickie had a drink in his hand and Vickie made her move. She found herself sliding into the cushy loveseat next to Dickie. She forgot she was supposed to be passing out the corporate holiday gift to chamber members, the new pocket Radisson calendars.

With her most alluring smile and a tilt of her pretty head, she positioned herself in her seat as she managed to allow her Miss Bunny Rabbit skirt to ride up past mid-thigh. She introduced herself, offering him a pocket calendar, "Hi, got room for something else in your pocket?"

The attraction was mutual. The next day that same alluring smile beckoned Dickie into her College Park townhouse for lunch, after Dickie located the safe parking spot Vickie had promised him on the phone, the one hidden around the corner.

From then on, he parked there, by the leasing office, twice a week on extended lunch breaks.

On the first day's "lunch," he stayed the night.

Over morning coffee, Vickie said casually that she was married to Johnny "Boss" Martin.

"Oops," he blurted.

"Oops what?" she asked, "You know Johnny? He's a bad dude Dickie. Be careful."

"Oh, I meant, oops, my socks don't match."

Dickie flashed on a mental image of lovely Vickie sunning herself at the backyard pool of his future McMansion on the

Potomac, cupping a cool drink in her hands, as Johnny arrives with a pistol looking for that no-good Randim fellow.

"I've heard of him, yes," he said coyly to Vickie.

Their affair was torrid and not well concealed. Co-workers at the Radisson snickered whenever she and "the newspaper guy"—like a hooker with her pimp—failed to be discreet in the hotel lobby. He would show up for every public event, from a political gala to a local Girl Scout troop fund raiser.

Peeps Martin was too self-centered to notice anyone else when Randim was near, or technically, when he just happened to be tracking yet another story for the Inquirer at the hotel.

"Does he ever cover anything else?" her co-workers would ask with a chuckle and a wink. "Yeah—Vickie," they'd laugh.

Chapter 16: Dreadful Gathering

Again, Saturday, May 12, 7:45 p.m.

Nearly two months after Dickie met Vickie at the spring mixer, Johnny still didn't know about Vickie's affair.

He was preparing to meet with Samuel Johnson and cronies at the Radisson Hotel. It was to be Johnny Martin's show down meeting in the big second floor conference room, with Juan "Knife" Garcia listening in behind the thin, folded divider wall of the big room. He was armed with incriminating evidence of Johnson's fraudulent practice of giving blacks bad lending deals, while Johnson was acutely aware of Martin's evidence and intentions to use it against him.

Entering from the first-floor lobby, Martin and one of his executives waited for an elevator to take them up to the board room.

At about the same time, Dickie and Vickie entered an elevator on the second floor, on their way up to a fifth-floor guest room, or, so they thought. Dickie had not seen Vickie for a month, while he spent much of his absence from the Inquirer in the Caribbean as his father had promised Chuck Bear.

The lusty lovers locked eyes as soon as the elevator doors closed and Dickie lunged for her. He lost himself in their passionate embrace and accidentally pushed the wrong button on the elevator wall, or forgot to push any buttons at all, except hers. Regardless of which button was to blame, the elevator did not go up to a love nest/guest room she had reserved and stocked with champagne, oysters on the half shell, and Dickie's favorite cheeseburgers from Ruby Tuesday on a hot plate. Dickie loved cheeseburgers.

Instead of going to the love nest, the elevator took them down to the first floor.

When the elevator door opened at the lobby, Martin, while talking with his colleague, stepped in without looking up at first. He stopped cold when he saw his trusty snoop Dickie Randim locking lips with his estranged wife Victoria. Dickie's right hand was in her red silk panties, holding tight on her firm ass, as her skirt twisted up at her waist.

According to witnesses near the elevator, Martin went first to Vickie. He reached over Dickie, who caught the full force of Martin's knee in his crotch. Martin grabbed Vickie by the neck. He quickly ripped off the diamond necklace Martin had given Vicky at their wedding. He then clutched an ample clump of Vickie's fiery red hair and violently pulled her out of the elevator and onto the hotel's fine cream-tinted Italian ceramic tiles, to the surprise of gathered guests who collectively gasped, still waiting to ride up to their rooms.

Witnesses later told police that Martin grumbled, "You ungrateful bitch." He was shaking his bloody hand, which he had cut as he tore off the diamond necklace from his naughty wife's neck. Blood spattered inside the elevator, said witnesses, then onto the lobby tile.

The violent man had attracted quite an audience as others rushed over to see the fight. Several people later identified him as "Boss" Martin, the real estate developer.

Dickie, stunned and afraid, managed to brace himself against the elevator walls as he tried to slip out to the hallway, but not before Martin turned to Dickie and screamed, "So this is the kind of inside scoop you're doing for me Mr. reporter."

The door closed behind the two men. When it opened onto the second-floor conference suites, Dickie was bloodied and gasping for breath. Again, he tried to run. Martin pushed him back against the elevator wall and punched "L" with the back of his wounded fist, busting the mirror plate of the elevator control panel.

Met in the lobby by a sea of curious people, Dickie stumbled out of the elevator searching desperately for Vickie.

Martin, though, had a far different response to the confrontation. Satisfied that he'd taken command and punished Vickie and her lover, Martin composed himself quickly. He took fast, decisive action and felt fine about it.

Within minutes he was in the conference room glad-handing his invited guests from LFD, who were Johnson and his cronies.

Earlier in the evening, Martin had asked the catering manager to provide a full bar and dinner to smooth over any ill feelings by his guests, but explicitly not to tell Peeps of the catering or his meeting.

Martin also thought it necessary to add a listening bug to his meeting. His assistant Knife Garcia duct-taped the transmitting device to the underside of the conference board table. Martin assigned Knife to remain in the adjacent room to secretly eavesdrop with earphones linked to the transmitter. "Just listen and witness what goes on, in case something goes wrong," Martin, always the attorney, told his young assistant.

Martin dismissed his two employees who set up the conference room. One was JDR's Chief Operating Officer Col. Humphrey Hurt, who was African-American and whom Martin never wanted him at the meeting with Sam Johnson.

Hurt was at the hotel only because he had driven Martin's father Vincent Martini there. Several hours earlier Vincent Martini had been in Johnny's office fussing. He was always unhappy with how his son ran the business after Vincent left it to him. He lectured Johnny constantly about it. In the heat of their arguing, Hurt, unaware of Vincent, entered, giving Johnny an out. Hurt heard him say "Papa, don't worry yourself. I will be at Vickie's hotel Saturday. Come, you'll have the best suite in the joint."

A meeting with Johnson was of no consequence to Johnny Martin's other executives.

But Martin especially didn't want Col. Hurt around for his meeting with Johnson because Hurt may cause Johnson to bolt. Hurt was Martin's corporate brains, with a Ph.D. from Harvard Business School. He was also a pillar in the African-American communities in King's County, the richest, majority black county in the nation. In Martin's firm at that time, all seven senior executives, all black, idolized COO Hurt.

In the previous five years, Hurt transformed Martin's JDR Builders Inc. with solid management. For the first time the firm, known for sloppy construction and cheap materials, was building with reputable architects, and the best materials. It was an arrangement that had been long overdue.

"Hump, I just don't want you around with that damn racist Johnson and his thugs," Martin said as he dismissed him.

But there was more to Martin's insistence. He wanted Hurt gone that night because of a secret he was keeping from his senior staff, including the Colonel. Martin had started to blackmail Johnson to get him to clean up his act before any related scandals might affect Martin's business, which was more likely during the current housing bust.

Boss Martin, and perhaps his secretary, was the only person at the company who knew that the monthly checks that had been arriving from LDF were the hush money and not the housing construction advances recorded by Martin himself.

Strapped for incoming cash in the economic recession, Sam Johnson was growing wary of Martin's blackmailing and wanted it stopped. He took the whole issue as a supreme threat. He was livid about Martin.

The meeting began with a false air of friendship. After 25 minutes, laughter and the loud talk grew bolder as Martin and his guests drank. Martin wanted to keep at least part of Johnson's blackmail money coming and was confident he could keep Johnson on the string. Johnson was breaking federal housing discrimination laws big time, according to Dickie Randim's research.

* * *

Meanwhile, a battered and stumbling Dickie located Vickie downstairs in her office. They sat licking their wounds sobbing with big helpings of mutual pity, chased with swigs of Crown Royal whiskey on the house. Oddly after Boss Martin had terrorized the couple, Vickie showed no fear and kept her office door half open for Dickie to find and comfort her.

After a few drinks, Vickie began priming her drunken lover's masculinity as if he would somehow defend her from the monster. She chattered on, ranting over Johnny's attack. "Dickie, listen to me! That bastard doesn't care about me. I'm just a toy he brings out at cocktail parties to entertain his thugs, fair weather friends and crooked politicians. He had no right to hit you."

"He's still your husband," Dickie said.

"Johnny and I have not been together in three years. God, we even live in separate houses. He whores around. Everybody thinks I'm a fool. The girls here say I'm his trophy wife. Well, sir, I'm sick of that bastard Johnny Martin. I wish someone would kill the bastard and set me free. I hate him for hitting you. You are twice the man he will ever be. I love you, Dickie. He had no right."

Her words felt good to Dickie. He was not a fighter of course, but he was drunk enough to be bold, to defend the fair maiden from the beast named Johnny.

They rested and napped briefly in each other's arms.

Dick then slurred. "Yer right Vickie, baby, Johnny had no right to do that to you in public, right here at your job place, ah you know. Yeah. No right, yeah." But his words fell on deaf ears. She was still passed out. After a few minutes, he shook her awake.

Vickie, equally drunk, egged him on further, "Johnny just snapped. He caught you red-handed. Dickie, before tonight, he didn't have a clue about us."

"So, you're saying what he did was okay?"

"No, I'm saying I understand what he was thinking. That's what you men do. But, not you, Dickie. You are too smart to mess with him."

"Oh, yea?" He was on his feet.

"Where ya going, Dickie?"

"I'm goin' ta teach the boss a lesson for what he did to Vickie," he mumbled.

Dickie was out the door before she realized it.

As he left, Vickie tried to pull herself up from the couch but stumbled. She tripped over a small table of whiskey glasses and the bottle. It took her a minute to gather herself. And then she took time to get a quick check of herself in a mirror, arranging her hair and clothes. She then went after him.

Dickie rode the elevator up to Martin's meeting.

Vickie missed getting his elevator and waited for another. "Damn it." She blamed herself for the incident with Johnny and realized her mistake in building up Dickie, the lover, into a blundering fighting man.

When she got to the meeting, Dickie had already kicked in the locked conference meeting room door. She staggered in behind to rescue him, only to witness a ridiculous scene.

Vickie later told police that Dickie was "just simply stumble-bumble drunk" when he busted in on Johnny's meeting. She said she followed him there because "Dickie was lookin' out for me. You can all understand that can't ya?"

She also told the police that, in front of the guests, Dickie crept in close to Martin, screaming "all kind of cuss words, ya see? 'cause of how Johnny hurt me, ya see?" she pleaded with the cops.

Chapter 17: Primary Suspect

King's County Sheriff's Office, Loweville

"Did Randim threaten to kill Martin in your presence at that meeting, Mrs. Martin?" asked a police detective.

She was honest and answered in the affirmative. She also admitted that when Martin lost his temper with Dickie face to face, Randim held out his hand and said, "I'll kill you, you bastard," Her deposition was consistent with those of Knife Garcia, Sam Johnson and two of Johnson's men, whom police noted had also been present at the meeting.

"Yes, Dickie, poor boy, said he'd kill him, my husband, John, if he laid another hand on me," Vickie nodded in agreement with the police interrogators, as the beautiful woman pouted, tilting her head to the side and added, "But you fellas know how you get sometimes over us girls, don't cha, huh?"

That's all she told the police.

But in later police interrogations, Knife Garcia also recalled that Dickie Randim ended his tirade with "So, there, you bastard" and then took a swing at Martin and missed. Dickie collapsed to the carpet "like a drunken teenager, Mr. Officer," Garcia offered. He also remembered that Vickie then called hotel security who took Randim back to their office for coffee to help sober him up.

Despite all the witnesses corroborating his threats against Johnny Martin, Randim was released from custody after spending another sleepless night in jail and a bail hearing.

The Inquirer's CEO Chuck Bear made bail for Dickie with money from Dickie's father Jimmy Bob Randim. Dickie's mother Belle Brooks-Randim didn't want any publicity for her husband Jimmy Bob at the jailhouse or courthouse. They let Bear bail out their wacky son.

After hours of interrogating Garcia, Dickie and the others, the police cautiously accepted Randim's stupid alibi of "Hey man, I was stinkin' drunk, honest. I was passed out."

Some female police officers at the county level couldn't stand the sight of the slick talking Dickie Randim. They expressed disappointment when Vickie's mother and young daughter gave Randim a tight alibi. They said he spent all weekend at Vickie's.

Neighbors also told the police they saw Dickie on the condo's balcony several times. They said they had worried that they didn't know "that big blonde man at Mrs. Martin's place." No one could say they saw him there on Saturday night but it was well-established by others that he was indeed at the Radisson of course.

* * *

Chris read all the depositions as he continued to piece "his" story together in his mind. For the first time, he could trace Dickie's tracks, that is, just why Dickie was at Chris's desk so early that Monday morning, May 14.

Chris reflected on his ill-advised ride that morning to Loweville with Dickie. It became clear to Chris that Dickie was likely sobering up the day before at Vickie's College Park condo from his drunken and violent encounter with Martin Saturday night. Hiding out at the condo, he would have had plenty of time to plan his scheme for Monday, using Chris for cover, taking him on a tour of the real estate beat first thing Monday, and perhaps righting himself with management after his six-week banishment. The newspaper people would think better of him then, perhaps. *Yes, that must have been Dickie's plan*, Chris thought. The logic and timing of Dickie's behavior clicked. Chris cringed at being used so easily. *Lucky me*, he thought.

Chris figured that the women -- Vickie and her mother -- nursed Dickie back to health and then sent him packing early Monday morning once they perhaps filled Dickie with black coffee and breakfast. That explained his earlier than usual arrival at Chris's desk Monday morning as well as the dark shades and cuts on Dickie's face. Chris sat at his desk with a triumphant feeling after piecing together the events in his mind. *Yes, I'll be an excellent investigative reporter one day. Yes, indeed,* he thought.

He shook his head vigorously as if dismissing the entire explanation. He realized that Dickie was lying about wanting him to meet Johnny Martin that morning because Martin had beat up Dickie two days earlier.

He wondered, *Was I his alibi? Did Dickie know about the bomb on Martin's pickup under the tower?* Chris asked himself. He thought, *Maybe, he didn't figure it would trigger a second blast in the gas lines of the building and knock the entire structure to the ground endangering himself in the process. It was damn close to both of us dying right there, right then. Whew.*

Chris settled on a preliminary theory that Dickie on that Monday morning was out to inflict vengeance on Johnny Martin. There was no other logical explanation why he and Chris were there. On the other hand, Dickie might have been sincerely wishing to wash his hands of JDR by showing Chris the tower and where Martin and the crooked lenders worked.

* * *

Several days passed as Chris banged out cream puff stories handed him by Benny Bradley.

He grew more and more upset over light-weight Fayme fumbling around with his story.

He asked Benny Bradley, "Why haven't the police, the FBI, or Homeland Security apprehended anyone else about the bombing? This is not right. Something is screwy. I want my story back."

Bradley reminded Chris he was still banned from the story, "and that also means making no calls or emails to your sources on that story," he said, "I'm trusting you on this. It is now in the hands of Fayme."

That hurt.

Benny's marching orders were Benny's marching orders. Chris felt pinned down.

Still, the whole Dickie-Vickie-Boss Martin triangle intrigued Chris. Why did it take so long for Martin to know about Randim and Mrs. Martin, if Knife Garcia was working for him as his private detective, like he told the police?

Chris thought, *Surely Martin was smart enough to have somebody tailing Dickie. And, why would Dickie still be working for him after he started banging Vickie?*

All of this made no sense to Chris, but, then again, the young man had never known individuals quite like those characters before. He made a count: Lloyd said Dickie was risk addictive. Benny said Vickie was dangerously "hot." Business editor Steve said Boss Martin was "totally corrupt." Martin adopted a murderer named Knife. The heads of the local mortgage firms were a racist Sam Johnson and total slob Bernie Madinoff. And, those were only at the top of the bizarre list of characters Chris contemplated as involved in the crimes.

Chris laughed, reflecting just for fun on his Nick at Nite heroes, *These locals were certainly not out of Mayberry, Petticoat Junction or Dodge City. This is the Twilight Zone.*

"What's up Chris," Steve Mothershart had been watching him daydreaming. "Writer's block?"

"Just thinking about all the bizarre character's around these parts," Chris said. He was embarrassed.

"Oh, these parts, eh?" Steve smiled and let it go, exchanging a head shake with Benny.

Back to business, Chris continued scheming. He came up with another puzzle piece missing in his mind about "his" story. *I just don't get that Knife was actually working with Dickie on his investigation for Martin. Knife likely knew about Vickie and Dickie. Too weird,* Chris thought and dismissed the crazy puzzle again.

* * *

Another two days passed, and another Thursday deadline arrived with no break in the case. It was all too much for Chris.

He was still muddled in the mediocrity of small, mundane assignments from Benny.

He looked up from his computer screen, bored, and was once again staring at Melissa instead of his tedious copy. He couldn't take his eyes off the shape of Melissa's amazing breasts, tightly ensconced in a pink wool sweater. That was surely too tight for her frame, he thought to himself, not considering that her posturing was deliberate power posing by the popular Mel. He knew he was getting nowhere by just sitting there at the Inquirer by just dreaming.

Wrenching his eyes away, he resumed his latest copy on a national spelling bee finalist in Frederick County, an 8th grader, who was the daughter of Jean Spicer at the Bioscience Tech Council. He was being careful not to spell Spicer as splicer, Dickie's nickname for her.

In the corner of his eye, Chris caught a glimpse of a small wiry figure racing into the newsroom. It was feather-footed Fayme Lovelace flying across the newsroom and alighting at Michele LaProbe's office. He stood to see Fayme, overly excited, hopping up and down and waving a sheet of paper at Michele. Chris walked over, watched and listened.

Michele's body seemed to fill half the room when she was angry. She was scowling. She was always there, but not always in a perky, no never, in a perky kind of mood, especially for greeting flighty Fayme, for whom she showed no patience at all.

"Michele, ah … Michele, I'm sorry to bother you on deadline, but it's ... it's.... [Fayme lost her breath]."

"For Christ's sake, what is it, girl? What can possibly be so important to disturb the whole damn newsroom half-hour before deadline. You know I'm busy." She caught herself, didn't want to shout at the girl any more than necessary; the door was open to the newsroom. Michele geared down her tone in deference to Lloyd Sollem sitting nearby and listening. Lloyd adored Fayme. "Sorry Fayme, what's so important, dear?" Michele said matronly.

Fayme shouted out, loud enough for motorists on the Beltway to hear her, "I just learned that Boss Martin didn't die in that bomb blast. He was ... he was... I mean I think so, he was..."

"For God sakes girl. Spit it out."

"... sh..shot!! He was shot!!!"

The newsroom fell silent.

Without stopping to pause, Fayme continued. "I got an advance copy of the autopsy report. You know that guy Steve knows at the forensic center? I'm tellin' ya, Martin died of gunshot wounds. Michele! (gasping for breath) He was killed before he was found in that rubble. Somebody put his body there. I mean, I think that was it, I guess. I don't really know, but …"

As if in a trance, Chris leaned into the doorway of Michele's office. "Are you sure?" he asked.

Michele, gave him a cross look while encouraging Fayme to continue. "Go ahead Fayme, what else? Chris, you just listen. Don't start taking notes. This is not your story!" Fayme said, "I checked with the police and they won't deny it. Said they will release the autopsy report at 3 o'clock. There is a press conference," Fayme said excitedly.

"Well, what are you doing standing here? You need someone to confirm that. We won't need a God damn press conference. Benny, did you know this? Get out in front of this, please."

Bradley was now standing shoulder to shoulder with Chris as they tried to hear what was going on. He said to Michele, "No, I didn't." And then to Chris, "Did they say anything was unusual about the body when they dragged it out last week?"

Chris shook his head no.

Back at the business desk, Steve Mothershart flipped through a crumbling roll-a-dex he'd started 25 years earlier, finally stopping at the H's. He dialed up his best police source, Jamal Henry, Who was Mothershart's neighbor's son. They both attended Mount Zekiah Baptist on South Dakota Avenue in northeast Washington, D.C. Jamal was a police radio dispatcher in King's County.

Henry returned Mothershart's call in five minutes and confirmed that the autopsy revealed gunshots to the right eye and in the chest of Boss Martin. "The shooting occurred sometime between midnight and four a.m. on the night before the bombing, Mr. Mothershart. You didn't hear it from me, sir, but whoever shot Martin had access to the tower and maybe to the JDR builders' basement parking. The guys here at the station think the killer managed to load Martin's body into Martin's own pickup truck in the early morning hours so darkness would mask their deeds. That's what I'm hearing. Don't quote me, Mr. Mothershart, okay, please sir?" said Jamal.

"Fine Jamal, thanks. We'll see you in church Sunday? Tell your folks I send them the best, okay?"

"Okay, Mr. Mothershart. Call me any time. When will this story come out?"

Before she let Fayme start writing her story, Michele held an impromptu story session in the editorial board room, gathering up her team -- Fayme, Benny, Steve and Lloyd who brought in Carrie with him in case an Op-Ed was in the wind. She would nail it with the current and correct information.

Thanks to Bradley, Chris stayed, too.

Why Carrie? Chris thought to himself.

Michele demanded, "Here is what we need to know. Get it all to Fayme in an hour." She possessed the sharpest mind in the room, and the sharpest tongue, too. She rambled uninterrupted until she fired out all the right questions as editorial bullets fired from her bright brown, level eyes to all the appropriate staffers. "Did the killer also bomb the building?" "Did the killer set a time bomb?" "Why wasn't Martin's body found before, that is earlier than the blast?" "Where was everybody else in his company?" "Did the bomber intend to knock down the whole damn building?" "Or was the sloppy construction vulnerable, maybe typical JDR construction, ready to blow over with a strong gust of wind whipping down through The Hole?"

Chris was mulling over dozens of other possibilities Michele didn't mention concerning the Johnny-Vickie-Dickie triangle and the predatory mortgage guys who lost their offices in the FUC&M disaster.

Michele summarily ended the meeting, in typical fashion barking orders to everyone in earshot to start digging fast. She started with Benny. "Benny, find out who else was working that day at JDR. Get anything you can on those people, but especially anyone out sick that day or just out on an errand. Get it? Also, ask the sheriff, ah, let me think, yes, to call you immediately after the press conference. We don't have time to drive there before 3 o'clock.

"And Steve, find out if that Jamal kid knows anything else.

"Fayme, just start writing anything."

Fayme looked puzzled.

Michele brushed her hands out toward her office door, shooing, "Yes, anything at all, just to get started. Your life story, if that's what it takes to put the fingers to the keyboard. Why, girl, you take the cake. Nice tip. Surprising but nice. Stay away from the mortgage fraud stuff Chris reported and anything about Mrs. Martin's love life in this one, be that as it may. You all know what I mean?

"And, Chris?"

"Huh?" Chris was not expecting a piece of this story.

"Stay out of it." Michele stomped out of the ad hoc story conference that had spilled out to too many ears in the newsroom. She marched back to her office and closed the door behind her. Benny and Steve knew for sure then that she still didn't want Chris's name attached to any stories on the tragedy. The fact that other newspapers and TV reports placed him at the scene while on his untimely journey with Dickie Randim that morning was still prohibiting any encouragement she might give the boy. She had to ignore his feelings on it, they told Chris later.

Chris knew the ground rules, even before Michele's final edict. The problem for the paper was that he was part of the story, by sheer accident, but still enough involved in the public's mind to cloud the Inquirer's coverage, especially to county and state officials.

"You okay with this, Chris?" Steve asked.

Moving past the question, Chris waited until he, Steve and Benny had distanced themselves from the others and settled back into the business cluster of desks before asking again, "Why did Lloyd bring Carrie into the meeting. She doesn't report news."

Benny admitted quietly that he was puzzled by Carrie being there too, that he "frankly, he said, "questioned management's judgment bringing Carrie into the mix. She hates Dickie's guts. That's the word around the newsroom," Benny said dismissively. "And, Dickie is still a suspect."

Chris said, "Yes, but wouldn't Carry coordinate any eventual op-eds on the story anyway? If Lloyd didn't invite her to the meeting, it might weaken trust in her to everyone else. Maybe it was in the best interest of the story to not exclude her. She was standing close by when Fayme told Michele about Martin being shot. After all, in a newsroom, don't you have to assume Carrie's hatred for Dickie may not influence her objectivity. I'd check what she writes on it with Melissa or Trichina if it looks prejudicial."

Bennie was wowed, "Young man, where DID you come from? Quite an analysis of the situation." His tone said he didn't care one bit about all that, leaving Chris wondering if he liked his analysis or thought it foolhardy.

Steve hung an arm around Chris's shoulders, "By Gosh West Virginia. Right, Chris? He may be right Bennie. Let's see what happens."

Dejected, Chris slumped back to his desk and ducked behind his computer screen. But his restless mind was still all over the story. He felt it would eat him alive until he did something. But what?

When the other reporters and editors dug into their assignments from Michele, Chris pulled out the little notebook, the gift from Dickie. He'd thrown it into the bottom desk drawer days ago, like it was trash, and had not yet retrieved it. *Probably useless,* he figured. He began to mull over the names and contacts that Randim, or maybe some female friend of his, wrote down ever so neatly and all with the same pen and penmanship.

"What's that?" Melissa Cushen asked. She was standing over Chris. She stretched and arched her back as she reached out to snatch the little book from Chris, who was startled by her unusually rapid movement. She clutched it tightly. He let it go, not wanting to struggle with her.

"Yea, thanks. Ah," Chris started to say something, anything to hide his surprise. He thanked Melissa for everything nervously without thinking; she never corrected him; thought it cute. "It's Richard Randim's little notebook of his best sources," he said.

Melissa and some female reporters at or near the business desk, her girls as they were known, laughed and covered their mouths or rolled their eyes.

Chris's face reddened. Noticing his embarrassment, Melissa said, "Look Chris, far be it for me to tell you anything about your reporting, you'll probably be twice the reporter I could ever dream of being."

She dreams too, then.

She continued, "But, that can't possibly be Dickie's real source book. He's up to something. Listen, we all know that guy. He even asked me out about five million times, or was it six million. He is a sleaze. Carrie knows for sure he's a sleazeball."

"Well, I really didn't think it was a book of his best sources. It's brand new. Every note, every number, every email address is neatly written in the same ink, possibly at the same time," said Chris, highly flattered that Melissa's ringing endorsement of his potential came out of her mouth and seemed to him loud enough to bounce off all four walls. He smiled, feeling a bit embarrassed and wondered if he'd revealed any affection for her—a clear violation of his personal vow to nix any romantic thoughts about his attractive colleagues.

"Now you're thinking," said Melissa, as Chris could not help but watch her bounce down into her chair, still clutching the notebook.

"Now, let me see. Maybe you ladies can help me here," she offered, "a little insight into the sick mind of the Dickster, our Mr. "role-the dice" Randim." A shot at his middle name.

Chris was impressed. He sat back to listen, amused.

Melissa, Rebecca Guthrie, Trichina Brown and Chris formed the real estate/business desk group, which reported to Bradley, then Mothershart, in nearby cubicles.

Skinny, stern Rebecca was highly competitive and determined to win awards for her reporting. She regularly trumped the other reporters during editorial meetings, questioning their facts and offering additional information to them, all to one-up her colleagues. She was irritating but desperate enough to accept bonding from the other women on the team. The women were delighted with Rebecca's clever emasculating of male egos, Dickie's especially.

Trichina's beat covered southern Maryland, including exclusive King's County deals. Maryland-wide issues from that county and the others were new real estate Chris's beat involved.

Trichina had strong African features, a sign that her family, from slave origins in North Carolina, never married outside of their race. She loved African-American history and issues. Her peers at the paper admired her pride. Once Trichina mentioned "African-American" as a noun or a modifier ten times in a 13-inch story on the election of popular Joe Collins, the first black County Executive in King's County. She also ran training sessions for reluctant young reporters and editors.

Melissa covered profiles of newsmakers in central Maryland, including Rhodesville, but rarely left the newsroom. Her Rolodex was full of contacts she could easily access and her charm and persuasive telephone skills guaranteed fruitful interviews. With her chair cranked high and desk in a good position to view the newsroom, Melissa was the queen, overlooking her followers, it seemed: the entire newsroom staff.

Carrie often joined Mel's girls to socialize and sat at Chris's desk when he was not there. She was not in the group discussing Dickie's little book that day, though.

After studying the book for just a minute, Melissa turned her attention to Chris. "First of all, why does that sneak Randim want to help you? He's never helped anyone," Melissa said.

Rebecca chimed in. "He's a total ass. Typical man, I'd say. Sorry, Chris, no offense intended."

"I probably know him least," Trichina jumped in, "but it seems to me he's covering up something."

"Yea, that's what I think," said Melissa. "Meanwhile, he's got Chris in the middle of something. I don't like it, Chris. It's just too weird. Listen to me now carefully." She addressed the group: "If he knew it or not, he managed to drive Chris to the best story ever to drop into our laps, like forever. I say Dickie had him there on purpose."

Chris's mind drifted: *Lap, hmm. I'd still trade any story to be in Melissa's lap. Why does she have to talk like that?* Then, *Get serious, fool.* He hated being so lonely and horny and realized once again how much he wanted a girlfriend despite his vow to focus all his energy the first year at the paper on reporting.

Rebecca's high-pitched voice cracked with, "Do you all think Dickie would kill Boss Martin for Vickie's sake?"

Trichina slowly responded, "Wouldn't have the guts, I would think, from what you all have told me about this guy. Though he had guts enough to be with Vickie for months I hear, right under Boss Martin's nose. That's nervy, risk addictive, as Lloyd says."

Rebecca: "That wasn't guts. It was hormones, girl. Get real. Besides, the Martins lived separately."

Melissa: "Wait a minute. Didn't you say he was here at 8 a.m. that day sitting right there waiting for you Chris?"

Chris: "More like 8:30. I remember checking the monster."

Melissa: "Maybe he was up all night, up to no good. Could have been involved with the Martins somehow on Sunday night? Possible? Yes? No one knows when Boss Martin died yet."

Chris: "He didn't look tired at all that morning; the opposite really; tanned and refreshed it seemed to me, from all that time in the Caribbean. He had some facial cuts from a surfing injury, he said. It did seem like he was overly anxious to see me; talk with me. Don't know why."

On Melissa's cue, the ladies picked up the pace. She said, "I know. He was on a campaign to clear his name around here, I bet. His parents are big advertisers, you know, and his father is best friends with Chuck, went to college at Charlottesville together. I bet Dickie wanted to guide you through his beat, his way, because he's definitely done something he doesn't want us to know about. Where's the book? I passed it to Trish."

Rebecca: "Here, I've got it. You know, this is not even Randim's handwriting. It's a female's I think. What'd ya think, Mel?"

Melissa: "Well, I know the man never seemed to be in the newsroom, but when he was here, I could see his notes sometimes--just out of morbid curiosity, of course. I say this is definitely not his writing."

There was a weighty pause before Melissa continued, "If these names don't represent his best sources and were written by someone with noticeably neater handwriting, then he's trying to steer Chris to only these sources, or at least to them first. He could mess you up, Chris, just as you start your statewide real estate beat. And, I bet these are not his real juicy sources, but softballs you could write, leaving him looking good after reporting better stuff."

Trichina: "This is why you are the best, Mel. You read people well."

Unfazed by flattery, Melissa brought the book to her heart as if to channel its meaning, then thought, "Mmm, I've seen him tug at a similar size book from his jackets, but it was a beat-up breast-pocket notebook. If *that* was his real source book, then there are surely names in it that he didn't want you to see, Chris."

She shot a sharp look at Chris, who had forgotten he was part of the discussion, "Chris, did you see anything in his breast pocket," asked Melissa, tapping the top of her left breast inadvertently to indicate a full pocket.

Her motions caught Chris off guard, a symptom of his pathetic naiveté. "Huh? Oh yea, maybe so." He recovered quickly, as usual, and rejoined the probing conversation, "The real Dickie notebook, if there is one as you say, would be helpful. It might help to know why he was so intent on seeing me before anyone else showed up last Monday. Has anyone seen him lately?" he said glancing at the reporters, one by one.

Rebecca: "We've been spared that pleasure all week, thank you."

Trichina, laughing: "You guys have raised more questions, wow, about a guy you can't stand! I think there is something that is intriguing you girls about the charming Mr. Dickster. What do you think Chris? They're fascinated with Dickie," she teased.

Melissa and Rebecca responded in unison, "Oh, my Gawwwd," as they covered their faces in mock shame, while the animated exchange at the real estate desk drew attention from the entire newsroom.

The conversation lapsed into purely girl chatter about each other, essentially dismissing Chris. He reverted to his normal position, his thick brown hair drooping over his eyebrows as he sat hunched over his computer. He zoned out the women, even his growing annoyance with Fayme who had walked across the newsroom to hear what the girl talk was about. Despite his good nature, Chris shot her a disapproving glance, making him think unkindly, *She'll never get it. Look at her. Doesn't have a clue where to start.*

He had no personal gripe with Fayme. It was professional. Fayme and Chris were the newest hires and he feared that management thought of them together, as the same. A major annoyance to his pride.

The two youngest reporters, Chris and Fayme, were opposites in more ways than just their reporting abilities. When Chris joined the paper's staff, his first beat, just like Fayme, was crime and courthouse for his first six weeks of his employment.

Typically, a fledgling reporter had the beat for much longer. But Michele LaProbe hired pretty Fayme Lovelace hastily just out of the University of Maryland 'J' school on a request by Lloyd after popular veteran reporter Benjamin Fortnight, the paper's best overall reporter, retired at age 45 years old. He signed a sweetheart Hollywood movie deal of $400K for his second vampire novel, the comedy "Let's Have a Bite Together Sometime after Dark, OK?"

With one reporter shy facing a heavy schedule of stories, Fayme might help fill in on crime and police, under the immediate and close supervision of executive editor Lloyd Sollem's more-than-willing tutorage.

Regardless of Chris's private disapproval of the girl, light-hearted Fayme was like a firefly at the paper who could always light up the room with her personality and genuine femininity. At 93 pounds, all in the right places, she was a looker, with shiny waves of raven locks below her shoulders, porcelain white complexion, mahogany eyes, and a cheery, girlish grin.

Her hiring did bring along one advantage to reporter Christopher Gilley because the girl clearly, yet so far as anyone knew, just figuratively though, charmed the pants off stoic Lloyd. Chris noticed instantly and logically concluded that cute Fayme was more than enough to divert Lloyd's original discontentment with Chris as too youthful and inexperienced at 19. Fayme was 22 but more childlike and adorable.

When Chris arrived, had Lloyd recommended to Michele immediately, "That boy should be a proofreader on the copy desk. He doesn't fit our image. He doesn't look like a real well-grounded reporter I would send out." After circumstances at the paper pushed Chris's reporting beat to statewide real estate, Lloyd was still too stubborn or proud to admit he was wrong about the remarkable boy reporter.

But Fayme, who looked just as naïve and innocent, was a different breed entirely to Lloyd who was charmed at first glance.

The arrival of affable, flirty Fayme--pronounced "Fay me," and not fame--though the reporters nicknamed her 'Fame' on her first day--pushed young Christopher to cover real estate in King's County and parts of other counties if a development deal was big enough. It got him his first real desk and his exclusive computer, which was a step up from the intern's corner. And of course, he was then in position for Dickie's statewide beat after Dickie screwed up by seducing Martha Read, the executive publisher, and getting caught by publisher Chuck in the act.

Chris hated Fayme covering 'his story' on the seeming terrorist attack and murder in Loweville. But overall he was agreeable about Fayme for bumping him "up" in advertently to a more responsible beat.

* * *

As far as Dickie's whereabouts, no one saw him at work after the Inquirer took him off the statewide beat and bumped him upstairs.

After all his trouble and arrests, he was anxious about his employment with the paper. He was determined to stay put in public relations so as not to further embarrass his parents. He now knew he had gone too far with his affair with Martha Read, before leaving for his "vacation."

He was also a little worried about Martha. Without further contact with his persuasive charm, would she squeal to others, including her husband, a big advertiser in the Inquirer?

But, why should she squeal? CEO Bear already knew about the affair, at least he saw what he saw. Dickie hoped that knowledge of the affair had ended with Chuck Bear, and it did -- for the most part -- except that the Dickie/Martha rumor further fueled Carrie's continuing hatred for Dickie.

* * *

Melissa's girl talk, so close to Chris's desk, went on and on. They chatted about clothes, Carrie's latest babies and newsroom gossip. It all bugged Chris silly.

Instead of listening, he tried to put his mind into again considering what was missing in the bombing story, i.e. the latest talk surrounding the Vickie-Dickie-Boss triangle and the unsolved tragedy of the FUC'M tower. He also reflected on his female colleagues' deductions. He contemplated, *So, there must be another little notebook. Notes in Dickie's real source book could unravel some of the puzzle on this damn thing? Fayme will never get to the bottom of this.*

He sat motionless as he mulled over recent events.

"Damn it, anyway," he said as he pounded his desk with a fist. The girl talk stopped and they all turned to Chris who made up a lame excuse. "Oh, it's my mechanic. He can't get the Mazda fixed yet. Parts … yes, needs parts."

Privately though, Chris pounded his fist on the desk when he made a fateful decision to defy Michele. At that very moment, Christopher Gilley made up his mind to look into the mystery of the tower himself, to go underground so to speak. It was really his story! *Damn it, anyway,* he thought again.

His first step would be to pay Randim a visit upstairs. Maybe there WAS another notebook.

* * *

Upstairs meant the executive suite. It was uncharted territory for the writers and editors. Inquirer editorial staff rarely, if ever, chanced a visit into the paper's inner sanctum (upstairs) where the suits made all the deals, made the money, signed the meager checks for editors and reporters. Especially sacred were the suites of advertising and publishing staff on the third floor. That was the Inquirer's Land of Oz, its kitchen of the oracle, tomb of the holy newsprint grail, source of its mystical revenue stream!

Once he committed to going "underground," Chris chose to visit "overground," that forbidden third floor by way of the rarely taken back stairs. He figured if he used the lobby elevator, it was very likely he'd bump into the paper's executives and have to make small talk. "What the hell would I say?" he said to himself.

"What's that, Chris?" Melissa peeked over the top of his screen.

"Nothing, more car trouble," he said.

"You have a good mechanic? Let me see who you are …" she popped around to look at his computer screen.

Chris quickly clicked to the Weather Channel. He told her he needed to leave for an appointment.

He then walked out of the building. He returned, walked through the paper's morgue and recycling room in the back of the building, then ran up the back stairs.

At the top of the back stairs, he turned a dusty door handle to the third-floor suites. As Chris quietly opened the door, it caused a clatter. The door was pushing several stacked cardboard boxes and recycling cans aside. He peaked inside the door. No one was there. It appeared to be a corner catch-all at the far end of a hallway. Indeed, no one saw him enter.

A warm ambiance of the plush designed offices in the executive suite was an absolute opposite to the stark, fluorescent atmosphere of the newsroom downstairs Chris just left behind.

The hallway was soft and silent with a thick cocoa brown carpet and off-white walls. Hung at eye level were framed community awards by the Inquirer and front pages shouting the paper's Maryland coverage of the important events: "Reagan Denies Iran-Contra," "Gov. Scruppels Crushes GOP Foes in Primary," "Bush: Mission Accomplished?" and "Clinton Economy Soars."

Chris amused himself imagining "FUC&M Tower Falls on the Boss," fitting neatly on down the nostalgic row of liberal-slanted framed front pages. Few people knew that Boss Martin was a closet Republican businessman and his demise would well fit into this third-floor Hall of Blame, Chris thought.

He walked softly past office after office, catching glimpses of expensive hardwood furniture and fine draperies. The managers who occupied those offices took pride in displaying framed family photos and keeping lush tropical plants amid oceans of natural light from large office windows.

Chris was impressed by the contrast to the plain fluorescence lighting of the no-nonsense layout of the newsroom, which never saw the light of day. By the time, he reached the end of the hallway's fine décor and rows of appointed offices of upper management, Chris felt like Keanu Reeves floating through the Inquirer's matrix. Like Reeves' character Neo in the movie "The Matrix," he was The One chosen to see that his world was an elaborate cyber program with Charles Ivan Bear, the Inquirer president, as the Oracle whose spirit held the company's secrets. Chris would surely open the last door and see an industrial control center for manipulating a giant virtual keyboard working the company's 88 editions in 50 some towns.

Mr. Bear was that intimidating, at least to the boy reporter. Musing aside, Chris already knew the real story though, that the founder was an intuitive genius in placing and running local news operations tied to a complex matrix of editors, photographers and reporters who mostly stuck to their Maryland town beats and kept the company floating against an undertow that was taking away the nations newspapers at an alarming pace.

Chris walked by Bear's office quickly, but not fast enough to not see red leather chairs, a couch and a huge oak desk that would add class to the Oval Office.

On the very next door, he was amazed to see the nameplate of Richard D. Randim, MBA, Director of Public Relations, immediately to the right of Chuck Bear's suite. *Dickie is on a very short leash,* he thought. Randim's door was closed. *Why did I think he would be here anyway?* thought Chris. The girls said he was never at the news desk, so he is probably never in his new job either.

"Hello young man, can I help you?"

Chris jumped. It was CEO Chuck Bear himself coming out of the men's room across the hallway. He didn't extend a handshake, just a look of suspicion over the skinny boy whom he caught reaching out to grab Dickie's doorknob.

"Oh hello, sir. No. Have you seen Mr. Randim by chance?"

"Yes, he's in the bathroom there washing up. He'll be out momentarily, I'm sure. He's always here."

A surprising statement indeed. Then Bear surprised Chris again with, "If you want to visit people at the newspaper son, have the receptionist Monica buzz Dickie or whomever you come to see. How'd you get in here so far? She's out to lunch or something down there?"

Whomever? Formal, isn't he? Chris thought as he pondered his next move, while his heart raced. He just shrugged without answering Mr. Bear. He figured it would be no use identifying himself. The Oracle would likely forget him anyway since Chris, an unknown, is clearly not Neo, the One in "The Matrix,", or even a familiar reporter.

He was impressed with Chuck's physical presence--a big-framed man, as tall as Chris. Clean shaven. Gray and brown hair, balding. He was immaculately dressed in a pinstriped Italian gray suit with a bright blue tie with red stripes and blue stars, polished black wingtips. An American flag pin on his lapel. *Very patriotic*, Chris guessed.

Before Chris could muster an excuse for his presence or tell his CEO that he worked for him, Chuck Bear just turned and ignored him, went into his big papa-bear den and closed the door behind him without further hesitation, or as much as a snarl or growl.

"Whew. I guess he doesn't know my name. Just as well," Chris murmured out loud.

Dickie Randim stepped out of the men's room and said, "Who doesn't know your name? I thought we took care of that one day in Loweville," he said sarcastically. "Everybody knows you now, Mr. Gilley. What's up Chris?"

Chris spun on his heel quickly to invent his next move as Dickie opened his office door and slipped in, beckoning Chris to follow. "Hey, Dick. How ya doing? I came up to thank you for showing me the ropes, though we got cut short a little, eh?"

"Nothing," he shrugged. "Thanks for returning my camera and laptop. Bradley brought them up. He also brought up a bunch of stupid questions."

"He needed to hear what happened that weekend, I guess, huh?" Chris said cautiously, not wanting to cut bait just yet.

Dickie also said, "More than that. He all but accused me of stabbing the paper in the back. Said something about me compromising the paper by getting involved with Boss Martin. Hell. I hardly knew the man. What did he mean by involved? What a bastard. I don't know how you can stand him."

"He just feels passionate about the integrity of the paper," *Oops*, Chris thought. He immediately knew he made a mistake.

"So, you think I don't have integrity? Look buddy boy, I wanted to help you and now you turn on me. And those cracks you made at the police station."

Randim was not usually so sensitive.

Chris wondered why he was so prickly and chose to ignore the opening to crack another Elvis suit joke.

Randim then said, "Look, just scram. I've got to attend a board meeting, every Wednesday at 1 p.m. in Chuck Bear's office. I'm late."

Chris let him go into Bear's office and then went for the elevator. Other suits passed him by going into Bear's big office. Chris shook his head as if to cast off demons and headed back down to the newsroom as quickly as possible in the elevator, shaking his hands outward as if to say 'enough, enough.'

Once alone in the elevator, he smiled with satisfaction, knowing he had accomplished more than he could have expected. Before Dickie escorted Chris away from his office, Chris had indeed spotted another little notebook, maybe Dickie's real source book. It was sliding halfway out of the inside pocket of Dickie's bomber jacket, thrown across on his nice oak wood desk.

The elevator doors opened and Chris sighed with relief to be back on terra firma, well sort of. He looked up to find a delightful, unexpected surprise.

"Liza, oh hey Liza, can you help me with a little favor?" Chris couldn't believe his luck. He'd run into his friend as they each arrived at the lobby at the same time. Community reporter Liza Leah Lopez, who convinced Steve Mothershart to hire the kid several months ago, was just arriving for work.

As he stepped off the elevator, she was entering the newspaper by the front door, which was rarely used by editorial personnel.

Chris new Liza was someone he could trust to help him find Dickie's real source book. Liza Lopez was 28 but looked 20, a Puerto Rican-American from Brooklyn, N.Y. with a big heart and an interest in getting into business reporting like her friend Chris. She had recently changed her career path to journalism from advertising she had started in the tough New York City market and then gave it up.

"Hey Chris," she said with a big smile. "What's up, buddy? I've been shopping and parked out front so I can sneak out early today. Won't tell on me, will you?"

Chris admired Liza's up-beat spirit and idiosyncrasies, such as her insistence that she did not know any Spanish. He guessed without ever asking that it was Liza's way to avoid being typecasted and stuck in an exclusive Latino reporting beat. There were just a few Latinos at the paper.

On the contrary, Liza didn't need any special help. She was a good reporter and had a way of lightening everyone's day, getting the most out of an interview. She dressed mostly in skirts and fine blouses, classy business attire mixed with a colorful scarf or bright colored jacket. Liza was tasteful in dressing, yet not emphasizing her hourglass figure.

Since their days as companions on The Hill, Chris always tried not to see his buddy Liza as an attractive woman, but rather as his best friend at the paper. The friendship was solid and he counted on her always being there for him. Chris assumed she felt the same way.

Chris had a big sister-like relationship with Liza that she also cherished. She worried over him as if he was family. She was already aware of Chris's strange joy ride with Randim which worried her, but she hid her dislike of the playboy reporter. She was too smart to mouth opinions on personalities at the paper.

This might be tricky, Chris thought. He knew Liza as well as anyone, but he was not clever in dealing with determined females, even close friends. He thought over his chore rather pathetically and with considerable guilt, *I should convince Liza to help me by exploiting Randim's weakness for the skirts.*

Facing her in the lobby, Chris couldn't ignore how nice she looked. Liza wore a short tight black leather skirt, a blouse with white puffy sleeves adorned with a gold chain around her neck. It sparkled under her jet black, long hair. She had dressed up more than usual to cover a rock concert in downtown Rhodesville that evening.

Perfect; she'll knock Dickie off his feet, thought Chris. Exploiting her feminine wiles was something friends would do for friends if necessary, immature Chris figured incorrectly perhaps.

They walked into a vacant office for privacy and Chris began, "Liza, Dickie gave me a book of his contacts, his good sources. But he was lying. I just saw his real source notebook I think halfway out of the breast pocket of Randim's bomber jacket laying across the top of his desk upstairs in the exec suites. I need to get a better look at it, see what's in it. Can you help me?"

"You went up there? Nobody goes up there. It's the dark side of the moon, Mister Christopher," warned Liza. "Did Papa Bear see you?" she laughed.

"Liza, you can get it for me?"

He told Liza the notebook was the same kind of notebook Dickie offered to him on their joy ride to a disaster, but the one on his desk was old and worn. Chris was sure it was Dickie's real source book.

Liza frowned as if she had tasted sour milk. "Me, why me?" asked Liza. "No way, Chris. Are you crazy? I like you my friend and all, but that's asking a lot. Why me?" Liza pressed.

"Because I can't ask Melissa to help or any of her sisterhood buddies. They're great. Don't get me wrong, they are on my side about me being stupid to go with Dickie that day. But if they helped, word would spread to the Orient in a second that I stole something from Dickie's office. It would put me in Dutch further with Michele. But, if Dickie sees you, he'll just hit on you because he'll be blinded by your looks."

"Oh, that's just great. And what's my looks, Chris? Am I so attractive, do you mean? Am I just irresistible?" leaning toward him, barely touching his arm, smiling devilishly. She meant nothing seductive, just a stick-in-the-eye sarcasm to annoy her friend. In fact, Liza was engaged to an Army officer who had just transferred from Maryland to Texas. He had proposed marriage to Liza before he left for the Texas base.

"Liza, please. I would only want you to borrow the notebook, hop back into this elevator, and hand it to me in the copying room, all while Dickie is still busy kissin' ass in a board meeting he's in right now. That meeting is always two hours long, Dickie said. It just started. He'll stay in there to ass-kiss the whole room, right? You know our Dickie. No shame. All the brass is there Liza, please. We can put it back by the time they finish in there," pleaded Chris.

"Yea, probably yes, that's him alright. No shame, for sure."

"Will you do it? I will stand outside the men's room, right across the hall from Dickie's office, which he left open by the way. I will signal you if someone comes out of the board room. It gives me a clear view from the men's."

"Okay, Chris. But don't you dare leave me in there with that wolf, you hear me?" Liza said.

The two rode the elevator up to the third floor and their plan went without a hitch, at first. Dickie was not in his office. She grabbed the notebook. They rushed back to the elevator. Downstairs in the newsroom Xerex copying room Chris copied all 60 pages of Dickie's coffee and food- and beer-stained notebook.

They took it back upstairs.

Just as they got to Randim's office, Dickie exited from Bear's meeting. Chris slipped into the men's room doorway as he said in a loud whisper, "Liza, watch it, here comes Di...," and then Chris had to slip back into the men's room, leaving Liza one step into Dickie's office, in a panic.

As Chris peeked from the men's room, it was just as he'd predicted: Liza's smart outfit helped. Randim was pleased to see Liza leaning over his desk, her young, tight bottom still facing him as she turned to see.

Dickie was intrigued. "Hey, there girl. I thought I recognized you," he said laughing. Whatcha doin'? Looking for samples of Dickie's hair or somethin'?"

She turned toward him. "Hey Dick, I came up to see you, yeah. Ah...just leaving a note. I'm... I'm looking for a pen. You still write things down or are you smart enough to remember all the fine details of being Mr. big PR director man now? How's that going for you anyway?" she joked nervously. She felt sweat dripping from her underarms down onto her nice white blouse.

"Not as much writing up here, Liza darling," he said, still looking at her legs below that tight leather skirt. Hey, you free for dinner? You look really good. It's a shame to waste that outfit.

I've been meaning to see you but I just got back from an awesome cruise to all parts Caribbean. You want to see some pics?"

"Sure," Liza replied, her hands still behind her desperately feeling for the zipper on Randim's bomber jacket pocket so she could slip the notepad back without him noticing.

"Sure, dinner? Or sure, pics? Which? Both right?" Dickie asked enthused.

"Let's try the pics first, then we'll talk, Dick," she replied with a wry smile. She was getting her usually dependable composure back. "Are the pics in the computer yet? Send them to me through Picasa."

"No, they are printed" he said. "They do still have one-day developing, even in Jamaica, Liza." He paused and stared. "Yea, you are a sweet sight. They are in my jacket, I think. Well, shoot me dead, I don't know where my jacket is though. Oh yeah, they're behind you. Sit all that down, Liza [giving her body the up and down] and hand me the jacket," he said gesturing toward her bottom half with an open hand.

With his eyes momentarily downturned, Liza swiveled, slipped the notebook into the jacket pocket with her right hand, and then handed the jacket to Dickie with her left.

Chris slipped by in the hallway behind Dickie, but not before he was plastered by Liza's ugly glance over Dickie's shoulder. Chris left her there, figured correctly that she could handle the dumb blonde Dickie Randim.

She wriggled out of Dickie's tentacles an hour and a hundred snapshots later.

Chapter 20: What's the Code?

Chris held only a slim hope of getting to the bottom of the FUC'M story if he remained content to crank out uninspiring copy.

Doing the stories Benny fed him would allow Chris to keep his job at the Inquirer. He understood that. But it was not enough. He was young, talented and hungry to apply himself to more than average newspaper drudge work. What to do?

He sat at his desk, reflecting on how he once felt that day when he arrived at the Inquirer, brimming with the right stuff, the best-taught ethics of the trade. He had been eager to start his journalism career on an honest and upright footing. This was his pride, his anchor.

But instead of riding the high road, getting established on his strengths, he had made a rookie's mistake of unwittingly stumbling into the din of Dickie's decadent network of schemes and sordid sources. *I'm becoming Dickie*, he dreaded. *I thought nothing of stealing that notebook.* It was almost as if he was preordained, he feared, to wade into filthy waters with his new beat, a beat Dickie had soiled by unscrupulous, dishonest reporting habits.

He thought of his mother's warning about wasting himself in newspaper work. *Sas right*, he thought. In just a week after the FUC'M tower bombing, he was already losing the prideful principles he learned at Northwestern. So far, Benny Bradley had caught Chris in a bald-faced lie about why he was with Randim the morning of the FUC'M tower collapse. Now he'd stolen another reporter's notes. Worse yet, he was stealing Dickie's confidential sources. And he had recruited his best friend Liza in his scheming, possibly compromising her career too if she was caught. *What kind of friend risks his best friend as I did to Liza.*

Chris put his head on the desk to hide his face. His disposition toward his work had changed. Never had he felt less than optimistic. So, he was only 19 and employed as a working reporter at a newspaper, his dream. But now, in his paranoid state, he felt that his life was already in a dark, cold pit at the Inquirer. Things didn't start well. He had a great story in his hands and Michele grabbed it away. He supposed *She doesn't trust me. This doesn't feel right. I didn't plan for this.*

Thanks to his splendid training, however, Chris recovered his wits. He wasn't discouraged enough to lose an urge to keep following the story, HIS story, clandestinely. It was his only way to keep self-respect and maybe even get back into good graces at the paper and save his career, he thought.

Yes, this is the way to get out of the doldrums, he thought.

It was only his youth, which was betraying his confidence. He had never faced such a crisis.

At 7 p.m. that evening, and after Melissa and her girls left for the day, he unlocked his desk drawer and leafed through the Xeroxed pages of Dickie's real source book. He discovered that Liza had stapled them together for him in perfect order.

Finally, alone by himself in the newsroom, Chris began reading it. He wasn't disappointed. Unlike the fake source book, the real one was filled with telephone numbers and email addresses for company CEOs and government officials, even cell numbers, home phone numbers and home addresses of sources. It was indeed the pages of a typical well-used, weathered little source book. It looked like it had been shoved in and out of pockets and through all kinds of weather hundreds of times. The writing was masculine, though neat and carefully organized.

Chris concluded, *This is my ticket out of this mess and maybe back onto the bombing story. Dickie knows all the players I will need. When I get to the bottom of the story I'll confess to Bennie and hope I don't get fired.*

Yet he had to guard against being too naive and trusting. So far in his fantasy to crack the truth of the messy story and miraculously get it published, Liza was the only human being he'd trusted so far. He had asked Liza to swear to secrecy. But, then again, why wouldn't she be quiet? She stole the notebook.

He swore not to involve Liza anymore. Instead, he needed to start by finding somebody else to help him get to the truth about Johnny Martin's murder. Two truths, who murdered him and why would explain the destruction of the tower, he was convinced. The press, including dizzy Fayme's coverage, was chasing the opposite reasoning: that the tower collapse would reveal the murderer.

Chris studied the notebook for patterns, threads of a storyline.

The information in the book included Boss Martin's cell number. A surprise. Also, there was a number for Knife Garcia,

Martin's once-juvenile-delinquent adopted son, now a detective of some kind for his foster father.

There were cell numbers for Randim's part-time lifeguard lover at the community pool, another for Mrs. Read, and other women in his sex life, Chris figured. Victoria Martin's name and number were not in the book but didn't need to be.

There also were theater and sports ticket office numbers with names. There was Teresa at the Strathmore Arts Theater; Monique, W. at the Washington Nationals, D.C. baseball park; Flo at Redskins and others. There were sexy names of places that sounded like strip clubs with numbers, too, associated with names like Bruiser, Ace and Tuffy -- bouncers, Chris guessed.

Most intriguing of all, there were several numbers marked "cell" adjacent to the two predatory mortgage and finance companies whose offices took a tumble with the FUC'M tower collapse: Best Opportunity Mortgage, Corp. (BOM) and Lifetime Financing Deal, Corp. (LFD) Those entries did not lead to names but were telephone numbers highlighted by colors. Green highlighted numbers under BOM. Red highlighted numbers under LFD. The same colors appeared sparingly elsewhere in the book. Code of some kind, Chris guessed. *So, Dickie didn't trust his own memory. He color-coded all the mortgage contacts in his little source book.* Chris imagined that Dickie feared getting contacts for the shady lenders confused.

Chris found another surprise. When he Googled several numbers written in purple ink, they were similar to numbers Dickie had entered for federal agencies, including the U.S. Treasury, the FBI, and, of all places, the White House or possibly the Executive Office Building next to the White House on 17th St. N.W. These were totally out of place and puzzled Chris. *Maybe this story is bigger than Boss Martin, bigger than Dickie and Vickie, and bigger than the Inquirer's myopic radar. Well, of course, that one is obvious, Chris.* He started to converse in his thoughts on the forbidden story with the other Chris, the straight and narrow Chris from Glasgow who had no business defying his editors' ban.

He had sat still, so to speak, for nearly two weeks since the FUC'M tower collapse, and the story was under the radar of national media after the first few days and not well covered in the region either. Meanwhile, his perception of the story was expanding. Each time Chris would open the Inquirer's website and see Fayme's coverage of HIS story, he'd cringe.

Putting the pages of Dickie's notebook aside, Chris checked Fayme's latest lackadaisical coverage online.

Loweville Tower Collapse Called Crazy
by Fayme Lovelace, staff reporter

LOWEVILLE, Md. (May 24)—Experts are getting mixed messages from new clues as to what caused the collapse of the First Union Credit & Mortgage tower in Loweville on May 14.

There are no clear ideas yet on how the building went down and the local investigation of the collapse was progressing, said King's County fire chief...

"My God, Fayme," Chris said to himself. "Must you go from clues to messages to ideas on the bomb? Who killed Martin for God's sakes, girl?" He was suddenly talking very loudly and caught himself.

The monster clock read 7:56 p.m. No one was around, of course. He continued the self-inflicting pain of reading her dreadful story:

Engineers from the Deekim, Doke and Ramsit, Inc. of Ft. Washington, state contractors, have determined that building codes had not been met by construction methods and materials. Structural weakness was the cause of the collapse.

"That is no great surprise there to that crazy collapse," said Donald Doke ["Title Jayme?" mumbled Chris.]. *"JDR's reputation is famous for cutting corners with poor quality materials and suspect dealings with building inspectors."*

Chris said louder this time, "Fayme, dearie, did he say famous or INfamous? And reputation is famous? Come on, girl."

U.S. Homeland Security Department investigators have reported that bomb fragments found at the scene were from a U.S. Army ordnance designed to be set off remotely or on a timer...

Even louder, Chris said, "Any chance this could be the lead, Fayme? God, I can't stand this."

After 11 days ["After what?"], *no suspects have yet to be arrested and held responsible, but the King's County Sheriff* ["Does he have a name Fayme?" he was talking aloud again.]

expects an arrest is imminent. ["How hard could it be with local, state and federal law enforcement involved?"]

He read on. Fayme's story rambled about theories on the bombing and little on the murder. Chris couldn't stand any more of Fayme's botched story. It was worse than high school journalism. It was killing him.

He pondered why a lot of news on the crimes was not being reported, even in the big papers—the who, what, and why? The killing of Martin could have been by nearly anybody in the county. The 'where' was now in question too, unless Martin was plugged at the tower before the bombing, not placed there.

Chris had not done anything stupid yet about his plan. Just thinking through how he could possibly investigate the story undercover. That was at least comforting.

But, he had no experience with flying solo into the dark clouds of a murder and possible a terrorism story. His only hope was steering toward Dickie's sources. He guessed correctly though that talking directly with sources listed in Dickie's source book would be difficult, perhaps dangerous.

After all, there was a murder involved, unless, that is, Martin shot himself in the eye and then the heart and then drove his pickup to the tower, opened his office garage in the dark, and laid down to die. He laughed out loud, "Nah, not hardly the suicidal type." He was getting his sense of humor back as his resolve stiffened.

He thumbed through the pages from Dickie's notebook and put them back into his desk drawer and locked it.

How did my life get so complicated so quickly? he thought. He leaned back and gazed across the empty newsroom at nothing in particular.

All the lights in the editors' offices were out. Only the stark bluish fluorescent lighting over the beat reporters in the middle of the newsroom left on, glaring lifelessly. He used to think journalism was supposed to be exciting and fun. He shielded his eyes from the glare off several dozen desks and PCs and rested his head in his arm on his desk. He thought of home and his path to the spot he found himself in so early in his career.

* * *

Even as a young boy, Chris had always been the intense, inquisitive reader and writer, never self-centered or conceited, but focused on the lives of others. People found him reserved, even quiet, and comfortable to be near.

Teenage Chris delighted his family and his small circle of friends when he won scholarship money from his literary writing in high school.

Judges were swayed by folksy essays Chris published in his local newspaper. The essays were on familiar stereotypes in TV sitcoms from the 1950s and 1960s in rural settings, like "Petticoat

Junction," and country music movies, such as Kenny Roger's "The Gambler." The boy loved corny, harmless stories. Perhaps they provided escape from the struggles of a large, impoverished family.

Chris intended the essays to be taken seriously. He was addicted to reruns on the Nick at Nite channel and identified with loveable and naive characters like Goober on the "Andy Griffith Show;" Uncle Ernie on "I Love Lucy;" and local sage Uncle Joe in "Petticoat Junction." His essays transcended the foolishness of such characters, inviting readers to love them. The local clowns survived in humble places of which Chris was familiar--like Glasgow. Television's old black and white sitcoms became part of his upbringing.

Literary "experts" on the lower East Side of New York, a universe apart from Chris's world, received essay entries to a national contest that were mailed in by "that clever boy in West Virginia." The editors labeled Christopher Gilley as that kid with that "fresh and deliciously new style of satire. A budding literary star."

He won first prize in the Harvard Essay Awards and the Dorothy Kilquiken Prize for new essayists worth $5,000. He was given a plane ticket to New York and an opportunity to talk with the editors. They had written to him stating that his use of down-home satire on "folksy fools" in TV shows was original and innovative.

No worry, he told his Ma. He was already familiar with people misunderstanding his meaning.

Therefore, when he met with the editorial board, he faked it so he would receive the cash prizes. Young Cristopher was aware that they had mistaken his genuine admiration for the values of TV's dimwits for clever pretentiousness thereby dismissing shows' redeeming values.

But Chris was different from young writers who were schooled at elite schools where the editors were prone to follow styles of so-called intellectual masters of northeast literary circles.

He knew what to expect in New York. Didn't even want to go, but wanted the money. Ma insisted that he go.

Chris had already learned to play the game in high school. In front of his senior English lit class, he read a warm tribute to Uncle Joe as might have been recited by one of the lovely, "Petticoat

Junction" girls who wore skin-tight jeans and puffy blouses. He characterized Joe as stabilizing the family of girls without a father—a trusted, dependable, yet delusionary figure to the pretty daughters of strong-willed Kate Bradley, typed cast by motherly Bea Benaderet.

At one point in his classroom reading, he let his heart take charge when giggling by his classmates began to irritate him. Chris started to explain his admiration for the sincerity of the characters, all the while knowing they were cast in the shows mostly as clowns. But his delivery was taken by the teacher and students as a mockery of the characters and resulted in uproarious hilarity. The teacher took a cue from the class and gave Chris a C-
.

Christopher figured he deserved the low mark and just accepted the grade.

Ma thought otherwise and sent the essays to the Glasgow Gazette where they appeared in print in no time at all.

Considering that he had few or no expectations, Chris was lucky. Things just fell into place for the unassuming young Gilley.

And, his good luck continued uninterrupted to landing the job at the Inquirer: Liza had Sen. Schumer's office call with a recommendation for him. The call was answered by none other than business editor Stephen Mothershart on Presidents Day when few staffers in editorial were in the newsroom, except for Liza who just happened by accident (on purpose) to be sitting nearby and heard Steve accept the call from Schumer's office.

The way things worked out for Chris, it could only have been Mothershart taking the call, taking a chance on a kid who was totally green.

At the other end of the staffing spectrum on the business desk from greenhorn Christopher Gilley was the unflappable Steve Mothershart, editor.

Steve was a man steeped in an ongoing arts renaissance in the black Washington, D.C. community. But he didn't know it. True to his foster dad's odd name, which he privately abhorred, Steve put his full heart in his relationships with others.

He was a tough-minded newsman, but smooth and likable at all the big receptions and business grand openings. He loved mixing and mingling. He'd often accept a networking invitation instead of a reporter in the appropriate beat and return the next morning to assign that reporter a story tip from the event. No one cared. He was the boss, but also polite about fishing in his reporters' beats from time to time.

He mystified people nevertheless as he normally carried an expression of a tired, grumpy middle-aged black man, that is, until he smiled, spoke and extended his hand. Steve was a natural networker because he showed genuine interest in people. He was always on the lookout for personalities to feature in his special column, popularly known as 'One with Steve.'

In his relations with his reporters, he never showed his cards in planning stories and giving direction and had an ability to get new information from people without them realizing they had just been talking too much.

He was way over extended and multi-talented.

He was raising his second family of three young children with a pretty, new wife. He was a keyboardist with the jazz combo The Five Brothers. He was an amateur oil painter, poet, and a regular music critic for the City Paper, and of course a full-time editor with a nasty commute to Rhodesville from Northeast D.C.

Women who met Steve seemed to like him for his warmth, sociability, and good humor. He loved women and was easily charmed by them. He feared no one and was interested in everyone.

Steve secretly didn't like the demands for detail but respected the paper, respected the role of the fourth estate in society, respected the readers and used his superior intelligence to fight that small bit of laziness typical of any newspaper man on a less than exciting lead.

Chapter 23: Not That Ben Bradley

Steve never missing a deadline was in large part due to his dependable assistant business editor Benny Bradley. Steve realized he relied on Benny too much. Not that Benny couldn't handle the pressure; he thrived on it. He didn't want to complain and thus show himself as somehow weak.

Benny Bradley got his way with copy editors, stiff executive editor Lloyd, tough and brilliant managing editor Michele, the photo journalists, and just about anyone associated with the Inquirer, editorial and otherwise.

On Chris's first day on the business desk, Melissa was first to fill him in on his scary-serious new boss, Benny Bradley. She said, "You'll see that Benny Bradley is REALLY married to the paper 24/7."

None of Bradley's four wives could compete with his love for newspapering, and, specifically, the Inquirer, Melissa observed. "He will eat, sleep and breathe newspaper work and rarely spend quality time at home with a wife. Why? He loved the newspaper more," she said.

Melissa further revealed to Chris, "Actually, I think Benny is extremely charming. I know his third wife Hilda. As a fan of the BBC's Britcoms, Benny would always mumble that Hilda was 'She who must NOT be obeyed' mimicking the British drama/comedy "Rumpole of the Bailey," you know? Starring Leo McKeon?"

Chris, who still preferred Nick at Nite's innocent old comedies when he did watch TV, didn't know Rumpole, but nodded in agreement to keep Melissa cranked.

Melissa went on, "Benny's charm gets 'em, his wives, and then his neglect repels them. That's just my take."

Melissa's comments on Bradley's personal life confirmed what Chris already uncovered doing due diligence on the man who was to be his new editor.

Before Chris even met assistant business editor Robert "Benny" Bradley, Chris knew his new boss was an old-school newspaperman. Early in Bradley's career, he had decided to exploit the similarity of his name to famous Watergate-era editor at the Washington Post, Ben Bradley. Benny worked hard to emulate him.

The Inquirer's Bradley was so much a true-blue newsprint devotee that management jokingly accused Steve Mothershart of finding Bradley at Central Casting.

The joke gained legs when Bradley, who lives on the same block on Capitol Hill as D.C.'s Central Casting office, met film personnel manager, Dagmar Falkenrath at Starbucks one Sunday morning. Mrs. Benny Bradley, wife number four, had gotten her fill of living life virtually alone. She returned to her native New Hampshire with a young, handsome copy editor.

Benny began dating the big German blonde Dagmar in no time.

Was it just lucky for Chris that he was hired by Steve and Benny, the top editors at the Inquirer? Chris always thought so. They interviewed and hired him only one day after Steve answered the call from Sen. Schumer's office set up by Liza Lopez. The interview was just a formality. Chris had faxed news copy from his scant experience at Roll Call and Northwestern.

They loved the copy and decided to see him live. It was better than anything published by the paper in recent memory, Steve said.

Chapter 24: Forbidden

Friday, May 25

Chris sat motionless on the old couch in his tiny apartment staring at the door. It was another Friday evening, alone again in Rhodesville.

What to do next about the lost story? Find out more about Vickie Martin? He wondered. Now that she was a prime player/suspect in the story, he could not stop thinking about that lovely strange woman's voice on the phone two weeks ago. What was her real story? That sultry whispering voice still haunted Chris.

He'd practically memorized Dickie Randim's source book by then. Mentally cataloging Dickie's notes, Chris's thoughts landed again and again on thinking about the Radisson Hotel.

After three cans of cheap Red, White and Blue beer, he chose the new hotel as his first destination. He launched his secret investigation, and with any luck, Mrs. Victoria Martin herself would be there.

He drove the old Mazda to the Radisson and parked at the far end of the parking lot, near the exit to I-495, the D.C. Beltway. It was to be a reconnaissance trip, no more than that, to get the feel of Dickie's beat, he rationalized. But he mostly wanted to see this notorious woman for himself. And, he could not deny to himself that he wished to see if she was as gorgeous in person as she was on the TV news shots.

He walked into the hotel's main entrance carrying a big mailer envelope as a prop to trick the doorman. "Sir, is there a Victoria Martin working here? I have a package for her," he asked.

"Mrs. Martin is stationed at the concierge desk," the doorman responded.

Chris soon learned that Vickie didn't mind being known as a walking peep show. Vickie liked being called Peeps; it was her pet name, he had heard from the newspaper guys. He had also heard that Vickie was a delight to have around, though a bit flashy, according to what the other Inquirer reporters got previously from her co-workers.

Chris walked to the side of the lobby opposite the registration desk, glancing back toward where he would expect the concierge station to be located. He hoped the doorman would bring her out about the man with a package. He hid and waited, then …

She was indeed quite a pretty sight. Chris had no doubt that the woman walking out from behind the desk was Vickie. She wore a tight white sweater top that revealed upward curves of her breasts. *She's got to have something holding them up,* he thought and wondered if they were God's gift or implants.

Vickie greeted some new guests as they checked in and by their gestures were asking for information. She was very animated, always flashing a warm smile, even shaking hands as she answered their questions. Guests responded well to her; seemed happy.

Chris remained in the shadows watching her, while he reflected on Vickie's biographical sketches he read that afternoon. It came from Style section clippings that appeared in the Washington Post and Baltimore Sun, and in the hospitality trade newsletters online about the flamboyant Vickie Martin. As he watched Vickie greet guests, walk about the lobby, and direct people, Chris settled into a stuffed chair and let his mind review what he had learned earlier. He didn't mind covertly watching Peeps do her thing, making people happy. She was a sight to behold.

* * *

He had read gossip that Johnny "Boss" Martin did love his Vickie, not as his wife, but as a possession, according to several quotes. They were a business team: he was a highly competitive industrialist and she was his trophy. At business parties and receptions, Vickie had always been the best looker, the flashiest, shapeliest woman in the room. Johnny was the smartest man in the room.

The first thing men would say to Martin at those parties was 'Hey, where's the real boss? Where's Vickie?'

Chris learned that Boss Martin managed and developed commercial properties in Chicago, as had his father, Vincent Martini, who began as a poor immigrant from Italy.

Johnny had not always been respectful of his father.

Real estate entrepreneur Vincent Martini was legit in every way, and lucky, too. He married the daughter of famed Washington defense attorney, F.B. Bailoff, who defended Chicago police captains after the infamous 1968 police riot outside of the Democratic National Convention hall.

Vincent was a grateful friend of the Chicago police force. They protected his tiny real estate office in a racially charged district during the turbulent 1960s. Minorities learned to trust Martini to get fair and decent treatment.

A turning point in Vincent Martini's life and toward his success in business occurred when he attended a trial to support the cops accused of crimes during the riot.

In that courtroom, he incidentally met Sonya Bailoff, 18, who would be his future wife. When her father won the case, Vincent rushed to the front of the courtroom to shake his hand. Vincent accidentally knocked her down as he pushed through a crowd of well-wishers to reach Bailoff. Embarrassed, Vincent mustered the courage to politely make up to Sonya for his clumsiness.

Young Sonya, already leery of the manipulating, girl-prowling men associated with her father's company, saw something special in Vincent as he lifted her back to her feet to apologize. She ignored him but nudged her father, "Papa, thank the man for his kind apology. He didn't see me."

F.B. invited Vincent to join them at the victory celebration at a nearby watering hole, a tavern frequented by attorneys. Vincent's eyes never strayed from Sonya, captivated by her.

Two months later and with Bailoff's support, Vincent transferred his business to the Nation's Capital even before proposing to Sonya. Over the next 25 years, he built a formidable empire of development projects, largely through F.B.'s contacts.

Vincent's business, V. J. Martini & Son Inc., was entirely legitimate, with many federal contracts, the favorite clients for Vincent, who was a proud new flag-waving American.

Chris read that Vincent Martini's company took a turn downward after about two decades in Washington when son John Martini took over the firm and began calling himself Johnny.

Johnny started out pretty green. Initially, he didn't want to bid on government work. Instead, he trusted his cronies to give him business in the building boom of the late 1980s.

Johnny was lazy and careless, but his father left a bankroll in the business that made it easy to build upon.

Yet, Johnny often said, "I don't need no stinkin' Godamn gov'ment contracts." He became quite cynical dealing with Washington bureaucrats.

As a businessman, young Martini was a different kind of businessman. He had a swagger and arrogance from being raised as a spoiled rich kid.

Vincent had projected his son as the company attorney and sent him to George Washington University Law School in downtown Washington, D.C. In law school, he drifted from his father's influence and he fell in with the wrong crowd during his first-year.

Then, Johnny Martin completely shamed his father when he was falsely accused of rape. Yes, he was a playboy in his youth, lazy and rich, too. But, he was no rapist.

On a summer night in the city along the Potomac, the weather was typically humid. He dated a nurse at the GW Hospital just off campus for six months and then proposed to her.

The rape charge surfaced when his fiancé nurse attempted to shake down the rich kid when she discovered he was unfaithful.

On that day, they had sex in his room in the afternoon.

Later that evening, he and his law school buddies celebrated John Martini's 24th birthday at the Wisconsin Avenue Grill. He got sloppy drunk and took a woman at the bar back to his apartment. His nurse girlfriend came in with her key and caught John in the act with the woman.

Angry, the girlfriend went straight to the police station nearby after tearing her blouse and scratching her chest and shoulders. She was examined at GW Hospital where she submitted to a rape exam and DNA samples from semen were taken. The tests revealed a match to Martin, not from her vagina, but her underwear.

His playboy student reputation hurt his case. He was convicted, but his sentence was reduced to a two-year term in a minimum-security prison just outside Great Falls, Va.
Court witnesses painted a profile of an angry young man fond of drinking and who had abused and forced himself on his woman.

Finding himself in jail after a regrettable one-night stand, Johnny Martini, bitter and simmering with anger, lost any last thoughts of running his father's business the way his father Vincent did—legitimately. From then on, Johnny was a man out to screw the world, especially the government, get all he could get, in any way he could, legally or otherwise.

His new business plan was one of payback: take what he deserved from the community. He hated the hypocrisy of Washington power brokers.

He focused on housing at first, then commercial buildings. Johnny retained some of the same compassion for the downtrodden that his immigrant father had given to everyday people dreaming of owning their own home. He found more profits in the suburbs of King's County and liked helping the burgeoning African-American population become homeowners.

But still, Johnny's rather slipshod-construction strategy was a well-oiled cash register.

Vincent watched from the sidelines in horror. Finally, after a couple of years, he sued his own son to take his name back from Johnny's unscrupulous business practices.

In an out-of-court settlement, Johnny agreed to change his name to John C. Martin from Martini and to change the company name, too, to JDR Builders, Inc. for "Jobs Done Right."

* * *

While reviewing what he'd learned about the Martins, Chris stayed hidden so long he had downed an entire pitcher of water from on a nearby table. Again, it was a pleasure. The whole time, he kept his eyes glued on the lovely Mrs. Martin flitting here and there around the lobby.

Still mostly hidden behind potted trees in the Radisson lobby, Chris continued watching his target from his stuffed couch at long distance. He continued reviewing his mental notes from his research in newspapers' style sections and began his first outlines of story angles into his reporter's notebook.

From what he'd learned, he figured that Victoria loved Johnny's money and stayed married.

Gossip columnists had concluded that Vickie no longer loved her husband, and yet, probably didn't dislike him either. Johnny seemed to ignore her most of the time, reportedly preferring to pay for lovers he could dominate and, in return, receive undivided admiration he no longer got from his trophy wife.

The Martins' rift occurred early in the marriage and was well covered in the newspaper clippings. Johnny had made it crystal clear that he didn't want any children. But she ignored him. She gave birth to a child, a girl she named Gigi, in the first year of their marriage. The child often stayed with Victoria's mother in a townhouse that Johnnie bought for her, a block from the Martin's College Park townhouse.

* * *

Chris realized that just watching the alluring "Peeps" Martin from afar was not getting him anywhere as the budding Pulitzer Prize investigative reporter of his fantasies.

Once she left her concierge station, he again understood why they called Victoria Martin "Peeps."

Holy cow, she's Ginger on Gilligan, Chris thought, picturing actress Tina Louise as the seductive movie star marooned with the crew of the SS Minnow on the goofball '60s comedy, "Gilligan's Island." Redheaded Ginger wore skintight dresses and high heels on a sandy island beach. Sipping his beer, Chris got a kick out of remembering how much he loved Gilligan reruns on Nick at Nite, as a kid in Glasgow.

But it wasn't Vickie's clothes that reminded him of Louise on Gilligan. She had on slacks. It was her movements. She would sashay about in a wiggle walk much like how Gilligan's Ginger perhaps imitated a Marilyn Monroe wiggles from "Some Like It Hot" as Jack Lemmon in drag exclaiming to his 'girlfriend' Tony Curtis also in drag, 'Will you look at that! Look how she moves! It's like Jell-O on springs. Must have some sort of built-in motor or something. I tell you, it's a whole different sex!"

With a strong beer buzz working on his mind's imagery, Chris didn't realize he was laughing out loud and clammed up. He thought, *Okay, so much for the sexy look. She doesn't exactly look the part of the grieving widow.* He took a closer look at how she had prepared for working that day so soon after the tragedy. A post-adolescent Britney Spears would have been envious of Vickie's school girl get up--a white angora sweater opened at the top and cinched tight at the waist by a wide leather belt that showed off her shapely long legs that were wrapped in baby blue slacks. She knew how to move her body to catch a man's eye. That was not a woman in mourning.

Chris lost all courage to approach her. He needed a stiffer drink, but on his budget, a beer would suffice.

Chapter 25: Fat Kid's Story

When he was sure Vickie had disappeared into the hotel interior, with little chance to spot him sneaking around, he slipped into the hotel's principal watering hole, the Congressional Lounge.

Yea, like senators drink here, Chris chuckled to himself and then ordered a draft Yuengling at the bar. The popular Pittsburgh area brew was the reported favorite of former Steeler fullback Franco Harris.

"Hey what's funny," said a fat kid sitting on the stool next to him at the bar. He wore a green golf shirt that was much too small for him. It exposed more than a biscuit of belly fat over his belt.

The kid seemed to be with a young woman on the other side of the kid. She had curly red hair pulled taught in a ponytail. She wore a parka, open over pink medical scrubs.

"Hi. How ya doing," Chris answered the kid. "Funny? Oh, yeah. It's just the name 'Congressional Lounge.' Seen Senator Byrd here lately? Or George W?" Chris was feeling good for a change, getting out drinking, although he worried about spending $5 a draft beer on a reporter's salary.

"Huh? Who's he?" said the kid, slurring his words.

Chris figured that the kid, maybe 18, had been there drinking for a while. Looking past the kid, Chris saw the girl toying with her Blackberry phone while sipping on a bottle of Bud Light. The kid looked back and forth a few times between the girl, preoccupied with her device, and curious Chris.

"You two know each other?" asked Chris.

"Why? You like her? She's here all the time, drinking buddies."

"Well, she is pretty, but I didn't ..."

"I'll put in a good word for you, alright?" the kid asked Chris, then turned to the girl quickly.

"No, no, that's okay, I was just…." Chris said. But it was too late.

The kid nudged the girl roughly and mumbled something to her about Chris, nodding toward him. She extended her hand to greet him. Chris's hand was waiting for hers.

"Hi, I'm Amy."

“Chris. Nice to meet you,” replied Chris, forgetting to ask for the kid’s name while introductions were going on. Amy’s smile and green eyes were far more intriguing.

The fat kid in the golf shirt asked Chris, “What do you do?”

“Newspaper.”

“You deliver them?”

“No, I write for them. I’m a journalist,” said Chris, who thought it still sounded strange when he said it. The word ‘journalist’ seemed lofty, grown-up. *Shoulda said reporter.*

The girl with the nice hair returned to her Blackberry and bottle of Bud Light. Chris watched her guzzle from the bottle with gusto.

“Journalist, eh? I got a great story for you, man. Best story you will ever hear,” said the kid. He seemed to be getting fatter as he settled in to talk with Chris. His body seemed to mushroom out like a tire going flat as he got shorter slouching on the little stool. He blocked out the cute redhead from Chris’s view.

“Will it win me a Pulitzer?” Chris tossed out.

“A what?”

“What about the story?” asked Chris as he surveyed the bar, crowded with young people. Men at the bar were dressed casually. The few women in slacks. They were mostly various shades of brown skin, he noted.

“Which one?” he said finally.

“The Pulitzer one, remember?”

The kid continued, “I’m gonna tell you the story,” as he slugged at his beer. “It’s one that people don’t wanna hear. S’bout my father, who wasn’t elected to nothing’ but ran the only factory in town, computer parts for cars. But it’s ‘bout lots of people really. I should also tell ya he is an alum of the University of Michigan. You sure you a reporter? Look too young.”

“Ann Arbor? And I’m 20 next month,” said Chris.

“Yeah, Ann Arbor, Michigan. The factory wasn’t in Ann Arbor. My dad lost his job, his house, and his health all at once. So then, my parents’ friends ran a benefit and the whole town helped him because he is such a, such a great guy.” The kid was intoxicated, to the point of saying only one thought at a time without connecting to other thoughts well.

Chris felt uncomfortable as the kid was about to cry. *Maybe I should change the subject.*

Instead, Chris tried harder to be nice, "You mean the whole city of Ann Arbor helped your dad get out of financial trouble? How? What did they do? How come the whole of Ann Arbor knew your dad that well anyway?" Chris was also hoping to unravel the kid's story quickly so he could talk with Amy again.

"No, a town near Ann Arbor. Everybody knew him 'cause he was a town councilman or somethin' or 'nother. He worked for them people up there all his damn life."

"You mean he died?"

"I hope not. Try to pay attention will ya, paperboy?"

"Oh, I misunderstood. Sorry, go on."

"Well, trrry..ee to pa-pay attention, as I said."

No sense being overly nice, Chris switched to, "Do you two hang out here much, know this hotel at all?" asked Chris. He didn't want to completely forget his goal there was to start investigating a murder.

"Yeah, but I wouldn't say hang out. I'm here sometimes. She is sometimes. I don't know. But here's the story, see...." he rambled on.

Chris understood that they weren't a couple but friends, maybe siblings; both looked Irish and had a certain resemblance. He wasn't taking the kid's story seriously yet but decided to help him feel better by hearing him out. "What did your dad do for a living where he lost his job?"

"Ya wanna know? Well, he was the plant manager, in charge of all production. Then they decided to contract out jobs to India and he lost his job, so he told the bank mortgage guy what happened and got nowhere. He was a foreign guy too, I think."

"The bank guy?"

"Yeah, fuckin' foreigner. So, my dad had this new house and the interest rate doubled and he got behind on the payments. He needed the house to raise my brothers and sisters cause my mom died of cancer, you know."

"I'm sorry, ah ... what did you say your name was?"

The kid ignored the question. "And so, this predatory mortgage guy at the bank said they would look into getting some help for my dad. He thought they would refinance or something. Nothin'. Nada. Not a damn thing. Months passed us by."

Chris fixed on the word 'predatory.' He listened more closely. The kid was then dead serious, angry and talking about lending predators like Johnson and Madinoff, Chris figured.

"My dad kept going to the bank and they kept sayin' they were workin' on it, see? My dad had to then start working as a custodian at my ol' high school at night even, then sellin' insurance or som'in in the day. It was killin' him. No sympathy from a predatory bank, you know."

"Yeah, rough," Chris said, while he also wondered.

Another guy started talking with Amy. Chris was distracted.

"Then he had the stroke," the kid said, almost crying. Chris felt bad for not paying attention. The new guy was stealing his time with Amy. "Is he okay now?" Chris asked, putting his hand on the kid's shoulder to look past him.

"Yeah, cause of the neighbors. They put on a benefit at the Lion's Club and raised a hundred and twenty thousand dollars for my dad's medical expenses. It was the biggest thing ever in our town. It was big enough. Big enough, hey, you listening? Big enough that the secretary of state for the whole fuckin' state of Michigan was there because my dad once did work for him."

"Did he get to keep your house?"

"Nah. That sucker belongs to the bank now. Dad and my brothers and sisters live in an apartment near his work at the school. Even somebody as important as my dad, no luck with a refi and getting help to keep his home. Even him, see? A real American. Not some fuckin' foreigner mortgage predator. Think that's a story for ya? Do ya? If you think that's a good story, I'll give you the whole story later. ... Nobody believes it."

"Yes, I do. I mean I do think that's a story," said Chris. "What's the unbelievable part?" he asked, regretting it.

"What's the unbelievable part? Give me ten seconds of your life and I'll tell ya. Man, where you been?" The kid was getting worked up and angry. "This shit is happenin' to people every place in this country. A guy, my dad, any guy, who worked his ass off, doesn't matter who it is, makes sure he has a job, health insurance, did everything they asked of him in his career, gets talked into a mortgage he thinks he can handle, maybe. Then things change, loses health insurance, and before he can breathe, they kick his ass down the road, and as a 55-year-old, they keep kicking' his ass, because he can't kick back. Could be anybody like him. He did everything he possibly could do to follow the rules, take care of his family, then they say get the fuck out of OUR house," he said, shouting the word 'our,' as he pounded his fist on the bar.

The kid was getting very loud, capturing cross looks from security guards outside the bar in the hotel lobby. Chris slouched down in case Vickie Martin looked over too. That would not be the way to meet her.

The kid saw Chris duck and then notice people looking and calmed down. He continued, "My dad had a stroke finally. Now we take care of him. No house. Fuckin' mortgage loan vultures, man, they are all over." He had finally captured Chris's full attention. The idea energized him. The story hit home. If in Maryland, it could have been one of the lenders from the FUC'M tower.

Chris asked, "What kind of work are you in?"

"I do grounds at Beechwood," said the kid pulling his shirt emblem out for Chris to read: Beechwood National Country Club. Although there is nothing national about the golf course, except maybe that it's just 10 miles from the D.C. line.

"Like it?"

"The job? Yeah; a lot. They can't get by without me. I am in charge of the grounds around the clubhouse and all. The place is filthy with politicians, judges and other criminals," the kid managed a laugh.

"I'll bet they are," Chris said, wondering exactly who the kid meant. Chris decided not to mention the FUC'M tower and its mortgage companies. He was thinking there's a good chance people at the kid's golf club would be close to the situation.

He thought *It might be good to get to know this kid better first.* He was pondering an opening to make friends with him better.

In the pause, the kid threw Chris a curve. "Not much dough in bein' a reporter, I hear," he said.

Chris teased, "I don't know. Can't be too bad, I've got two homes and drive a sports car." As he lied, he thought of his dumpy apartment as house number one, his mom's house in Glasgow as house number two, and Dickie's car in place of his old Mazda.

Chris was painting castles in the sky, but it felt good to see the pretty redhead toss her hair around, suddenly making eye contact with him, abruptly ending the conversation with a dark-haired pale kid in a Baltimore Ravens' jersey, who had come up behind her.

The kid leaned back and said, "Wow, that's pretty good."

Knowing she was still listening, Chris went on. "It's a Boxter 3, a Porsche," He saw the girl's eyes light up and she agreed with the kid's assessment, raised her eyebrows, and gave Chris a big smile. "Yea, that's pretty good," she added.

The kid ordered beers for Amy, Chris, himself, even the pale kid in the Ravens' shirt. A few gulps of beer later, the kid asked Chris what he was doing next. He meant after having beers at the bar. A dejected look on his face made Chris squirm as the fat kid leaned over to Chris's ear.

"You wanna go out?" asked the kid barely loud enough for anyone to hear him.

Jesus, he means me. Do I act like I'm a homosexual? thought Chris. He was a bit freaked out. He'd never been hit on by a male. *I've got to get out more.*

Chapter 26: Why Love Amy?

Chris immediately leaned in front of the kid, as if nothing just happened, found the face of the cute girl also leaning out over the bar looking for him. "Amy, what is that elastic bandage on your wrist, some kind of wound?"

She said something he thought sounded like "car accident." Then, "I've got scars to prove it. They are ugly scars. I was taken to Shock Trauma in Baltimore."

With the kid's sexual pass still pinballing around his mind, Chris steered himself toward Amy, a bold move to a more comfortable 'port of call' for Chris.

He surprised himself and cast off his vow to stay clear of dating at the beginning of his work at the Inquirer. He stepped off his bar stool in a determined manner and said to her with clear intent, "They are probably very sexy scars. Got to be." He grinned suggestively as he focused on her nice face and beautiful blue-green eyes. "That's how you should think of them; sexy scars."

She pulled her Blackberry out of her pocket and signaled with her other hand for Chris to come beside her so he could see the screen.

Much relieved not to have to excuse himself, Chris maneuvered around the large kid—by then lost in a beer mug—to see what Amy was holding. Her Blackberry had photos of her totaled SUV.

"There's my baby, my car. Nice, huh?" The maroon Blazer was horribly smashed in from the front driver's side and dents all around as if it had rolled. "It's in the body shop."

"You're getting it back? Really? It looks totaled," said Chris as he maneuvered around close to the girl's shoulder and arm to view the pixel pics.

The two oohed and awed over shots of the mangled vehicle. Then Chris motioned to her wrapped wrist. "Pretty fancy wrap, Amy."

"I did that myself. I didn't like theirs at the hospital. They didn't do it right. I work at the Southern Maryland Hospital in Clinton in orthopedics.'

"Is that color salmon?"

"Paalease, it's pink, to match my scrubs. I bought these pink scrubs special. Like they wear at Shock Trauma in Baltimore," she pulled back her jacket. He could see she was solidly built.

"Goes with your hair; very pretty, Amy," said Chris as he hoped she would warm up to him. He felt his body chemistry tingling, changing as he looked at her. It felt good; he hadn't let himself make time with a girl that near to him in a very long time. Gone was the resistance barrier he wore around the pretty young women at the paper and on his reporting beat.

He gasped a bit for a comfortable breath of air, feeling a little weakened, "Work at a hospital, huh? Did you get another car to get you there? Quite a ways from here, huh?"

He was stalling, time to think as he just remembered that her hospital took in most of the injured from the FUC'M tower collapse. Although infatuated suddenly with Amy, Chris was never far from his lost story.

"Not so bad. I came here with him," she said, motioning to the fat kid next to her. "He knows my brother."

The kid smiled and Chris smiled back to make up for abruptly halting their conversation.

Amy continued, "Where do you work, Chris?"

"All over. The paper's in Rhodesville, but I've also worked in King's County further south, after the office building disaster in Loweville."

"The FUC'M tower? That's what they call it you know, because it fucked over everybody. Now, it's fucked," she seemed to love saying the word 'fuck.'

It was delightful to Chris. "You don't say."

"We were swamped with broken bones from people mostly falling down, thrown around by the blast, getting the hell outta there. The stairways were leaning, ya know. From what I hear, the name FUC'M fits the creeps who worked there."

The fat kid was listening, "I'll say. Ya got that right. Just like back home in Michigan."

Chris acknowledged the kid's comment with a polite smile.

He then leaned in close to Amy and whispered in her ear, "I saw it." Her hair was intoxicating, sweet, fresh. She stayed close to him. He felt her lean into him softly. Ever so lightly, he pulled on Amy's good arm, drawing her away from the bar.

She gushed, "Saw what? The crash? The FUC'M Tower crash down? No fuckin' way," as Amy followed him to an empty table.

Chris paid close attention to the pretty young woman with the light red hair and matching pink scrubs. Was it her story, or her sexiness he wanted? He didn't care which. He needed to know Amy now.

"The crash, the explosion, the hysterics. All of it," he said.

"I didn't know they had video."

"Not on video. I saw it live because I was there at the back parking lot when the bomb went off, very close in fact. It could've blown off my head," Chris inadvertently faked pain in his face.

"You saw the whole thing? Get out!! Tell me, tell me. What did you see?"

A waitress wearing a Washington Wizards tank top and shorts located the two at a table. Chris ordered a pitcher of Bud Light, his least favorite beer, but her preference.

He was thrilled to be with the girl, but stayed cool. He soon learned that Amy's work at the hospital gave her access to all the names and addresses of the injured, as well as the extent of their injuries and where they worked, their complete charts. It was a treasure trove of potential clues. And, Chris didn't have to press the matter. He had a strong physical attraction to 18-year-old Amy. Or, maybe it was the story after all.

As they talked, Chris sensed that Amy seemed impressed with his manners and intelligence. She wondered, "How do you know such things? You are so smart, Chris!"

He believed he was the most well-mannered guy in the bar, but his surprising charm helped mask over being the loneliest damn male in the bar.

In no time at all, he felt a growing sexual desire for her, while also aware that any information Amy knew about the FUC'M wounded could help him with his story. He gave his intellect a momentary chance to decide which was motivating him and decided to let himself go with simply the sexual attraction.

After more talk and more beer, she said she was "tickled" to be with a journalist from Scotland.

She politely said goodbye to her friend, the fat kid at the bar, and enjoyed a ride to her apartment in Chris's dinosaur Mazda. She laughed off his lie about the Porsche. It finally lost its muffler somewhere near the darkened Rt. 301 gated entrance to Charmington Village, one of Boss Martin's developments. "Damn Porsches are for shit, eh?" he quipped.

She loved it.

Chapter 27: Thrilled

Amy sat down with Chris in her kitchen and put down two cold Bud Lights, perhaps deliberately keeping her small Formica table between them. She watched his reactions and waited for him to squirm for affection before she would show him to her bedroom. She was smart enough to chance playing with his shyness.

Chris waited and listened to his pretty pick-up girl, feeling quite proud of himself.

Meanwhile, Amy talked about the hospital on the day of the tragedy. She said several injured patients at Southern Maryland Hospital's orthopedic surgery were employees of the Best Opportunity Mortgage Company. Oddly, there were only a few minor injuries to employees at Johnny Martin's JDR Builders, Inc. and none from Lifetime Deal Financing, Corp. Chris explained that the explosion occurred at noon on a workday, though on a Monday, a slow day around Loweville, a town run by cavalier attorneys and politicians.

"Odd, huh? she said deadpan with a shrug.

The two stopped talking and stared at each other adorably.

"Come on Chris," she stood and dropped her jacket to the floor.

"Yeah, come here you too, Amy," he said, no longer needing to act boldly. She nodded for him to follow her.

* * *

Orthopedic assistant Amy Steinholder was eager to help her new lover with his investigative journalism, which she didn't fully understand. He never did tell her he was forbidden by his newspaper to report on the tower story but told her it was all confidential. She was thrilled to be privy.

She confirmed that among names of those injured was Best Opportunity's President and CEO, Bernard Madinoff, of 102 Riverfront Drive, Bay Ridge, Md. She had memorized his address because she had to write it down many times for him. His hands were injured.

Why, Chris couldn't figure.

Amy said Madinoff got his jaw broken when the blast came from one story below his office at BOM and on the other side of the First Union Credit & Mortgage tower. Madinoff said he was taking his sauna, after just arriving from his regular Monday morning round of golf at the Country Club at Beechwood.

She heard Madinoff tell the orthopedic surgeon that just as he had placed an extra wide towel on the Finnish spruce bench in his office sauna, his world was rocked. "He had a great story to tell, Chris. You should interview him," Amy said as she lay naked in her bed, sheet pulled back to frame her pretty face on a yellow feather pillow.

"He said he was 'God damn glad to be alive,' blabbing incessantly. The man knew everything. He said the soft spruce paneling in his sauna likely saved his life as he bounced around in the hot room."

Later, Fayme Lovelace told a similar story to Melissa's lady reporters at Chris's cluster, a story some witnesses told to Fayme on the day of the explosions. Fayme said witnesses saw Madinoff, in living color, bloodied from head and neck injuries, wearing only his flip flops, running, and then falling down a circular stairway onto the lawn. Wooden slivers were embedded in his flabby flesh. Then, he fell again, screaming, into the malodorous overflow hole from the septic system that Fayme said inspectors found to be in violation of sanitary codes. Madinoff instinctively ran downhill and away from the leaning tower, she had said.

Chris later crossed-checked Madinoff in Dickie's notebook. His name and phone numbers had been highlighted in green. He wondered why, if BOM had anything to do with the bombing, Madinoff had not been privy to it. Instead, he was sitting naked, sweating off a few pounds of his considerable blubber.

Amy also said Madinoff had head injuries, which required emergency surgery. "The stench on his body was so overpowering that doctors, nurses and other patients all like gagged."

She had copied official photos of Madinoff and other patients onto her cell phone secretly.

Chris could not believe his luck. It was a reporter's fantasy come true. Some photos showed surgeons suiting up in their scrubs and surgical gloves in preparation for the operation on Madinoff.

"Please Amy, do not delete these. Better yet, let me download them into my desktop, please," Chris implored.

Amy added more color to the story. She said that in the recovery room, Madinoff was delirious on the anesthetic. "He said he dreamed he was in outer space with actors Gary Sinise and Tim Robbins, like in that Mars movie?"

"Mission to Mars?"

"Yea, that's the one, but this time the three were partners in real estate development. About to reach Mars, the three argued, he said. They were betting their NASA salaries on the first land development deal ever on the red planet. And just before touching down, Madinoff described it as 'just as pretty a landing as you'd see in the movies. Perfect, no dust, no sound and no glass stuck in my ass'." She added, "Then, he said 'Hey, I'm a poet,' and he laughed about his own story for like 10 minutes."

Amy said "the corny scene in the O.R. was, well, just as good as one of my favorite childhood TV shows, "Hee Haw," the Nick at Nite rerun comedies with Buck Owens and Roy Clark. You've seen them, Chris?"

"Yeah, of course. And, you watched "Hee Haw," when you were a kid?" Chris asked.

"God, yeah. It was insane."

"I liked Lulu and Minnie Pearl on the show," Chris said, as he conjured up his own images. As silly as it may seem, an hour of sharing Nick at Nite comedy episodes sealed Chris and Amy's love affair. Just a couple of kids and their old-time TV shows.

Chris saw Amy almost every day for a week. She was thrilled with him as a sexual partner. She was falling in love with nothing held back. His pent-up energy and the repeated installments of lonely boy sex sometimes lasted all night. He exhausted her, while he energized himself. It was great sex and he thought he cared about her a lot. Love? Not yet. He was too focused on his lost story.

Chris didn't analyze the relationship. He didn't stop to think whether he was just using her for information or for sex. Did he really not care? He thought, *No. I'm good to Amy; she's good to me. That's enough.* He just knew it felt good to be close and care about a woman who cared for him. He hadn't had a girlfriend-sort of serious relationship since college, and that was three years ago, and it was not very physical like his lust affair with Amy.

* * *

Ten days after Chris met Amy and back at the paper, Melissa Cushen spotted a framed, 4x6 picture of a mystery girl half hidden next to Chris's computer.

Amy had made him promise to keep a picture of her at work. When he at first refused, she whined and pouted. She accused him of not caring anymore. He couldn't grasp the urgency of displaying a photograph, just less than two weeks into their love affair. "Oh well, sure, the picture is fine at my desk. I'm sorry. It will remind me of you," he said. He was then puzzled that she responded with, "Oh, so you need reminding?"

After Mel spotted the photograph, the ladies at the business desk were into it in no time at all.

Melissa asked, "Who's that Christopher?"

Chris, "Oh, I'm sorry. I thought you saw that before. Just a girl I know in West Virginia. You wouldn't..."

"Oh."

That was the end of that. But Melissa and her gang of Brenda Starr wannabes loved how after seeing Chris get past losing the FUC'M story, their boy seemed to be more contented, enjoying himself more at the paper lately.

Unlike men who might have guessed, "Gettin some now Chris?", there was no kidding from the women.

For once, he appreciated his gender minority status and didn't have to explain anything.

Chapter 28: They Call Me Peeps

Friday evening, June 1

After meeting his deadlines quickly during another week of easy assignments, Chris was able to free himself for several hours each day to himself.

He began putting pieces together, thinking about Madinoff, Boss Martin's death, the fat kid's story about his father, predatory lenders, and more to investigate. He created a dummy file on his office PC called "Family Contacts" and another on the laptop he got from Benny called "Cold Tips."

He sensed story patterns forming. His nerves were on edge when he considered there was no turning back. To try to relax he imagined being the mild-mannered reporter in the day, and super sleuth hero of Nick at Nite, seeking truth, justice and the great American crime story. Fine fun for the imagination, he thought. But yet, he knew he had the reporting tools to be a hero, except the cape, he mused naively. He settled on his strength, thinking, *It should not be difficult to pull this off. I just need to file my story notes I collect into my secret files, organize them and present a finished story to Benny when done. Nothing new about that.* Whether Chris and his plan were delusional or functional. His mind was set.

The next Friday evening, he returned to the Radisson, this time not so much to watch Peeps at a distance, but to talk with people who knew her or even to talk with Vickie herself. He needed information from her, hopefully without Dickie finding out. He needed a clearer mental portrait of Victoria Martin, the central figure in the story developing in his mind, the femme fatale perhaps.

He made sure Amy wasn't planning to be at the hotel that night drinking, with or without her friend, the fat kid. Chris still didn't know his name. And he would avoid the Congressional Lounge, where he might have to turn down a date with the kid again, although without that nice kid's unwitting help, Chris would not be on track. *Am I on track?* he wondered. *Shoulda been more polite to him.*

To get close to Vickie, Chris decided to pose at the hotel as a tourist.

He carried his old faux leather suitcase, empty, into the lobby. It was a hand-me-down from his dad. He walked directly to the registration desk.

A petite Filipino woman greeted him, showing off sparkling white teeth in a forced grin as she stated in a monotone, "You can check in here, sir." She resembled a mannequin as she froze with a blank stare waiting for his answer.

Instead of answering directly, Chris asked, "I'd like to see a choice of rooms. I just want to be as comfortable as possible, ma'am."

Chris wondered why he was feigning a bit of a Texas drawl. His nerves were getting the best of him. He feared being exposed as a newspaper writer.

"Well," said the little woman, without yielding one millimeter of her fake smile. "All of our rooms are extremely comfortable," she said matter-of-factly.

"Are they all the same?" he pressed. *Damn, that's a mistake*, he thought.

"All the same," she responded, maintaining her plastered smile, which translated meant *'I'm going to reach into your wallet and get that credit card sooner or later, mister. You may as well give up now.'* She stood rock still as did her smile.

"Yes, but they can't all be the same size, can they? The same window direction? The same view? The same...."

Another woman's voice from behind him, a familiar voice, added, "Same mattress?"

Vickie floated up to the desk from nowhere to help.

He tried not to act surprised, but Chris was nervous that Vickie was giggling a little, enjoying the conversation. "Is there a problem, Marlenna? Is this gentleman checking in today or making a reservation?

"You've been at the desk for a while now, sir. I couldn't help noticing you. Maybe I can be of some assistance." She was wrapped tightly into a short red dress with a glossy wide black belt girdled around her tiny waist. Her pink lipstick was wet, Chris thought. The short-sleeve dress opened at the neck in a wide V and plunged to the middle of her breasts in a narrow slid, which showed more as she turned. Chris couldn't help peeking.

This time, it was Chris who froze like a mannequin.

Vickie's smile opened into a wondrous ah-ha rounding of her lips around an open, pondering smile with a mouth of perfect teeth. She stroked her right index finger across her lower lip, and then said, "It's okay, Marlenna. I'll take him. I'll take it from here." She turned to face Chris and gave him a lovely, reassuring open-mouth smile that seemed quite genuine to Chris. Yet, he sensed she suspected something fishy about him. She kept her head slightly cocked to one side, looking up at him at an angle.

Well, that went smoothly, Chris thought with cautious sarcasm. *What am I doing this for, again? She is beautiful, no question about that now.*

He took a deep breath as quietly as he could, and said, "I just wanted to see the accommodations because I like to wake up in a room that's within my Feng Shui."

She said quickly, "Oh, the ancient Chinese practice for, eh, good health and fortune. Wonderful."

That was fast. Was she playing him already? He wondered, *God, does she know who I am?* He took another breath slowly.

Marlenna spoke again, "Vickie, he wants to see the rooms. I don't think we do it ..."

"Course we do. I'd be happy to help. Can our boy take your bag, sir?" she took him by the elbow gently, walking forward.

"Oh no, that's okay," he said as his voice reached high falsetto. He clutched hard on the feather-light, empty suitcase. "I have some personal items I want to keep on me at all times. I mean with me."

"Well, in that case, walk this way," said Peeps.

I do, and I might get arrested, he thought as he followed, watching the back of Vickie's skirt sway as she walked towards the elevators. *Is this really happening? I think she winked at me. Stay focused, she probably winks at everybody.*

He stayed quiet until the elevator reached the fifth floor, calculating that silence might draw the most information from Mrs. Martin without revealing anything about him. He knew at least he had an impression to build upon. His silence, however, did nothing for him but make him think he was in over his head with this mature, witty woman. She said nothing.

He thought he was making a huge mistake. He focused hard on his responsibility as a reporter and the tragedy of Boss Martin and the glass tower in Loweville, of the estranged odd Martin couple, Fayme, Michele, the paper, and the public. He then proceeded confidently and feeling more like a grown-up.

She took him into a guest room on the fifth because she said that floor has its own bar, pool and game room. "Here we are. This room is one of our best. It faces east for the sunrise," she said, twisting the upper part of her body so she could direct his attention to the window at the same time watching Chris to see if he was watching her, he guessed.

Another wink. "Come on in," Vickie half held back a snickering laugh that put Chris on edge.

She brushed against him as she moved toward the door. Vickie closed the door behind them. She locked it. She put her hands on her hips and demanded, "Okay, Mr. Gilley. What the hell are you doing in my fine hotel? Spying on me or something?"

"How do you know my name, Mrs. Martin?"

"Dickie Randim, Chris. You're the boy who answered Dickie's phone on that embarrassing call I made. I guess you know about Dickie and me then. You will be kind enough to tell me please what you are doing?"

"I didn't tell Dickie I was coming here tonight," said Chris.

"Dickie didn't tell me your name. He didn't have to. I recognize your stuttering voice. Dickie told me a couple of weeks ago who you were, before my husband was shot. Dickie described you. You two saw the Loweville tragedy. Oh, he also said you are destined to be the best reporter at the Inquirer. He said you were the youngest. He said you look like a choir boy. So here you are and you do ... sorry kid. Hey, you asked."

Chris, thought, *Interesting. She said 'before my husband was shot, instead of 'killed', or blown up*. He was visibly shaking now, "Okay, Mrs. Martin ..."

She lightened her tone, "Please call me Peeps, Chris. Everybody does. Dickie does, so I like it. Peeps, okay?"

"Why did you play along with me, bring me up here, wink at me, pose so beautifully and then lock the door? Pretty odd behavior I'd say, Mrs. ... ah... Peeps."

"Not so odd, for me that is. Just a routine. I thought I'd walk you up here because I recognized your voice. I needed the time to put two and two together. And heeere weee arrre," she said, lilting, as she sat on the side of the king-size bed in the room.

She leaned back and propped a pillow under her head. She raised her legs up and crossed them at the ankle on the bed, putting one hand behind her neck so she could balance herself. She laughed at Chris again and said, "Well now?"

Chris gasped for air in the stuffy room. It was the effect of that sexy voice again, he mused. And she was lying on the bed looking amazing. His knees were week; he wanted to sit but there was only the bed and no chairs nearby.

She swiveled onto her hip, bracing herself on the edge of the bed. "Chris, I'll ask you again. What the hell are you doing here? Did you come to see me? If so, why? Dickie would not like that at all, you know."

He tore his eyes away to a hard chair at the far side of the room near the telephone table and dragged it closer to her. In the meantime, he ran his mind through three rather adolescent reactions he might try to play through the game she seemed to be playing: *One: I could run back through the door and escape and then have all this get back to Dickie. Two: Try a clumsy move on the beautiful woman; no, stupid. She'd scream and call security. Or, three, trust her with my story and take a chance on blowing my cover.* He decided to come clean with the third choice.

He propped his right foot on his left knee and folded his arms. "Peeps. I can't help the fact that I know about you and Dickie. You called me by accident and gave it away big time, okay? That is not my fault. Also, I couldn't help being with Dickie when the building blew up and killed your husband. I am so sorry and you have my condolences, I mean it. But..."

She put up a hand, palm toward him. "Listen Chris, don't be sorry. I didn't love my husband. I wonder if I ever did. But, I didn't want him dead. Well, maybe sometimes, but not really. And, he didn't die in the building anyway. You know that, right?"

"Yeah, he was shot first, I know. It was in the newspaper." He made a mental note that she said 'didn't die in the building.' That was not clarified by any reports. *She knows something,* he thought. "Like I was saying," he continued, "I didn't ask to know so much about all this. Can I ask you to keep this to yourself?"

"What?"

"What I'm about to tell you."

She nodded yes and took on a more matronly expression.

Chris rationalized his situation. He decided that she was, basically, a good person. He had been rude to intrude on her. He continued, "I'm a newspaper man. It is in my blood. Okay, I look like a choir boy, you say, but I've been in training to be a journalist all my life. I've read all the reports of Mr. Martin's killing and the building bombing.

"Here is the deal: Because I was at the exploding building with Dickie that morning, for whatever reason, my bosses won't let me report this story. But it is my story. I reported it first! Peeps, it's killing me not to write it. I just know there's got to be a whole lot more to this story than people are fessing up to. I've decided to find out by myself. I just know there is more, but I haven't gotten far yet." He paused, looked for her reaction, but her face was expressionless, yet showed some curiosity, he thought. Was this a mistake, he thought again. *Maybe she can hurt me if I find out she is involved. Oh God, I'm stupid.*

"Go ahead, Chris."

"Well, the police have not said much either. So, I thought I'd find out about you, for starters. I mulled it over and over and decided, well, why not try to meet Vickie Martin and see what she knows?"

"Stop right there, Chris. There IS more to the story," she said, straightening up as if at attention, shoulders back, head up, to sit on the side of the bed facing him. Her body language quickly shifted from sexy to studious and compassionate. She pulled a pillow to cover her legs and was now very curious about what Chris might know. "Chris, do you know who killed Johnny?"

"I'm not sure. Some people said you did," Chris felt his blood rush to his head. *Are you nuts, man? The door's still locked. She might have a weapon.* Then, he glanced at her outfit, *Dummy, where would she hide a gun in that tight-fitting dress?*

Vickie Martin noticed him narrow his eyes and scan her body again. She showed a little apprehension herself. Here was an anxious young, viral male in an inappropriate time. Suddenly, she seemed a bit scared, too. Chris noticed and was ashamed.

"I didn't kill him, I swear. Why would I? There are guys who worked in that awful building who would want to kill him more than I would. He had a meeting at the hotel with some of them the night he died."

"Who was in the meeting?"

"Stupidly, Johnny came here by himself for the meeting, I think—well, maybe with a couple of his men, who he sent away—to confront these mortgage creeps from one of those two flim-flam companies, Best Opportunity--oh yeah, you say? [She chuckled.] Or Deal of Your Life Incorporated—oh, yeah, that's a good one, too, sounds like a TV game show or something, get that? I don't know which."

Chris was surprised that she was opening up, as she tossed her arms up in bewilderment.

She continued, "Dickie might know. Well, that night Johnny didn't tell me ahead of time that he was coming here to use the hotel for a neutral meeting location with those thugs. I should have been told. Otherwise, I would not have had Dickie sniffin' around all goofy and stupid looking. We hadn't seen each other for weeks. God, he was a mess. Dickie just couldn't wait to see me and me him. What a disaster."

"Hmm," Chris mumbled under his breath about notes in Dickie's source book, "Could be the Dickie's greens or it could be the reds?"

"Huh?"

"Oh, nothing. Go on," he said.

She continued, "That's about it. Then Johnnie and Dickie got into a shouting match. He already knew Dickie from the paper, you know, even before Dickie met me. No surprise there, 'because Dickie did things for him, I think. I don't know what. But Johnny found out that night about me and Dickie. Yes, I do love that crazy dumb blond, even if he is a dickhead. Yeah, I guess I do."

After an audible, rather self-conscious sigh, she continued, "Hey, listen. How about if you come by tomorrow for lunch and I can give you some background for the story. That'll be okay? I've got to get back to work in the lobby."

He thought about the idea, *Oh, great, a date with the infamous Peeps Martin.* He couldn't say anything; girl stricken, like the teen he still was for a few more days at least.

"Come on now. That won't hurt, will it?" she said with a coy smile, the sexy whispering voice there again. She got up and unlocked the door. "I'll have the chef whip up your favorite kiddy meal. A big plate of French fries? Some nice chocolate pudding with whipped cream, cherry on the top," she chuckled. "I'm sorry, just kidding, Chris. You're no choirboy; you're quite a man alright. Lots of guts to show up here tonight, then to talk with me about this stuff. This is no kid's game we're dealing with.

"But, hey, they will be getting suspicious downstairs if we don't come out of here soon," she said. "They'll have me arrested for attempted statutory rape. Sorry, again. You're okay, Chris. Thank you for coming. I mean that. Let's get out of this bedroom, eh?" She raised and lowered her eyebrows repeatedly. "Ouwww, they'll be sayin' Peeps is up there with that boy, don't ja know," she quipped.

They both laughed with ease and relief. Chris was glad he finally met the voice that was attached to the phone call but had a lot more to learn from her. He had come to the hotel expecting to dislike Vickie Martin, but instead, she seemed like a nice woman. He figured she must be outstanding in her job helping people find things and places to go. *On to tomorrow,* he thought. *Did she just say 'game WE'RE dealing with'?*

They took the stairs down to the rear entrance to the parking lot. Strangely, it seemed to Chris to be romantically lit and maybe she'd taken boyfriends, maybe Dickie, out that way sometimes. They walked out to a small patio, nicely landscaped with the sweet smell of June roses and honeysuckle. The kind of place young lovers kissed goodbye. But, not this odd couple.

They squeezed out the doorway together, barely touching, but close enough for Vickie, without him noticing, to slip something into Chris's jacket pocket.

He walked out quickly, careful not to be seen "See you at noon then," he said.

"Oh, Chris," Vickie said, as he glanced back for one last look at her pretty figure silhouetted amid fake gaslight lanterns. She pointed down to his hand-me-down suitcase, and smiled, "You really don't have anything in that thing, do you?"

"No ma'am. I mean no, Peeps. I just wanted to meet you," he said, and immediately regretted saying it. Then thought she was the kind of woman who expects to hear such things.

Chapter 29: Liza Warns

Vickie waved goodbye, twiddling fingers affectionately from both hands, and went inside. Clearly, she liked the young man.

Chris exhaled many times, his breath having been held more than he might have expected.

Once outside, on the dark side of the Radisson in the shadows, Chris stopped next to his old Mazda and looked back at the hotel, as if he'd use his super sleuth man x-ray vision to see clues to some ugly incidents that happened there on that fateful Saturday night.

He wondered if he had his killer, or at least a group of them--the mortgage creeps. But why? Maybe Vickie did kill Johnny and was blowing smoke in his face. Maybe she was protecting Dickie. No, he was cleared. *Much left to do*, he thought.

He didn't get into the car. Instead, Chris walked across the parking lot of the Radisson, studying the layout of the hotel. It was a habit of his. He still couldn't afford a cell phone and had already given Amy's back to her after downloading the pics of Madinoff and other people during surgery from their wounds at the FUC'M.

He walked away from his Mazda and into Chili's Restaurant next to the hotel to make a call. Amy answered. He needed her.

It was nearly midnight, but after two weeks of wild lovemaking, that wouldn't bother the girlfriend. The two were tight.

Amy said in a bossy tone, he'd not yet heard, "I was damned worried that you haven't called for two days. It's Friday. Get over here, would ya?"

He cringed to hear a hint of domination in her voice. He didn't want another doting mother. But he willingly went to her.

* * *

The next morning Chris cleared out of Amy's without breakfast. He let her sleep. He decided to go to the paper to enter his notes and thoughts into his computer. He normally didn't work on Saturday but there was too much running through his mind on Vickie's comments to go back to his apartment yet. He'd dump them into his secret "Family Contacts" file. The newsroom never closed and several reporters were typing away when he arrived at 11:15 a.m.

He was exhausted after more than a two-hour drive in traffic from Amy's home in Clinton to Rhodesville, plus he got a late start because he and Amy had argued. First, in the middle of the night, after she said he "seemed different" after sex.

And then in the morning, Amy had demanded to know about a gift certificate for a meal at the Radisson, which Vickie had slipped into his pocket. The gift certificate had slid out of the pocket and onto the kitchen floor the night when Chris threw his jacket on one of Amy's slippery metal chairs. She was incensed. The envelope smelled of Chanel No. 5 perfume.

Finally arriving at the paper, Chris sat at his desk and immediately found a post-it note "From the Desk of Liza Leah Lopez," on his screen. She had written in big letters, *Coffee in the Café. NOW!!*

He headed into the café where coffee is free to the editorial staff. He was starving and joined a few Saturday employees in the breakfast line and picked up four glazed donuts and put them on a tray. Liza spotted him and pulled him out of line. She rushed him off to a distant table by his elbow. Chris in tow was puzzled. Before they sat, Liza shoved a folded newspaper hard into his gut--Metro Section, Washington Post.

"Did you see this Chris? I think you should forget about all this business. I know this Juan Garcia guy. He's a bad dude."

"What are you doing here on Saturday and what are you talking abou ...oh."

She shoved the paper closer to his face. "Just read," said Liza in a pushy, yet protective way. She touched his forearm helping bring the newspaper closer to his eyes.

Chris was stunned by a big 40-point headline:

Wife Charged in Boss Martin Killing

KING'S COUNTY, June 2--Victoria Peoples Martin was arrested at her College Park townhouse early this morning and charged with the shooting death of her husband John Martin, a prominent Maryland builder.

Martin's body was found in his vehicle on beneath rubble of the destroyed office building complex containing the offices of his company, JDR Builders, Inc. An explosion caused the collapse and destruction of the building, the First Union Credit &

Mortgage (FUC&M) Tower in Loweville. JDR constructed the tower in 1998.

In a curious twist of the case, forensic physicians later determined that Martin did not die in the building as was first reported. He had been shot twice at close range and placed at the scene, likely under the cover of night, according to Sheriff Barney Standard of the King's County police.

"We now have considerable evidence linking Mrs. Martin to the killing and more than one witness who can place her with Mr. Martin before he disappeared on May 12," said Standard.

Mrs. Martin maintains her innocence, said her attorney.

Bullet holes were discovered on May 20 in the badly burned body of Mr. Martin, known in the building trade as Johnny "Boss" Martin. From exit holes in the skull, forensic investigators believe he was shot by a small caliber pistol.

Mrs. Martin's 22 caliber pistol was recovered with her fingerprints on the handle in the dumpster at the Radisson Hotel where she has been employed as concierge since a partial opening of the hotel resort complex in November.

Mrs. Martin previously worked as a cocktail waitress at Blue Heaven Gentlemen's Club on Auth Road, next to Andrews Air Force Base in Allentown, where she met Mr. Martin in 1996.

The forensic report also matched blood found on Mrs. Martin's shoe, stockings and hair and also found on the hotel parking lot matching DNA of her deceased husband.

Harrison Verdi, an employee of the Lifetime Deal Financing, Corp. mortgage company, formerly based in the FUC&M building, placed Johnny Martin at the hotel and in the parking lot near the dumpster late at night on May 13 before Mr. Martin's body was found in the rubble of the destroyed building. His statement was unconfirmed.

Juan Garcia, a personal aide to Mr. Martin, told the Post that Mrs. Martin is not capable of the shooting. Earlier, at a closed casket wake for Johnny Martin at Omens Funeral Home in Northeast Washington, DC, Garcia repeated to the Post his statement to the police that the shooting was an execution-style killing, with just two shots directly through Mr. Martin's heart and right eye. Garcia said Mrs. Martin was not skilled with firearms and that the pistol was a deterrent that she kept in her car, but had only fired it once to practice. He said he had shown her how to fire the gun only last year.

John Martin ran his construction in Maryland after buying out his father, Vincent Martini, who founded the company.

Before being transported to jail, Mrs. Martin asked police if she could leave her five-year-old daughter with her mother, Mrs. Eloise Peoples, who lives nearby in another townhouse owned by the Martinis.

On the counsel of her attorney, Redmond Dundeili advice, Mrs. Martin made no statement at her arraignment. However, she previously told police that she kept a pistol locked in the glove box of her car for protection because she works late hours at the hotel.

Mrs. Martin drives a top-of-the-line 2007 Infinity LS46L all-wheel-drive sedan, with a special-order pink-silver hue.

Chris's first reaction was that the article made it clear that the police case was air-tight.

Liza frowned. She saw the puzzled look on Chris's face.

He finally said, "Why drag her luxury car into the story? To make a statement about her character? Besides, it's not true, Liza. She didn't kill Boss Martin," said Chris with more conviction than Liza would likely have thought necessary.

"And how do you know? No. You don't know that," Liza was protective, reaching her small hands toward him to find some focus in her friend.

"I saw her last night," Chris said reluctantly.

Liza shifted gears, calling on her defiant New York City attitude as she ending each phrase in a sharp inflection: "You talked to her? Where? Not in her house, I hope. Are you crazy?" She was steamed.

"No. At the Radisson, in one of the guest rooms."

"Oh, so now you are in love with this bimbo, Chris. You bangin' her? You're bangin' her, aren't you? Oh God, you are crazy," she said, half talking to herself looking across the room for a second. "You've got to back off, boy. You don't know what you're doing."

Her fists were clenched to the lunch table. She wanted to pound the table or pound on Chris, but instead kept her hands on the table, shaking. Her angry brain bypassed a dumb thought that her friend Chris could not possibly 'be bangin' her.

He retreated, "No, no. You don't understand. I went there undercover and had to act like a tourist with a suitcase. I acted like I wanted a room. She showed me one. Boy was I nervous. But, she figured out I was from the paper. I don't know-how. From Dickie, I guess. I mean, well, she's smart as hell and pretty nice, actually. And, no way I had sex with that woman, Mrs. Martin." With those spontaneous words, Chris instinctively thought of Bill Clinton and his Lewinsky affair.

"Oh, now I feel better. Way to go, champ. What a guy? Thank you, Mr. President, for the explanation."

"Liza, seriously, I don't think she did it, kill Boss Martin."

"I repeat. How do you know?" she asked.

"I just feel it. Before I saw this piece in the Post, I was fully engaged in finding out more from her today. We planned to have a quiet lunch together. She knows I'm interested and wants to help. Martin met with some predatory mortgage creeps, she said, at the hotel the Saturday night before the bomb at the tower on the following Monday and all." He was shaky in offering his far-fetched explanation.

"So, you ARE dating this bimbo?"

"She's not a bimbo, Liza. Well, I guess she is, but I believe her. She is quite nice when you get past all her flashiness."

"You're not thinking clearly, Chris. You can't start messing around with the greens and the reds, whatever that means, in Dickie's little source book. I looked at those marks and they are in all the wrong places. Those marks are for the creepo mortgage guys and they are dangerous. And, stay away from Knife Garcia, I'm tellin' ya. He's big time trouble. His parents were criminals from San Juan. He is the same, according to Latino sources I got in King's County."

"Okay."

"Chris, remember, I'm involved with this, too, thank you very much for making me a thief in my own place of business," said Liza, as she flipped her long, jet black hair back from her eyes and dashed off.

She's right. He zoned out and ran his mind though his transgressions, the compromises he was making for the stupid story: Lying to his boss, stealing from a colleague, unethically researching another reporter's (Fayme) story under false pretenses at the Radisson, using his girlfriend to steal hospital charts, compromising the employment of his best friend at the paper, Liza. He was not proud of himself.

Liza stormed back and clamored on, "You take the cake, Chris. This is crazy stuff." She stood over him still sitting.

Chris wondered, *Is it worth it? This is certainly not the Daily Northwestern in college.* He remembered the day Christopher Gilley, youngest editor ever of his college newspaper, was honored at graduation by his dean, who read from a script, "For three years of highly principled and honest reporting; editing that set new, higher standards for young journalists who follow Christopher."

Chris knew the words by heart.

He shook his head and extended a handshake to Liza, who did not take his hand.

She was set to lash out again, but said in a calmer voice, "Chris please promise me that …"

Chris put his hand up to Liza politely and said, "Let's move on, okay? I'll be careful Liza and consider what you are saying. You are probably right. I should forget this nonsense."

She smiled affectionately, "I'm so happy for that." She ruffled his hair slightly and made a slight move to hug him then thought better of it while at work. She looked around and said, "See ya."

Chapter 30: Vickie's Version

King's County Detective Lieutenant Colonel Jones asked, "Which is it? Mrs. Martin or Mrs. Martini?"

Vickie, sullen, responded, "Martin, please. My husband changed his name. Floyd, all you guys know that from all the free stuff you scarf up at the hotel to satisfy your appetites and foil-filled pockets. Please don't patronize me."

"Just for the record, Ma'am. Thanks. Tell me where your husband went after his meeting on the 12th at the Radisson."

"Not sure. I know that he went home, or at least left the hotel before me. When I left, I saw that his truck was gone."

Detective Jones, upbeat, "But you said earlier he planned that night to stay at the hotel with his father."

"Yes, but they had words," she replied. "Coulda changed their minds."

"What about?"

"Vincent, his dad, doesn't like how Johnny is running his business."

"How so?"

"It was Vincent's business once. You know how that goes," Vickie said, pouting. She knew it always worked well on the policemen.

They backed off.

Even after being summoned out of her house before dawn, booked and arraigned, then after several hours in jail, Vickie looked radiant.

She had dolled up just for Detective Floyd Jones, who had admired Peeps from a distance for years. She knew he favored her and wore her hair down and made up very pretty but tasteful. She wore a modest burgundy and gold designer dress she often wore at parties for Washington Redskins players or their management.

One chance to quickly choose a dress from her walk-in closet that morning as Jones and his uniformed cops waited, she wisely picked the dress that would give her an edge, or at least some chance to change the subject from time to time. Men love football and she was a persuasive woman.

Det. Jones caught himself staring and paused before saying with a clearing of his throat, “That’ll be all, for now” in a soft tone and left the questioning room.

Trichina Brown wore her interest in King's County's black history tranquility, confidently. She had nothing to prove and had no anxiety being one of only two blacks on the editorial staff, with Steve Mothershart the other.

Like everyone else at the paper, she was monitoring the excruciatingly slow pace of the Johnny Martin/FUC'M tower story. Was the race card being ignored? she secretly wondered. The predatory lenders were not being profiled.

Trichina did a little digging and found her angle with no bias; just reporting facts. She recalled covering the new King's County Executive Joe Collins when she learned that he had traced his black ancestry back to slaves on a plantation in Mercle, in lower King's County, owned by the White family.

Fueled by the Martin murder story, she worked the editors into letting her write a follow-up piece on Collins' discovery, partly to get the bigot Johnson's name more in public view, much to the delight of her colleague Chris Gilley. Since reports had placed Johnson at the Radisson meeting with Johnny Martin on May 12, Johnson had attracted no additional ink.

Trichina's angle was perfect to advance the story. It happened that the White family plantation where County Executive Collins black ancestors lived, was the former home of the ancestors of Samuel White, who had changed his name to Samuel Johnson before Johnson founded his mortgage company. She worked it in gently and the editors kept it as is, despite Johnson's higher profile since the disaster and murder in Loweville.

Black Heritage Big Business in King's County
Collins Linked to Slave Ancestors of Lender Johnson
by Trichina Brown, staff reporter

LOWEVILLE, June 30--Newly Elected King's County Executive Joe Collins "can't help but find it both ironic and joyful" that the southern Maryland County has become a business and residential magnet to African-Americans.

Collins, the first black county executive in King's County, tells anyone who will listen that in "Lincoln's day" the county had the state's greatest number of black slaves. "And things were especially slow to change for the next 100 years, even slow to integrate after Brown vs. Board of Education in 1954. I attended all black schools in the back roads of King's County until the '70s," says Collins.

His great grandparents were slaves in the southern end of King's County until 1869. "Apparently, they even stayed on the plantation after emancipation," says Collins who, with wife Helen, hired a genealogist to trace their family roots. "Who could have known what was going on down there, and this close to the Nation's Capital," said the new executive.

Collins has asked the County Council to put aside funds to continue an archeological dig and restoration of the site of his family's slave quarters on the former White family plantation in Merkle.

The Inquirer has learned that home loan financier Samuel Johnson of LTD, Corp. is a descendant of the White family that owned and lived on that plantation. "This is not unusual, though interesting that the Collins and Whites once lived and worked together on the same land, though in much different ways," said Maryland Historic Society archeologist Richard Leakless. "There is a treasure of ruins from slave quarters and artifacts, you know, such as pots, pans, tools and such, in many places in King's and other southern Maryland counties."

Johnson changed his name from Samuel White after his service time in the Army.

In more recent years, Johnson has negotiated more home mortgages to blacks than anyone else in Maryland.

County Executive Collins told the Inquirer that he is not considering Johnson, who is white, as part of the irony he sees in King's County. Instead, a more important irony is the fact that the county has the highest per capita income of any black majority county in the United States, yet progress for blacks was very slow for people of color in the county until the economic boom years of the 1980s, he said.

Collins was raised in the 1960s when the county was still largely agrarian, he said. "We now have a booming, suburban-based economy that is making people wealthy and secure. However, as African Americans migrated into the Nation's Capital for employment, many have found King's County to be like going home. We have affordable housing, good parks, integrated neighborhoods, and lots of role models for new professionals in our county."

Collins said another draw for blacks is the diversity of churches. With so much black heritage rooted in the church, blacks have built strong religious institutions and extended activities of all denominations in the county, said Collins.

The Collins' family heritages are part of a strong growth business in the county of reviving histories of its African American families who have lived in the county for hundreds of years, said Leakless. The Maryland National Capital Park and Planning Commission lists 34 preservation efforts in the county, including Collins' family site on the former White property and 18 other historic slave sites. In 1998, the MNCPPC listed only one slave family preservation site, near the home of Dr. Elvin Lanchester, now inside Pine State Park.

Collins said he and his wife know individuals from six African American families who have lived in the county for seven generations. They recently held a family reunion for descendants of those families at the Collins' home in Loweville. They said they did not consider inviting Samuel (White) Johnson.

The economic numbers for the county's emergence bear out Collins' assertions. The average per capita income in 1980 was in the bottom 10 percent nationally. Now, the per capita income is in the top 10 percent nationally, says Henry Polk, managing director of midAtlantic region of the U.S. Census Bureau.

Chapter 32: Risking the Low Road

Heeding Liza's advice, Chris laid low for a few days. He just did his job covering little real estate stories for his editor and mentor Benny Bradley. But in his mind still, was the salacious press coverage of Vickie, which to Chris was another layer of insult. He believed he now knew more than the Post reporters did about the story.

He couldn't shake the idea that it was still his story and began to press it again. "The coverage of this story has gotten cheesy with Vickie Martin's arrest," he told Benny Bradley one day. "They're dragging her to the gallows." Benny gave him a funny look and shrugged. Steve Mothershart noticed too but said nothing. The three returned to their computers.

Chris thought it unfair that the Post started its Vickie coverage by painting her as a gold digger. The Post kicked in a description of her new $90,000 car she drove, as a "customer relations staffer" at a hotel in the county. "They're cooking her alive," he mumbled.

Chris's mumbling did not go unnoticed. "Huh? What's that Chris," asked Steve, but he'd heard every word.

By 5:30 p.m. that Thursday, June 7, he had met his weekly deadlines, and then the tower story began to eat at him again. As soon as Melissa went home and the coast was clear, Chris unlocked his desk drawer and peeked once again at the pages of Dickie's notebook. His fingers took him to a cell phone number next to 'Knife.' No green or red dot.

* * *

Meanwhile, far back of the mostly abandoned Charmington Village, a JDR housing development, Juan "Knife" Garcia, the former Boss Martin spy guy, was relaxing. He was lighting a joint in the spacious kitchen of a large, foreclosed six-bedroom, four-bath, white brick house.

The house was situated at the rear of a cul-de-sac entirely populated with foreclosed homes that were surrounded by lush woodlands.

Knife was on his way to the backyard deck to lift the world off his mind when his cell phone buzzed against his pants pocket. "Yeah, who eez it," asked Garcia.

"This is Charlie Sanford," Chris said in his best juvenile voice. "I'm a journalism student working on a story for the Diamondback paper at the University of Maryland. Are you the gentleman who said in the Post that Mrs. Martin didn't kill her husband?"

"Don't bother me now."

"Is this Mr. Garcia?" Not waiting, Chris stated flatly, "I don't think she did it, Mr. Garcia. I would love to put that in the newspaper also."

Garcia grumbled, "Yes sir, I am him. But I'm in meeting. Don't want to talk to you. Busy."

"Can you tell me first if this is the best number to reach you, Mr. Garcia, sir?"

"Who gave it to you?"

"Vickie Martin."

"Okay, call me back in 15 minutes. I talk to you. Busy now."

"In 15?" Chris asked.

"A half-hour, busy. But maybe then." Knife hung up.

* * *

Chris used the time to check the latest Vickie bio stories appearing on the wire.

The former Victoria Peoples and John Martin were married for eight years. She had the schoolyard nickname 'Peeps,' short for Peoples, long before the Radisson or Dickie. *Ah, of course*, Chris realized.

Martin was Victoria's second husband.

When she just turned 16, she married a Navy pilot, Captain Peter Foresquen, two months after he seduced the beautiful teenager at age 15 at his Air Force-issued house at Andrew's Air Force Base near Washington, D.C. Her mother Eloise Peoples worked housekeeping in the officer housing including for Capt. Foresquen.

Only three months later, young Vickie Peoples' flyboy died when he missed an aircraft carrier flight deck somewhere in the Persian Gulf. The Navy listed him as killed action over Baghdad, though media reports consistently reported that no American planes had been shot down in the battle for that city.

Vickie continued to live on the base with her mother after the death of her flyboy.

Without a high school diploma or a job, Victoria's exceptional beauty was her only career ticket. She began waitressing at The Classic, a strip club a short walk from the base, where she met Johnny Martin a year later and shortly thereafter married the rich real estate developer. He was dark and handsome and very exciting to be around, she said in one clip.

An Associated Press story revealed that when Vickie got pregnant with their daughter, Johnnie Martin moved out of their condominium in College Park, where she wanted to attend the University of Maryland, and into a house with a live-in girlfriend near the FUC'M tower in Loweville.

At the time of Johnny's death, the Martins hadn't lived together for six years.

Neighbors said they argued over having children. He didn't want any but she disobeyed his wishes. Vickie got off the pill and got pregnant, thinking he would warm up to having a child if it happened.

But, Johnny left her.

However, Chris deciphered that the couple probably maintained a businesslike marriage and never formally declared a separation or filed for divorce. They remained friends, of a sort. SEC filings showed she had a minority interest in his business.

Best of Maryland magazine article reported that Johnny paid handsomely for Vickie to be hired as concierge at the Radisson even though she didn't have any experience. Martin was proud to say he had advised her that all it took was to look "tasty hot."

Her charm and fishnet stockings won the interview over, Martin said she told him. Vickie was quoted joking, "It troubled me that that handsome hotel manager, James Strait--single, very manly and, yes, straight--never hinted at making a pass to me. He actually seemed a bit scared."

She had worn a sexy, gaudy leopard print skirt suit with top buttons of her silk blouse open to a hint of cleavage. It didn't matter. She was going to get hired anyway. Boss Martin said so, according to sources reported in the Capital News Service of University of Maryland journalism students, which Chris vowed to double check but forgot.

Chris's quick research also revealed that Boss Martin employed almost exclusively African-Americans and Latinos, the later for hourly wages rumored to be paid under the table as illegal immigrants. Though he paid low salaries, Martin was popular with his employees.

Newspaper clippings online only dated from 1996. But Chris found a clip from the Inquirer's morgue, which was a glowing account of Martin receiving an award in 1989 for advancing labor rights and training in the building industry.

Johnny in essence treated the public badly with poorly build homes and commercial structures. But readers were treated to an image of a strong, dynamic and caring employer in an industry better known in Maryland for construction delays, payoffs to government officials, and labor strikes.

Chris also found an article that appeared in the Washington Times listing dozens of lawsuits against Martin and his JDR Builders Inc. for home defects allegedly resulting from using inferior and less costly building materials. Rotting decks, leaking basements and roofs, lime stain from cheap brick mortar, installing manufacturer's recalled appliances, even lack of insulation was cited. Two homes exploded and burned to the ground from gas leaks from faulty installation of tanks and gas fittings. Some of the suits also listed Madinoff's Best Opportunity Mortgage, Corp. or Johnson's Lifetime Deal Financing, Corp. as co-defendants.

No wonder the FUC'M tower collapsed so easily after the bombing, Chris thought.

* * *

Armed with 30 minutes of background research on the Martins, Chris was ready to call back Martin's odd-ball spy man, "Knife," again to learn what he knew.

"Hello, Mr. Garcia. Thanks for taking my call ... Yes, this is the newspaper student, Charlie Sanford. Thank you, sir."

Juan Garcia had gone outside of the foreclosed Charmington Village house to the edge of the woods directly off the back yard and was enjoying the long, warm June evening. He was sitting in a bed of soft ferns with his back against the smooth gray bark of a mature beech tree. The bark still held the carved out initials of a young couple framed in the shape of a heart. Once in love, their love now gone, home foreclosed, carving now surrounded by poison ivy vines.

Knife didn't know about poison ivy. He was stoned surrounded by the stuff.

"I kinda busy right now," said Garcia, who punched "speaker" on the cell phone and put it on his thigh, so he could get back to "being busy."

On his agenda, at that moment, was burning big black ants with his cigarette as they crawled onto his arm, then pinging them off with his forefinger-thumb flick at an increasing distance. He was busy getting the carcasses to fly four and five feet into the forest duff. It was an acquired skill and required a steady hand. He did it all the time. He was stoned all the time.

"Can we talk," Chris asked boldly.

"Okay, now we can. But I'm kinda busy here."

Curiosity was killing Chris. "Mr. Garcia, if this is a bad time maybe we can meet for a few minutes. I understand you were close to Johnnie Martin, who considered you like a son he never had."

"That's right. Mr. Martin was a fine gentleman. He was not very lucky with doz guys, you know, in the tower in there wid him. Things got outta han. Who is dees again on the phone? I'm sorta tied up now. Ouch! We can talk, I guess. Okay, come over before it gets dark 'cause ... ah, I dunno why, but okay."

His openness surprised Chris. Knife was obviously stoned, but that was enough of an invitation for Chris who smiled triumphantly and pumped his fist. He self-consciously looked over his screen at the newsroom. His chums would wonder why he was excited. Everyone has to know everything in a newspaper office.

Chapter 33: Charming

He drove the old Mazda down Route 301 and braced himself for entering the infamous Charmington Village, a ghostly development of unfinished houses and foreclosed homes, with only a few original residents holding on to their properties, likely at gunpoint.

His colleagues at the paper had nothing but bad reports to say about it. The housing market collapse, poor economy and bad mortgage ethics had transformed Charmington Village--the latest outcropping of nice homes, originally promised to be the best, and perhaps the last, JDR Builders' development in the hilly, planned community of the town of Charmington, central King's County—into an eerie collection of shells at best.

As Chris drove south to visit with Juan Knife Garcia, he reviewed the facts he knew so far. At the time, 2006-7, home foreclosures washed a red tide of debt over many neighborhoods in the county. The result was decreased spending by consumers, loss of tax revenues for state and county services, a busted economy, leaving hundreds of first home buyers back in apartments, often living with relatives, or on their last financial leg to save their beautiful new mini-plantation-like homes, many in white brick with two-story pillars in front.

New middle-income blacks were especially hurt by the housing crash. Black families were drawn to King's County by the earlier success of thousands of the new-rich African-American business and government workers who had transformed the southern Maryland landscape on the Union side of the Potomac, which long ago had ironically been full of farms with black slaves.

But as more and more homeowners, black or white, foreclosed and drifted away from their dream homes, a new, tougher crowd of renters moved into many of those big houses. Vandals stripped many of them of built-in furniture and appliances, even recreation room paneling and the wood on their outdoor decks.

Mortgage fraud in the region became more rampant with the rise in foreclosures, as adjustable rate mortgages (ARM) interest rates skyrocketed and property values plummeted. Of those eager people who did put a down payment in some equity, many ended up using the house like an ATM to plug the dike against a rising tide of bills until it was all used up.

One of the most notorious mortgage frauds was perpetrated by Sam Johnson's Lifetime Deal Financing, Corp., at one time, one of Johnnie "Boss" Martin's developing collaborators. Martin had used LDF to snare new home buyers and later regretted the collaboration because of the LDF prejudicial lending practices. When times got tough, LDF bought back thousands of houses throughout Maryland, using fraudulent low appraisals. The firm's CEO, Johnson, pleaded guilty to mail fraud two years earlier, leaving 313 homes in central and southern Maryland in the hands of a court-appointed administrator and, which now sat empty, contributing to the huge glut of abandoned properties and therefore compounding the crime problem.

The history of the housing disaster in King's County gave Chris cold chills on a warm June evening as he drove to the notorious Charmington Village he'd heard so much about in the newsroom. He had read accounts of vacant houses that were poorly patrolled by police or sealed up and subsequently taken over by gangs who used them as warehouses for fencing stolen goods, drug dealing and prostitution. Blatant drug dealing was ongoing in Charmington Village and some of the hidden-away cul-de-sacs were completely vacant and hidden from view of the main roads.

There were unconfirmed reports in one Washington Post story that houses in certain cul-de-sacs at Charmington Village were one-stop drug shopping sites, or convenient places to pick up a cheap whore, or a well-stocked basement—a virtual discount store for anything from the newest wide-screen LCD television to bling, stolen jewelry.

When high numbers of houses had gone through foreclosure and lay abandoned in some of the new McMansion neighborhoods of Charmington and new developments of King's Grant and Coachman's Path Estates, hardened criminals from D.C. and Baltimore moved into the neighborhoods. In some places, where original buyers had abandoned their properties, the gangs moved in and ran their operations openly. New gangs formed and they competed with one another.

Both mortgage firms in the FUC&M office tower, LDF and BOM, were widely accused of predatory lending in the 1990s, by promising no-money-down or no-questions-asked loans to people with no chance of paying their mortgage when it finally adjusted to a higher interest. They gave money to clients with weak credit or no credit.

Predictably, new homeowners, often excited first-time buyers, could not pay mortgage and other financial commitments, and they are forced to vacate their houses. Maryland's anti-predatory lending laws and federal assistance to underprivileged homeowners later in the decade came too late for most of them.

Could a disgruntled former homeowner have bombed the blue tower, a symbol of the greedy lenders? Chris wondered as he approached Charmington.

Chris put aside his fear of driving into Charmington Village and once again felt emboldened by the thrill of exposing the unreported story of the bombing.

He knew the gravity of all the mortgage fraud in King's County. But a little knowledge can be a dangerous thing for a zealous and naïve reporter. He also realized then that Boss Martin could have been killed by just about anyone angry enough with him in the foreclosure-epicenter, King's County. Chris felt overwhelmed as he drove into Charmington Village a former gated community. Its gates were no longer closed to outsiders and half-covered with Virginia creeper and trumpet vines with clusters of big, orange buds waiting for the full warmth of summer.

He saw a stocky, short young man he took for Garcia walking up the hill toward the gate. Chris pulled his car over next to a large billboard.

Knife was in his early to mid-twenties, dark leathery skin, wearing an old grease-stained tee shirt that read *Conch Republic Cafe, Key Largo*, baggy jeans and sandals.

"You da guy?" he said.

Chris extended his hand, "Hi, I'm Charlie Sanford, sir."

Garcia didn't shake his hand. He just moved his toothpick from one r in his mouth and said, "Dis way." and started back down the hill.

"But, I can take you to your house in my car, sir."

"No, leave it here, behind the sign, where we can't see it from down there. We walk."

He told Chris to slip the Mazda behind the peeling sign on the billboard, that read, "Welcome to your new life in Charmington Village," featuring a pretty, mixed-race model resembling an intense, unsmiling girl holding a golf club over her shoulder. She could have been African-American. She could have been white. She could have been Asian, Latino, or Native American.

Perfect diversity ad for King's County, Chris thought. As he hid his car behind the billboard, his mind flashed on Marty McFly in the movie "Back to the Future," hiding the time-traveling DeLorean behind a billboard at the entrance to the town of Hill Valley to find it later.

He walked down the hill with Knife toward a circle of McMansions with overgrown grounds. Most of the three dozen or so Charmington Village homes had boarded-up windows, lawns of tall weeds, bright yellow dandelions, and taller smartweed, and an occasional auction sign. Some houses had flyers with forewarning messages, such as, 'Keep out or be prosecuted' taped to the front doors. It was a sea of foreclosed properties with an occasional 'normal' home still maintained by an original signer. *So many dreams sunk as people drowned in their debt*, Chris thought.

Tall vegetation was everywhere uncut, untrimmed. He thought of his favorite country comedian, Jeff Foxworthy: *If you find a car when yer cuttin' your grass, you might be a redneck.*

His chuckle didn't last. Chris's eyes were drawn to a big man in a Pittsburgh Steelers hooded sweatshirt and jeans and a woman in wraparound goggles ripping the aluminum siding from the back of an empty house halfway down the hill. *Nope, no rednecks here,* Chris concluded. Like hundreds of King County foreclosed properties, that one was likely already gutted, stripped of kitchen appliances, copper piping, wiring and any upgrades, perhaps even doors and carpets. Most of it already loaded on a flatbed truck behind the former home.

Chris, aka, Charlie the student reporter, and Knife stepped up the pace as they neared a house that served as a gang's crib.

Chris was very scared. He saw two scraggly men, most certainly killers, he feared, sitting on crates in the open garage, likely to check out Garcia's unwelcomed guest. One of the guys pressed a remote device and the garage door began closing fast, nearly hitting Chris in the head as it closed. *Did he do that on purpose?*

"Yo, dis, Barney. I know dees kid and he want some weed," said Knife, in more of a black, street accent than Latino. "Said he saw some growin' roun' here. He okay. I gots him from da road 'cause he don't look so good out dare. N'ma sayin'? No white kid ought be nosin' up in here."

Chris thought Garcia, mixing in black lingo, was playing up to one of the two rough guys, a black kid, no more than 17 years old, with a hooded sweatshirt pulled up to shadow his face.

'The killers' bought Knife's story at first.

Chris had gotten instructions from Knife on the way down to the house. Knife said not to reveal himself as a reporter. To let him do the talking. But he had not said anything about buying weed. Chris didn't want any marijuana for sure on such a delicate, fact-finding mission.

The two thugs followed Garcia and Chris into the house. They were joined by a fourth young man, another gang member for sure, Chris supposed. They all sat down in an eclectic ring of brand new La-Z-Boy recliners of styles, colors and sizes.

The guys were scowling at Chris without moving a muscle. He took it as a game of chicken and tried to limit expression while he looked back at them. *Maybe this was not worth it after all. I'm dead,* he thought.

He was in bad need of a haircut, sported a three-day beard and had the same wrinkled shirt and pants that he took off next to Amy's bed the night before. *Maybe I blend in some here. No, I'm dead,* he concluded again.

Compared with the others, Garcia was practically in his Sunday best, Chris noticed. Next to him was Mitch, bald white guy, say 20, cigarette in his mouth while he started rolling a joint with an eye on Chris. He resembled the original cartoon Mr. Clean television character on retro commercials on Nick at Nite, without the muscles. Mitch was skinny, with a shaved head except for one four-inch bolt of red hair dangling like a fat worm down the back. He was bare-chested and in baggy jeans. *This guy's been angry for a very long time,* Chris judged by Mitch's fixed, sullen face.

His most distinctive feature though was a green and blue tattoo of Neptune's mermaid daughter and her spear on his arm. Chris turned away from Mitch to keep from laughing at the tattoo.

It closely resembled a wild-haired Elton John in big glasses screaming into a microphone.

Next to Mitch was the black kid, Jerome. In no time, Chris realized Jerome was the gang leader, with his arms folded across an old *Iverson 76'ers* tank top. He wore dark sunglasses and several gold choker chains and one wrist bracelet that appeared to be West African. He was the only member not wearing earrings. Jerome had mid-shade African skin, clean-shaven, with neat cornrows that would require careful styling and care, *maybe coiffed by his main squeeze*, Chris thought. He was trying to remember any street lingo he'd heard or read about.

And the bulkiest, most dangerous of the quartet was Julio. Chris could not make out Julio's deep-set eyes. Where there should have been eyeballs were black holes in his skull. He wore a sweatshirt with arms and neck cut out and an oversized, sweat-stained Florida Marlin's cap, bill to the back, over a blue knitted skull cap. Julio wore diamond earrings and tattoos of indistinguishable imagery in great detail covering all the flesh on his folded arms.

Jerome let the others talk. He watched closely as a marijuana joint reached Chris.

If Chris, aka 'Charlie,' declined, they would certainly suspect him of spying and he would possibly never leave alive, Chris deduced. But, if toked, well, Chris thought, *Damn, shouldn't. I need a clear head. I'm in a tough spot here.* But Chris had no choice. He took a modest toke and pretended it to be a long drag. He was grateful that the smoke was mild and he didn't cough.

"Thanks. Is this what it is, what you guys have? The weed, that is." He was showing his nerves, wondering what was stowed away in the rest of the house. The place looked very sloppy from where he sat, with piles of clothes and trash bags thrown on stuffed furniture.

They stared menacingly in response to Chris's comment. He was pressing too much.

Mitch snapped, "Who says we got anything?"

Knife said, "Ease up, Mitch, I asked him up in here, man."

Julio jumped in anxiously, "So what? He came here why? Just to score some smoke? He's a fuckin' college boy.

"No, he ain't," said Knife.

Mitch and Julio put on mocking smiles, while Jerome just kept staring at Chris as if the visitor was something he'd never comprehended on the planet.

Chris was getting paranoid as he got high. *He knows I'm a phony. I'm dead; may as well get stoned.* He thought again, *No, got to get away from these guys. Bad idea, bad, bad, bad....*

Another pass of the joint, Chris shook his head slightly in the affirmative, involuntarily. He liked the buzz, and then turned toward Jerome, who looked at Garcia with a quick, upward head movement, then brought Garcia's fist across his chest, pumped twice on his heart, and pointed to Chris, without moving one facial muscle.

There was a prominent tattoo of Jesus Christ on the underside of Jerome's forearm. Chris found himself locked into it, staring. The image surprised Chris. The smoke had had its effect and he couldn't move his eyes off Jesus. *Am I seeing that right?* he thought, *or am I tripping.* The image seemed to stare back at Chris. *This guy is close to Jesus? ... needs to stay with him? Doesn't compute. Maybe it's me who needs Jesus to help me right now? What am I doing here?* One of the thugs coughed and Chris recovered his stoned-rambling mind.

Chris was hoping the image of Jesus meant that Jerome won't be the one there who kills him. He found himself staring at the tattoo again. Jerome noticed.

It irritated Jerome to be the focus of Chris's attention.

No, don't look again, no matter how strange this is, Chris disciplined himself. *But it is a very ordinary image of Jesus, no funky style or weirdness. Strange for such a tough looking dude. Such a beautiful picture, wow.* Chris was quite high and frozen in a stupor.

Knife nodded to Jerome and then said to Chris, "Hey, kid, that's it, let's go."

That's it? I'm dead, yes, if not Jerome, it'll be Garcia himself. I'm dead. Shaking, Chris followed Juan "Knife" Garcia out to the back deck outside.

Chapter 34: Born Again

Knife and Chris sat down on a Cherrywood bench on the backyard deck. Before Chris could get him talking about Martin's killers, Garcia lit up another joint.

Damn this anyway, Chris thought, *I didn't figure on getting wasted.* "Ah, listen, Mr. Garcia, ..."

"Call me Juan. You are again?"

"Chr... ah, Charlie Sanford, from the school paper at Maryland?"

"Yeah. You dun have ta buy weed, man. Just try this. It's my stash from the backyard; see over dare, growin' in the sun. Cool? You dinnent hear that, okay?"

"Okay, Juan. Why did they call you Knife?"

"I like the name. Reminds me of my father. I killed him with dis knife here." Garcia pulled a hunting knife from his baggy jeans. He waved the 6-inch blade in Chris's face.

Knife's knife had a nicely polished oak handle. Carved neatly into the handle was just one word, "Knife," not Juan, or J.G. or anything that would tell a finder that the lost knife belongs to Juan. It just said Knife.

Chris stared at the knife called Knife and wondered how anyone would not know that was a knife, yet Garcia had labeled it so.

Garcia said, "See, I put my name on it, people back off when they see it?" he said with a crooked Lon Chaney-like menacing smile. "I was 14. Always carried knife, very sharp, man, in school, all over when I growin' up. Cause my Popi, he beat me and he beat my mama. Too many time, man. So, I kill him with my knife to help save mama."

He paused, took a long drag off the joint, and then looked up again at Chris, passing the joint as he stopped to admire the blade of his knife and said nothing for a couple of minutes.

He then continued in a sad tone, "Mr. Johnny Martin was in court one time to help some friend's kid out of da joint--dat's Jerome, in there. We tight, Jerome and me."

"Saw his Jesus tattoo. Beautiful, man," Chris forced out words that he hoped made him seem cool.

Knife continued, "Yea, dat's good, yeah. So, as I said, Mr. Martin heard my trial and he like me, 'cause he know about my Popi bein' a fuckin' bastard, man. Mr. Martin dinnin like him neither, man."

"He got you off?"

"Nah. Spend some time at juvenile place in D.C. and worked in the chapel. I found Jesus, like Jerome in there. No backslide to bad stuff for me again. Then did some time on work details at Cheltenham Detention Center, where Mr. Martin came. He hire me and Jerome both, man. Jerome was at Cheltenham, too. We partners, but don't tell nobody, okay?"

"You two work for Mr. Martin now, or, I mean you did. Right?"

"He got me released and him and Mrs. Martin took good care of me and gave me work."

"That how you know that Vickie Martin didn't kill him?"

"Mr. Martin, he own dis house here again here after buyer dropped out a sight. He own all doz too, unfinished down there, too. No buyers, man. I am workin' for him in secret, me and Jerome checkin' out what goin' down roun here. Dem other fools in dere don know 'bout us working for the man. (pause)

"Then Mr. Martin got killed. It was those people man, loan guys, I know it, sure. Somedin bad bin happenin, man. (longer pause)

"I gonna stay clear of it, but Jerome, he crazy. Wanna hurt somebody bad for dis, man. He would kill dim. But I toll him wait. See what they do about it, see?"

"Who shot Johnny Martin?" Chris asked abruptly.

"All I know es dat they musta got Miss Vickie's rod from her car. I never heard no gunshot, and I was dare, man, at dee hotel. Listen Charlie, err, whatever your name ees, I can give you de story, but you gotta help me. Do you know Randim from the Maryland paper?"

Chris felt a shiver run through his body. He looked at the woods for a path. Maybe he could run away and escape. He didn't answer before Garcia continued.

Garcia said, "I know of Mr. Randim because of Mr. Martin. They were gonna do this story, I think, on those mortgage bastards and then Mr. Martin got killed. I think they tried to blow him up, the evidence, you know? You see what happened to dat goddamn

FUC'M tower, man? Mr. Martin had sometin on dos guys, dee mortgage guys, Mr. Sandin."

"No Sanford"

"Whateva, don know what. But he thought Dickie, 'cause he's a reporter, could blow de lid on 'em, you know, in de newspaper. They got him first, I guess."

Chris thought, *Boy, he's got Dickie all wrong. What a crock Randim must have laid on this guy. Dickie wouldn't have the balls to expose anybody like those loan creeps.*

But instead of sharing his thoughts, Chris said, "Yeah, I saw it. What a mess. I mean I saw it on TV. Do you know what Martin had on the mortgage guys, Juan?" Chris asked, thinking a little more clearly. Amazing how a little adrenalin can clear the brain of THC. "And what the hell are the feds looking at, Juan, I mean Knife, I mean Juan? That what they call you?"

Garcia looked puzzled and ignored the question. He picked up on Mrs. Martin. His tone got tender. "She wanna help me stay on with the company and keep helpin' out with some problems Johnny having with "da fuckin mortgage guys" and to keep spying on the gangs in Charmington. Martin needed to protect investments, say Mrs. Martin. Da cops don do nothin' bout all dis, man." He circled his hand over his head indicating the neighborhood.

That part of the story, a side story, intrigued Chris, aka Charlie Sanford. And he considered fessing up; admitting he was with the Inquirer. After all, if Knife was telling the truth, Chris was in a far better situation than expected because Knife was hanging with buddies in a stolen-goods home in the cul-de-sac under false pretense. The gang thought Knife was their ticket to the goods, being an insider at Martin's company. But, Knife had been infiltrating the crime ring for Johnny Martin, using his streetwise wits that Martin lacked. Quite an ingenious setup.

Chris imagined that Martin might have failed to get Sheriff Standard to clean up Charmington Village, put it on 24/7 marshal law to save his investment. Instead, Garcia was spying for him. Thus, Knife was still a very useful employee to the Martins and to JDR Builders.

Knife took the long walk with Chris back to his Mazda and sat in the car with him.

"Let's make a deal," said Garcia. "I'll get you Mr. Martin's company records on a bad dude called Bernie Madinoff. He run the Best Opportunity Mortgage group up in the tower. Don't know where now. If you fuck Madinoff over in the newspaper, I get you the records. Madinoff was Johnny Martin's enemy in business 'cause I heard Mr. Martin cursin' him every fuckin' day, man."

He thinks Madinoff killed Martin, Chris pondered without looking at Knife.

Because Garcia confided in him, Chris took a chance. He came clean. "Look, Juan. I have to confess that I am not Charlie, but Christopher Gilley. I just got hired by the Maryland Inquirer early this year and fell into this story because me and Dickie Randim saw the FUC'M tower bombing. He took me there that day to meet Mr. Martin and before we got into the building, it exploded. I hope you are not angry with me for lying about who I am. I had to chance it."

Chris paused and held his breath as Knife glared at him far too long for comfort. Then he added, "I think we can help each other." He exhaled and looked fearfully at Garcia's angry face not two feet from him as the two men in Chris's little car sat hidden in shadow of the billboard, hidden from the world, hidden from any witnesses if Garcia hurt him.

Garcia pushed his left hand down on the car seat to lift himself toward Chris so he could pull his right hand out of his right pants pocket.

Chris noticed a bulge in Garcia's pants pocket. Chris expected to see the oak grain of the knife called Knife any second.

Instead, Garcia tapped Chris on his knee and said, "Jeez. Okay, gotta get outta here," as he opened the car door. He stepped out without further comment and slammed it shut. Garcia then turned, still holding on to the Mazda. He thanked Chris for coming and told him to ask Dickie to call him. When Chris dropped his head to think, as was his habit, Garcia repeated, "Please, please. Do dat for me, man, and I will get you your story. I promise, Mr. Gilley. I not angry with you. I angry wit dose guys who kill Mr. Martin."

As Chris drove off, he thought of Amy's comforting love, her caresses and willing pleasures. He chose not to stop at a phone to call her though. Too stoned. He would be lucky to make it back to Rhodesville without crashing and sacrificing his old junker to the body shop once again.

It got dark. The roadsides were pitch black on a moonless night. He motored slowly into a pool of bright light from shops at the main corner. The lights were from the pink and yellow Dunkin' Donuts where he'd seen cute Kizzy make all over dumb, handsome Dickie. At the traffic light at Maryland Route 301 and Marlton Road, street lights brighten the car's interior.

For the first time, he saw it on his car seat, a nickel bag of Garcia's backyard pot, a gift from his odd new partner, Knife. That was the bulge in Garcia's pocket, Chris realized.

Chris looked at the red traffic light again, hoping to move on quickly. But, a state police cruiser pulled out of the Dunkin' Donuts parking lot and stopped next to the Mazda. A heavyset, graying cop surveyed Chris's old junker, likely for violations, Chris figured. Chris reached down without moving his shoulders, slipped the baggy of pot under his leg and instead of waiting for the traffic light to green, turned right into Arby's fast food restaurant. The cop drove on.

At the Arby's drive-thru, Chris ordered two large roast beef sandwiches with cheese, a large fries, chicken nuggets and a mocha coffee-flavored milkshake. He figured the caffeine would keep him from dozing off at the wheel. It was a long way to Rhodesville.

Chapter 35: Liza Reprise

Chris was typing away on yet another creampuff real estate story from Benny. It didn't take much concentration. He thought of Juan Garcia's request and wondered, *What am I going to do about Dickie's dope on Madinoff... Liza! I need Liza. Damn it anyway, she won't like this.*

He wandered over to Liza's desk.

"Hey, Chris. How ya doing?"

"Got a minute, my friend."

"Oh my, my. What a way to say hello, 'my friend.' Okay, what is it you need," she said with a mocking laugh. Perhaps safely nestled among fellow reporters, Liza didn't press him, just flashed the smile that lit the room as always.

"Can't say here. See me when you finish there, Liza. Please."

She met him in the nearly empty café, where he whispered that he needed a favor again.

She whispered, "You could have sent me an email for this. Come on, Chris. I told you. I'm through with this nonsense. I'm in line for a great job with Port America now, you know, that new luxury resort on the Potomac? I need to get a good word from the Inquirer. I don't want to mess it up, okay? Goodbye, have a nice d..." she said as she started to leave her seat.

He grasped her forearm and coaxed her back and she sat reluctantly with a smirk.

He whispered. "All you have to do is come up with me again to the exec suites when Chuck is away on business and help me ask Dickie if Chuck is in today, and … Oh, what did you say, Liza?" It dawned on him that Liza had just said the magic words 'new job'.

"Maybe, okay? Bye." She got up again.

He'd ask about the new job later, he thought as he luckily reached her hand this time flying away and pulled her down to another chair next to his, and whispered. "Here is the plan..."

She raised her voice, "I said NO." It drew surprise and concern from others nearby.

"Shish. Come on Liza, are we buds or what? We always look after each other, don't we? I need you."

Two office working ladies from upstairs sitting at the next table said in unison, "Ooooh."

He ignored them. Chris figured Liza might remember his favors for her, like covering for her, writing for her community beat with her byline for three weeks, when she was with her sick mother in New York City.

Her face softened, and he said, "Okay. All the editors are out this afternoon, right? At the editor's powwow in Laurel, right? So, I ask Dickie if Chuck is in because we wanted to get his opinion on which stories to submit for the annual Suburban Newspaper Association of America awards. We will tell Dickie we need Chuck because all the editors are gone. We always win a bunch of those awards, right? It's a legit question. The deadline is tomorrow and we don't want to miss it, we'll say."

"I still don't know why you need me. Leave me out, please."

"No, no. You gotta go. You are just there to get his attention. Then you can go, so I can talk with him some."

"Why me, Chris?"

"Because of the way he looks at you." He gestured toward her outfit with an upward palm. Liza was wearing a smart black skirt suit and white buffy blouse for an interview at Port America, which she had scheduled for that morning. "And you do look great today, Liza. I mean it."

"Oh, fuck you, Chris!" she said loudly.

Sarah Jenkins, the cashier at the register, turned to hear more.

Embarrassed Liza finally said, "Okay, when?"

"Right now. The advertising director upstairs just told me Dickie's in. I think he is scared; hiding out up there. Our timing is perfect because Chuck is away. He is in Barbados on some junket and not with the editors in Laurel like he is supposed to be. Carrie told me the Laurel meeting would be relaxed. I asked why. She told me it is because he's away."

Liza shrugged and let out a thin, "Okay, as long as Papa Bear won't be up there."

In the elevator, Liza calmly confided that she had almost certainly landed a nice job in PR with the new Port America on the Potomac River, a 500-acre multifunction vacation town of upscale shops, five hotels, and an expansive pleasure boat dock with luxury water taxis running the five miles north into the Nation's capital.

“I got to have that job, Chris. This would be the absolute last time you will get me involved in all this nonsense,” she insisted, slugging Chris in the arm hard enough for him to fall into the elevator wall.

He could not help noticing Liza was quite pretty when angry. Never saw such an expression on her. He quickly looked away.

Dickie’s door was closed. After just a moment, he shouted out and unlocked the door to let them in.

Seeing the two at his door, Dickie said, “Liza, I knew I’d see you again real soon. Come on in, sweetheart. Chris, what’s up?”

“Actually,” said Chris, “we both came up to see Chuck. Is he around today?”

Dickie looked puzzled, “He’s not here. What, want to use his office or something? He doesn’t have any whiskey in there. I looked.”

“See you guys then. I’ve got work to do,” Liza said while sprinting out, Chris closed Dickie’s office door behind her.

“What the hell, Chris. What’s goin’ on anyway?”

Chris had rehearsed for this moment. It was the only thing that would get Dickie to open up. “Dickie, I’ve got to know. Did Vickie Martin do it?”

“You came all the way up here to ask me that?”

“No, we came to see Chuck about the newspaper awards, which pieces he wants us to submit.”

“Isn’t that Bradley and Mothershart’s job?”

“They are out at an editors’ meeting and the entry date is tomorrow. Liza and I have some pretty good pieces to enter,” said Chris, knowing it was a lie, which Randim was not likely to catch. They calculated that Dickie probably didn’t even know about the SNAA awards and never would win one even if he reported an exclusive of aliens landing in a pink space ship on the White House lawn.

Chapter 36: Playing a Player

PR director's office continued

Chris pitched, "But listen, Dick, remember Mrs. Martin calling my phone and thinking I was you because it used to be your line? She sounded like a nice woman. I can't imagine she had a motive for such a blatant shooting because if convicted, she'd lose any claim to Johnny Martin's estate. She has a piece of his business too. Am I making any sense? I just feel since we witnessed the bombing, and, and I figured that, well, you and she ... well, you know."

He was playing Dickie as Garcia said to, but was out of his league. He could see in Dickie's placid face that he was losing his attention.

Dickie yawned and said, "I'm sorry, Chris. I can't talk about this. Why'd Liza leave? I thought she wanted to take me up on my dinner offer. She looks hot today, doesn't she? You and she?"

Happy to sidestep Dickie's stupid innuendo, Chris took a big risk, "You can't talk because you are involved in Martin's murder, right?"

"God, no. That's why Liza left?"

"No, damn it, Dickie, you can't talk because you were part of his murder; that's what I was asking."

"Chris, no I wasn't. I liked Johnny. We had drinks sometimes."

"Sorry. I had to ask so I could at least cross out some questions in my mind about you. You cool with that?"

"No," Dickie turned his back on Chris and sat behind his desk.

To Chris, Dickie so far seemed to be innocent of the killing. But he still didn't have a killer and both he and Dickie thought the police had the wrong suspect in Victoria Martin. He slugged on with his difficult visit to Dickie's office, "I also got a call from Knife Garcia who you claim not to know, but he knows you very well. He told me you were working for Mr. Martin. Dickie, if you don't help me or at least help that pitiful Fayme—a neophyte who can't tell her ass from a hole in the wall and the girl will never find the truth—the state is going to hang your lover for a murder she didn't commit. Am I getting through to you?"

Dickie's mind was mush most of the time, but he was smart enough, or self-absorbed enough, to perhaps realize that Chris was still focused on the story. "When did you get back on the story, Chris? I heard Michele kicked you off it, and, man, was that ever stupid. I saw how you responded down there at the tower bombing. It was really something. Read your stories on it too. Good thing I wasn't in them though," Dickie said, eking out admiration with some discomfort.

"I'm not on the story officially, and please, please Dick, do not tell anyone I am researching this crazy puzzle. I still don't understand what's going on, but the paper is ill-equipped to investigate, the police are idiots and frankly, my instincts as a journalist tell me I've got to find the truth. I trust only myself with this. I don't think anyone else wants to work hard enough to get to the truth. Everyone has concluded that Vickie did it, that's the end. It's killing me. They are wrong."

"I see." Randim did seem to see.

Chris continued, "Knife, I mean Juan Garcia wants to meet with us. He also wants Vickie out of jail as we do. His job depends on it and, frankly, he loves the Martins like parents."

"I know, Chris. Okay, but you need to respect my anonymity in this. I could be in big trouble with the cops. I know too much. Are we cool? Knife turned on me once you know, with the police. Damn fool."

Chris was surprised at Randim's eagerness to join the hunt. Was he sincere? Still, he wondered, *What's he so afraid of that makes him stay locked up in the crow's nest up here all the time?*

* * *

The next day, Dickie visited Vickie in the county jail. He told her that he'd been finding dirt on Johnson and Madinoff for Johnny for several weeks. Chris and Dickie had agreed that Vickie needed to know.

Dickie got back to Chris eager to share new information from Vickie. She told him she had asked Johnny's father Vincent to beg his son to please stop criticizing the crooked lenders over their civil rights violations. Johnny could get hurt and they might lose their business, she had told Vincent.

She said Vincent then confronted Johnny about it on the afternoon before Johnny met with Johnson and his cronies at the Radisson.

At the time, Chris could not understand the significance of a father/son meeting over business matters, it would become crystal clear later, at Vickie's trial for murder.

Chapter 37: Carrie and Martha

Chris took Liza out for lunch at the Silver Diner on Rhodesville Pike to thank her for helping him get Dickie's attention, he said. The real reason was that he wanted to tell his best friend that Dickie had signed on as an ally, if for no other reason than to save Vickie from being convicted for murder.

Liza was suspicious but said she thought Chris did the right thing. "Rumors were getting ugly about Randim and something had to be done to help Dickie," she added.

"I can't believe what I just heard you say, Liza. Are you taking up for Dickie?"

"Well, it's just too bizarre to be true," Liza told Chris. "Carrie says he did it, tells everybody. She really hates that bastard and wants him hurt bad."

"Badly, Liza. It's badly."

"Shut up, Chris. I hate you too," Liza said laughing and punching him lightly in the stomach.

* * *

Back at his desk, Chris mulled over Liza's Carrie comment in the perspective of a few days earlier when Martha Read mentioned Carrie during her rare if perhaps the first ever visit to the newsroom.

The refined publisher lady was completely lost in the newsroom. She hadn't a clue who was what or where no matter how. In her position, she didn't need to. Just run copy past her and she'd okay it to publish.

Two steps into the newsroom, Martha asked the photo editor Getty Light if Carrie Amora worked "down here." She wouldn't have located the name Carrie Amora, op-ed editor, in the directory of the regular list of reporters. With no telephone number to call then, Martha sought out Carrie.

Getty told Chris, "Somebody's messing with Mrs. Read's head. She thinks Carrie and Randim are good friends. She came here to find and 'talk with the young lady,' she said, and learn what Carrie, of all people, Chris, knew about Dickie. Hey, let me know if she goes after the old gal, okay? Love to stay for Carrie's fury, but I've got to go out to a shoot."

As Mrs. Read approached the business desk where Carrie happened to be visiting with Melissa, Chris leaned in to listen. He slouched further behind his big computer monitor as usual.

"Hi, Carrie, I hope this is not at a bad time."

"No, Mrs. Read."

"Sit down please, Mrs. Read," Melissa motioned her to a nearby chair.

"Girls, call me Martha, please. Carrie, may I talk with you in private?"

"Have I done something...?"

"No, it's about your friend Mr. Randim."

Ears all around perked up.

"Martha, anything having to do with Dickie Randim is hardly private, said Carrie, "You can talk. We know who he is."

Melissa, and Rebecca, who'd come within earshot, both nodded. Rebecca added quietly, "And what he is." And then barely audibly, "Fine fella that Dickie, yes."

Read continued, "We in the boardroom are worried that Randim was involved in some way in the Martin murder. I don't know how, but it has come to our attention that he was intimately involved with the Martins."

"I'll say," Carrie said under her breath.

Read heard her and responded, "I would appreciate it if any of you learn anything about Mr. Randim's involvement, that you tell us first before putting such a thing in our newspaper. Is that clear, ladies? He is still an employee of the company."

Melissa said firmly for all, "Yes ma'am. We will."

Martha, still thinking Carrie and Dickie were an item, ended with, "Carrie, when you see him, today, tonight, or whenever, please be careful not to mention I was asking. I hear you know him the best."

"What? I hate the ..." Carrie shot a look at Melissa shaking her head violently, "the idea of ratting on one of our colleagues."

"Of course, you do, dear."

The minute Martha Read bid them, "Good afternoon ladies" and walked away, Chris heard Carrie begin immediately to spread the rumor around nearby desks that "our publisher Martha Read thinks Dickie did it, killed Boss Martin for Vickie."

Following the visit, Carrie spread the word that Read had surefire reasons why Dickie could have done it. She told everyone who would listen that Randim had confessed to Read. Carrie made it up, but it was a logical conclusion from Read's visit to the newsroom.

Carrie wore such an affected Shirley Temple pout that the skeptical reporters she approached surely dismissed her claim. Everyone knew Carrie longed for the day when a thug would plug Dickie in the head like what happened to Johnny Martin. The perfect dream never left Carrie's mind.

Chris could hear Carrie confide in a whisper to Melissa, "After all, Dickie mucked up my reputation at the paper. I should be in management by now if it wasn't for him making a fool of me. Everybody knows, damn it. I hate that bastard. I'd like to kill HIM."

Melissa tried to tell Carrie, "That was a while ago and not everybody knows or wants to because he is just a jerk, Carrie dear. We all love you."

Meanwhile, Chris figured that Carrie's campaign to paint Dickie as the killer was just the kind of distraction he needed. Maybe it would throw Fayme off track long enough for Chris to swoop in and get the real story.

He still passionately wanted the story back for himself. He was tasting it.

Chapter 38: Falling Behind

Wednesday mid-morning, June 20

The e-mail from Dickie Randim to Christopher Gilley at the Inquirer read, "Garcia is missing. Going to find him."

Chris deleted it quickly and erased it from his delete folder. He called Dickie's office phone. His out-of-office message said he would return on Monday. Chris realized he probably had every phone number now in Dickie Randim's life, except Dickie's cell.

He called Knife. No answer.

He didn't know that Garcia and Dickie had gone to visit Vickie in a Washington, D.C. prison cell after she was permitted to call Dickie about being transferred from county jail in Loweville to federal prison.

Dickie's email then to Chris was an obvious diversion. Dickie still didn't trust sharing with Chris.

* * *

By Saturday, there was still nothing in the Washington Post about Victoria Martin being moved.

To find out why she was no longer at the county jail, Chris called Harry Blalock. At one time, Blalock was the best crime reporter in Maryland. He was sliding into retirement with a plum-easy job at the Inquirer, specializing in police matters. He was old but still needed money for his double alimony.

Chris went to Harry's home and found him on his couch complaining. He told Chris that Vickie was in a federal prison, but that he was too tired to help him.

He said he'd just helped Eli, the Inquirer's intern, with two domestics in Riverdale and Mt. Rainer on the D.C. line, reputed to be the home of Linda Blair's character in "The Exorcist." After the assignment, Harry took the kid to see the location where the movie was filmed at the kid's insistence.

"I'm bushed, Chris. All I know is she's in federal prison. Can it wait?"

Hear lies my future, Chris thought seeing Harry lazing around unshaven in a tank undershirt, pajama pants and slippers and still broke after a lengthy newspaper career.

Old Harry was adored by the news staff for his tales of cops and robbers. Instead of leaving, Chris got the old scribbler talking nostalgia, reminiscing about how he had busted up the toughest crime rings in the region in the 1960's while working a crime beat for major papers.

Finally, after a beer with Chris, he said, "Okay boy, I'll consider the Martin transfer Monday." First, there were baseball games on TV Sunday that demanded his undivided attention, he said. "Wanna stay and watch? Another beer, son?"

Chris was too antsy to wait until Monday. He drove to the paper to look at Dickie's source book for more clues.

The only reasons he could think of to make the feds take over Vickie's custody were Vickie's financial interest in Johnny Martin's shady company or a possibility that a terrorist bombed the FUC&M tower on May 14.

* * *

In the best of circumstances, newspaper reporters are self-motivated. They want to scoop up the big story and get it on A1, or at least the front page of the business, style or sports section. They are dedicated to filling the news hole with their stories, strong or weak. But mostly they want their byline to dominate page one.

At a good weekly newspaper like the Maryland Inquirer, the Tuesday afternoon story meetings put a competitive fire under the reporters at least until the next week when they find out the stories are not as earth-shaking as they had pitched to the editors at the Tuesday story budget meetings.

The meetings help the editors prioritize the importance and placements of stories in the next edition.

The down side of the story meeting for a new reporter like Chris, who is not yet in the editor's complete trust to crank out several stories a week without prodding, is that stories meetings can be dreadfully exposing.

At the regular Tuesday story meeting on June 26 of the editors and a half-dozen other reporters covering business and related topics, Chris was slouching so much so he was in danger of slipping completely under the table. He didn't say much because he hadn't been doing much official news reporting. He hoped no one would notice. When it was Chris's turn to update his stories, he said little.

"That's it?" said Steve Mothershart. "Benny, it seems Mr. Gilley must be working on that big centerpiece." Steve was up to one of his best tricks to motivate the writers. It bugged him that talented Chris Gilley had contributed just one story for each of the past two weeks, and not very good ones at that.

Before Chris could speak, Benny Bradley spoke for him, to punctuate Steve's initiative. "Yeah, that's right Steve. You're pretty far along with it, right, Chris?" There was no such centerpiece from Chris in the works.

Again, before Chris could utter a word, Steve offered, "Oh, I see. (a little chuckle) "So, next week then?" He seemed to sense a problem and moved on.

Chris was freaking out that they were referring to a center feature he'd forgotten all about due to his preoccupation with his secret Martin investigation. He said nothing.

Mothershart bailed him out, though. "And that Gaithersburg Science City story this week too, Chris?" he asked.

Chris responded, "Okay." However, Chris had no idea what that was either but was used to the light-handed way Steve and Benny managed the editorial meetings, anything to keep an even keel, support the troops, and layout the deadlines without too many cuts and bruises.

Benny glanced at Chris and nodded as if to say, 'we'll catch up.' That should have been all for Chris.

But, Rebecca, the emasculator, jumped in, perhaps couldn't help herself, "You know Chris, the council voted on that Science Center yesterday. Didn't you want it this week, Steve?"

Liza, sitting in for community tips, eyed the downtrodden Chris across the table and said quickly, "They delayed the vote. Nothing happened at that city council meeting, Becky." Rebecca hated the nickname Becky. Liza knew it and continued. "We do know, Becky, (pause) they will vote next time. I think the story should hold, Steve."

Steve said, "Well, thank you, Ms. Lopez. Did you hear that Chris? And while we are suddenly on the topic of our Liza, are we about to break any other news at this point? Maybe personal news?"

Liza's face flushed, "Yes, indeed we can, Steve. As I told you this morning, it's official."

Steve replied, "My friends and colleagues, our own Miss Liza Leah Lopez will be leaving us for a hot job at Port America."

“In the Peabody Hotel, no less, guys,” Liza said. “It’s not something I planned, but it is closer to where I live. I’ll miss you guys a lot.”

“And all the fame and fortune that comes along. Congratulations to Liza. You’ll be doing what?” Benny chimed in.

“Thanks for asking, Benny. I was hoping for an opening on the business desk here. But this new job will combine my two careers so far, marketing and journalism. I’ll be doing some writing, but mostly public relations.”

Chris sat quietly because he remembered seeing some Port America telephone and email addresses highlighted in red in Dickie’s source book, likely meaning that the new resort was perhaps linked with Sam Johnson and his LFD company. He worried about Liza while others congratulated her. When she noticed his reticence, he joined the others in applauding, grateful that Liza took the focus away from his poor showing at the story meeting. She had bailed him out once again. He looked hard and fondly at Liza as he nodded his head slightly in the affirmative with his best winning smile. He also realized that he was going to miss her more than he’d anticipated.

He caught himself staring too long and remembered why he was so lethargic that morning. The whole truth was that the night before he and his hot new girlfriend smoked up much of a certain bag of marijuana dropped on him by some whacky Latino character in Charmington Village, whom Liza told him to stay clear of. He was flush with paranoia for a moment. What would happen to him if Steve knew about the pot? He imagined explaining: *It’s no problem. Me and Amy got stoned together, stayed up all night talking, and ate her refrigerator clean. So, I flew in here at noon on my magic carpet.*

“Chris...Chris,” Benny wanted his attention. “Hey, Chris,” louder.

“Huh, oh yeah, sorry. What is it?”

The others Steve had left the room with Steve, leaving just Benny Bradley and Chris behind. “Stay a minute. I want to talk about your story budget,” Bradley said firmly.

When alone, Benny whispered, “Hey what’s up with you, Chris.”

“Didn’t Mel tell you?”

“I’m not normally in Melissa’s circle, kid,” Bradley said. “What’s going on? Your stories are a little flat recently. You got a problem or something? Not that’s it’s my business, of course.” It was obvious to Chris though that this was plenty of Bradley’s business.

“New girlfriend. She lives in Clinton. Bad commute when I stay over, Benny. But don’t say anything to Steve or anybody, okay? Sometimes, I’m a bit slow in the mornings.”

Bradley laughed and faked a punch to Chris’s arm. “You go on, boy. Enjoy yourself. But don’t let it show around here. There’s only so much Steve can do for you. Give us more copy. Earn your big salary, eh?”

They returned to their desks.

Steve Mothershart sat behind them at his desk. Without looking at Benny, he asked, “Benny, you gave Chris that profile on the IT guy in Rhodesville; Jackson, rising black entrepreneur award guy, didn’t you?” He filled in enough for Bradley to get his drift, though Benny didn’t know what Steve was talking about. It was another of Mothershart’s polite tricks to move things along.

Benny checked the email and there was an assignment note on the IT story from Steve for Benny to pass to Chris, but not copied to Chris. There was a PS: “What the hell’s gotten into your boy?”

Benny laughed, turned to Steve and said, “He’s got a girlfriend. That’s all.” Chris heard, shook his head and laughed, back to slumping over his PC.

His editors still didn’t think Chris was seasoned enough to find most of his own stories, yet they knew he could if he tried. But Steve didn’t want to dance around with Chris again at the next story meeting. Chris shouldn’t need incentives. He got the message without further nudging, polite or otherwise.

“I’ll send the black guy story to him again, Steve,” Benny said, after he read over a previous story on Jackson.

Chris knew enough to not admit his ignorance. Just take the assignment. It was a gift. He had good bosses, almost considered them his friends.

Chapter 39: Making Due at Denny's

Chris preferred to talk with Mr. Jackson in person, but Jackson was out of town until Thursday. The editors had put it in the weekly budget. On Wednesday, the day after they gave Chris the assignment as a kind of vote of confidence, Benny assured Steve that Chris could still get it on Thursday on deadline.

That night at Amy's, Chris set her clock radio alarm for an earlier start. He didn't want to miss a 9 a.m. phone interview with Steve's profile guy, the black entrepreneur Jackson, especially because it might mean something special to Steve Mothershart.

The previous afternoon at the newsroom, Chris left his handwritten questions taped to his computer screen for a phone interview with Jackson, set up by Jackson's secretary. He realized that the story carried special significance to the black business community. Chris sensed it without Steve saying so.

Cummings G. Jackson was the kind of story Steve enjoyed publishing, though he wouldn't likely admit it. He was fair and open about proposing story ideas about African Americans, Hispanics, Asians, and women to give the paper diversity appeal for its readership.

But, significant story or not, Chris was supremely contented when he slept in Amy's feather bed that night, and thus, he got a late start in the morning. Amy was pawing and cooing when Chris woke angrily and slugged the annoying alarm clock that was suddenly demanding more attention than Amy with her pawing and cooing.

He rolled back to his girlfriend's arms.

Result? Chris didn't ease out of his love nest until 8:30 a.m., not nearly enough time to call Jackson from his desk at the paper where all his notes and questions were ready for him. Rhodesville was 45 minutes away on a good day with no rush traffic.

He woke up cursing and fuming about misplacing his car keys, his shirt was on backward, and he yelled at innocent Amy, "No, no, this is not happening; I told you I was charging your cell and you unplugged it. Damn, Amy."

"I put it next to your wallet," she said weakly as she tried to hand him a coffee mug for the road. He dropped it.

His head was derailed. He had gone to sleep imagining his byline had already appeared over a pic of Jackson on the front page. His story would read like 'Yet another successful black-owned business in remarkable King's County, the richest majority black county in the United States.' A slam dunk, A1 for sure.

But in the morning, he had left himself no time. Steve Mothershart's Inquirer business edition was published every Friday and it was already Thursday, nearly 9 a.m.

Chris was not properly prepared, way late, hung over again.

Jumping into his car, he closed the door on his right hand, enraging him further. He drove with his left hand and right knee, reaching across to shift gears with his left hand until the feeling returned on his right hand.

Time running short to meet his 9 a.m. call to Mr. Jackson, Chris's only option was to ball-ass it to Denny's Restaurant in Allentown, ten minutes away, armed with Amy's cell phone low battery, Benny's old laptop, half a brain, and maybe two hands.

He was also famished. Denny's seemed to be the right thing to do.

Once his hand stopped throbbing, his mind waffled—Grand Slam breakfast at Denny's then 'what were those questions,' then Grand Slam breakfast, then questions, then breakfast, then questions. He was sweating on a cool morning, nervous and upset. Rhodesville was still 30 miles north and traffic was horrendous.

One question, he remembered, was something about revenues at Jackson's firm, Entre Systems Inc., growing a whopping 400 percent the previous year. *No, no don't lead with that. Too serious. Better to go with: Mr. Jackson, did the company start as a dream when you attended the Smith School of Business at University of Maryland? Is your family involved? How old are those kids I see in your portrait on Entre.com? Yes, that's it, Chris. That's it.* Preliminary chatting up in interviews was his standard operating procedure before lobbing hardball questions.

8:49 a.m. He arrived at Denny's parking lot. It was jammed full. He parked on the street and sprinted in.

What's the deal, free pancakes or something? It's just Thursday morning, not even the weekend. Probably like this every day, he thinks, nearly panicking. He had to write the story that day, before the Thursday noon deadline for his edition.

8:55 a.m. He was waiting by the 'Wait-to-be-seated' sign. There was only one, tiny empty table left. There was one counter seat open, but the cash register at that space took up all but about eight inches of counter space. Not enough space even for his reporter's notepad, not to mention the laptop, breakfast plate and coffee, he thought.

One customer, a little Mediterranean-looking middle-aged guy dressed like a construction worker looked at Chris as if he knew him and wanted to reach out to him, but didn't. He had finished a cup of coffee and had six or seven torn-open sugar packets scattered around the empty cup. He was looking up and down the counter, waiting to put in his order.

9:02 a.m. Chris was still at the sign, which could have then read, 'Wait-as-long-as-we-make-you-wait-to-be-seated.' While he stood alone by the sign, he reached into his pocket for Amy's cell and called the phone number for Jackson's company.

"Mr. Jackson is not in yet. Can I be of some assistance?"

"Yes, this is Christopher Gilley at the Inquirer. We set up an interview for nine. Did he confirm that to you about that?"

"He most certainly did, Mr. Gilley. Do you have a number where he can reach you when he gets in? He's on his way."

Chris checked the back of the phone to find Amy's cell number and gave it to Jackson's receptionist. He thought he knew the number but didn't have the luxury of time to waste on the phone battery if he got it wrong.

"Okay, Mr. Gilley. You have a blessed day, hear?"

Cummings Jackson was also known as a devout Christian, a leader in his church and community. *Maybe Jackson's religion rubs off on employees, nice,* thought Chris. He was not familiar with people ending conversation with 'have a blessed day'.

At 9:14 a.m., Chris was still by the 'Oh-we're-sorry; are-you-waiting-for-a-table?' sign.

He saw another table open, but a big waitress rolling by made no eye contact with Chris who was still first in line by the 'We didn't-see-you-there' sign.

He called Bradley, "Hello, Benny? Yeah, it's Chris. No, Jackson is not in yet, so I'm going to Gaithersburg first to talk with Dr. Amir at Johns Hopkins, Shady Grove, okay? It's about the science center." He hated himself. Lying to his best ally Benny Bradley was getting to be a bad habit.

9:24 a.m. Chris is still standing by the 'Excuse-me, you're-blocking-the-aisle-now" sign.

He was watching a very large waitress in yellow walking slowly toward him, not looking directly at him. "You not seated? Come on honey."

The waitress, with a yellow name tag, "Else," seated Chris in a small table, dead center of crowded, cluttered dining room tables; chairs jammed close to one another.

Okay, great, I think I can eat, make my call, take notes, and maybe open the laptop.

"Thank you so much, Ma'am. I'd like orange jui..."

Else was gone, tugging at her receipt book dangling from a side pocket. It caught on the shoulder of another customer's sport jacket, which fell to the floor.

Chris, thinking he would never, ever want to work in a restaurant, turned on his laptop and checked the battery on Amy's phone. It was flashing LOW.

He smelled fresh coffee.

The warm aroma of coffee made him think of the two women in his life at the time. He wondered if he was more in love with Amy, or the voice and mannerisms of beautiful, Vickie Martin. There was an emotional attachment there too. The young journalist was worried about the latter. *What did she talk about with Dickie and Garcia at the Washington jail?* He started dialing Garcia and stopped. *Can't. Low battery. Got to save it for Jackson. Where is Jackson?*

The cell phone rang. The number for Entre.com was on the phone.

"Mr. Gilley? Mr. Jackson had to return home. His wife is sick and he must take his child to school. Can we reschedule?"

"No, no, I mean, I, ah ..." a waitress accidentally bumped his arm holding the phone. It flew off and slid under the table next to him. Two young mothers and their children sitting there were unaware of the projectile. Another boy, about four years old wearing starched green overalls, crawled over to see what Chris had dropped.

"Get up off that floor, boy!" a mother screamed. "Oh, this yours, sir? I'm sorry. Here's your phone. Is it broken?" The mother smiled summarily and turned back without hearing

Chris's response. She was trying, unsuccessfully, to control several children.

"Hello, hello, still there? I dropped the phone. Hello."

Nothing.

The phone rang. It was the Entre receptionist again.

Chris quickly responded. "Ma'am, can I get ten minutes with Mr. Jackson today, this morning wherever he is now? Does he carry a cell? That would be okay because he won't need to give me any figures or records." Chris couldn't reschedule and still file the story by his deadline that afternoon. He was picturing the sour expression he'd encounter at the Inquirer on Steve Mothershart's face.

Jackson's employee promised to call back.

9:40 a.m. Chris spoke to a waitress. "Miss, do you have any orange juice? And I'd like to order."

"I'll get your waitress."

Chris saw one waitress approach another behind the counter and gestured toward him.

Another yellow-clad waitress arrived with an order pad in one hand and a small orange juice in the other. "Sir, I'm sorry to keep you waiting. Can I take your order?"

Chris ordered scrambled eggs and toast and told the waitress that he was in a hurry. She was not exactly delighted with that comment.

He continued, "And can I have a large juice, please? I can pay for this one too if you want." She picked up the small orange juice and was sauntering toward the counter again without writing down his order.

Chris looked around and saw the little man still at the counter looking back at him, still unserved too.

Chris imagined the little stranger thinking, *Hey, guess what? We're the only two white people in here. Must be patient, mister.* Chris laughed almost audibly. *This is amazing. I wish I wrote fiction. Can't wait to tell Steve. Oh, maybe that would be insensitive. I don't want to laugh off discrimination. White hillbilly boy gets slow service in black community Denny's? Big deal,* he pondered.

The irony might amuse him, but Steve may not appreciate Chris taking racism, one way or another, so lightly, Chris considered.

A large glass of OJ finally arrived on his table.

Chris started to reach for it, but Else, who had seated him, came from behind, walked through an uncompromising space for a big woman between his table and a man seated at the next table. Her hip clipped Chris's table. Juice poured onto his laptop and lap as he jumped to his feet.

No one noticed.

He flipped over the laptop and shook the liquid off it quickly and shook it out of the keyboard. He then walked to the counter to grab a handful of paper napkins. Two waitresses noticed him standing up and rushed to clean up the juice.

9:55 a.m. Breakfast arrived. Two eggs easy over, a short stack, biscuits and home fries--not close to what he ordered. Chris again asked for coffee.

He ate the incorrect order hurriedly—it was something, at least. As he waited for the Jackson call, Chris punched up from his computer files Trichina's piece in the Inquirer quoting Denny's executives about their PR campaign following racial discrimination problems in the 1990s. Some frustrated black customers had sued the company. She reported that the company worked with black radio personality Tom Joyner who ran an on-air promotion for his Joyner Foundation offering college financial aid scholarships to needy students of single parents.

Well, it could not have been this Denny's, he thought with a smile.

Finally, Mr. Jackson called Chris at 10 a.m. sharp, with a sincere apology. Chris quickly flipped the laptop upright, stacked his dishes, walked them to the counter himself, and returned to his table.

Jackson, a spirited businessman on the rise in the Rhodesville community, granted Chris an amazingly informative interview. He organized his comments well on describing his products and a unique approach to customer service and family history in business. Chris wrote a very comprehensive outline directly into the laptop nearly in real time.

Back in the Mazda, he located Wi-Fi, with a great sigh of relief, at a coffee shop in the next strip of stores. By 10:45 a.m. he filed a 13-inch profile of Cummings Jackson, emailed it to Benny Bradley and headed north to Rhodesville.

King's Black Chamber Names Jackson Top Entrepreneur
By Christopher Gilley, staff reporter

RHODESVILLE, Md. June 29--Ten years ago, a teenage entrepreneur named Junior Jackson was making good money and expanding his produce business in front of his father's house in rural King's County.

But it wasn't enough for Junior. Each fall, he put his profits toward business school tuition.

Last week, the Maryland Black Chamber of Commerce named Cummings G. Jackson Jr. its 2007 Entrepreneur of the Year for successfully founding and building the rapidly growing IT firm, Entre Systems.

"I didn't even know what information technology was when I marketed apples and tomatoes," says Jackson, CEO of Entre. He discovered that he was a natural entrepreneur when attending the University of Maryland Robert A. Smith School of Business.

At Smith, his first computer course inspired young Jackson to start up his own IT business to streamline the business side of small Maryland farms, including that of his father. The senior Jackson was running his son's still expanding produce business.

The 28-year-old entrepreneur credits meeting his wife Marion at the Grace Baptist Church of Bowie Heights as the "secret" of his success managing the fastest growing IT business in the state.

"I wasn't even attending that church but helping a buddy set up computers there. My buddy's dad was the minister. I heard Marion singing solo at choir practice one day. I walked upstairs to the chapel, discovered my angel, though she didn't like me at all."

Cummings and Marion Jackson are raising three children in their home near Grace Baptist. She is the president of Entre Systems.

Revenues for Entre last year increased more than 400 percent as Jackson landed contracts with the state agriculture department and the Jessup Wholesale Food Warehouse in Anne Arundel County.

Mrs. Jackson accepted the award at the Maryland Black Chamber Banquet on June 12, for her husband who was at a contract signing ceremony in Chicago, she said. "Cummings' faith and his wonderful gift for helping people translate into helping people help themselves in business many ways every day of the year. Our children and I are so proud of him," she was quoted on the chamber website.

Reached by phone yesterday, Mr. Jackson, said, "You know, there were 32 nominations, all fantastic new black enterprises, and I was just fortunate enough to be one of them. It's great to be recognized as one of the great companies in Maryland."

The company has a staff of 15 and sales of more than $1 million.

Entre Systems already had corralled nine clients by the time Jackson graduated from Smith. He then earned an MBA from American University.

After developing a unique IT framework for small farm businesses in 2003, Jackson has developed and patented similar frameworks of efficiency in more than a dozen other industries, including manufacturing, education, and interior design. "That interior designing one was developed by Marion. I cannot take the credit," he said.

The Jackson's home in Bowie has won several awards for home décor and innovation, and neighborhood leadership. Marion Jackson has a master's degree in design.

Laticia Harland, chair of the chamber, said the greatest contribution of Jackson to the community is his willingness to show people how to communicate information technology well.

The next day, Friday (after the deadline pressure was off), Chris told Benny and Steve about his "very odd, sort of ironic" experience at Denny's. He wasn't sure how "ironic" involving racial discrimination would go over. He was still underexposed to racial undercurrents of the city.

There were not a lot of black people in Glasgow, W.Va., except travelers lost or tanking up under the blinking Phillips 66 sign that likely still just read "hill 66" at night within the familiar company badge shape icon.

Chris told Steve and Benny the Denny's discrimination scene occurred that Friday morning instead of on the critical deadline day. No need, he thought, to explain his early Thursday indiscretions of smashing Amy's jarring alarm clock just to capture just one more oh-god-it's-so-good-to-be-a-man sex, instead of leaving for work on time.

He didn't have to explain the "irony" of being that young, stupid white, hillbilly sitting patiently as black waitresses, just doing an honest day's work, grossly neglected him, blatantly discriminating it seemed to Chris, while he was only there in the first place to interview the latest young black business star in Maryland. Some things just run deeper than surface awareness, he reasoned.

Chris was fascinated with it, but cautious as he told the story.

"Did you ask for the manager?" Steve said sharply, protective of his protégé.

What do I say? Chris though. He didn't want to sound flippant, as if he didn't take racism seriously. He hadn't been offended by the experience, just annoyed by delaying his deadline. It hadn't been a race thing to him. Desperately clueless about Steve's thoughts, he was sorry he had even brought it up. He could only whimper, "No, I didn't have the time to complain, just muddled my way through it. I don't think the employees were aware they were ignoring me."

"Nice story on Jackson, Chris," Steve turned back to reading the Life Section of the Washington Post and said quietly to Benny nearby, "That's our boy, lucky hire for us."

Chris took home the Xeroxed copies of Dickie's source book from his locked desk drawer to call some numbers from it over the weekend.

The lost story and wound to his pride had then become a sort of mental paralysis, an immovable force overriding everything else in his life. He couldn't enjoy reading, watching TV and certainly not going out for pleasure or a nice meal without THE STORY following him. Like some kind of inorganic predator, it was baiting him, daring him to act more boldly and attack. He knew it was nothing more than his training and dedication to excellence making it so.

"Get it done, soon, or lose the opportunity," he said to himself as the old Mazda coughed and backfired, then went silence at the curb at the apartment. He jumped out of the car and dashed inside, determined.

There were no new press stories on Johnny Martin's killing in the national newspapers he'd grabbed on the road. He tossed them aside and flicked on TV. Broadcaster news announcers led with an anguished face of Vickie, obviously rendered as guilty.

He felt desperate. But until the next Friday's paycheck, he was broke. For gas money, he borrowed $25 from Amy's nerdy brother, who never spent his paychecks from his part-time stock boy work at K-Mart. For spending money, he sold Vickie's Radisson weekend guest gift certificate to his landlord José Cruz for $50. It was worth about $300 because it included three free meals and a free night's stay.

Newspaper ethic dictates that he should have given it back to Vickie, but oops, she was in jail. To spend it would be a very serious violation of the reporter's code at the Inquirer. He mulled it over and rationalized it. *God damn it, Chris, you got a bribe when not even officially covering a story. Forget it, take the 50 bucks!* he told his conscience.

Despite his ethical compromises in the name of secretly investigating his story, Chris revered the rules of reporting and was tortured by his compromising with increasingly desperate behavior. But much was at stake—investigating a murder, a bombing, and more—than Christopher Gilley's petty reputation, he figured. He tried to be true to his humble roots, but this was his duty as a journalist. *Screw it; I can crack this bad boy,* he thought.

He figured he would serve the community by exposing the guilty, no matter what. He'd thought it through and through a million times. And it always came out the same: expose the bastards at all cost, even losing his job. As he fell asleep, he tried to stay focused, *This is my destiny, not laying low, squeaking and purring over cream puff stories for Benny.*

On Saturday afternoon, Chris popped a beer and studied Dickie's source book. Some of the green and red highlighted telephone numbers under M for "Mortgage," he guessed, matched numbers under S. Those were labeled "SC's and were consistently highlight green linked to BOM, which Chris interpreted as Best Opportunity Mortgage, Corp. The numbers marked in red, such as those under L for LDF, for Lifetime Deal Financing, Corp. had no matching SC's numbers.

Curious, he called one of the many SC numbers, a 202-area code for Washington, D.C.

A gruff voice answered with disco music blaring, "Voting Booth, Gentleman's Club, what's your vote, red, blue or purple?" said the man on the phone, disco music blaring.

SC for strip clubs, of course. Thinking quickly, Chris asked, "Hey buddy, I've got a group coming into town. What's that address again?"

The man said it was on 19th Street Northwest, Washington DC, only a few blocks from the White House. The man then asked Chris if he was a member.

"No, but my buddy is though."

The man said "come on up. We got an election for your erection every night. Cast your vote for the liberal college girls or those sexy conservative business girls. Frankly, Bud, I'd vote the big business types, they are hungry for some action, if you know what I mean. But, that's just me. You know the deal, show your voting' registration card and get your first drink free."

"Thanks, very civic minded," that's all Chris could say before bursting with laughter and hanging up.

I don't think that number will give me much on the story, he thought. Although the same number for that strip club was also next to the number for Bernie Madinoff of Best Opportunity Mortgage, Corp. *I've got to find Dickie. This is outrageous.*

He called Juan Garcia. “Hey, Juan, it’s Chris. Did you and Dickie see Vickie?”

Juan said, “Dickie did. She wanted to see him by herself. I seen her quick. She look okay.” He said Dickie was very upset that “she ain’t talkin’ much. Lawyer, he not helpin’ much.”

Garcia said Vickie warned Dickie to stay out of sight for a while because her lawyer said the prosecutors had a new subpoena for Dickie. Garcia said Dickie went in hiding in Vickie’s condo in College Park where he drank up all of her liquor worrying. After that, Dickie typical of fugitives from the law, aimed to keep moving to the Florida Keys in his case. “He’s gone now to his parent’s summer place in Islamorada Key, Fla. I been … nice place,” Garcia said. “Don’t tell nobody, kid,”

Garcia gave Chris Dickie’s cell number.

Chapter 41: Tickle My Pickle

Before he had a chance to call Dickie, Dickie rang him, "Chris, listen, Garcia and I are going to Madinoff's company to steal a peek into his files on loans. You need to come too."

"Dickie, where the hell are you, Florida yet? I've been trying to find out something about these mortgage guys. I think they had Boss Martin killed."

"I didn't go to my folk's house in Florida. Told Garcia but changed my mind. Been at Vickie's, been sort of hiding out because she said I should. Chris, we think we can bust this case open with Madinoff and get Vickie off, Johnny didn't like Bernie Madinoff big time. The man is so fat and rich, he's no more than a buffoon, leaving himself open. I bet he was involved. He has killed before, I hear."

"What the hell are you talking about, Dickie? We can't go to Madinoff's office. It's in a million pieces, down in the hole of Loweville, like a giant construction dump in front of the courthouse. Besides, he was in the tower when it blew."

"Doesn't mean he didn't kill Johnny. Maybe the dumb shit forgot the bomb he or his guys set. Maybe they didn't tell him. Maybe his people didn't do it but did kill Johnny. He had motive. Anyway, not now."

"Not now what?"

Dickie paused for emphasis, "I mean his office. Not now in the tower. Madinoff runs his office now in one of his seven strip joints. You might have heard of the *Tickle Your Pickle* gentleman's club in Arlington?"

Chris remembered initials TYP in Dickie's source book pages and likely with green highlighting nearby. "Yeah, so what?"

"The damn fool opened his operation again right above The Tickle, one of the clubs he owns. He used to run girls up there. You know what I mean?"

"Sure, Dickie. What's that got to do with us?"

Dickie said that when Madinoff lost his cushy headquarters at the FUC'M tower, he had little choice but to move it to his unofficial headquarters at the strip club. "And it's in Virginia, out of state, out of mind for the cops, I guess," said Dickie.

"Yea, yea. Like I said Dickie, what's that got to do with us?"

"Me and Knife have a plan. Bernie Madinoff and I know each other pretty good. He trusts me."

"Why would anybody … never mind. Go on."

We'll meet you there Thursday after your deadlines. It's amateur night, so there's lots of fun and confusion. The man is a pig. He plants strippers in the audience who dress as ordinary housewives and professional women and invites them up on stage to compete for a phony prize. It's a riot, Chris. We'll see you there. So long, call me if you get lost."

Dickie, caught up in his own vivid imagination, forgot why he called, to tell Chris about Madinoff's files and why they can get them there.

"Dickie, Dick! Hey, Richard, hold on, don't hang up. What's the plan?"

"We'll tell you Thursday. At 7."

"Isn't that a little early for a gentleman's club, Dickie?"

"They start with Karaoke. I just love that stuff. Anyway, we'll get a bite first. Meet us at Boob's Barbeque then, across the street at 7 p.m."

"You mean Boog's Barbeque, don't you? Boog Powell's, the old ballplayer in Baltimore?"

"No, Boobs. Get it. God, you're slow, kid."

Yeah right. This is nuts, sure folly, Chris thought and hung up, not thrilled with staging a theft at a place called Tickle Your Pickle Club. "Geez, what a name, that's classic Dickie alright," he said to himself, then chugged the remaining half of his bottle of Yuengling and flipped through the pages. *Yep, there it is under 'S' in green.*

Chris wanted to pass on the strip club idea. Then on Monday morning, he changed his mind as he sat down at his desk at the Inquirer and read Fayme's latest train wreck of his story on the top line of the online Inquirer. "Horrible, horrible," is all he could mutter:

Peeps Denied Bail, Remains in Federal Jail

by Fayme Lovelace, staff reporter

LOWEVILLE, July 2--Judge Harry Scarree of the 4th District Court in Loweville, denied bail for Vickie Martin in a pretrial hearing in the murder case of her husband, building magnet Johnny Martin.

Judge Scarree said due to the additional federal charges against Mrs. Martin, he was ordering Mrs. Martin to remain in custody at the Fort Balmoor prison in Washington, D.C. until her trial, which he now has set for a date of July 4 in his court.

Mr. Martin's body was found on May 14 at the bottom of rubble from the building collapse where his office was in Loweville and where there was.......

Chris stopped reading. That was all he could take.

He jogged into Michele LaProbe's office to complain. He'd finally had enough humiliation.

But she was not in yet, no editors were at the paper yet.

As he sat at her desk to write a note, Michele suddenly cast a large shadow in the fluorescence over him.

"Well Chris, anything interesting on my desk this morning?"

"Michele, I'm sorry, but where is Fayme? Did you see the... "

"Fayme's bail piece? Yes, that's old copy. We were just over at the copy desk, Lloyd and me. It's being changed. Fayme posted that Saturday somehow. God, can you imagine? Trial to open on July 4? Where was everybody in copy? These mistakes are just too much. I told that girl to take a few days off. Then we'll talk. Do me a favor, Chris, and don't say anything about this okay?"

"So Fayme's not covering the FUC&M story now?"

"I don't think so. But I know you won't play that tune in the newsroom. Be cool, Chris. Blalock said he could pick up the pieces. That is if Oprah can spare him off the couch for a few weeks. This thing will be over by August. Vickie's peep show is toast."

"Michele, I should have that story. Benny thinks so, too."

"You and Benny, what a pair. Nice. Look, you know I can't do that."

"No, I don't!"

"Chris, lower your voice. This is not good. Your copy is just great and you are doing very well here. You are very, very young. Don't ruin it for yourself. Be patient."

He slid out of her chair and eased around the desk to let her sit while saying, "Okay, I'm sorry. No disrespect intended. But can you believe this piece? That Vickie's trial is in the courtroom of Judge Scarree? His name is Scarley, not Scarree, as Fayme wrote! The whole story is scary! And she wrote that Vickie's accused of killing a magnet? Come on. Someone should have caught that. And what ARE the federal charges against Vickie? No, there may be interest by the FBI because of her shadow role in Johnny's company by marriage only. There are no federal charges. Not yet anyway. Can't we do better?"

Michele perhaps needed to lift his spirits. She said, "Well, Fayme at least has a magnetic personality."

They enjoyed the laugh, and then she added, "Meanwhile I don't know what I'm going to tell Lloyd about getting Fayme off the story, though. Oh, well. Mr. Excitement will just have to find something else to keep his interest, poor boring soul."

Chris just smiled and returned to his desk. He thought Bradley was right about Michele. The Oxford-educated boss can be okay at times. He returned to his PC wondering why she didn't react to his mentioning of no federal charges against Peeps. He hoped he didn't blow his cover. *Maybe she knows something. Oh, well, I can't push it. Dickie will know.*

Suddenly, Dickie Randim's Tickle Your Pickle idea seemed more appealing. Nothing else was coming up. He laughed out loud about Dickie's idea.

Heads popped up from desks and over computer screens to look at him.

"What is it," asked Melissa, "Share, dearie, share."

"I don't think so."

Boy wonder was getting bolder, even with lovely Mel.

Chapter 42: Gimme all of your lovin'

Thursday, July 5

The old blue and rusty Mazda pooped out once again.

While crossing over to Virginia, destination Tickle My Pickle, the car sputtered to an oily, smoky stop at the top of the Wilson Bridge over the Potomac River, on the draw. Chris was going to be late to his first strip club. He didn't want to go anyway. Well, he did. And then he didn't. Then, and so on …

He sat on the side lane of the bridge deciding while fumbling with Amy's cell phone. *Who to call? Why was he there?* Anyone he called would want to know.

The decision was made for him.

He showed his press badge to the policeman who stopped. Chris took a chance and told the middle-aged heavy-set cop he was on his way to a story at the Tickle Your Pickle. The cop laughed, "Oh sure kid. Here, call this number tomorrow to claim your car." He handed him a card for the police impoundment lot in Virginia.

He drove Chris the rest of the way, lights flashing, sirens blaring and was soon joined in a caravan of five squad cars deep. They dropped him off across the road from the club.

At the same time, the surprise police motorcade scared the crap out of Bernie Madinoff who watched from the window of his second-floor office over the strip club.

He might have expected another bust? Liquor license violation? He likely couldn't grasp why they were practically surrounding his place in the early evening.

He continued to watch as all but one of the police cruisers left. He saw a tall, skinny civilian climbed out of the back of the last squad car. The skinny guy pointed toward the Tickle club. And then he waved back to the cop driving off.

Chris then walked into Boob's Barbeque.

Madinoff frowned and his jaw tightened on his smarmy, round face, as he left the window.

Chris found Juan 'Knife' Garcia in the first booth at Boobs about to enjoy a pulled pork sandwich which proprietor Pepper Bubre touted as her "Famous New Awe'lins Recipe." Chris saw a striking resemblance in her to John 'Boog' Powell, giant

Baltimore Oriole first baseman from an era unknown to most of his generation, but now doubly famous in Baltimore for his Oriole Park at Camden Yards Boog's Barbeque. "There is order in the universe after all," Chris muttered, approaching Garcia's booth.

"What? Ah, yeah, Chris, hi. Dickie's already over dare," Knife said as he downed shredded pork ravenously, slathering hot sauce dripping down his chin. "Let's go. I'll carry dis wit me. You hungry, eat over dere. Pretty good dere, too. Where you bin, man?"

Back outside on the street, Chris finally noticed that the entire block was daylight bright from the dancing lights that lit up of Tickle My Pickle, otherwise a seedy little 2-story converted movie house, and an animated neon sign across the street of huge pink buns over Boob's Barbeque that repeatedly captured red barbeque meat between them, over and over.

Chris entered the club excited by the prospect of naked dancers on stage or a catwalk close to customers. He'd made up his mind to at least enjoy himself, yet he tried to focus. With serious business at hand, he just couldn't help getting caught up in the carnival-like atmosphere.

Blue and orange lights spun through the room of mirrored walls. The air was dank and cool, smelled like a gym, Chris thought, a gym with apple cider incense. Lights were rather dim except for the old movie theater stage straight across one side of the room.

Instead of catcalls and whistles for a sexy girl stripper, which he'd anticipated, there was hilarious laughter. A shocking performance was on and it was breaking up the place. Chris recognized the long-haired blonde dancer as none other than Dickie Randim himself on the stage.

Dickie, bumping and grinding, was the focal point of a ring of red and white spotlights. He was dancing in tight yellow, sparkly pants, shirt open, with a microphone in hand. Scantily clad women danced behind him.

He was belted out Def Leppard's 1987 hit *Armageddon It.*

"What the hell?" Chris turned to Garcia.

"Chris, we didn't want to tell you. He closes out de karaoke every Thursday night, man. He usually does Elvis Presley.

"In a white jumpsuit and Elvis wig and all?"

"Yeah, how'd you know?"

"Just a guess."

"Good one. Ain't he great? Girls are next. They all love Dickie."

"Chris had to admit, Dickie did look and act like a great entertainer as his blond mane swayed left, then right, then left again, hips bumping and grinding to the rhythm of the music. He sang just like Def's Joe Elliot:

You flash your bedroom eyes like a jumpin' jack
The play it pretty with a pat on the back
[Four girls smacked Dickie's butt all at once.]
You know you, you can't stop it
So, don't rock it.......

Chris took in the ambiance and shouted to Knife Garcia over the music, "The man is definitely crazy. He is supposed to be in hiding."

There was no denying though that Dickie was a good act. The routine was polished and very funny. He sang:

Gimme all of your lovin'
Girls' refrain: *Every little bit*
Gimme all that you got
Girls' refrain: *Every bit of it*
Every bit of your lovin'
Girls' refrain: *Oh, c'mon live a bit*
Never want it to stop.

And then, the girls shouted into Dickie's ears, cupping their hands at their mouths:

Yeah, but are you gettin' it?
All together: *Armageddon it*
Girls: *Ooh, really getting' it*
Together: *Yes, Armageddon it...*

Garcia and Chris were still standing in the back by the club's entrance.

Garcia shouted to Chris, "He's hiding in Maryland, si? But, this is Virginia. He thinks it's different. Yeah, loco, man."

"I just hope he doesn't take off all his clothes."

"Oh, no, this is a gentleman's club, Christopher. The girls. They will take his clothes off. Watch."

Oh, sweet Jesus, take me out of this dump, please, Chris thought. He needed some fresh air. He turned to go back to the lobby. A huge bouncer stopped him. "Can't leave during Dickie's number, guy."

He was stuck there and returned to Garcia to watch. Three gorgeous dancers in red, white and blue sequenced costumes pushed and pulled on Dickie, fighting over him until they got his shirt off, still pawing on him. He sang to them:

Take, take it, take it from me
I got an itchy finger following' me
Pull it, pull it, c'mon trigger the gun
'Cos the best is yet to come, I say
'Cos the best is yet to come

Dickie was lovin' it.

The girls, now on their knees around him, unzipped his pants, and started to fold them down off him. They sang over and over

Never want it to stop
Never want it to stop.

as the lights went out with Dickie, in just briefs, laughing, the girls clinging to his thighs.

Could have been a lot worse, thought Chris.

The room brightened again to an up-roaring approval of applause and cheers by the full capacity house. Dickie was gone and the girls were posed together topless wearing only sequined pasties and shorts that showed off their pink, round, bare asses. The evening was on.

Dickie, clothes back on, appeared stage left, on top of a few steps, waving to Chris and Knife to join him in front. The three sat at a table just three feet from the stage, their favorite drinks already in front of them. There was a fourth chair unoccupied.

After the shock of seeing Dickie's routine, Chris for the first time scanned the room. Many of the off-duty strippers milled around bars on both sides of the room, dressed just in bikinis or skimpy tops and panties. He was enchanted with the flirting expressions and sexy posing.

Most were clearly sporting their wares to get men to buy them drinks. Others partied among themselves. Chris was dazzled by all the eye candy. He momentarily forgot why he was there.

Soft jazz began with the next act.

Dickie caught Chris's eye and motioned for him to follow him.

Chapter 43: Shaky Plan

Dickie led Chris and Knife Garcia to the men's restroom and shared his plan with them.

"Listen, Chris, I've already spoken to Bernie Madinoff about you guys coming here tonight. Hope you didn't mind my classy act. I do that sometimes, but tonight it's part of my scheme to loosen up Bernie. Have him trust me."

Chris said, suppressing most of his sarcasm, "You missed your calling."

"Yeah, I know," Dickie replied, mocking his act with a head shimmy. He composed himself and said, "Bernie knows that the Inquirer had just hired a young, naive reporter."

"What!!" Chris wanted to smack Dickie.

"Relax, will ya. I told him, tonight, dildorf. I said you have never seen strip tease before and that Garcia and I want to show you how to have a good time. He likes fun so the idea appealed to him. Bernie told med, 'Hell, yes. I'm always up for corrupting our youth. Bring him over.' Now Chris, listen. I want you to get sick after a while. It is part of my plan."

"I'm already sick after your performance," Chris sniggered, looking down and hiding his mouth with his hand.

Dickie took offense, "Wasn't that bad, was it? I like to have fun. As I said, it's a classy act."

"Dickie, it was actually very good. Next time we'll get Getty to send a photographer down from the paper to snap some shots for the comics page."

"Get serious, Chris. Juan will volunteer to take you to his car when you fake getting sick, but you won't get to the car. Then a stripper named Joy will help get you and Garcia up to the finance office by the fire escape in the back alley, while I keep Madinoff occupied."

"Sounds risky," Chris said, "This Joy can be trusted?"

"Yeah. Hey, it will be easy because Joy is scheduled right before the amateur night contest with the fake ordinary gals, strippers in street clothes Bernie planted in the audience. It's always a riotous act, which guarantees that the boss will stay put, to keep an eye on the proceedings hoping to maintain some semblance of order. Joy will go back upstairs to the files. You got your girlfriend's cell phone like I asked?"

"Yeah, got it." Chris patted the pocket of his blue jeans.

"You good, Juan?"

"What?" said Knife, who had been preoccupied with the strippers serving drinks.

"You got your cell?" Dickie asked.

"No problem, bro," Garcia muttered never taking his eyes off the girls.

"Well, now that that is settled," Dickie said. "I will stay with the table and keep Bernie occupied. Meanwhile, my stripper friend—remember, her name is Joy—is also a clerk for BOM in the daytime. She will finish her act and unlock the back door to the office for you and Juan. She will have the files we want from the BOM files."

"My God, Dickie, I don't know. She's a stripper, probably a hooker, too!"

Dickie tried to assure Chris they could trust Joy, "Hey, you'll like her. She is a graduate student in business administration by day and a stripper by night to pay for her student loan debt. I don't think she does tricks."

"What?"

"I will call her upstairs now to make sure she's got the files for you before I get back to our table, alright? Hopefully, Madinoff will still be with you there.

"When you and Juan clear out of the building with the files from Joy, call me back from Boob's and I'll come by with the car. You are sure you have Amy's phone?"

"Yes, yes, here it is. See. Do you have YOUR'S?" Chris was tired of Dickie's bossy tone and remembered vowing on May 14 at the scene of the tower disaster that he'd never get missed up with the fool Dickie again. *What am I thinking? This scheme all depends on Dickie.*

Back in the main room, directly in front of the end of the three-foot high stage lined with round light bulbs, Chris got a look at Bernie Madinoff, who was then sitting at their table. To Chris, he was none other than the Mayberry town drunk, Otis Taylor in the '60s "Andy Griffith Show" and one of his favorite stumblebum characters from Nick at Nite. There was a strong resemblance.

He shook Madinoff's sweaty hand and sat across from the big man. Dickie sat across from Garcia and close to Madinoff to maximize his signal calling nods and pointing when necessary, Chris guessed.

"Good to meet you, kid. Thanks for coming," said the big guy. He nodded toward the stage where the next stripper popped out from sequenced black curtains and threw her skinny arms out.

The stripper girl was a pale-skinned redhead in a skin-tight cream-colored pantsuit. She proceeded to gyrate along a fireman's pole. She swung around and fell clumsily. The skirt of her suit ripped open.

Part of the act? Chris wondered. A lone, shapely leg slipped out of her skirt. She swung it back on the pole and pulled herself up legs first as her jacket fell off. She fell again.

That time Chris thought the poor girl hurt her head. But she shrugged off her necktie, popping a couple of buttons of her white blouse exposing a bit of her small breasts, then crawled over to Madinoff.

She tossed the necktie around Madinoff's neck seductively and feigned pulling it tight.

Ripping her bra off, she fell back and hid her eyes in shame. She pretended to slap the boss, then crawled stage rear, wagging her bottom.

Back on the pole, the skirt came off.

Shaking her breasts and screwing her hips round and round, the open blouse also came off.

The beaming patrons were tossing bills her way. Chris was intrigued.

She ran her finger down her side, slowly removing her panties, then crawled off into the shadows to only polite applause.

Chris figured, *They must be waiting for the fake amateurs.*

"She's a lovely girl," Madinoff said, spilling beer down his stretched-out Tickle Me golf shirt, wetting the center of his considerable belly, again reminding Chris of Mayberry's Otis Taylor. Chris hid his laughter again in his hands.

During the end of the striptease, Chris spotted the next girl standing in the wings. She looked familiar, maybe because the good-looking brunette carried a charming innocence of Natalie Wood in the 1960's hit movie about stripper Gypsy Rose Lee.

Chris shook his head in wonder over why he constantly romanced over classic TV and movies.

He caught another glimpse of the next stripper. She was certainly not a plain girl from the audience. Chris took a deep breath. Much to his surprise, this Natalie look-alike was also looking directly at Chris from a side door across the entire stage. She had noticed him and kept staring.

Dickie, annoyed that the girl was looking at Chris and not at him, whispered, "That's Joy, Chris. She's the one." The girl kept staring at Chris. "Outrageous!" muttered Dickie Randim under his breath.

"Huh?" Chris muttered without looking at Dickie, eyes glued to the glorious woman looking at him.

The lights went off.

Two orange lights came on, accompanied by the tune "Jump Up" by the Pointer Sisters. Every time Joy would jump and point at the audience as she danced on, the audience of maybe 99 percent males would point back. She was wonderful to watch, Chris thought. Great fun. An adorable, yet alluring dancer.

After the most sensuous dance Chris had ever seen, Joy was nude, except for a G-string and spike heels. She laid prone, belly down, snaking her firm body in a waving motion from head to calf, then pumping up and down her rump as if in a heated moment of sex.

Chris was losing his sense of purpose as an investigative reporter and was more of a bedazzled adolescent, lost in wonder as she danced again, nude. To Chris, she was by and away the most beautiful woman in the club. Oddly, he felt he knew her because she continued to make eye contact. *I guess it is obvious that I'm damn mesmerized. She has spotted the youngest guy in here for the act.*

In the bright light, her eyes squinted to relocate and the find Chris time and again. She smiled at him when her head met a shadow. She winked at him, and as she leaned her body toward him, leaning over the edge of the stage, he heard her whisper clearly, "Say there, Mr. Christopher Gilley. What are you doing here anywaaaaa... oh no!"

Joy's high heel broke, causing her bare body to twist unnaturally. She fell off the short stage right into Chris's arms as he rose to save her. He was thrilled and thought, *Wow, what a great act.* But it wasn't an act. She was injured with a sprained ankle.

Chris didn't yet recognize Joy. Her real name was Denise Delmonico from Glasgow, West Virginia, the same Denise who once dated Chris's older brother Nathan.

Denise last saw Chris when he was a handsome boy of 12. He would be sprawled out on the living room floor eyes glued on Nick at Nite's "Gunsmoke" or "Hee Haw" as Nathan brought Denise home from a date.

Now held firmly in Chris's arms, Denise looked closely into the frightened boy's eyes and laughed. "Thanks, Chris," she said as Madinoff got up from the table to find something to cover the girl.

Chris was puzzled.

"It's me, Chris? ... Denise. From Glasgow? Nathan's friend, Denise?"

The slightly drunk boy was suddenly, easily in love again, or was it in lust. Then, he remembered Denise by her voice. He reverted to feeling like that 14-year-old gawking kid again.

Denise was naked in his lap! All he managed to say was, "Hey, how are you doing, Denise? I mean, are you alright? Yeah, how could I forget you? Especially now." He lapsed into uncontrollable giggling spurts of nonsensible syllables.

A waitress brought a clean table cloth and handed it to Madinoff. "Not me, stupid. Put it on Joy," said the sweaty, rotund Madinoff. He covered the stripper, now in his chair.

He rolled himself up the four steps to the now empty stage and tried to calm down the audience. Everyone was standing, cheering. He announced, "Joy Ecstasy, gentlemen. Quite a finale' huh? Give it up for Tickle's little bundle, and what a little bundle, eh? of Joy!"

Another loud cheer.

He gestured to Dickie, cupping his hand shouting, "Dickie, carry her upstairs and then get her to the Wilson Boulevard Medical Clinic. No funny business or you'll be eternally sleepin' with our friend Johnny Martin. Got it?"

Chris perked up. *So, that fat slob may well be Martin's killer?* he wondered.

He looked around the room and tried to figure how to get away fast. He sized up the bouncers and got a bit frightened. They were fearsome looking brutes. He was still sober enough and eager to take a look at the BOM files before splitting but couldn't figure how. He thought, *Would Denise still be able to help us? I'll sit still for Dickie a while.*

Dickie returned in 20 minutes, way too long for Madinoff's taste. "Well, took you long enough. Dress her yourself, you sly bastard?" Madinoff smiled knowingly with raised eyebrows.

"No, I didn't Bernie. One of the girls upstairs, one of your girls, is a nurse at INOVA Fairfax Hospital. Didn't you know that? The nurse said there were probably no broken bones and wrapped her ankle. Can't tell for sure until the swelling goes down. I watched."

"Bet you did," said Madinoff.

"Nurse said she'll be okay," Dickie added. "She needs to lay on a couch or something for the rest of the day. I said I'd check on her when Judy, I think is her name, the nurse comes down to perform her operation."

Dickie missed catching a harsh glance from Chris.

Chris was thinking, *It's a mistake, you idiot!* He and Garcia were supposed to go upstairs by the fire escape to meet Joy, not Dickie, after she opens the back door. He didn't yet know that Dickie had already unlocked the back door as he carried Denise to a couch to rest upstairs.

Chris figured he alone knew that Dickie's shaky plan may be unraveling. *What now you fool?* Chris wondered. He stared at Dickie to try to convey a nonverbal message.

But, Dickie was more concerned with Madinoff's bombastic attitude toward him. He excused himself to check on Joy.

Dickie winked at a panicky Chris and nodded his head upward.

Meanwhile, Juan Knife Garcia was transfixed at the stage where Chesty GoDeep was stripping off her football pads and pants, already topless. He had missed all the talk and gesturing, as Dickie was evidently adjusting the plan on the fly.

Chris wondered, *Where are the amateurs? That was to be the distraction, not Joy's fall.* Chris watched Dickie leave hoping he hadn't totally miscalculated.

The normal raucous amateur contest was delayed.

Dickie, at last, saw Chris looking his way. He mouthed the words silently, "Change of plans." He winked and with a turn of his head, Dickie signaled for Chris to get up and follow him.

Into the men's room again. Dickie met with Chris first and said he would help Chris with the files from Joy, not Juan because Madinoff expects him to stay with Joy. "We all can't leave the damn table," he said.

"I'm out Dickie," Chris said, "because this is crazy. You just want to be with Denise, right? You always let the skirts run your life you damn fool. I'm not a part of this anymore."

Juan arrived then separately to avoid suspicion. He said, "You guys fuckin' up, man. Mr. Bernie thinks things fishy with you. Thees not good, Dickie, not good."

"Ah, he's nuts. Don't worry about him, Juan," Dickie said. "Chris, stay with this, will ya?"

He sent Chris and Juan back to the table as he returned upstairs to Joy.

When Madinoff finally announced the amateur contest from a cordless microphone at his table, the joint again exploded with cheers.

Meanwhile, at the table near the stage, Chris got a text message from Dickie upstairs: "Got files. Get sick." Chris then coughed, stood, and turned away seemingly to vomit. Instead, he staggered and shook hands with Bernie Madinoff, saying goodbye and thanked him for a "real good time, sir."

He only assumed Knife knew to stay this time and he did. But only after saying, "It's Boob's Barbeque, Mr. Bernie. Dee boy ate in that trash dump tonight. I'll take you to your apartment, Chris."

Oops, thought Chris. "No, no, Juan. Stay and enjoy the show. Dickie will be back down to take you home later."

But Garcia didn't understand, dismissed what Chris said and kept on gawking at a 'housewife' in curlers under a head scarf on stage losing her clothes by stumbling around.

Chapter 44: Pinched

The back door was open for Chris as Denise was standing at the top of the stairs to the second floor waiting, leaning against the wall. She was looking gorgeous in black and tan sweats, Chris thought. Her hair and laughing eyes matched her dark brown hair.

"Come on, quick, Chris, let's go up to the office," said Dickie. "What've you got to show us, Denise?"

"I thought I showed you everything already. Isn't that right, Chris? You catch many stripper jokes, mister?" She gave him a warm hug and a kiss on the cheek and then asked about Nathan and their mom. Chris was relieved that she was fully dressed. He still had a boner as Denise pressed against him and his crotch with her full body hug. "They're just fine, Denise," he exhaled.

Dickie picked her up in his arms and carried the stripper/accountant Denise into the office room; glad to take her attention away from home boy.

Entering the musty smelly little office space, she said, "Okay boys. Here are the files for all the loans from the last five years. As you can see, they fill three file cabinets. So, I stayed late all last week, telling Mr. Madinoff that I was studying for a graduate exam. I even snuck in here over the weekend ... and wa la!! [She spread her arms to encompass the universe.] Here is a chart of all the loans--names, locations, interest rates, totals, and most important, race and religion, as best I could determine. Do you need anything else?"

"My God, Denise, marry me this minute," Chris blurted, relieving a long-days' ball of built-up tension. He hadn't wanted to do the Tickle trip, but after what happened it would be quite a story to tell one day. He only had one question. "Dickie, Garcia was supposed to be here with me instead of you, remember? Does he have his cell or not?"

Dickie's face flushed red.

Chris pressed, "Does he? The man is in a drunken stupor over those naked women, man!"

"Don't worry. Let's work fast and get outta here," Dickie said thinly, avoiding Chris's eyes.

Chris tried not to show his fear, his displeasure with Dickie's mistake. (Up to that moment, his day had been full of bad omens:

Benny disliked the story he turned in at deadline. His car likely expired for good. Dickie's plan was screwed up. And the look he was getting downstairs from Madinoff had been more than just frightening. It was chilling.)

Denise, proud as she could be to see Nathan's little brother from Glasgow, joked, "I think we almost consummated that marriage down in the front row, Chris. Hope I didn't crush any personal items when I plopped into your lap, boyfriend." They all laughed nervously and got down to business.

"Yea, yea, let's do this," Dickie said in a rare serious moment.

She hobbled over to a table and they sat among papers she had pulled out as possible evidence of BOM criminal activity. It became evident to Chris that she was no longer planning to have much of a future with BOM.

Meanwhile downstairs, Knife was panicking, and for good reason. After the 'housewife' act, he realized only he was left with handling Madinoff and the big guy was getting antsy.

Dickie would have easily controlled Madinoff.

Garcia had no chance.

Madinoff wanted to leave the table to check on Joy.

Garcia made several clumsy attempts to delay him in half-English/half-Spanish conversation and could not keep his attention.

Bernie Madinoff stood, "Hey Juan guy, I don't want to talk to you anymore; got to see Joy. She's my precious, best dancer and she was injured," he said as Garcia tugged at his sleeve with one hand and pulled his cell phone out with the other. He punched Dickie's speed code number 3.

Madinoff stared down angrily at Garcia and became more and more annoyed as the Latino made excuses.

Garcia said, "Dickie says she need sleep. She fine, Mr. Madnuff." He was able to glance at his phone for Dickie's reply. The phone screen was black, no light. It was dead.

Madinoff yelled at Garcia, "Why are you here anyway," he asked, determined to get away from Garcia and attend to his precious commodity. "Who the hell are you … Oh, so calling Dickie, are ya? Why?"

Madinoff stormed up the front stairs.

Knife slipped outside and ran down the street from the joint as fast as he could, turning the heads of beefy bouncers sitting by the entrance.

Madinoff reached his upstairs office, unlocked its security door and swung it open, expecting to see his prized stripper stretched out quietly on his red leather couch. Instead ...

"What the fuck?!!" he screamed at the top of his lungs.

Before him was his clerk/stripper Joy, his reporter guests and piles of confidential papers spread out on tables and the floor. He did nothing at first, perhaps in shock by what he saw. Slowly, calmly, with the downturned face of an angry guerilla about to pounce, Madinoff reached into his pants and pulled out a huge cell phone, circa 1995, and pressed one button.

"Bruiser, get Slugs and Big boy. You guys get up here to the office in one second, if not sooner. Leave the front door unguarded. Get up here. We have burglars; send Mash around back, too."

A menacing, contorted smile crept across his face, his massive body filling the door frame. Madinoff just shook his angry head and muttered, "Mm Mm Mm, thought you boys were up to sommim."

Almost before he could say, "You're fired, Joy," the three bouncers came running in as Madinoff stepped to the side. Three came from the front security door and one from the back stairs. They also stood staring for a moment, tormented grins spreading slowly across their mugs.

Madinoff growled, "Lock the doors, men." His menacing expression broadened into a diabolical smile as he corralled each muscle-bound brute with a head bob gesture. He then simply nodded his head toward Dickie and Chris as a cue to the bouncers to earn their keep.

The bouncers quickly began to pound the daylights out of Dickie and Chris while Denise scurried off limping, nearly falling down the front steps into the lobby, as Madinoff stepped aside to let her by.

In the mayhem, Madinoff, shaking his head in disgust, gathered the papers and locked them in his office safe. He took particular interest in Denise's three lists of first-home loan purchasers, which his company had marked 'personal information.' One list was all African-American mortgage signers. Another was all Catholic buyers. Denise was Catholic and made a separate list because she had made a point in her research to find out if her boss hated Catholics, as Dickie had suspected. A third was a complete list, all the home loans for the past five years.

Ex-heavyweight, local boxer, crew-cut and muscle-bound Bruiser Boy Lenox landed a solid punch to the jaw of wiry Christopher Gilley, knocking him out cold immediately.

Dickie Randim wasn't so easily subdued and tried to talk himself free, running like a scared rabbit around the furniture, "Listen, listen guys, we didn't mean nothin.' Bernie, you don't want them to hurt me, do you? I'm sorry. Please, please, please."

Bruiser and his companions, turned on by Dickie's display of cowardice, finally closed in and pummeled Dickie unconscious. Still, that was not enough for Madinoff.

As Dickie lay on the carpet, Madinoff put his left foot on the small of Dickie's back and stomped on his back with his right foot. He handed them barber's scissors, and then ordered, "Cut the bastard's hair off, Bruise. He's still too pretty."

They cut off all of Dickie's beautiful locks and stuffed much of the fluffy yellow stuff into Dickie's mouth as Madinoff went into a nearby bathroom.

He returned in just a few seconds with an old fashion straight razor and a can of shaving lather, "Lather him, Slugs," he said.

With Madinoff's big shoe still on Dickie's back to hold him, they shaved him bald.

"Now, let me have that thing," said the fat man. He took the straight razor, got on his knees, and cut deep gashes on the back of Dickie's bald head while all four bouncers stood by laughing.

Minutes later, with Dickie's head bloodied and Chris still out cold, one of the bouncers asked what to do with the bodies, "Boss, you want to call the cops or somethin?"

"Don't be so stupid. Toss 'em out back in the dumpster. Let 'em wake up with the rest of the garbage."

Chapter 45: Denise and Joy

Friday late morning, July 6

Chris was the first to regain consciousness. He was in Denise's king size bed awakened with ungodly pain. When he opened his eyes, he had a close-up view of Dickie's bald and bloodied head six inches from his face on the same pillow.

Denise and her stripper friends had pulled them from the dumpster in the alley behind the Tickle club and drove them to her place.

Dickie had a broken jaw. He still had strands of his blonde hair coming out of his mouth.

Chris was alarmed by the blood on the pillow under Dickie's bald noggin. He sat up and leaned over to peak behind Dickie to see if he was alive.

And then he saw it.

As he lifted a loose bandage on the back of Dickie's head, he saw the bloody gashes Madinoff had carved with his straight razor. Looking closer, there was a message in the cuts. The carving was in the shape of a big bloody heart on the top back of Dickie's bald head. On the left side of the heart was a capital 'I' and inside the heart was carved 'Juan.'

"Did you see this?" Chris said to Denise, who sat in a stuffed chair dozing.

"Yes. I cleaned him up as well as possible while he slept," she said with teary eyes.

Chris sighed and tried to get out of the bed but couldn't. He said, "What a stupid thing. After all the planning, all the trouble we went through, hoping to find clues to Boss Martin's murder or any clues from BOM company's loan records of racial profiling, what did we get? Well, we got beat up, nearly killed, and bounced into the alley like so much garbage. I guess Dickie told you the plan. Stupid, huh?"

Except for some cracked ribs, bruises, and a bloodied mouth and face, Chris was going to be okay. It was 12:30 p.m. Chris was late for work. "Got a phone, Denise?"

Denise already had her right hand on the handle of a coffee pot where she had put it next to her on a small table with three mugs waiting for the men to regain consciousness. "How do you like it?"

"Black, please," Chris said. He didn't know where to start a conversation. The fight? Her ankle? Glasgow? His mom? *Oh, don't encourage her. Don't want Ma knowing.* Although she was the seductive Natalie Wood look-alike stripper the night before, now she was the wonderful West Virginia Denise from Glasgow who used to remind adolescent Chris of the '60's "Leave It to Beaver" TV character, the very pretty and matronly Miss Landers, Beaver's teacher, on Nick at Nite. Same dark, wavy, styled hair covering most of her neck. Same laughing, penetrating dark eyes. Same sweet, loving smile. She had been difficult to ignore then and now.

But the adult Denise was far sexier than Miss Landers. As a kid, young Chris had always fought the fear welling up inside when he spotted her coming through the door with his brother Nathan. Even at 13 or 14, he would stand, stunned by her beauty and sex appeal, when his big brother brought Denise into their home. He'd feel his young body inexplicably warm at the sight of her movements. All those memories ran through his mind as he sipped her coffee and watched her sympathetic expression toward him for his bruised body and ego.

But now, in her apartment, under far different conditions, of course, Chris no longer feared such feelings. He was grown up. He was nonetheless fumbling around in the irony of seeing Denise, his older brother's fabo-girlfriend, his teenage fantasy girl, in a real-life fantasy-like situation.

What to say?

She spoke and broke his spell, "Guess you're wondering how I got here? Well, it was the only way I could get out of Glasgow and to make decent money, Chris. People always said I was pretty."

Chris rolled his eyes, recognizing her invitation for a compliment. He was growing up now and knew enough about flirty women to let it go.

Denise asked, "Chris, is your mom okay these days? I haven't been back in three years, since your brother dumped me."

Nathan is the biggest dope in the world, Chris thought. "Ma's fine. You okay, Denise?"

"Me? Don't be silly. The question is, how are you? It was awful, just awful. I think we need to get Dickie to the hospital. I don't think he can talk."

"Okay, I'll help you with him. Just some caffeine first, please. Thanks. Too bad about all that work you did for us. Madinoff destroyed it? Did you see him in that rage?"

"I don't know, Chris. I ran, afraid of him and his boys, though now that I can think, they wouldn't have hurt me physically. I'm part of the show at Tickle. By all the work I did, did you mean the mortgage buyer lists?"

"Yeah, the list of loan buyers by all those categories and stuff."

"Oh, I have copies, I think. Sent them to my computer here yesterday before you guys showed up. Couldn't email such things to you of course."

"So why did we have to ....?" said Chris, indignant.

"Dickie. He insisted on picking them up, printed out. He's not so smart, just a handsome devil. Well, he was. Oh, look at him. Poor Dickie."

"They say he has a mental condition called risk addiction. This closes the deal on that!" Chris offered.

Denise and Chris fired up her home PC and sent copies of the BOM lending lists to his computer at the Inquirer in a folder marked 'Auto repairs.'

She added, "You know, you guys were my second request we got for stuff like that. Some government guys called. They talked with Mr. Madinoff. He had his secretary working on it."

"Oh, my God, the fed connection," Chris said as he also wondered why he didn't know this before.

"What's that?" she asked.

"Nothing yet. Hey, what can we do to patch up Dickie? Come on, he needs to go to the hospital. The back of his head is all bloody."

Denise cleaned Dickie's head again and looked again at the 'I love Juan' cut into his skull. "Oh my," she muttered sadly.

"Oh my, what Denise?" Chris asked as she pointed to Dickie's head.

"Oh my, that! They really shouldn't have done that to him," she said, covering her mouth with both hands.

Chris shivered thinking of the sort of people he'd been messing with. And the sort of people he had chosen for help. "Shouldn't Dickie or Juan have known Madinoff was a target for the feds?" he said softly.

"What?" she asked while taping gauze over Dickie's cuts.

"Nothing."

Denise then pulled a yellow and black Pittsburgh Steeler knit cap over his scarred up bald head. Chris said it was a good choice.

Dickie woke. He was unaware he had been branded as Garcia's lover. "Wha thaa for." he tried to say in pain.

"They took your lovely hair Dickie, cut it off. I just think you need to get used to no hair for a while, might get a chill until it grows back. Besides, my Steelers cap matches your old blond hair color," said Denise.

Dickie convinced them not to take him to a hospital. "Ah fine. Ja bruised up." He gave up trying to say anything more and passed out.

When he woke again Dickie managed to mumble that he didn't want the Maryland authorities to track him down at a hospital where he'd have an admission record. Chris understood Dickie's concern and agreed.

Chris called in sick to the Inquirer. It was Friday, a day past deadlines for the weekly and he wouldn't be missed.

Denise convinced Dickie to see a doctor at the home of a physician whom she knew. "Doc is a big spender at the strip club," she said with a shrug of her shoulders and a slightly wicked smile that Chris noticed and kinda liked.

She dropped Dickie off at the doctor's to get treated, and then took Chris to the police impoundment lot to claim his car. She put up the $200 to have it towed to a garage of Chris's choosing, Al's Auto Repair Shop in East Rhodesville, walking distance from Chris's apartment.

"Call it payback for all the fun I had with your family in Glasgow," she told Chris. "Remember?"

"Not really," he said. He didn't need to admit he had always been secretly thrilled to see his brother's gorgeous girlfriend. He'd had been in enough embarrassment during the past 24 hours for a lifetime, he figured.

* * *

The next day was Saturday. Chris spent the day at his apartment in bed, watching Nick at Nite on the Nickelodeon channel. He watched old detective shows like "Naked City" and "Peter Gunn."

He felt better by escaping into his boyhood with stress-free TV. It had become painfully clear that his quest for *his* story was getting much tougher than he'd expected. He had a beauty of a shiner over his right eye, sore ribs, a swollen upper lip that was cut badly. He couldn't lift his left arm over his head.

Chris had asked Dickie not to say anything about the strip club fiasco, not that Dickie could say much for a while anyway. With his broken jaw, all he could say was a series of moans and groans with an occasional decipherable word or two. Chris told him anyway that as far as anyone should know at the paper, Chris was in a serious car accident and his Mazda in the shop once again.

Chapter 46: Peeps Goes to Court

July 30, U.S. District Court 9 a.m.

During pre-court strategy sessions, defense counselor Redmond "Reddy" Dundeili begged and pleaded with his client, Vickie "Peeps" Martin to dress "respectfully" in court. She was insulted and said she wanted to dress "attractively, as I always do."

But the attorney convinced Vickie's mother, Eloise Peeples, to have a word with her daughter who was facing a good chance of life in prison. Mrs. Peeples and Vickie's little girl Gigi went shopping. They brought to the jail a conservative gray-blue business suit with the skirt that would fall below Vickie's knees.

The murder trial was rushed to court in record time by the state's attorney general. No one at the Inquirer could dig up why the rush. Courthouse personnel was mum on the subject. Chris asked Benny, "Where's our unscrupulous Dickie Randim when we finally need him to charm the information out of one of his pretty court clerks?"

Benny saw no humor in the crack. Then lightened up to ask, "Okay, I give. Where is he?"

"I was kidding, Benny. Dickie still can't talk, but he is better. Must have been a hell of a fight he got into. Spends all his time doing PR upstairs."

In fact, Dickie was ashamed and stayed locked away in his third-floor office and then getting drunk every evening at his condo.

Somehow, Fayme finally said casually at a story budget meeting that she'd been told by the cops that the trial was put on the fast track by federal investigators.

"For God's sake, girl, how long have you known that," demanded Carrie.

"Few days. That's all," said Fayme. She continued to file her nails, oblivious to a key fact in the story. While still looking at her nails she said meekly, "They wanted Maryland to resolve the murder trial quickly because of the FBI's broader interest in civil rights violations in the home financing market of King's County. The federal agency had targeted Vickie as a potential prime witness, just as they would have targeted husband Johnny, had he not been killed. They needed her full cooperation, I guess."

"Good God," Lloyd muttered under his breath.

* * *

The trial began with opening statements. Defense lawyer "Reddy" Dundeili offered, "This woman is not the perpetrator of a murder. This woman is a victim."

Chris, who was sitting in the last row corner of the courtroom, heard a deep voice in the audience say, "Well, that's original." He couldn't tell who said it but noticed there was snickering near the voice.

Dundeili pitched hollowly, "This woman had less of a motive to kill her husband, John Martini than I do. And I didn't even know the poor man," said Dundeili. He smiled as he lied through his bleached white teeth.

Others now heard the deep voice again, "The bastard is Johnny's golfing buddy." The voice laughed with others in the back of the courtroom. Chris thought it was a large man in the front row with broad shoulders in a dark blue, pin-striped suit. He sported a thick white crew cut.

In the press the next day, "Weak," "Stale," "Lame," and other hopeless adjectives led the media barrage against the defense attorney's weak effort, leaving readers and viewers the impression that Vickie "Peeps" Martin had little or no chance of acquittal. Most legal analysts didn't give Vickie much of a chance either.

Unless her attorney could produce a surprise witness or new evidence, she was already guilty in the court of public opinion and in chambers too.

All the evidence pointed to Mrs. Martin. The prosecutor Lawrence "Bones" Jarboe painted her brilliantly as the estranged wife of a bully construction developer who had refused to give his beautiful wife a divorce for five years, resulting in five miserable years for their daughter to grow up without really having a father who cared.

What was left unsaid was that Johnny Martin doted over his daughter Gigi whenever Vickie let him see her. He even took the child he never wanted on vacations with him from time to time. Vickie trusted him with the child.

With Lloyd assisting Fayme, the Inquirer published:

"Peeps" Pleads Not Guilty of Boss Martin Murder

By Lloyd Sollem and Fayme Lovelace, staff reporters

LOWEVILLE, July 31--Victoria "Peeps" Martin pleaded not guilty today to the murder of her estranged husband, John "Boss" Martin, president and owner of JDR Builders Inc. construction company, at the 4th District Court presided over by Judge Scarley.

Mrs. Martin, well known for her showy outfits in her position as Radisson Hotel concierge, wore a plain, conservative gray suit with a hemline below the knee.

She is accused of shooting her husband twice sometime between 10:35 p.m. and 1 a.m., Saturday, May 12 at the hotel, where he was meeting with clients.

On Monday, May 14, Martin's body was found after the explosions destroyed the First Union Credit & Mortgage tower in Loweville. The FUC&M tower was constructed by Martin's firm in 1998.

In an opening statement, defense attorney Redmond "Reddy" Dundeili said Mrs. Martin was not capable of such a crime and that potential motives would be sketchy and unrealistic.

Prosecutor Lawrence "Bones" Jarboe countered by promising evidence to convict, including the murder weapon, blood tests, and firsthand witnesses to violent arguments by the Martins shortly before John Martin disappeared.

Johnny Martin was not seen again until his body was unearthed in his pickup truck in the basement garage of the crumbled tower, with bullet holes in his eye and heart.

Newspaper reporter Richard Randim, and Johnny Martin confidant Juan Garcia, are listed by the defense as potential witnesses by both defense and prosecuting attorneys. Chief operating officer of Martin's firm, JDR Inc., Humphrey Hurt, and Radisson Hotel manager James Strait are also expected as defense witnesses. The prosecution list of witnesses includes King's County Sheriff Barney Standard, two Radisson Hotel security guards, and Mr. and Mrs. Harvey Jones from Orlando, Fla., who were guests at the hotel on the weekend of Mr. Martin's disappearance and death.

Chris was desperate. It didn't look good for Vickie.

He did due diligence and appropriate math on hundreds of BOM loans from Denise's charts and, surprisingly, didn't see any clear discrimination by Madinoff's finance company. *What the hell were we doing then? Dickie steered me to Madinoff because of the girls and his unscrupulous lifestyle. Dickie just guessed. Damn him.*

He realized that any day there could be a conviction of Vickie. He seemed to be the only person, besides Dickie and Knife, and maybe her mother, who believed she was not guilty.

Dickie still couldn't talk much with his jaw wired. Michele didn't care. Neither did Lloyd, or anyone in the newsroom.

Carrie was delighted, "What's with Dickie's Steelers cap? He shave his head or something? He's not even from Pittsburgh, ha."

Meanwhile, 'Mama' Melissa doted over Chris and his sudden injuries, worrying him with questions in front of her girls about his confessed car accident.

Chris Gilley, the intrepid investigative sleuth, now had little time to change Michele's mind on the story assignment. However, she would soon be taking her annual three-week vacation around Labor Day. Maybe he could take over, he hoped.

Chapter 47: Blood Evidence

July 31, U.S. District Court, 9 35 a.m.

"Your first witness, Mr. Jarboe, please," said Judge Harry Scarley.

"Your honor, the prosecution calls to the stand the King's County Sheriff, Barney Standard."

Sheriff Standard testified that he'd known both John and Victoria Martin since before they separated, more than five years ago. He said that previously his officers were called to "domestic situations at the Martins' homes" many times before they were separated and several times since.

"Frankly, I don't know why they didn't divorce. They just never got along," said Standard.

"Objection, your honor," barked defense attorney "Reddy" Dundeili.

Said the judge, "The court recorder will strike that comment from the record. The jury will disregard Sheriff Standard's opinion about the Martins' marriage status. Sir, I agree. It's not relevant. Please confine your answers to the questions."

Standard shrugged and replied, "Yes sir, Harry, ah, Judge; sorry. But everybody in this county knows ..."

"Aaa-aa, Barney do you want me to slap the county sheriff with contempt of court before you say what you've got to say?"

"No, Harry, ah, no your honor ... sir."

And he said plenty. The sheriff testified that blood found on the dress that Victoria Martin wore the night Johnny disappeared at the hotel was Johnny Martin's. The same blood was also found on her hands, dress, shoes and hair. The sheriff observed, "Obviously, Mr. Jarboe, the body was moved, but there was no blood in the conference room where Mr. Martin met with clients that night. As far as we could determine from many people who were at the opening celebration of the hotel that night or over the weekend, that was the last place anyone saw Mr. Martin alive or dead, in that conference room."

Prosecutor Jarboe asked, "Is it possible, Sheriff, that the murderer would have gotten Mr. Martin's blood on her hair, hands, shoes...."

"Objection, Mr. Jarboe is leading the witness to a female killer and Mrs. Martin has not been convicted as a murderer," said Dundeili.

"Objection sustained."

"No need for that of course," the man with the white crew cut could be heard saying. Chris heard it as he sat in the third row, closer to the action. The man's sarcastic comment triggered laughter from men sitting near the white-haired gentleman.

"Order! There will be no more laughing during witness examinations. I will clear the courtroom with one more outburst," Judge Scarley said while pointing at the man with the white hair.

Jarboe said, "I'll rephrase. Is it possible to get the victim's blood on Mrs. Martin's hair, hands and clothes if she moved or had helped move the victim?"

"Absolutely," said Standard.

He testified that the bullet holes in Mr. Martin's eye, skull and chest were of a small caliber, though the exact caliber could not be determined. "The lab found fragments of the bullet in the brain of Johnny and it could best be described as .22 caliber, like Mrs. Martin's handgun."

"Sheriff," asked Jarboe. Can you identify this weapon I am holding in my hand?"

"Yes sir, that's the .22 pistol registered to Mrs. Martin." He testified that her fingerprints were on the barrel and the handle of the gun and no one else's.

Jarboe completed his questioning of Sheriff Standard, asking if he or his officers had any knowledge of altercations at the hotel the night of Mr. Martin's disappearance.

"No sir, just what I've read in the newspaper," said the sheriff.

"The same paper, the Inquirer that employs Richard Randim who was at the hotel that night, correct?" Jarboe asked.

Dundeili shouted, "Objection. One cannot assume bias by the Inquirer."

Judge Scarley rolled his eyes and just said, "Oh? Objection sustained." Chris detected a slight snicker in the judge's comment.

But the implication was out.

Bones Jarboe for the next several minutes soundly demonstrated how he earned his reputation of tearing down defenses to the bare bones. He painted a scenario of cover up.

Police were never called by the hotel the night of Boss Martin's meeting, which was also the night of the celebration for the opening of the full Radisson resort hotel. Through a series of witnesses, Jarboe gave the jury a complete picture of Johnny Martin throwing Vickie out of an elevator by the hair while threatening her lover Richard "Dickie" Randim. Martin had caught the couple engaged in sex in that elevator, witnesses said.

Hotel security guards testified that hotel management gave orders not to call in the police. They said a disturbance at the opening celebration or Mr. Martin's meeting could be handled by hotel security. They also testified seeing Mrs. Martin and Mr. Randim in her office late in the evening before each of them were said to storm into Mr. Martin's meeting, where angry words then ensued.

Jarboe concluded for the jury that no one saw Johnny Boss Martin leave the hotel that night. Yet, security testified that his custom-designed pickup truck was missing from the parking lot by 11:45 p.m. From hotel files, written reports from security rounds indicated that Mr. Martin likely had driven his pickup home and that Mrs. Martin's metallic pink Infinity was also gone by midnight.

Defense attorney Dundeili used his cross examination of Sheriff Standard to establish Vickie's movements after the Radisson meeting. He handed Sheriff Standard a court copy of Vickie's police interrogation deposition. "You may paraphrase it, Sheriff," offered Dundeili.

Standard said, "Mrs. Martin said that Mr. Randim was very drunk after being attacked by John Martin in an elevator earlier in the evening. Randim insisted that she drive Randim home, even though it was not yet midnight and her shift at the hotel was to end at 2 a.m.

Mrs. Martin said that Mr. Randim really wanted to get to her car to obtain her gun in the glove box. Mrs. Martin kept it for protection on dark nights at the Radisson. Before Randim could reach the gun, she grabbed it away. She was afraid he might use it on Mr. Martin. So, she argued with him and put the gun in her purse and returned to the Radisson. Then, she said Mr. Randim fell asleep in her car. She said that is how she had the gun in her possession and had her fingerprints on it."

Standard stopped reading and said, “But, we did not get anyone to corroborate her st ...”

“Thank you very much Sheriff. That will be all for this witness, your honor,” said Dundeili. He then asked the judge for a recess because his next witness Richard Randim was ill.

Jarboe objected.

But the judge overruled, saying, “Yes, I would like to hear from Mr. Randim myself. This case will resume on Tuesday, August 7 at nine a.m.”

He left the bench with a smile on his face that Chris could not interpret.

Chapter 48: Will Call

Friday, Inquirer newsroom, August 3

Chris called Dickie and asked him to come down to the newspaper conference room after hours. Dickie refused. He walked up to Dickie's office instead.

Dickie unlocked his door and faced Chris with a scowl, "What now?"

"Dickie, how can I get as close to Sam Johnson as we did to Bernie Madinoff, without getting hurt, of course?"

Randim shrugged and growled as if he were a mad dog. He still could not talk much.

Randim retreated to his office and locked the door, still wearing Denise's knit Pittsburgh Steelers cap.

"Well that was a waste of time," Chris said leaving Dickie's office and returning to his desk.

"What?" Bennie heard Chris passed by him.

"Nothing."

Sam Johnson now loomed large and alone in Chris's mind. He was close to dismissing Madinoff as a suspect because he didn't seem capable of such a complex crime. Chris still did not believe Vickie did it. That left the dangerous Johnson, as far as Chris was concerned. Finding a way to poke into Johnson's Lifetime Deal Financing, Corp. somehow may be Chris's last chance to get ahead of the story of who killed Johnny Boss Martin and knocked over the FUC'M tower, he figured.

So far, he had not found anyone who liked Johnson. The nasty bigot was the Teflon mystery man behind thousands of unfair loans across central Maryland and Virginia. He'd never been held accountable, never been the one to actually sign mortgage documents. His loan officers did all the paperwork.

Chris needed a plan, a cover. It was late summer, months after the crimes. Maybe he could latch onto the truth when a criminal's guard is down, he thought, on his vacation, golf course, strip club—no, not that again—or some business mixer somewhere. It was a crap game.

He started dialing red dot numbers with no luck, just realtors, officer's clubs, chambers of commerce, and the like.

When he tried dialing a red highlighted phone number that matched a "Tickets," he got, "Good evening, Washington Redskins Will Call, window one? May I help you?

Thinking fast, Chris asked, "Do you have your tickets for the four pre-season games yet?"

"Yes, sir," a young woman said.

Chris thought all Redskin games were sold out. And will call? Why will call? He took a chance, "Tickets for Chuck Bear?"

"Don't see that name, sir."

"Maryland Inquirer?"

"What? I'm sorry."

"It's a newspaper. Any of my tickets there yet? Mmm. My name is Randim?"

"Richard Random, sir?"

"Yes, tickets for Randim. It's my name. Dick Randim." Chris swallowed hard.

"Yes, sir. You say you are Richard Randim, is that Dickie, you say?

"Ya-yes, Dickie, sure I guess I am. I mean, yes, I am ma'am. Dick, Richard, one and the same."

"Okay then, Mr. Randim, I've got your ticket on Will Call for Sunday's game with the Baltimore Ravens. Just show up 30 minutes before the game Sunday and pick it up, sir at Will Call window one. I guess you won't need to arrive any earlier to tailgate, huh?"

"Why's that?"

"Well, you know, sweetie. [Chris cringed with the sweetie talk like Vickie's voice again.] You'll be getting plenty to eat and drink in the skybox suite. Great view sir, isn't it? I took a tour up there once. I see you are a regular to the LDF box."

"That's right. Can you tell me, ma'am, if my buddies have checked on their tickets for that box yet?"

"No sir, I'm not allowed."

"Thank you and see you Sunday. Against the Baltimore Ravens, you say?"

"Yes, sir. First preseason game. You knew that, kido."

Chris suspected she knew Dickie. *Sweetie? Kido?* He reminded himself not to meet that ticket girl at Will Call window number one.

Chris thought it over, *Certainly, Dickie was in no shape to use the tickets. He won't be going. So...*

Chapter 49: Make Mine Beck's

Sunday, noon, August 5

Christopher Gilley—the naïve country boy, just turned 20, was again taking a tremendous risk among dangerous characters—sordid sources certainly for his story—and this time by himself, no Dickie, Juan, Denise, no Liza. He was perhaps still too green to know what he was doing, but he carried a secret weapon, sheer determination. His scars from the strip club incident were his badges. He believed he was going to be a famous reporter and still felt he had landed on his opportunity.

Chris arrived early at FedEx Field, the Redskins' new, 90,000-seat stadium. It was near the Radisson Hotel, on the other side of the maddening public speedway called the Capital Beltway, I-495, and near the very spot where he and Dickie took flight in the Porsche in May.

He picked up Dickie's ticket at Will Call window three using his Inquirer press pass and wearing a Redskin cap well down past his eyes as he faced the ticket lady.

He walked all around the stadium immersed in thought, then sat on a barstool in an island cafe within the circle of luxury suites, deep inside the stadium. He sat behind a pillar, in case anyone from the newspaper came by or anyone else who might know him. He had a view through the bar's mirror of anyone entering or leaving the LDF skybox just across a hallway.

He carried a burgundy and gold Jan Sport backpack he'd filled with clothing for his costumes of sorts. That morning Juan had helped Chris plan the strategy because he had been to Johnny Martin's luxury box at FedEx Field many times and knew the ropes. Juan also gave Chris $200 to "dude you up," he said, for the rich skybox set of Redskin fans. Chris wore a Washington Redskin burgundy and gold tie with the team logo, a maroon jacket, and pleated khaki dress slacks. In the backpack, he carried gold pants, a waiter's vest of gold and maroon and John Riggins' sneakers with big number '44' on the heels for the former Redskin great fullback. Also in the backpack were five Redskins mugs and a small burgundy tray.

He had in mind alternative plans.

Plan A: If the box was crowded with chaotic partying, he didn't need to masquerade as a waiter, just a Washington Redskin employee servicing the suite, busing tables and cleaning, he figured. Plan B: If the box turned out to be orderly and not crowded, he would lie to the stadium staff that he was hired by the mortgage company as a personal waiter for the executives attending the game.

In either case, he first needed to make a quick in and out inspection of his targeted space, the skybox, to assess the layout. He also brought a steno pad he borrowed from secretarial services at the paper.

He entered the luxury box and was immediately flagged by a few guests.

"Hello, sir, I'm with the team's owner, Mr. Snyder's office. Can I take a quick survey of your pre-game needs?" Chris said to the first of only eight men and women already in the box.

"Son, you old enough to work here?" said the crew-cut, tall, 60ish man, dressed in a double-breasted, polyester sport jacket, in Redskins' burgundy and gold plaid.

Chris froze.

The man broke out laughing. "Oh, of course, you are. Just a joke, son. What do you want to know?"

"How many guests are expected?"

"You should ask Mr. Johnson. It's his party, but he's not here yet. I expect this room to be packed, though. It's the battle of the beltway, after all, Baltimore versus D.C., big fuckin' deal, right?" he said sarcastically as if that meant he would be doing no more than glancing at the game on the field below. The party in the suite seemed to be the real game. The Baltimore Ravens had not been in the National Football League long enough to create a great rivalry with the mighty Washington Redskins, but the two teams' home stadiums are only 30 miles apart.

Nevertheless, the broadcasting sports voices in the Baltimore-Washington region generated some interest by promoting the Battle of the Beltways, the massive, interstate highway moats circling each of the two cities.

"Yes, sir. Right. No big deal indeed. Which is why we want to measure the corporate interest in supporting the game. Does that make sense, sir?"

"Son, yer okay. Let me tell you, this is the best party at the stadium every damn week."

"Does Mr. Johnson cater the games or rely on stadium caterers?" Chris asked. "That's important to know for the remainder of the season. I am one of the help. I assume each party is pretty much the same?"

"Thought you'd know how Sam caters the suite."

"I'm new, sir, and yes, it's a bit off script," Chris flashed a big, phony smile. "What I was getting at was to make sure things were to everyone's satisfaction."

"Aren't we all wantin' soma that." The man grabbed the shoulders of a platinum-blonde woman, about 30, wearing tight jeans, was braless in a white formfitting t-shirt. She at first acted like she didn't know him, but then gave the older man an obedient flirty smile.

Chris asked them both, "Are the arrangements here satisfactory?"

"Guess so, yes," the man said as the young woman walked down to the railing to lean over it for a look at the field presumably, or to show off her bottom in the skin-tight jeans.

Chris tugged his eyes from the woman in the corner of his eye to the man again, "Do you have clear vision and sound for the game?"

"Sure, but who cares about the game, right honey?" The woman turned from watching the football athletes warm up on the field and nodded yes with another obedient smile.

"Do you visit other lounges in the building during the game, too, and which ones?"

"No."

Chris wrote down nonsense answers from five of the men and two women, in his fake survey, then told the first man he had a good sample. "See you folks during the game. I'll be working this side of the stadium boxes." *Mistake, damn. I'm supposed to be working for LFD.*

He breezed by the bar to inform the bartenders employed by the stadium that he was working the room for LFD Corporation. They gave him blank looks. He informed them that Johnson's company wanted him to take drink orders and serve them to the ticket holders at their seats to ease the stress of "losing again to the hated Ravens," he said with a wink. With that, he was gone. Chris was becoming quite the actor.

Once out of the skybox, he sprinted to the men's room where he had hidden his knapsack in a stall. Earlier he'd locked it from the inside and crawled out, leaving a makeshift sign that read 'Out of Order' on the outside.

He tossed the steno pad and pulled out an old-fashioned dining check pad from his backpack, complete with carbon paper between the pages. His mother had packed six of the pads once used by one of Chris's sisters in a Glasgow café into his car in case he needed extra note pads, as was typical of his frugal mother who raised nine kids and saved everything, even of minimal possible value.

He changed his outfit to khaki trousers and the new "Arrington" Redskin uniform shirt replica of the one worn by Skin's All-Pro linebacker, LaVar Arrington. He would wait for Johnson to arrive.

In his new 'costume' he sat at the same bar across from the LFD box to spy on Johnson's guests as they arrived.

He held a mug shot of Sam Johnson in one hand at his lap and a Yuengling in the other.

The more he looked at the mug shot of Johnson's scowl, the more the picture resembled the TV character of Frank Nitti on "The Untouchables" in Chris's mind. Chris felt rather stupid sitting there as a local scribe gunning for Frank 'The Enforcer' Nitti, the successor to Chicago mob boss, Al Capone. The role was played by big, loud-mouthed Bruce Gordon in the black and white drama series, "The Untouchables," which aired on Nick at Nite weeknights at 11 p.m. when Chris was a kid. Chris stared at Johnson's Nitty-like photo and realized, *This may not be pleasant.* The Nitty played by Gordon was big and burly with deep-set angry eyes, just like Johnson.

Chris watched the luxury box fill up quickly and the activity inside become more spirited by the minute.

All the guests looked pretty much the same. They were conservatively dressed, 50ish and older, mostly men, with a few skanky young women. What caught Chris's attention, though, was that everyone was white. No blacks, no Asians, not even Hispanics, as far as he could tell. Very much unlike the diversity in the stadium's general crowd.

Soon, the room was packed, but no Johnson. Chris decided he would make his move anyway, while he could still slip into the crowded luxury box, maybe unnoticed.

It worked.

He did slip in nicely and pulled the server tray from the back of his waistband under his Arrington shirt. First, he said hello again to the hired bartenders and told them they could stay by the bar if they wished while Chris personally serves the guests as he was told to by Mr. Johnson.

They bought it; didn't seem to care one bit.

There were about 50 people in the luxury box, which had two rooms, a larger sort of lounging room, and a small private room to the side. Outside and below three steps there was a balcony overlooking the football field. Chris immediately began to take drink orders from the farthest reaches of the balcony at the rail that overlooked the field.

Two 20-something women ordered sweet, girlish drinks while the older men with them ordered whiskey or Beck's beer. All the guests who ordered beer ordered Beck's. *Only Beck's, the German brand, how weird*, Chris noted. Older women, a few there, maybe wives, ordered mixed drinks with little umbrellas.

He took the drink orders and walked briskly with his head down until he arrived at the top of the lounge to give the order to the bartenders. He didn't want anyone to detect the terror he was feeling.

He was at the entrance of the suite closest to the field when he heard a commotion at the entrance behind him. He looked up to see Johnson and two cronies coming in resembling angry stevedores ready at the drop of a hat to beat up Marlin Brando's Terry Malloy character in the roughneck classic movie, "On the Waterfront." They marched in, chests out like peacocks, smug smiles and surveying the suite, presumably for any trouble for the boss.

Suddenly, the room exploded with cheers when everyone saw the CEO.

Being very close to the suite entrance himself, Chris had his answer to his question to Dickie—how to get close to Johnson. He was face to face with the notorious mortgage financier. Johnson ignored him and took three quick strides to the bar. Chris instinctively followed.

"Ah, it's the good service this time, boys. How you doin', sonny," Johnson barked to Chris, sounding a bit like the big cartoon rooster Foghorn Leghorn, Chris thought, despite his chilling sudden presence.

"Best I can. As you wish, sir," said Chris.

"Good, now get out of my way so I can get a Beck's and make sure nobody's thirsty, eh?" He then screamed. "Everybody got enough to drink? … eat?"

Chris turned away and smiled over his nervy ploy. He was in. *Still an all-white crowd in a mostly black city. Strange*, he thought.

Being a Steelers fan, Chris knew enough about the Ravens--big-time Steelers rivals--to hold his own in football conversations. *Too bad there aren't many Baltimore fans to jab at*, he thought.

Meanwhile, he overheard snippets of conversations.

It seemed that many of the guys at the party were longtime friends of Johnson, most were about his age of early to mid-60's, and many from all the way back to their Army days when Johnson was an officer in ordinance supplies in Vietnam.

One man stood out, Chris thought, because he wore a Navy-blue cap with the service logo and bright gold lettering "U.S.S. Dragonfly."

"Take your order, sir? Sort of outnumbered here, aren't we?" Chris inquired.

"Yeah, say, you're too young to be a vet. What? You just like the Navy? Great career, son."

"My whole family's been Navy, sir, but I've not heard of the Dragonfly. That a battleship? I know it's not a carrier."

"Cargo. Mostly ammunition reloads for ships. Goes all the way back to dubya dubya two at Okinawa Harbor. Before my time, though."

"When did you serve?"

"I was with Sammy during Vietnam on the Dragonfly, under Commander Pappy I. Doolittle. His real name wasn't Pappy. We just called him that. George, I believe it was. Yeah, you can laugh. Funny name. He took more of a beatin' than the gooks did for that label."

"So, Vietnam. Mr. Johnson was Army though."

"Yeah, he was an ordnance officer at Saigon Harbor. We drank together, whored around and tried to make the most of rough duty. Sorry, dear," he said to a downcast older woman nearby.

"You've stayed in touch," Chris asked.

"Sure. I'm here, ain't I? Sammy's real people. Has the right outlook on life."

"What do you mean?"

"You work for him, too, don't you, son?"

"Yeah."

"Well, then? You see any niggers here?"

"What? Oh. No, of course not."

"Only thing black here, son, are them niggers we're watchin' down there and the poor souls' money what's paying for all this. Well, I didn't really say that, did I?" He turned to the woman again. "Did I say that?"

No response from her. She seemed to be drunk already.

The former naval officer laughed heartily. "Make mine a double Jack D on the rocks, son, and some of them Bavarian pretzels," he said.

It was tough for Chris not to follow up with questions about Sam Johnson's so-called 'right outlook on life.' And the other crack, about blacks paying for the luxury box. Didn't make sense to Chris until much later.

There were other former military buddies of Sam Johnson. Sitting together at a table of empty Beck's was his former supply clerk Joey Stowitt, age 62, from Manchester, New Hampshire; a former Marine MP once assigned to Johnson's ordnance duty named Frank DuShayne, age 68, from Lake Charles, Louisiana; and the scarred up puffy face of Lightnin' Lou Lomax, 1976 military heavyweight boxing champ, from Montgomery, Alabama, the most dangerous looking human being Chris had ever seen close up.

Nearby, there was Brick "Face" Wall. This brute was Johnson's bodyguard, from Brooklyn, New York. It was said to be his real name. *What mother would name her kid ... never mind, don't go there. Chris, stay focused,* he thought.

Wall's side business was Brickhouse Security. Chris would have recognized the company name had someone mentioned it. He had quoted a Brickhouse security guard on the day of the FUC&M tower bombing who was at the disaster.

There was also a guy with a gold 70's style ban-lon golf shirt inscribed with the name 'Verdi.' Chris remembered him from Vickie's trial. Harrison Verdi was the big, fit man with the white crew cut and top wide blue pinstriped suit, who was cracking mocking remarks and leading all the laughter.

Chris took Verdi's drink order and learned with some effort that Verdi had been Johnson's intelligence officer in 'Nam.

Verdi ordered a Beck's.

When Chris asked if he was another Army buddy, Verdi said simply in a brutish tone, "Intelligence was ma thing, boy."

Chris turned his head quickly to hide his smile. Everything about the odd behavior of Johnson's guests—not the least of which was their blind loyalty to a racist resembling gangster Frank Nitti—signaled to Chris that normal logic didn't apply here, in this place, at this time. Naïve as the country boy had been, this story investigation was making Christopher Gilley wise up quickly to nasty, urban realities of behind-doors ethnic slurs and boldfaced racial prejudices, far worse than outward prejudice he'd hear sometimes at home.

What do all these guys have in common? he wondered. *They look kind of angry or at least rough around the edges, sharp edges. They love Sam Johnson; many still work for him and seem very inflexible and unflappable.*

He scanned the crowd again. No blacks. He was getting scared and needed more courage to continue. He tried to duck into the skybox restroom for a breather. Meanwhile, Johnson hurried back to the entrance of the luxury box and Chris stopped to watch. He saw Johnson greet and immediately huddle closely with two fit young white men in suits. Instead of ties, they wore dress shirts with the top button open and carried glum expressions and body language charged with anxiety.

Unlike Johnson's other guests, these men did not instantly perk up by seeing Sam Johnson. Quite the opposite. They seem to tense up and become very apprehensive as he approached. They could have been dreading a life-changing encounter with Dracula.

It was clear to Chris; these two men had arrived with a different purpose in mind. He was intrigued and made a move, "Can I get your guests a drink, Mr. Johnson," he asked, his heart pounding.

"Where'd you come from boy?" he likely used his divergence to Chris to tamp down the nervous pair. "I love this boy, right on the spot. Yeah, bring us three Beck's over there," said Johnson, without asking if the other men wanted Beck's. He pointed to a carved oak door leading to the smaller room inside the luxury box.

As Chris carried the beer on his Redskins tray, he noticed that the private room had a small wooden desk and chair, which were clean of anything that might hint of paperwork. The room also had a small conference table and four chairs, Chris noted. The room had a huge window to the game, which was by then late into the second quarter approaching halftime. Johnson and the two men sat at a table, not watching the game through the window, nor on any of three large TVs.

There were empty bottles, glasses and dishes on small countertops. Chris turned back. "Excuse me, gentlemen, can I clean this up for you and get more drinks?" He was dying to eavesdrop.

He had already detected that they were talking finances. They ignored the young waiter boy. Chris slowed to a crawl, glancing around for a reason to stick around. He spent time at the room's shallow sink, washing his hands and toweling slowly, all the while listening to the conversations.

Johnson finally realized the boy was speaking to them and replied, "No thanks, son." Johnson was irritated by something, probably not Chris, so Chris stayed at the sink.

The conversation was rapid and competitive.

Johnson, impatiently: "We can get by. Things will pick up and cover us."

The first man, about 35, black hair, clean shaven: "We need more, Sam. You know that."

The second man, a little older: "What Reece means is that we can't buy more loans right now. We are getting pressure from New York. Give us a few months."

Johnson, face taut, voice strained: "You guys make promises and don't keep 'em. You said you can buy as many as we sell. Then you come here, upset my party, and say you can't come through." His voice grew louder and could be heard by others outside on the balcony.

Reece: "Sam, that was six months ago. Get real. If you hadn't lost the Port America condos..."

Johnson: "You're full of fuckin' crap. I was squeezed out of the condo mortgage deal at Port America by my former partner, that scumbag, Madinoff. I don't know how the man stays in business with a mind as dull as dirt. Besides, that's done. I need some support. We lost our entire office in that accident."

Other man, Chad: "Accident? Not what I hear."

Johnson: "What the hell? So now you're a cop. Who's talkin' to you? It was an accident. Those explosives were set for Johnny but too close to the gas tanks. Nobody would have known about those tanks right in the fuckin' garage."

Chad: "You seem to know a lot about how it worked there, Sam."

Johnson: "Oh, fuck you. Fuck you both. It was my office too, you know. I just read the papers too about the gas tanks and all, fuckhead."

Brick "Face" Wall, the bodyguard, opened the door a little and asked, "Everything alright in here, boss?"

"Yeah, oh ... oh, yeah. Everything is fine, just watching the game and got excited. Go back to the party, Face," Johnson suggested. The football game was in a timeout and nothing was happening on the field for anyone to get excited. Brick Face looked concerned, shrugged and left, without closing the door behind him.

Johnson, leaning in, almost whispering, said "If you think I had anything to do with that mess ... I lost my office, records, everything, you fuckin' bastards."

Reece offered, "You guys, calm down. Sam, he's not sayin' anything. Let's talk some football, shall we? Skins any good this year?"

Chris, frozen at the sink by their exchange, moved to remove dishes and empty glasses.

Johnson admitted, "Not the foggiest. Don't tell my friends and colleagues out there, but I could care less about Redskins, black skins or yellow skins."

Chris mumbled instinctively, "Couldn't care less."

Johnson grumbled, "What's that boy?"

"I said, couldn't it be careless of me, ah, to take these glasses, I mean?"

Johnson ignored the stupid boy servant, turned to his guests. "Like I said, I don't even like football. The company writes this off as marketing expenses. Works too. I invite developers to share this private room, even plain old family landowners, like that fella over there.

Johnson pointed out to the lounge. "You're going to meet him. This fella owns 300 acres of land, right on the D.C. Beltway just south of here. Tobacco and soybean farmer, now he can't grow 'bacca' he says. State's outlawing it. Wants to sell but wants too high a price. I'll reel him in eventually. I'll give him a break, but he doesn't know it yet. I want the rights to rezoning, too, for a shopping mall. That's why I got the county planning director there talkin' to him, see? Makes it seem inevitable. Done deal. That's how I operate guys and it will continue with your loans. So …"

Chris knew he had connected with Johnson's financing world, after fully grasping that he had indeed unearthed a nasty nest of horrible racist partners in the larger room, all operating in King's County and likely preying on the predominantly black community. He remembered how strange that an FBI office was in the FUC'M building. His skin began to crawl. The flesh on his arms felt prickly and he felt his knees getting shaky.

He thought, *This may be a bigger story than I thought. Certainly, not all these guests are racists. But, they all must like Johnson's money enough to play his game. I'm getting sick.*

He figured that Chad and Reece were out-of-town investors whom Johnson sold mortgage loans to, perhaps part of a daisy chain passing along derivative loans.

It all fit, Chris reasoned: Johnson was just like his reputation, a predatory lender. He likely loved to prey on blacks especially, judging from the harsh conversation in the big room. The loans get passed on and no one knows about the discrimination, perhaps not Chad and Reese. And now that the housing market has crashed and Johnson needs more leverage. *Yep, that's the deal. Got to get out of here,* he decided.

Chris looked over the guests on the balcony and a window to the main room in the suite. Johnson's military buddies, now grouped together, sported 60's style flat tops or sparse remnants of Fonzie's D.A. (duck's ass) haircut from *Happy Days*.

Some guests had eagerly shared with Chris their undying admiration for Johnson with their comments, like, "he's got it right" or "he lives life right," interspersed with racial slurs like "gooks" or "niggers."

They made no effort to conceal their shocking attitudes and at the Johnson party they could feel free to say what they think. *These are Johnson's handpicked bigots*, Chris thought.

Chapter 50: Johnson's Wrath

As Chris took empty glasses to the sink, the big oak entrance door opened once again.

This time, it was Verdi, Johnson's former Army intelligence officer. "Sam? You asked me to bring in Henry Claggett, our farmer friend to meet your guests."

Chris turned around to see Verdi and the King's County planning director Brendan Boldman coaxing in another man who looked familiar.

The other man was lean and tall. He was an old man in jeans and flannel shirt looking out of place in the sporty crowd and out of step with his hosts. He wore an expression of disgust and his eyes darted about anxiously. It was the farmer, Claggett.

Johnson and the two finance guys rose to welcome Mr. Claggett, acting as if they had long been expecting him.

Chris stood staring as the man stared back, neither yet recognizing the other right away. And then, before he could turn away, Chris was first to recall the man. This was the same farmer that he and Dickie treated rudely when Dickie lost control of his Porsche on May 14 and flopped it onto Claggett's farm an hour or so before the FUC&M tower was destroyed.

After introductions, Claggett looked back at Chris and squinted to see him better. Chris quickly turned away again, but it was too late. Claggett's eyes flared and he said forcefully in a mean, spiteful tone, "Now, I know what the hell's goin' on here, Mr. Johnson."

Johnson was surprised. "What? What's going on with what Mr. Claggett?"

"You playin' a game with me to get me in the paper. With this here guy from the Inquirer, is what's goin' on. Now I recognize him. Hey you, come here, boy. I know you. You were the reporter come on my property in that wrecked sports car. I thought that was an accident. Well......"

"Mister, you must be mistaken, I'm just working here for the party," Chris's face turned plum red. He dropped a tray of glasses. They shattered on the tile floor, just short of the sink.

"Reporter!!" Johnson's jaw dropped. "You say this boy works for the Inquirer?"

The farmer pointed a finger at Chris and spoke to Johnson, "Them Inquirer boys came to my place in a beat-up blue sports car the day that buildin' in Loweville fell in pieces," said Claggett. "I think you sent 'em because they had no better reason to be on my land. Thanks for the beer, Mr. Johnson. Good day, sir."

He stormed out, leaving Chris and Johnson facing each other, Chris, wide-eyed, glancing about for an escape route. Johnson, slowly inhaling and clenching his fists.

"Son, if that's true, you are in a lot of trouble. Goddamn, Randim probably sent you in here, that gutless fuck up. Sports car, my ass, well yes, that's likely Randim's doing," he said menacingly. "Randim's car." Johnson pulled out his cell phone and demanded, "Get security in here immediately, if not sooner. My God, this sucks."

The two financing guests got up and bolted to the door. They found it to be locked and smashed into it like slapstick comics. They, like Chris, were frightened by Johnson's temper outburst.

Chris was trying to figure a way to talk himself out of it, but his disguise, which had been his ticket there, betrayed him. He was not aware that when he dressed in the men's room, Chris left his press pass in his wallet and stuffed it into his unfamiliar clothing. As Johnson confronted him, Chris repeatedly denied he was a reporter. "No sir, not me, sir."

But, when two wiry tall security guards quickly grabbed Chris his wallet popped out from his oversized Arrington uniform jersey, which he had partially stuffed incidentally in his back pocket cradling his wallet.

The men lifted Chris by the elbows. The jersey lifted. His wallet was free; its content scattered across the floor. His press badge fell, too, landing precisely on Samuel Johnson's right shoe, with a face shot of Christopher Gilley looking smack at Johnson looking down at it.

"Oh, not a reporter, huh? Take him to the police. He's trespassing. Have them search this boy for a recording device or weapons. God knows what he heard."

Chris resigned himself to his capture and being exposed. He reached out to Johnson for his press badge, but Johnson quipped, "No, no, my boy, I'll keep this, thank you." He jerked it back behind him. "I will deal with you later, Mister … oh, let me see here … Gilley, is it? I guarantee I will deal with you, son. You have made a big mistake crashing this here party."

The security guards hustled Chris from the box and onto an escalator to the lower level beneath the upper grandstand. They then walked him along briskly, each with an arm under Chris's arm, along the wide promenade, past rows of concession stands of the lower deck.

The stadium crowd let out a tremendous roar as the first half of the football game at that moment concluded with a dramatic touchdown pass from the Redskins' first-string quarterback Jason Campbell to wide receiver Santana Moss. The catch moved the home team into a one-point lead and sent the crowd into a cheering frenzy.

Moss's catch was Chris Gilley's good fortune. Perhaps his captures' grip loosened.

As thousands of fans came storming up the aisles of FedEx Field and into the lower deck, filling in all the space around them, the slender guards were finding it more difficult to rush Chris along. Hundreds of hungry fans stormed toward concessions. Hundreds more to the restrooms. Hordes of people were crisscrossing in front of the security guards and their prisoner.

Bumped and shoved along with the crowd, Chris shook loose just before the security officers approached their destination, a police desk in a small room inside the stadium, the holding station for violators of stadium regulations.

Nimble Chris quickly disappeared into the crowd. Like a stealthy, slim halfback, he reversed his field, and then slipped ahead of two very large African-American women heading to a refreshment stand. The two women essentially blockaded any sight of Chris by the security officers who trailed somewhere behind.

He crouched and slowed down to remain shielded by the ladies. He stayed slowed down as a crawl to stay just in front of the two ladies chatting and meandering toward the food line.

"Young man, you go any slower, and I'm calling the old folks home to come get cha," howled the larger of the two women. They laughed pleasantly.

When Chris turned to face them, she toned down the humor, "Hey, I know you. You at Denny's that day; it was so crowded like midweek, right?" she asked.

Chris recognized Else from the challenging breakfast he struggled through that deadline day at Denny's while he was desperate to get the black IT entrepreneur Jackson on a dying cell phone.

Before he could respond (He had no breath.), Else continued, "Yeah, that's you. Hey listen, I am sorry 'bout that OJ. We awful busy mornin's and... Hey, whatchu runnin' for? ... You doin' something' wrong, honey? Hiding with us? Fine. How 'bout we get you a hotdog, young man. Again, sorry for …"

* * *

Chris Gilley, greenhorn investigative reporter, had botched another one. This one, as they say in the trade, now had legs—the wrong kind for him—the wobbly, hurtful legs.

He had escaped.

But, as he sprinted to his old Mazda outside of the stadium, Chris knew he was now in a dangerous spot in his pursuit of the story. Sam Johnson knew Chris's name. Johnson also knew who he worked for. Johnson had Chris's press badge. Johnson knows Chris was listening and probing into his inner circle. Bottom line: Johnson was Chris worst nightmare.

He wondered if his clumsy investigation could get any worse. As he drove off, he decided that, yes, it could. *Why didn't I just leave all this alone? No, I couldn't,* he thought.

Chapter 51: Hopeless

August 7, U.S. District Court, 2 p.m.

The morning was uneventful in Judge Scarley's courtroom as prosecutor Jarboe laid out his case against Victoria Martin with no surprises. He called Radisson Hotel employees who gave the jury a mental picture of the crime scene and circumstances of the night of Johnny Martin's meeting while the hotel celebrated its grand opening.

After a lunch recess, the judge said, "Mr. Jarboe, call your next witness."

"I call Mr. Richard Randim to the stand your honor, please."

Vickie leaned over to say something to her lawyer.

Defense attorney Dundeili, announced, "Your honor, I have just been informed that Mr. Randim has a broken jaw. He's had it wired and will not be able to speak and present testimony for at least one week."

"Is this a doctor's report, Mr. Dundeili? My word, the court thought you were a lawyer."

"I am a lawyer, your honor. But a doctor gave me a note. Dr. Irvine Kildare of Arlington, Virginia gave us this prognosis." He walked up and handed the single sheet of paper to the judge.

"Mr. Dundeili, are you sure of Dr. Kildare? That's his real name?" the judge chuckled, trying to hide his reaction.

"What's the problem, Your Honor? It's is a real note from a doctor, sir."

"Never mind. Dr. Kildare, indeed it is," the judge said reading the note.

And, your Honor, Mr. Randim is my witness. I get to call him first," said Dundeili quickly.

Even the judge had been taken by Bones Jarboe's persuasive style. Embarrassed, the judge corrected himself, "Yes, of course. Have we heard from all of your witnesses, then Mr. Jarboe? Okay, then. You can question Mr. Randim after he is released from Dr. Kildare."

Laughter erupted from the older folks in the audience.

"Next witness Mr. Dundeili?"

"Your honor, the defense calls Juan Ramirez Gutan Garcia."

Dejected and slouching badly, Garcia shuffled to the witness stand where he reluctantly repeated for the jury his contention that Mrs. Martin could not have made deadeye shots at Mr. Martin in the eye and heart. "It is called execution style killin', I thin, sir. And dat would be impossible for Mrs. Martin. She always very kind woman. Never kill nobody."

Garcia described the night at the hotel that was supposed to be special for Mrs. Martin, the opening party from 6 to 10 p.m. "She very happy. Work very hard." He added that "Mr. Martin didn't want to interfere with his wife's job there. He say he don't tell her he was meeting that night after 10 o'clock with clients," said Garcia.

Garcia's positive testimony on Vickie's behalf was short-lived, however. Under cross-examination Bones Jarboe got him off message.

"Mr. Garcia, or should I call you The Knife?"

Garcia quickly responded. "It's just Knife, Mr. sir."

"Objection," screamed Dundeili. "What is Mr. Jarboe after? The question is not relevant."

Jarboe said, "Your honor, Mr. Garcia's nickname Knife comes from his criminal past before John Martin rescued him as a troubled teen in juvenile court and took him under his wing. The relevance is to establish his close relationship with both Mr. Martin as well as Mrs. Martin."

"Overruled, Mr. Dundeili. Let's see where this goes. Mr. Jarboe, please address the witness with his real name."

Jarboe continued with a sneer, "Well thanks to Mr. Dundeili quick draw, we have established that you knew Mr. Martin and still know Mrs. Martin. Is that well? Do you know her well, I mean?"

"Mrs. Martin a fine woman, sir."

"Isn't it true that the Martins are like parents to you since you were 17 and now you are nearly 10 years older, close to the Martins for nearly 10 years?"

"What?"

"The Martins have been more like parents than your own parents?"

"Si. I mean yes, sir. 'Cept me mother, she went back to San Juan."

"I would say that may cause some bias on your part Mr. Knife. I, ah. Excuse me, Mr. Dundeili, Mr. Garcia."

"I dunno, sir."

"Yes, okay then. Let's switch to your good friend, Mr. Randim. How do you know Dickie Randim, Mr. Garcia?"

There were a few more chuckles from among the gallery.

"What you mean? What's so funny anyway?" Juan was getting perturbed and nervous. He couldn't figure out what the court was trying to do to him.

"You know Mr. Randim through Mr. Martin, right?"

"Dat's right."

"When did you last see him?"

"Couple … er, ah … few weeks back."

"Where was that?"

Garcia squirmed and let out with, "He fell down broke his jaw, that's all."

"I didn't ask about his jaw, Mr. Garcia. Were you with him when he was injured?"

"Si."

"Where?"

"Tickle My Pickle," was the mumbled response.

"Please, Mr. Garcia. Speak up. I know you are not directing that at me. Or, are you?"

The audience laughed a bit.

Judge Scarley, "Answer the question, Mr. Garcia. Where did he break his jaw when you were with him?"

"Tickle My Pickle, a strip joint near the Pentagon."

The courtroom exploded in laughter.

"Isn't it true, Mr. Garcia, that Mr. Randim performs at this Tickle My Pickle?"

"Sometimes yeah, he do," he testified.

An uproar of laughter almost drowned out his answer.

Prosecutor Jarboe sat still and silent without objection to questions regarding Dickie's character, a stray off Garcia's expected favorable testimony on behalf of Vickie. Dundeili seemed to be shifting guilt from her to Dickie.

After Garcia's disastrous testimony, defense attorney Dundeili considered dropping Dickie from its witness list, but in the meantime wanted a delay to reset its case.

"Your honor," Dundeili was scrambling, "Dr. Kildare just informed me Mr. Randim will be released and talking in about a week.

"Are you sure it is okay with NBC," said the judge. His voice was dripping with disgust.

"Sir?" Dundeili was still clueless on the Kildare humor.

"Never mind," said Judge Scarley. "Mr. Dundeili, is your next witness well enough to testify?"

The attorney ignored the wise-cracking Judge and asked for Johnny Martin's former private secretary, Sara Parker, to take the stand as a character witness. His hope was to establish Vickie's unwavering compassion for her estranged husband and father of their child right up to when he disappeared.

"Miss Parker, how long have you known the accused," Dundeili asked.

"I met Vickie shortly after Mr. Martin met her."

"That was many years ago?"

"Yes, and she worked for us part-time after they married. I saw her a lot and worked well with her. Very pleasant woman. I was happy for Mr. Martin."

"How long have you known him."

"Oh, my gracious. I came from Chicago with his father, when Vincent Martini, his gather you know, brought his business to Washington and stayed with young Mr. Martin when Vincent retired."

Dundeili got to the point, "Could you tell the court about the last time you saw the father and son together?"

"Yes, it was the day of the tragedy."

"You mean the destruction of the First Union Credit and Mortgage office tower, the one Johnny Martin's company built and owned?"

Prosecutor Jarboe jump to his feet, "Objection, your honor. Relevance? I can't see what this has to do with Martin's murder suspect."

Dundeili answered, "Your honor, Ms. Parker has been intimately familiar with the Martin family. Her testimony will relate to Mrs. Martin, if you please."

"Overruled. Proceed.

Testifying under oath, Johnny Martin's secretary testified that the father confronted his son angrily, that he had rushed into the JDR offices on the first floor of the FUC&M.

"Did you hear the nature of their argument, Ms. Parker? asked Vickie's attorney.

"More than the nature of it. When Vincent marched right into Johnny's office, ignoring my pleas to wait, I stayed close and took shorthand. Johnny liked me to take notes of important meetings. I stayed back at the door and took notes just in case of legal trouble," she told the court. She admitted that she didn't want to lose her job with JDR she had held for 11 years.

She took her stenographer's pad from her purse and presented the court with her notes from the Martins confrontation, she called it. She relayed that Johnny Martin was taken back and said, "Papa, what are you doing here?" Johnny was on the phone and shooed him away, the secretary testified.

Ms. Parker further testified, "Vincent Martini yelled in anger, 'Vickie, she talked with me today, Johnny.'

"Johnny then said, 'Well, so what?'

"Then, Vincent told his son, 'Vickie heard you have a vendetta on that crooked finance guy Sam Johnson. She don't want you to get hurt. Me too. You got to stop dealing with this criminal Johnson. He is a bad man Johnny'."

Jarboe objected that Johnson was not on trial.

The judge, intrigued, asked Ms. Parker to continue.

From the witness stand, the secretary continued telling the court the conversation from her shorthand, beginning with Johnny's reply to his father, "He said, 'Papa, I have known Sam Johnson a long time, since he was Pinky White at George Washington University, and later at Ft. Meade when he tried to blow up a lounge for black soldiers. I know he is a bad guy. He hurt a lot of my people, Papa, including the blacks who work for me too. He deserves to be hung out. And he won't hurt me. Johnson thinks we are old friends.'

"Vincent said, 'Vickie told me Johnson's company is broke, can't finance any houses no more. Let it go. Please, son.'

"Johnny said, "I got the goods on him Papa, racial profiling, fraud mainly targeting all those blacks movin' into big houses down here. I can have him put away for a long time and he knows it, Papa.'

"Vincent said, 'Stop it, Johnny. There is a time for vendettas. This is not one of them. If you don't stop, I will turn you into Lt. Palumbo with the state cops.'

"And then Johnny asked, 'What kind of man turns in his own son? Even to cousin Tony Palumbo?'

"Vincent said, 'You know me, Johnny. I am a man who would never bring disgrace on the family or the family business, unlike you. I won't stand for it.'

"It's not your business anymore. Goodbye, Papa."

"Vincent repeated his threat to turn Johnny over the police. I'm not sure for what, though. And then he played his best card, your honor. Vincent said, 'I can't see this happening to you. They will kill you. What would your mother say?'

"Vincent's mention of Johnny's mother softened him," his secretary told the murder trial room. "And then he thought of Mrs. Martin, I think because he said 'Hey, Papa, I'll ask Colonel Hurt to take you for a nice weekend with Vickie at the new hotel, the Radisson, on Saturday, just opened Thursday. You'll see. Everything is fine Papa. Vickie works there, you know. You can see her theree, maybe Gigi too'."

Dundeili thanked Ms. Parker and added, "The testimony establishes regard of Johnny Martin for the care of his daughter and respect for his wife, the accused.

Judge Scarley asked the prosecutor if he had questions for Ms. Parker for cross-examination.

"Yes, your honor. Just two. Ms. Parker, can I assume you made a reservation for Mr. Vincent Martin for that weekend at Johnny Martin's request?"

"Oh yes, I called in the reservation."

"Did you speak to Victoria Martin who was the concierge there or the front desk?"

"Oh the desk, sir."

"Do you know if Mrs. Martin knew or facilitated his stay at the hotel?"

"No, sir. I do not."

The judge dismissed the witness and complimented her, but with another wisecrack. "You obviously take great shorthand. We could you use in the courtroom to help me keep all the characters straight ... The Knife, Miss Peeps, Dickie the stripper, his physician Dr. Kildare and so on.

“I just cannot wait for tomorrow’s cast. It is five o’clock gentlemen and ladies. Court is now adjourned.”

Chapter 52: Pinky and the Boss

Chris didn't make it to the trial that Tuesday morning because he could not get his Mazda to start, even after Al's garage had replaced its distributor and generator. He also called in sick to the Inquirer and stayed in recovering from his scary encounter with Johnson's creepy crew at FedEx Field.

He was flat broke and could not afford another repair. When he lifted the hood, he discovered that a wire from the new distributor to the coil had fallen off. He left the hood up as a reminder to himself to inspect the engine later. He would rather spend the afternoon drinking beer and feeling sorry for himself.

The next morning, he attached the car's wire to the coil but it was still not turning over. He took his then familiar No. 9 bus to the Inquirer.

When he finally arrived at the paper past 11 a.m., Chris skipped his cream puff assignments and quickly dove into some research online on Johnson. He was deathly afraid of the man. Rapid clicking through the Inquirer morgue produced Johnson's disturbing background, details long buried before the collapse of the FUC'M tower.

Johnson's true-life story left Chris shivering cold in a very warm newsroom in August.

He spent the afternoon matching bios of Johnny Martin and Samuel Johnson. He discovered that they attended GW law school at the same time.

He also learned that the birth name for the scary white supremacist Johnson, aka White per Trichina's profile of County Exec Collins, was James Samuel 'Pinky' White. *What an irony*, he thought.

Local King's County newspaper stories on Johnson revealed that schoolyard bullies called him Pinky, because his normally pale complexion would be burned bright pink after working his daddy's 'bacca fields. When he was a big teenager and probably still seething with resentment, James decided to adopt the derogatory nickname Pinky as his badge of honor after one of his bullies disappeared.

The school yearbook told the sad story titled, "Fondest Memories, Lost at Sea," of three boys (Pinky among them) fishing off a half-rotten pier on the White Farm. "As boys will be boys, daring to take risks, they cast their lines out into Patuxent River on the wrong day, just before Hurricane Agnes hit our region. The river was ragingly fast that day." One boy fell in and the river rushed him toward the Chesapeake Bay. The category 3 hurricane swirled right up the gut of the Bay and the boy was never found.

The boy lost was Pinky's primary bully.

Hmm, bet he pushed him in, planned the whole thing with the storm coming, Chris thought, reminded again of the monster he had put on his trail. *Ocean sharks probably took the boy's body.*

He noted that the high school account didn't mention the third boy fishing with them. Chris found that in the Maryland Gazette on-line. He was a black boy. Likely a worker on the White farm and terrified of Pinky, he guessed.

When Pinky White went to law school, he flunked out halfway into the curriculum. He hated blacks and was consumed by that hatred that only escalated when he attended George Washington University Law School in mostly black Washington, D.C.

The young man must have lived in a constant state of hatred, Chris thought. Never in his life had Chris experienced such raw hatred. White, aka, Johnson was a genuine throw-back Confederate-era racist.

White joined the Army and became a munitions officer, in charge of distributing artillery and explosives in the Vietnam War.

His hatred of blacks led to a dishonorable discharge amid rumors that he helped plan an explosion that blew up a recreation hall for black soldiers.

It happened on a Sunday morning in Saigon and everyone at the base was attending mandatory religious services required by the platoon. Mysteriously, the building was totaled by an explosion. No casualties reported. No crime was proven, according to press reports. However, White's defiance under oath in an official investigation led to convictions on 12 counts of perjury.

Chris read that Martin and White began operating in King's County years later, and collaborated, but White had changed his business name to Johnson, in honor of the Confederate President Andrew Johnson. He kept his legal middle name Samuel after a member of the proud White family who settled in Southern Maryland in 1688.

He remained business friends with Martin and when Johnson's second tour in the Army ended, Johnny Martin invited him to join his construction company and collaborating loan firm, which was at the time Bernard Madinoff's BOM.

Johnson split off from BOM to form Lifetime Deal Financing, a company that specifically catered to young, rising families that were pouring into the suburbs.

His business from the start scammed blacks and Hispanics.

Meanwhile, LFD also ran a local chain of highly reputable home improvement stores called Mitchim's Home Improvement. Johnson had purchased the family-owned chain solely as a public relations cover. He swindled the Mitchims, one of the most trusted of the founding families of the state, in a phony deal to share profits after the company filed for bankruptcy, but any profits were written off under the LFD umbrella in the 1990s, according to the Maryland Gazette.

Court records revealed that Martin turned on Johnson when Johnson ruined the financial lives of several of Johnny's top employees, who had taken his home loans, all of whom were African Americans.

Benny's voice cut into Chris's concentration on Johnson's history, "What's wrong with you Chris. You look like you lost a relative or something."

Though shaken by what he'd learned about Johnson, he managed, "I'm fine, Benny. Thanks. Just tired; think I'll call it a day." He figured that Benny was worried. As Chris got up to leave, he reflected on the mess he was in, *"Yeah, I might have lost a close relative. Me.*

* * *

Chris took the No. 9 bus home that evening only to find Dickie's brand-new silver Porsche Boxster ragtop parked behind his blue Mazda. Chris's car still had its hood up, in front of his landlord's Don Quantos Puerto Rican Restarante.

There was a note under the Mazda's driver side windshield.

But before Chris could read the note, which he assumed was written by Dickie, the man himself emerged with Juan Garcia from the eatery. Dickie was still wearing his yellow Steelers cap, with the hint of blond stubble around his ears and neck, "Hey Chris, we gotta talk."

Chris read Dickie's face: much more anxious than normal, Chris thought, as he greeted them coolly. "Hey, guys. What's up?"

Juan followed a rather glum Dickie, while holding the remainder of a pork-and plantain-filled mofongo, a Puerto Rican specialty of Don Quantos. He mumbled with a full mouthful. "Hey Chris, how you doin' man. I finally seen Dickie's head, man. We in love, man." His hilarious laughter made him spit a mouthful of goo on the sidewalk then step in it.

Dickie punched him hard in the arm. "Shut up Juan. Be serious," he said and quickly turned to talk to Chris.

"We had to see you, Chris. I mean I did. Juan told me about the trouble at FedEx Field. Does Johnson really have your press credentials?" Dickie asked. "How stupid is that?"

Standing awkwardly on the sidewalk in front of Don Quantos with people going in and out, Chris asked Dickie, "How'd you know where I live?"

"I looked it up. I'm a reporter too you know; was at least. You are getting paranoid or something?"

Dickie paused for an answer that didn't happen, and continued, "Hey, I didn't want to tell you before, but I think you should know something about Johnson...."

Chris cut him off and said, "I think I know quite enough now. You have no idea how bad I feel, Dickie. No thanks." Chris paused to think then said, "Okay, what? That you work for him, too? Don't tell me that," Chris shook his head and began walking into the building and his apartment, hoping to ditch them.

"Not here. Can we come in?" Dickie said. Juan was tagging along like a loyal puppy.

Dickie continued talking while they climbed up the dark, creaky stairwell and inside Chris's apartment, "Hey man, I should have told you this way long ago, but couldn't. You see, for several months, even before I met Vickie, I was helping Johnny Martin gather evidence on Johnson and Madinoff possibly profiling blacks and other minorities."

"I know that. You know I do."

"But you don't know that Martin was outlining federal civil rights violations, most of which Johnson never bothered to know or care about. I gave Boss Martin notarized copies of court records of Johnson's loans that clearly showed consistently far worse terms for black borrowers. The court clerks who signed the paperwork witnessed the notaries. I know those girls."

"I'm sure you do," Chris said.

Dickie said without commenting on Chris's sarcasm, "Johnny Martin had Johnson dead to rights on federal raps and, here it is: He was blackmailing Johnson."

"And, you didn't think I needed to know that?"

Dickie was not deterred, "I'm trying to help. You probably don't know that Johnny even gave Johnson copies of those legal statutes that he thought Johnson was breaking. I saw that file. Martin even listed potential prison time for each of them in the margins."

Right on time, Dickie, thank you very much, thought Chris. "Don't you think it would have been nice to tell me this earlier? I almost got killed. Hope you are happy? First, you destroy my career. And, now my neck. Johnson knows where I work, knows who I am, and probably has figured out what I'm doing and wants me dead. I expect his thugs to visit me at any time. Happy Dickie? Why the hell did I take that ride with you? Tell me, you ass. Why?"

For the first time, young Christopher Gilley was seriously jaded in his quest for the story. He was tired and exhausted.

"Sorry, Chris," Dickie said, showing little compassion. "Martin kept evidence of Johnson's fraudulent loans to King's County blacks and affidavits in his safe at FUC'M tower and it is all destroyed. I don't have that stuff now"

Dickie and Juan left without offering Chris any ideas, of course, to help him, except Juan shouting foolishly loud enough for all Rhodesville to hear, "Hey man, stay outta this guy Johnson's way now, man. He gonna hurt you."

Chris stood stunned. He closed the hood of his hopeless Mazda as the note on the windshield fell at his feet. It was not from Dickie.

The note was on an advertisement for a car repair shop in downtown Rhodesville, one that offered free, 24-hour towing and a telephone number to call for help. On the back, Chris read, "Call us for towing, guaranteed inexpensive repairs for the life of your car." *Boy, that's a joke,* he thought.

Chapter 53: Baited and Hooked

Chris still had the note from the repair garage in his hand as he plopped onto the couch with a beer in his other hand. Next to him on a small table, his telephone screen displayed 10:25 p.m. He made a call despite the late hour. He'd at least leave a voice message, but to his surprise, someone answered.

"Yeah, we can get your car. Yeah, the blue Mazda. I was out there myself today. Mr. Don Quantos said you work at the newspaper, not around much. My buddy says I should leave you a note. Okay, so you want your car fixed? We have a payment plan, no money for the first two months, with a major credit card. You want us to get it now?"

"Now?" The man seemed a bit eager, Chris thought.

* * *

While Chris was busy planning and performing his acting job as a Redskin waiter in Sam Johnson's luxury box, the Inquirer editors were getting agitated with the entire staff. For another solid week, they were still left begging for crumbs on the Vickie Martin murder case.

Fayme Lovelace's follow-up stories appeared with little or no news beyond Post coverage, except some real-life background copy on the principal characters involved, Vickie, Johnny, 5-year old Gigi and Knife Garcia.

Michele LaProbe was getting antsy for what she termed "raw meat," a real account in the story. No one noticed. Annoyed was Michele's prevailing mood those days.

One afternoon, she spotted executive editor Lloyd Sollem chatting in Steve Mothershart's group, sitting on the edge of Bradley's desk.

She casually walked over to visit with him, mentally composing her acerbic lecture as she marched into the conversation.

Steve recognized Michele's stern body language first. Her bulldog-like pace normally preceded a devilish conversational tone. She swung her arms as she marched with her reddish messy hair flying about as Led Zeppelin lead singer Robert Plant would prance toward a concert audience.

Steve knew something was afoot and kept quiet, waiting for the performance to begin.

"Well, here you are, executive editor Lloyd, he who writes frankly and honestly. Getting a few tips from these folks about real reporting from the trenches, in the field, out in the real world, on the waterfront, eh Lloyd?" She was in rare form and seemed to be enjoying it. Without a response, not even a facial reaction from the group, she added harshly, "I thought so."

Steve put his hands behind his head and leaned back to watch the entertainment.

She lowered her voice to a near whisper, "Mr. Johnny 'Boss' Martin—interesting label, huh? —is rotting in his grave. Mrs. Peepshow Martin is marching in high heels no doubt to the gallows, with flashbulbs—do they still use them?—primping herself like Norma Desmond in her final scene in the movie "Sunset Boulevard." Somebody, don't know who, knocked down a little, insignificant building called FUC&M tower, a tower hated by all the locals in central Maryland. It nearly hit the District Courthouse. And now the federal government, could be Homeland damn Security itself, is holding Miss Peeps and who knows why? Not me. Certainly, not you fellows. Are we havin' fun over here? What? Talking Redskins season opener? Have they got a good team this year? Huh? Can't hear you."

Only Lloyd, as her official superior, had the authority to cut it off. "Michele, what are you driving at?" he asked.

Her sarcasm was now razor sharp. She replied in a loud, high pitch, "Driving? Who's driving? I'm just coming over to talk some football with the guys."

Steve couldn't help but laugh, though he knew the hammer was about to fall on somebody, hopefully not him.

Finally, Michele threw a switch and the newsroom was suddenly cold.

She was livid. "Lloyd, I want you to get some goddamn news out of that Victoria Martin murder trial if it takes writing it with the point of Fayme's pretty little nose. She's sat in there at that trial for three days and has gotten squat. Nothing new. What possessed you to leave her alone in there? She needs you, man."

Lloyd muttered something incoherent, glancing from Michele to cute Fayme sitting in a short plaid skirt at her desk across the newsroom, facing him, bare legs crossed. (She had very pretty legs.) His heart skipped a beat.

Michele kept barking. "She's gathering up her make-up and checking her manicure right now. Before she finishes sharpening her three dozen favorite numbers 2s, go tell her you'll be with her today at the courthouse, OKAY?"

Lloyd looked back at Michele, concealing his wry smile, though he was dutifully ready to obey.

She continued, "And for God's sake, show her some court reporting skill before I put Chris back on this and get some real reporting on this story again. Poor kid, look at him. Pathetic. Look what we've done to Chris. Okay, we don't do investigative stuff. But, we can at least show that boy that we can do some reporting, too."

Chris was smirking and secretly hoping Fayme would fail again. Michele would carry out her threat and put a good reporter back on the Martin story—him.

Lloyd appeared embarrassed. Yet, he was silent until he uttered softly, "Okay, fine." Pleased to leave the group, he headed over to Fayme's desk. She wasn't looking, likely had heard none of Michele's outburst.

"God, the man's dense," Michele said. "Hell, of a writer, even if he dresses like an undertaker around here. Brrrrr, I feel a chill. Now, Chris, "I see you frowning again. I am sorry we can't let you do this, but Steve promised me you will have your day, young man. I am now exiting the stage, gentlemen, as thousands cheer." She threw her arms up in the gratuitous triumph of an opera diva exiting stage left.

Steve, Benny and Chris had a good laugh.

Benny uttered softly, "And it's whispered that soon, if we all call the tune, then the piper will lead us to reason."

Steve matched him with, "Ha ha. And as we wind on down the road, our shadows taller than our soul, there walks a lady we all know."

"Huh?" Chris asked.

"Stairway," cracked Benny, "Zeppelin. Let's cool it shall we, Steve?"

"Good idea. Check out Mr. Solem there," Steve said.

Lloyd seemed delighted with his 'assignment,' as such, from the woman who worked for him. He was going to spend 'intimate' time with Fayme. It was she who cranked his motor around that place, not drab newspaper editing.

At the trial at District Court in Loweville, Lloyd was to keep Fayme focused and asking all the right questions. She needed some top journalistic guidance in such a big case and Lloyd was the one who could provide it.

Chapter 54: Nowhere List

August 15 afternoon

Chris seemed blessed with finding the phantom "inexpensive" car repair guys who drove by and happened to see his Mazda sitting lame, he figured. He should have been suspicious. All he had was a phone number until Benny drove him by the place one day to see if the Mazda was parked there.

But it was not a timely repair. After calling several times for several days, Chris got a phone call from someone he assumed was a car mechanic. Repairs, the caller said, would take a few more days because parts must be ordered. He offered Chris a loaner.

At 5:30 p.m. Benny dropped Chris off at the repair shop to pick up the loaner.

The repair shop was small, wedged between two buildings just off Rhodesville Pike, the main commercial strip in the busy suburban town.

A man named Poko who wore remarkably greaseless, pressed mechanics overalls, was already walking out, smiling, "Hello Mr. Gilley, how you do."

Chris questioned why the repair would take so long, but he didn't understand Poko's answer in broken English. Chris desperately needed wheels.

Mr. Poko said, "I let you use my car. I ride with my brother. He is bringing it around for you. You got credit card?" To drive off with the lender, he had to have Poko record his credit card. "Sure, here," Chris said handing his Visa card to the pressed and starched mechanic.

As the loaner car turned the corner of the garage, Chris was stunned. "That's all you've got?" Chris asked when he saw the new silver Lexus LS 430 four-door sedan.

"You don't like?"

"Yeah, but this must be a $50 grand car. You sure you want to trust a complete stranger with...?"

"Actually, it is a $70 grand Lexus. But you're not a stranger, Mr. Gilley. No, I got your credit card number and address and I know where you work. You from West Virginia, right?"

That was frightening to Chris. "How do you know that?"

"I am so sorry. I looked in the Mazda glove box."

"And..."

"You are registered in West Virginia and relatives owned the car before you, right?"

This man was too familiar, Chris thought.

Against his better judgment, Chris agreed to take the Lexus. He was desperate for wheels. He would just keep it away from the Inquirer's parking lot.

* * *

Chris stayed at Amy's that night.

The next morning, he called Bradley to ask if he could work from home on the Gaithersburg Science City story, considering that the city council's vote was coming up Tuesday. He was surprised when Benny said "of course," without hesitation.

Benny knew that 'home' meant the girlfriend's house because Chris had no computer at his apartment. Benny and Steve had talked about Chris being settled in with a girlfriend, that the relationship might be good for their young prodigy and good for them in the long run, though neither would ever admit to being attached to the kid personally.

As Amy left for her job at the hospital, she gave her boyfriend sitting at the kitchen table some last minute instructions, "Hon, I left a list of a few things I need at Safeway. Can you be a dear and run over there at your break?" she said, backing out the door without waiting for an answer.

"I'm on deadline, Amy. You know I can't do that."

"I don't know that. In fact, I don't know anything about your whereabouts these days. You don't tell me about your stories lately either."

"Amy, please."

"Hey, I'm letting you stay. You should be a little nicer. Where were you last evening when you came home sweaty and smelling of beer and cigarettes anyway?"

"No place. Must be from that loaner."

"Chris, that is another thing. Where did you get that car? Are you holding something out on me? I thought you were a poor struggling reporter?"

"I told you that too. The Mazda, our Porsche, remember? is in the shop. A friend lent me his car. He's a rich guy I know?"

Chris dropped his face to the kitchen table in disgust. He realized that his lies were getting worse, even to his girlfriend, in addition to all his other indiscretions along his foolish drive to write a phantom story.

Chris also hadn't shared with Amy anything about his harrowing FedEx Field experience because he was conscious of not showing his high anxiety.

He stayed calm. Things had been cooling between them. They weren't seeing each other as much and the physical comfort from Amy was not as satisfying. She had become the kind of a smothering-mothering lover/friend that Chris did not want. He wanted the cute redhead with the ponytail at the Congressional Lounge back.

She stood in the doorway staring at him, perhaps wondering about his thoughts, why he seemed to have changed.

He wanted to tell her about the FedEx Field experience but knew he shouldn't. She might have become overbearing, he calculated. So, he avoided encouraging her and said instead, "Okay I can try to get out to the store later."

She exited with, "That is the least you can do. Be careful with my desktop, Chris. Don't clutter the place up with your writing too." And she was off, as Chris slouched and tossed the cell phone lightly on the table, exasperated with her bitchy tone.

He knew by then that Amy was a serious alcoholic. He was still fond of her, but he had learned that she came from a family of alcoholics. She was drinking more and more as their relationship progressed.

In bed, she had become the aggressor. He was not comfortable with the change.

Amy had begun to take more and more liberties with Chris's time and thoughts, as she tried desperately to tie his freedom down as he was less attentive. Perhaps loving Chris was more of a crutch than was the booze.

He thought, *jeez, this is getting bad.* He was torn. Having a girlfriend living within his reporting beat was a super situation but, he thought, *Damn it. I can't trust her with anything about my secret coverage of the Martin murder and FUC'M tower bombing. She works at the county hospital.*

He sat up straight and said to himself, "No, this won't do. I might leave something on her computer drive. Shit. This sucks." He walked away from the computer.

He realized the girlfriend tension was far more serious than hating Amy's controlling, mothering attitude. One mom was enough.

After she left, Chris stayed only a couple of hours and he made sure to save his writing on a floppy disk, though he was only researching mortgage scams on the web unrelated to Johnson for a new story.

His mind soon filled with thoughts of Johnson's rage and the murder story he may never get to write now. He saved the mortgage research notes on the disk and slipped the disk out of the computer and into his pocket.

With an empty feeling, sitting alone in Amy's apartment, he again started to wonder if he'd been stupid about his affair with Amy, but then he focused on his monstrous stupidity of trying to unravel his story, now infested with a cadre of unsavory characters.

He was compelled to write down a list of loose ends, more like troubling facts really, on one of his long reporters' notebooks. Maybe it would help him conceptualized some kind of pattern to help him.

He read it out loud:

- "Mad bomber Sam Johnson is likely behind the explosion that brought down the FUC'M tower.
- Racist maniac.
- Blew up U.S. things in Vietnam.
- Ran munitions for the Army.
- Johnny Martin probably shot with Victoria's gun.
- Her prints were fresh on the gun.
- Vickie likely to be convicted of his murder.
- Dickie afraid of Johnson; too eager to pin crimes on Madinoff.
- Before his murder, Johnny Martin was upset, say Vickie and Garcia.

- Loan predators ruining Martin's black employees.
- Loan sharks ruined whole neighborhoods.
- Martin built homes for good, law-abiding, young black and Latino couples.
- Martin's earlier buildings were slipshod.
- Martin was blackmailing the mortgage guys.
- Lenders met with Martin at the hotel weekend before bombing.
- Madinoff and his BOM could be Dickie's decoy.
- No racial profiling in BOM records so far.
- Madinoff was a greedy oaf.
- Madinoff voted Johnson off his board years ago.
- Johnson likely is my man! Or, somebody at his company.
- Johnson's mad as hell with me; would like me dead. Gotta keep moving, get to the bottom of this--FAST. It's my fatal deadline."

Study of the list revealed no new patterns to help Chris solve the crimes. He flipped the notebook closed.

After writing it all down and reading it several times, still unable to come up with a new plan, Chris felt insanely afraid. He lost all sense of reality for a few moments.

He flipped on Amy's computer again.

Minutes passed while he stared at the blank computer screen waiting for Amy's slow dial-up modem to fire up for the Internet.

He talked with the screen as if his fuzzy reflection was the last friend he could trust, "It all seemed so easy at first. I'd get the story, Michele would forgive me. I'd be the hero. How dumb. If I'd only stayed out of it. I've compromised all I was taught to respect as a reporter. I'm done.

"No, I had to try to get to the bottom of this story; just should have been more careful ..."

After a long, annoying flat tone of static, Amy's computer finally connected to the Inquirer's home page. He was shocked by the story that appeared. He spoke to the screen again, "Well, it's about time they reported something. Nice going, Lloyd."

Federal Probe of Racist Lending Links to Murder Case
by Lloyd Sollem and Fayme Lovelace, staff reporters

Washington, D.C., Aug 17—The U.S. Justice Department is closing a major investigation of lending practices of local mortgage brokers suspected of discriminating against minority borrowers, according to the Maryland Real Estate Association.

The MREA has turned over emails and mortgage records to federal officials as well as to the King's County police detectives who are investigating the murder of real estate developer Johnny "Boss" Martin and the bombing of the First Union Credit & Mortgage building. Martin's JDR Builders, Inc. owned the FUC&M.

Arrests are imminent in the bombing probe, said Sheriff Barney Standard this morning at a press conference in the 4th District Courthouse. The 13-floor FUC&M office tower, directly across Gov. Scruppels Blvd. from the courthouse, was destroyed by a bomb on May 14. Seven people died and more than 50 were injured seriously.

Only two months before the bombing the Federal Bureau of Investigation set up a small, covert operation inside the FUC&M tower, according to King's County records. The Inquirer has learned from JDR employees that Martin informed the FBI of blatant civil rights violations by two lenders, Samuel Johnson and Bernard Madinoff.

Martin's ties to Johnson, now CEO of Lifetime Deal Financing, Corp. (LDF), *date back to the 1980s when they were both students at George Washington University Law School. Martin and Madinoff, CEO of Best Opportunity Mortgage, Corp., have done business together since 1995. Both maintained their company headquarters at the destroyed FUC&M tower.*

According to sources at the Sheriff's department and confirmed by JDR employees, the U.S. Department of Justice is going after one, and perhaps both, lenders for seeking and granting minorities access to home loans that were beyond their means of payment and not to non-minority home buyers.

The justice department also found documents showing that Maryland companies have targeted minorities for mortgages with loose underwriting standards or high interest rates that forced minority applicants into an unprecedented number of foreclosures. Court records show that both LDF and BOM now own most of the foreclosed homes in King's County. Martin's company owns many unfinished and unsold units.

Lloyd was finally making headway on the story, while Chris had been getting beat up working undercover.

Lloyd, an executive level reporter, and Lloyd's heartthrob Fayme, were suddenly doing some good reporting. But the story was also inadvertently helping to dig Chris Gilley's professional grave.

Johnson is sure to see this, he thought.

* * *

Chris took the old reliable No. 9 bus to the paper early the next day, leaving the loaner Lexus parked at his apartment hidden behind the restaurant.

When he got to his desk, his phone light was blinking indicating a message from the previous day. He anxiously picked up the receiver, dropped it, and then held it with both hands to hear, "Gilley, this is Sam Johnson. I am kindly reminding you that if you print so much as one word of what you might have heard at my skybox party, you won't live to regret it. That's all. I mean that. Have a nice day."

Chapter 56: Featherweight KO

Same day, Thursday, August 23, noon

Chris then switched on his PC.

"Oh, my God," he said and quickly hid his head behind his computer screen.

It was the Inquirer's home page. The terror Chris was feeling from hearing Johnson on the phone the previous day intensified ten times over. He was shaking.

He missed putting his phone back on its receiver and it fell on the floor next to his desk. Cold sweat formed on his brow as he read the headline on the home page:

Johnson Firm Tops in Foreclosures, Seeking New Backers
by Fayme Lovelace, staff reporter

"I'm dead. This is not happening. I thought Michele was firing that featherweight," he whispered to himself.

His phone rang.

It was Johnson screaming, "Gilley? What part of my message yesterday didn't you understand? You are in a serious shit hole, my friend. Let me make myself clear. Don't you dare even think of any more stories on me or my company for eternity? Get it, boy? And, Mr. Gilley?"

"Yes?"

"Please don't scratch my Lexus. My man Poko tells me you like my automobile more than your old clunker you got from your generous big brother in Glasgow. We certainly don't want Mr. Chuck Bear to know about our deal, do we? "

"Wha … what deal is that?" Chris knew exactly what Johnson meant, but his reporter instincts told him to sit back and listen. And then, he was even more terrified.

"You know. You get the car. I get no coverage. *Now* do you understand? That's the way a good newspaper reporter works, right? Gifts for stories. In this case, a gift for no stories. And, you signed for the car on your Visa card, boy. Quite a nice expensive bribe for a hillbilly fuck up, so-called journalist. So, keep your nose clean, boy, you can keep the car and still have a newspaper career to look forward to. Goodbye, Mr. Gilley. I hope this is the last time we talk, got it? Give my regards to the big guy Chucky."

Chris was sitting in a pool of his sweat. At his wits end, he gazed out across the entire newsroom, a scene he may not be seeing much longer, his dreams, his vision to be a great reporter, gone.

He saw heads ducking who had been listening to Chris's nervous voice on the phone.

He considered his precious few options: Should he save that message, the first threat, a threat that is recorded on his phone? Should he confess that he'd been tricked into a bribe, a Lexus for silence? Who would he tell? How to explain things to them without blowing his cover that he was defying all knowing Michele and investigating the Martin/FUC'M tower affair on his own?

His blank stare across the newsroom turned to desperate searching for anyone he could consult. He needed a friend. The starkly lit news arena was filled at that hour with a handful of reporters, all clicking away at their computers. They all had a deadline to meet.

I wish I could trust somebody to put this story together before I'm killed. He's going to get me. I really am dead this time.

Chris glanced at the monster clock on the wall. He heard it ticking louder and louder. It was actually electric and emitted no sound. That was its raison d'etre: the deadline monster that sneaks up and gets you before you've finished your story.

11:48 a.m. Thursday, deadline day.

Oh, God, I'm fucked here, too. Got to get working.

He needed to crank notes from three inane interviews, assigned to him by Benny himself, into news copy before 3:30 p.m., or feel the brunt of Steve Mothershart's impatience. Steve wouldn't be so conciliatory this time because lately, their boy's stories had been too short and slow to develop into solid, compelling copy. He wasn't the golden boy anymore, he thought. *Is all this worth losing my job over? For a story with no ending, no deadline and no common thread, even after three months? If I quit, I still have my health and Johnson won't be looking for me. Yes, that's what I'll do, slip away. No. Can't. I owe these people. Oh God, if only I'd just turned down that joyride with Dickie*

Randim that day...Bastard set me up. The same thought had haunted him all summer.

"Aren't you going to get that?" asked Steve. Chris awoke from his daydream and convinced himself to grab the phone like a professional, not a nervous Nellie. It was another sexy woman's voice, "Hello, Dickie?"

Oh God, not this again. Chris was on edge. Not another sexy phone call. This was how his trouble began in May.

"Dickie, this is Denise, er, Joy, from Tickle My Pickle."

"No, no, no, this is definitely not Dickie!" Chris answered, much louder than he intended. Melissa and her girls snapped to attention by the sound of his voice. They'd never heard Chris raise his voice in the newsroom.

"This is Christopher Gilley. I have Richard Randim's old number. I am on deadline but maybe if you tell me what you want," he tried to make the call sound like there was a stranger on the line. He refused to picture the image of lovely Denise in his mind, especially the naked one in his lap at the club.

Denise spoke quickly, perhaps put off a bit by Chris's formal tone, but played along. After all, she'd already had one experience with the wacky reporters at the Inquirer. She told Chris that Madinoff hired her back, for both her clerk and stripper duties. And after all, she said, lots of customers were asking where she was, obviously missing her. Denise explained to Madinoff that she had been trying to protect him from the FBI agents who had been there looking for him. So, she thought she could get advice from Dickie and the rest of the newspaper guys.

Chris was suddenly intrigued. "FBI? What FBI? You mean THE FBI!" he asked incredulously. Ears again turned in his direction and tuned in. Melissa, for one, was on high radar.

Denise said Madinoff had confided to her that the government calls she had been getting were probably okay and that he didn't think the federal guys were after him personally, but maybe some or one of his associates. She said that Madinoff was tipping off the FBI on his own, after he inadvertently told a stripper hooker friend about Johnson.

She said that in the spring, Madinoff met the agents touring his building in the FUC&M tower and got them drunk at a club. He could always spot a law officer. The stripper he told about Johnson, in turn, told a customer with deep pockets for throwing tips, Denise said was an agent for the agency. As a result, the FBI opened an office at the FUC'M tower directly above Lifetime Deal Financing, Corp. Denise said that same stripper also called to warn Dickie, who knew of the FBI interest somehow too.

Chris listened carefully. He deduced that Denise saw Madinoff as a buffoon, but smart enough in his trade to know LFD was being squeezed by the housing and construction crash. She said Madinoff had nothing but disdain for Johnson.

"Thanks for calling. I'll relay your information to Mr. Randim," he said loudly to end the call.

Chris got up from his chair and headed to the conference room to make some calls in private.

Steve said to Benny, "Something's up with that boy."

Benny, head buried in deadline madness, muttered, "Yeah, I know."

Chapter 57: Liza III

For the first time, the young maverick reporter was certain he would never have his big moment at the Inquirer. He would no longer see the time when he would heroically put the whole story on Michele's desk exposing in one fell swoop the murderer, bomber, and character of the perpetrators. He would no longer have that chance to serve the community, save his career and perhaps Vickie's conviction. Johnson was surely going to hurt him, at best.

Chris desperately needed help to scratch and claw out of the fix he was in. Resigned to failure, he still feared his life.

In a lame moment, he thought to turn to Dickie, since he was involved up to his shaved head now too. When he called and heard Dickie whine and whimper on the phone, Chris told him Denise had called. Maybe he would be interested. He didn't tell Dickie what she said about the FBI, just that she was back with Madinoff.

"Madinoff is in the notebook I gave you, Chris because he was a good source of local development deals," Dickie admitted. "You are using my source book, right?"

"Oh, yeah, more than you'd ever think, Dickie," said Chris quickly, wishing he'd stuck with the fake notebook instead of the stolen one.

He got nowhere with Dickie. The coward on the other end of the phone line acted like he'd just like to pull the covers over his head and hide.

Chris then thought maybe Benny would help.

Even as tight as he was with his editor Benny Bradley, Chris couldn't tell him about Johnson's threats and the trouble he was in. He just didn't know how the edgy Benny Bradley, the newspaper's most ethical journalist, would react, despite his fondness for Chris. How could Benny possibly rationalize Chris using Johnson's Lexus? *He couldn't*, Chris then realized.

A familiar, comforting light flickered into Chris's foggy brain, *Maybe I'll call Liza, just to feel better*, he thought.

He had left a voice message for Liza two weeks earlier to see if she could find time to look into her company's records for anything on Samuel Johnson, aka, Samuel "Pinky" White, and Bernard Madinoff. With all that had happened since Chris had nearly forgotten that Liza hadn't returned his telephone call. He had an excuse to call.

This time, he was in luck. Liza answered her phone.

He was tempted to spill his misadventures immediately but didn't want to ruin her day by dragging her back into his dilemma. *Maybe Liza would be sympathetic,* he thought. No, instead, he imagined she may have followed up his earlier message with getting some dope on Johnson. He'd start there.

"Oh, Chris, I'm sorry," she said apologetically. "I've been so busy with this new job. It's great, but I haven't had time to call you. But I have something I need to show you. Can you get over here sometime?"

Liza told him she had gathered some background on Lifetime Deal Financing and Best Opportunity Mortgage concerning the Port America development. "You know those creepos in the FUC'M tower," she began. "They were bidding on financing a huge mixed-use condominium project at Port America. Bidders needed to file background checks because the project was federally subsidized for some affordable housing in the project.

"These creepos probably thought the indentured servants would huddle up in the affordables. You don't know the half of what these guys are about, Chris. They are scum. Can you come today about 6:30? That's when my boss usually has gone home and I can fill you in on the whole thing. It's Thursday and your deadlines are over today, right?"

Chris felt his body return to an upright position and his head lighten. As he agreed to drive over to see her at her workplace, he steeled himself against confessing anything to Liza about what he already knew about her 'half-of-what-these-guys-are-about' comment. He told himself, *Listen fool, don't get her involved again. She's the best human being you know in this town. Keep her out of this.*

Juices flowing again, he made a mad dash to file his stories before his ordinary deadlines, checking the monster clock to finish in enough time for fact checking.

3:39 p.m. Time enough.

For the entire afternoon, though, still burning in the back of his mind, there lingered his real deadline—finding a way of ridding himself of Sam Johnson. *My fatal deadline*, he thought, over and over.

Chapter 58: Desperation

The damn Lexis trick haunted him.

For several days after he knew Johnson had set him up, Chris would not drive it again, no matter how long the Mazda took to get fixed if it was being repaired at all, that is. But, he needed a car to see his pal Liza.

Desperately exhausted from late nights, long hours and extreme tension, Chris still had not lost his curiosity to learn the truth about the crimes he failed to solve. It left him no choice but to check out what Liza had for him. He thought he'd simply turn over the information to Lloyd and say Liza thought the paper should know.

Reluctantly, and full of guilt, Chris drove Johnson's Lexus into the maze of concrete canyons along the southwest arch of the circling Washington Beltway. From Rhodesville, he headed south toward the Port America resort on the shores of the Potomac River.

Every gangster car chase he'd ever seen in the movies flashed before him. *Are they following me? Do the cops know this car? Suppose it's rigged with a bomb?* The fear seemed to paralyze his spine. Images of gangster actors George Raft, Al Capone and James Cagney appeared in the windshield reflection. Only his arms worked to steer the Lexus, as his hands shook. He'd change his grip on the leather-covered steering wheel. His wrists pulsated with nerves.

He popped in a CD.

Blues guitar extraordinaire Stevie Ray Vaughn, laying down a heavy number, could be the right tonic, he thought, for the nerves.

His mind was a jumble of images, from the string of his messy failures to Benny's and Steve's puzzled looks at him, to the skybox of racist throwbacks to the old South. It was all too surreal while driving in absolute comfort and feeling the incredible power of the finest motor vehicle he'd ever driven.

Instead of achieving his goal of gaining clarity after weeks of investigating, he was in a fog of confusion and was disappointed with himself. There was the revealing story by the fat gay kid in the bar, which he didn't understand at first. He had taken full advantage of sweet Amy. He'd put Liza at risk in her career. He had smoked pot with hoodlums to no avail, stole BOM finance records putting family friend Denise in harm's way, lied to Redskin Will Call for Dickie's ticket to Sam Johnson's luxury suite, faked being a waiter to spy on Sam Johnson's private party, lied to everyone at FedEx Field, took money from Juan Garcia and Amy's brother, even justified driving a bribery vehicle to somehow salvage the story when prospects seemed dark and desperate.

During the summer, he'd lost 20 pounds.

And still, he would pursue more evidence, perhaps at Liza's expense? He believed that would be the end of her and she would be rid of him. He would keep her out of it.

God, I can't believe I've done all those bad things, and for what? he thought. *All that effort just so I can file lousy copy to Steve and Benny to keep my job. I'll likely lose it anyway.*

He felt bad mostly because he had sacrificed his principles, his reporting ethics. *Why go see Liza at all?* he wondered. *I'm a failure. Ma was right; I'm wasting my life in a dying profession.*

Chris imagined that the airtight, silent Lexus was a coffin. It symbolized the demise of his career, a short, too short and foolishly idealistic career, marred with enough ethical violations to get him blacklisted for every outlet in the industry, he imagined. He had been on the job, his first reporter job, his dream, for only eight months.

The Stevie Ray Vaughn CD did ease his mind some. It was a gift from Knife. "Here man, this will make you feel better for yourself, okay?" he remembered Knife saying. Until that drive down to Port America on the Potomac River shoreline to talk with Liza, Chris hadn't understood Knife's comment. Knife was right, the music kept him going.

He drove on in heavy Beltway traffic.

Liza, ah Liza. She was a bright spot in his brief journalistic adventure in the D.C. Metro area. Chris reflected how he and Liza became friends on his first day in Capitol Hill when they met in the Dirksen Senate Office Building cafeteria. The soulful blues of Stevie Ray made him long for those innocent days. Why she took an interest in him, he never understood. But he was grateful still.

Chris's eyes shut. His shoulders relaxed. He dozed off.

He woke with the riveting sound of the side warning strip of the highway. He slammed his foot to the brakes and stopped on the shoulder. "Oh, my God, I feel so weak," he said to himself. He hadn't eaten since lunchtime the previous day. "Maybe I should just get out and leave the Lexis here."

He drove on instead.

Stevie Ray changed pace. His rhythmic guitar kicked his band into a fast boogie tune.

Chris got a little excited to see the glow of the massive Port America searchlights against the darkening daylight in the east. He imagined he was driving to the music hall where Vaughn might have recorded the CD before a live audience. That was more fun than thinking about going to the resort on the Potomac to discuss his possible killer, Johnson, or Madinoff, for that matter. They both hated him.

On the final concrete ramp that led to Port America, crossing back over the eight lanes and three 2-lane ramps of the Beltway, Chris caught his first glimpse of the gleaming island of urban life against a backdrop of wooded hills. At that time of the evening, Port America loomed like the Emerald City in the "Wizard of Oz.". It was prosperous King's County's crown jewel. The Nation's Capital resort down the river from Washington, D.C. was a dazzling display of multicolored, flickering lights that illuminated towering hotels and office buildings.

He couldn't believe the smart configuration of real estate development that was surrounded by black green hills of suburbia and the gray waters of the nation's most notable river with Washington and L'Enfant's Potomac River at midstream.

As he drove the Lexus slowly into the five-lane veranda at the resort's primary accommodation, the Peabody Hotel, five valet parking attendants rushed to be the first to take the keys to his luxurious Lexus in exchange for a handsome tip. "No thanks. I'm waiting for someone," Chris said.

"Take your time, sir, and if you can pull the car into the far lane until your guest arrives, please? Thank you, sir. Have a nice evening and come again to the Peabody Resort and Conference Hotel, sir."

Before he could put the car in drive, he made out the figure of lively Liza hurrying out of the massive glass doors of the hotel.

"That's okay, Rodney. He's with me. He can park in Mr. Brando's space. Here," she said to the attendants, quickly waving a hangtag parking permit.

She was wearing a smart, cream-colored suit and silk blouse that coordinated with her white high heels. Chris saw she was also wearing impressive yet tasteful gold necklaces and a matching bracelet on her right wrist. Liza is left handed, he recalled. He had never seen his friend look so glamorous. He was extremely proud of her. She wore her wavy black hair pulled back off her face so it fell neatly down her back.

Liza waved for him to bring the car along as she walked slowly now only 50 feet with the car to the edge of the veranda. She stopped at the second of five "Peabody executive--reserved" spaces and waited for Chris to back in.

Chris was deeply aware of how he felt, very blue and hurting, and didn't want Liza to detect his sour mood or see how weakened he'd become. That was fixed quickly. He was delighted to see Liza's radiant smile again. Even in the evening driveway lights, he could see that Liza was tanned and happy.

She said, "Well, what do you think of my new digs?" Without waiting for an answer, she was wowed, noticing the top-of-the-line Lexus. "Hey, who'd you steal that car from, Chris? Here, hang this on the rear mirror inside. Hey, you don't look so good," she managed to say all that while rotating on her right heel to face him as Chris pulled his long frame out of the car. Liza's words kept spilling out. She always tossed out multiple thoughts at once when she was excited.

"You don't. I mean...you look like this job suits you, Liza. Good to see you and thanks for inviting me," Chris said.

"Hey, stupid, don't be so formal. It's me, Liza, Capitol Hill co-conspirator and confidant. And, Chris? Did you hear me? Hey, the car? What's with the car?"

"It's a loaner. The Mazda's in the body shop again."

"Oh, sure. What ya do, hold up a Lexus dealer?" She seemed to notice Chris was not laughing with her.

"They were all out, so the repair guy lent me his car. It's a year old; he said he was now driving a new one. Pretty nice, huh?" He wanted to get off the subject of Johnson's bribery car quickly. The thought crossed his mind to admit part of the sad tale, but no, she might not understand the dire straits he has been swimming in since they last saw each other. All he was thinking was how glad he was to be safe with Liza. She, whom he could trust.

"And, oh yeah, the Mazda's in the shop."

"Chris, you said that. This car ... this car is better than what my boss drives, Mr. Brando. It's fab, but it's not you."

They were still standing alone at the end of the veranda. He wished she would stop talking about the car. "It's the only car I could borrow to get down here, okay?" He slipped up with a cross tone.

In that flash of discontent on Chris's face, Liza might have seen the desperate and confused demeanor of her friend. She furrowed her brow a little and then let go of the subject of the car, "Oh, well, if you rented this okay, I am most impressed. Let's go inside. I've got some things to show you."

Unwittingly, Liza's words threw a protective cloak over Chris's troubles for a few minutes. He was not yet fully aware that he was coming apart at the seams. His emotions were in shreds. He felt tight, yet in denial that Sam Johnson could put a hit on him at any time.

He let her guide the way, as he would with his older sisters. He walked behind her into the vast Peabody lobby. Marble floors, marble walls. Everywhere marble. They stopped talking as they made their way through a majestic lobby.

Chris held his view fast to the shrinking image of Liza's cream-colored suit as he treated himself to glances at the extraordinary opulence of the Peabody. The floor was a pattern of four-foot squares of white marbled tiles striped in gold and black. It reminded Chris of the soft, striped marble-colored candy strips he used to enjoy at his brother's Little League games in West Virginia. None of the other kids liked that marbled candy. The other kids preferred Sugar Babies and Sugar Daddies.

Chris fell further behind Liza. He had never been in such a palatial setting. His mind drifted as his legs weakened with the brisk walk. The huge sparkling chandeliers proclaimed wealth. He was dazzled and felt more insecure.

Meanwhile, the shadowy cream-colored figure of his friend got farther and farther ahead of him in the belly of the luxurious hotel.

He saw Liza's fuzzy image swing to the left across the plush red carpet to the center of the lobby, stopping only by the hotel desk that Chris estimated to be 100 feet long. Weak from worrying instead of eating, Chris was getting dizzy as the lavish display of lights and colors was blurring in his vision.

He gathered up some energy and caught up to Liza at a glass-enclosed elevator.

"Like this place?" she said while poking him in the ribs. She frowned again seeing Chris's face pinched in with worry. "Hey cheer up," she added. "You ain't seen nothin' yet, boyeee," She laughed by herself again.

The elevator took them one floor down and deposited them into an atrium the size of an airplane hangar. The atrium was stitched together with a huge superstructure of white crisscrossing, reinforcing metal beams of a gigantic 7-story space of glass and steel. He was again lagging behind Liza. Looking up, spinning his head around, Chris nearly fainted. He was becoming very nauseous.

He continued to lag behind Liza along a brick, tree-lined path of the atrium. It could have been the set of a Grace Kelly romantic movie filmed by Universal Studios in the 1950s.

He was awestruck. The scenes in the hotel, which were astounding, also slammed home his profound sense of guilt and regret that he might have come there to once again enlist his most trusted friend into his misadventures, even by just sharing contract documents, as she had promised. He had no intention of exposing her to the truth of his investigation, beyond what she knew about Johnson and Madinoff's latest financial and personal lives. He was thinking, *This was wrong. She has moved on to bigger and better things. This is wrong, wrong, wrong.*

He stopped to catch his breath, pondering, while Liza kept walking way ahead, never glancing back for him. He heard music and people partying outside of a double set of side doors. Now was the time to abandon the visit, kick open those doors, and disappear before she knew it. *I'll let her go down that hallway to the convention side of the hotel, then make a quick exit. I'll explain somehow later.*

Chris was becoming so weak he was delirious from all the walking. Since Johnson's threats, his appetite was gone. Chris hardly knew his own confusing thoughts: *Liza won't be happy with me continuing this Martin murder craziness. No oh hell, what am I doing here? She'll scold me again for my stupid principles.*

Hell, with the story. Leave her out. Out. Got to go. She'll get things out of me; I know her too well. This place ... great for Liza. She's in her element now. I've got to beat it.

He leaned against a vine-covered pillar. He petted the leaves. *Ugh, plastic.* And then, he realized too late he was tripping out on the fake vegetation. He felt foolish, looked to see if anyone saw his stupidity, and focused again on the double doors to outside. He took a step to leave through the doors.

But, Liza retreated to look for him. For a minute, she didn't see Chris.

Chris spotted her first and changed his mind again. *But, I do miss sharing things with her. She's always good to me and this can't hurt her. She's tougher than I'll ever be.*

"Chris, you coming?" she asked.

"Yeah, just looking around at this amazing place."

She gave him a self-satisfied smile and flipped a lock of her hair back that had come loose. "I'll wait at the elevator, 'kay?"

He didn't know how much Liza had missed his friendship, too, and was very proud to show him her new daytime digs. She seemed to dance around a marble wall at a corner and disappear among the hotel's conference and convention center offices.

Chris felt very faint and wobbly. He made it through a large wooden door that separated the glow of warm yellow lighting of the hotel and the starkness of blue fluorescents common to a convention hall. The contrast was blinding.

Once in the convention side, austere hallways were leading to open doors to identical meeting rooms and coffee islands. The floor was carpeted in red, white and blue stripes, dotted with gold fleur-de-lis. Though the building was not yet three years old the carpet was already stained from spilled coffee and mixed drinks left by careless conventioneers. It bothered him and he began to study the stains without realizing it. His mind was on pause. He was too weary to think clearly.

His eyes involuntarily followed the stripes in the floor instead of where Liza had just walked. Before he knew it, he was lost in a childish game watching the stripes twisting and wrapping around themselves. The stripes made Chris dizzy. He then saw them waving and twisting with life.

He was hallucinating terribly and fell. He felt the stripes curving and spinning around and over him, and then the room itself was wavy. The stripes snaked up his back and shoulders as living entanglements around his neck and arms as he collapsed to the floor. He twisted to pull the snakes from his neck. But it was only in his mind.

He was unconscious.

When he opened his eyes again he was on the floor, dizzied and out of breath. *I know I'm nuts now. Snakes? God, these stripes don't even look like snakes,* he thought.

Liza ran back to him and slid down to the floor with him. "Chris, Chris! What happened? Was it this cheap carpet? It's buckling all over. I've got to talk to maintenance." She was on her knees, close to Chris, cradling his head. His face was ghostly white. She pulled his head to her chest and stroked his brow. She felt him perspiring.

"I'm sorry, Liza. I shouldn't have come. Now you'll get that nice white suit dirty."

"Oh, this ol' thing. Got it this morning at Good Will. It's just an ol' rag," she said feigning laughter as she bent to pull him up by one arm and stood hands on hips. They both laughed at her little show of strength as he briefly pulled her shoulder into him for a hug, then pushed her away just as quickly.

Soon they were at the elevator at the center of the business convention hall lobby.

"My office is in the management suite, top floor."

"Of course, it is," Chris said, managing a smile.

"I think you must have fainted, Chris. You are so pale. When did you eat last?"

Besides coffee at the newsroom, he couldn't recall eating since a Pop-Tart at his desk at noon the previous day. "Who knows? Not been eating much, Liza. Don't worry about me. Hey, look at this place. You must be doin' great here, huh?"

When they stepped onto the elevator, Liza stared at Chris for a prolonged moment. His downtrodden face might have told Liza that her friend was in deep trouble. He noticed her alarmed expression and reminded himself mentally that she would not want to know what troubled him. He'd never seen such a worried look on Liza's face.

"Chris, you got a buck?" She took a dollar from him and bought a Coke from the hallway vending machine. "Here, I'll pay you back later, kay? My money's in my purse in the office." Liza was too much the fashion bug to wear bulky pockets that would mask her nice figure. "Drink this, all of it. You look bad, man. You scare me."

Chris's penchant to repel such mothering led him to rib his good friend, "Did you really hold me that close on the floor? Shame on you, lady."

"You shut up. After we look at what Mr. Sam Bam Johnson (if that's his real name) and Mr. Mad Enough have been up too, we'll get some food in you at the hotel. You are ridiculous, man; coming down here looking like a starving refugee." She whistled a little Tom Petty tune.

"I get it," said Chris. "And it's Madinoff, Russian name. And right, Johnson is not his name. How'd you know?"

"I didn't. I just know people. He's a sleazeball if I've ever seen one."

"His name is White."

"Get out!"

"Really."

"That's just perfect." Liza sighed.

They sat at one corner of the company's 20-foot-long board room table long enough for Liza to wait until color returned to Chris's face. She brought him Wheat Thins and pretzels.

She then stepped to a credenza in the room to retrieve a plain manila folder she'd hidden in a brown paper bag under the furniture.

"Here's what you can take with you. These are all copies and you can have them, but first I promised you some good food and we'll come back for this. Trust me," Liza said.

Chris listened closely. He did not detect any enthusiasm in Liza to hear any more from him about the predatory lenders.

She disapproves of my interest in these fellows, he decided. The two friends were sensitive to one another's tone and inflections. It grew out a common bond of thinking of themselves as throwbacks to glory days of investigative journalism. As an endangered species, they had always shared that common interest to build a friendship. Their unspoken bond was that each knew there was an affinity for the other, an effortless channel to understand each other's thoughts. Chris was dutifully careful not to ruin their friendship over work issues.

Chris was frustrated in journalism but still young. Liza now at Port America was sidetracked from the profession, enticed by the bigger paycheck that newspapers surely wouldn't offer. She always told him she hoped to rejoin a newspaper someday and make a name.

As they sat at the board table catching up, they shared small talk about how in the old days of investigative journalism, hardcore digging--the stuff they both studied in J school--would uncover creeps like Johnson and Madinoff quickly, saving lives, keeping families from housing frauds, and preventing broken hearts.

Chris finally relaxed his mind and his conscience a bit.

She repeated her concern with his appearance, "You look stressed. Is the job okay, still?"

He said without thinking, then regretted it, "Yes, I've been a little stressed because I uncovered some dark secrets about the dealings of Martin and the mortgage guys. I keep it to myself and tell nobody. Well nobody, that is, except Dickie and Knife."

Liza's fists tightened on top of the tabletop. She said that "those predatory developer guys" tried and failed with bids to infiltrate Port America as "floozy financiers." She opened her hand and touched his arm. She pleaded with Chris. "I put together information on them to convince you to stay clear. Please, Chris, I told you before, these guys are dangerous. Please give this up. Tell Benny or somebody. Give these papers to Steve; you don't need this story. You're going to be the best one day. Besides, I want you to hire me back into the business." She laughed with him.

Liza said she learned that Madinoff, as a young man, had preyed on rich married women, got three of them to divorce their husbands and marry him. "He was pretty good looking at one time. Can you believe that?"

"Absolutely not. I've seen him close up."

"Damn it, Chris." She said Madinoff stopped the sport of preying on married women when the last one bit him back. In 1979, Liza said, he fathered a child by a stripper in Las Vegas, who then sued him when he didn't want to divorce and leave his millionaire wife for her. The stripper ragged on Mrs. Madinoff until she finally demanded a divorce from him. By then, Madinoff had taken the previous wives for fortunes.

"He had to placate this bimbo, Jeri 'Body Beautiful' Mansfield. Yeah, that's the stripper who sued him. He bought her a luxury mansion off The Strip. Our researchers here at Port America told me that this first taste of real estate was deliciously satisfying to Madinoff. He hired a ghost lender to set her up for expensive additions—heart-shaped pool, miniature golf on the front lawn, wine cellar, and a disco-room addition to the house. What she probably didn't know was that Madinoff was also on the deed, yet the construction loan payments would be hers as soon as construction started.

"A tiny clause in the contract made that happen within one month of completion, well after she was settled in and he was off golfing and laughing it up with the ghost lender, who was Madinoff's brother. Nice story, huh?" Liza said.

"That sounds like our boy," Chris agreed.

"Then he and his brother both skedaddled to Northern Virginia, where they had grown up.

"Earlier, another break for the Madinoff brothers was that their family-owned 45 acres of farmland in Northern Virginia, on the D.C. Beltway right where Tyson's Corner Shopping megamalls are now. Their parents were both dead, so the Madinoff brothers hit pay dirt by holding out for top dollar from the first developer at Tyson's when the construction was already underway."

Tyson's Corner is the largest shopping mall in the Baltimore-Washington area. As it expanded, the Madinoffs bargained well, selling pieces of the land. Bernie Madinoff never had to work another day in his life. He plays at work, she said.

Chris could have guessed, thinking back to the Tickle My Pickle episode.

Liza also unearthed much of the same dirt on Sam Johnson as Chris had collected, he told her, his bitter upbringing and his racist behavior throughout his life.

She challenged, "But I'll bet you didn't know that federal agents are investigating Johnson's practices, have been for more than a year, I think. So, we denied his application to bid on the Port America condo projects. Same with Madinoff, but minus the racism. Port America nixed him, too. He was just too unscrupulous and was in the process of defending hundreds of lawsuits, which began to pour in as the housing market crashed last year."

This is good stuff, thought Chris, *Port America as a second source for what these creeps are all about*. "Thanks for doing this Liza. I really appreciate it."

"Remember, Clark Kent, this is not for you, but for Steve. How do you feel now, Chris? Your head, that is? Still dizzy?"

"I'm fine, Liza. Thanks."

"Good," Liza smiled and jumped up from her chair. She brought back two ice-cold Pina Coladas she had put in her boss's mini-fridge. "After getting the dirt of Johnson and Madinoff off my mind, I knew I'd be ready for one of these," she said sipping first. "How about it?"

"Chris, I feel cleaner after getting that off my chest. It's all yours, pal! Don't forget to take it with you," Liza said with a generous slurp.

He motioned thumbs up, clicked her glass with his, and sipped. "Mind if we look around some before I have to go?"

"Are you kidding? You're not getting away without Liza's grand tour, my boy. Here, give me your hand and walk this way."

"Not sure I can walk that way, but I'll try," Chris said bumping his rump from side to side, quickly halting his impersonation once they reached the office hallway.

"Just bring that with you," she said as she eyed the drink Chris had in his hand. "They know me here."

Finally, Chris was happy he'd come. He told her he'd be delighted with a tour of the high-profile waterfront attraction.

Liza showed Chris the expansive atrium again, this time from the top-floor balconies.

Chris let his inquisitive mind wander and take in the architecture. The white superstructure resembled string art that had been tossed by a magician. On three sides were seven stories of balconies, each with 13 entrances to guest rooms. Three-foot wide red and blue banners dropped the length of three sides ending with a big, gold star, like giant copies of the ribbons awarded at a Boy Scout Jamboree in West Virginia, Chris thought, or a state fair, for the best dairy goat or cherry pie. He was dazzled by the spectacle of lights and colors.

She laughed and said, "Man, you are enchanted by this place aren't you. Come on outside. What you hear is a convention party. They hired a marimba band."

"Just for me, right?"

"How did you know?"

They zoomed back down in a glass elevator. Outside, on a massive patio of tiki bars, palm trees, and gas-fed torch lanterns, Chris looked up and over the atrium again. On each side were multicolored lights that gave the hotel an eerie resemblance to a Disney World fantasy set. Or, was it an illusionary exaggeration? He still wasn't thinking clearly.

Large panels of translucent primary colors gave the structure a definition of a child's toy, light-up keys to a toy piano, or a dollhouse for children of the wealthy. "Hey Liza, this is the strangest architecture I've ever seen. Clearly, this is my next real estate centerpiece feature. Fill me in soon on the creative minds who did all this, okay?"

They made their way across the floor to a tiki bar tucked amid palm trees in huge planters. Hundreds of conventioneers on the patio were in the midst of a raucous party. Casually dressed guests wore name badges hanging from their necks. At several improvised bars, bartenders dressed in crisp white jackets handed out free drinks.

Chris found Liza's laughing eyes, nodded and raised his eyebrows, tilting his head to the right in approval. He took a couple of very deep breaths. He allowed himself to have a good time for once in a long time. It had been weeks since he wasn't filled with dread and worry. Liza could not have planned a better distraction for the troubled young reporter.

"Okay, just one," she whispered in his ear, meaning one drink with the conventioneers. "I think we are supposed to be medical supply people, so be prepared to talk like you come from Topeka and know or want to know the latest in asthma inhalers and thermometers."

He smelled her hair as she whispered the plan. He couldn't help realizing it smelled delicious. He dismissed the thought. *Not the place. Not the girl. It's Liza, dummy,* he told his exhausted, vulnerable self.

He asked for bourbon straight. She asked for rum and Coke.

"Whew, I needed that," he said to Liza after he took a few steps away from the makeshift bar. The marimba music was loud and festive.

They exchanged a knowing oh-why-not smile and returned for a second drink.

Glasses in hand, they sat at a candlelit table at the Moon Bay Coastal Cuisine Restaurant. The window gave them an enticing view of the shimmering lights of the nation's capital, the Capitol Dome, and Washington Monument in the distance, and nearby Alexandria, Virginia. They could see the Masonic Temple reflecting on the river against the dark night sky. The seven illuminated, perfect Roman arches supporting the Wilson Bridge over the Potomac River were glowing yellow through the mist above the river and reflected in ripples on the water. The riverside park in front of the Peabody was gorgeous.

"Hey, pal, little too romantic for us, isn't it?" asked Chris, wondering, *She up to something? Nah, no way.*

"Don't be foolish, Chris," Liza said, wagging an index finger in his face with a smile. "This is far and away the best food at Port America. You need a treat."

"You are really proud of this place, aren't you?" Chris offered.

"Of course. Yeah. And, I want to show you around. It is so good to see you Chris, really good!"

"Me too."

"I got to say though, you did look dreadful when you arrived in that luxury pimp wagon," Liza said sternly, motherly.

God, I can't take yet another woman mothering me. "I'm leaving now, Liza," tossing his hands up.

"What? You can't."

"I was just kidding. Let's eat. But, no way are you paying for this dinner, Liza Leah. We'll split it. I've got money," he said and hoped she wouldn't be interrogating him about it. He had a $50 bill left from the money Knife gave him to buy his FedEx Field disguises.

"Yeah, from where?" Lisa queried. "Did Steve give you a big raise for not doing the big story," she asked, emphasizing "not" in her comment. She began a kind laugh and cut it short. She had hurt his feelings.

It threw him off his plan. "Liza, I'm getting the goddamn story, Miss, thank you very much. I've been talking with Michele. Don't worry about that."

Liza saw she had struck a nerve. "I'm sorry, Chris. I wasn't trying to put you down. You know that. Let's order. Okay, we'll split the check."

Chris lifted his head, "Hey, how about if we limit the talk to your new job as communications specialist for the Peabody."

"Plus, those crazies you still work with. I miss those folks at the Inquirer," she agreed.

"Liza, you will never get back to newspaper work after all this." Chris said.

"Like to get back to it, yes. The money here is, of course, good. But, I miss you guys. How's our favorite stickler?"

"Benny? He's Benny; married to the paper. The man is worth his weight in gold—dedicated, knows everything about current business and real estate news, and has been great to me. He and Steve have taught me a lot."

Liza laughed and put her left hand on his shoulder, looked at him with her chin down, and said, "Oh, yea. I bet they are learning from you, kiddo. I bet you are the best they've seen. I mean it."

"I'm a fuck up, really. Miss having you around Liza. I think we were a good team at the paper with your community contacts and my … well, my something," he laughed. You had to go ruin it," he said. "Just kidding. Hey, I'm a little jealous."

"Oh, this gig? You'd hate it in a week, Chris. No reporting, just PR bullshit. Propaganda for the hotel and Port America resort. It would kill you."

"I could use the money though."

Liza played with her meal a bit, thinking, and then said, "I think you will be fine. The Inquirer will be your springboard. You were born to be a newspaperman, Chris. I know this looks fantastic to do public relations for a resort. But, you … well, you, my good friend, are going to be a star journalist. I just hope you still talk to me when you are big."

They both laughed.

"You can be my literary agent, Liza, when I'm Mr. Big, okay?"

"Make that your byline, Mr. Big," she kidded. Liza put her fork down and raised her right hand to give him five and their hands smacked together and fingers grabbed on impulse for just a second.

They ate and talked for more than an hour and a half. Their warm friendship led to three more drinks and a carafe of wine before they realized how high they were.

* * *

Liza took Chris back to her office at the convention center to give him the manila envelope of papers she had dug up for him. She put it into a plain brown bag and suggested they go through the lobby separately to the parking lot. She would meet him at "that scrumptious car. Maybe I'll get a ride sometime," she told him.

Neither took notice that they were walking arm in arm, like uninhibited drunks.

At her office suite, she let go of Chris to lock the kitchen where she had iced the two special Pina collates hours ago.

"Is that the office stash?" Chris asked, watching Liza also close the liquor cabinet in the office's kitchen.

"Yeah. There is a bottle or two for special deals and visitors, but..."

"Oh, I'm not a special vizdor or a spech dill?"

"Deal, not dill. But I'd be in a pickle if we're caught," she said.

His troubles temporarily off his mind, Chris admitted, "We are now true conspirators. I see plastic cups too. Liza."

She poured some whiskey for him and water for herself as they made their exit. Liza locked the door behind, without thinking, and then realized what she had done. "Damn! How am I gonna get the parking tag back to my boss? The key is inside the office now with my purse."

Chris responded, "Well you're the newspaperwoman, always arriving top of the morning. Come in early Monday. Somebitty let you go in."

"Not funny. Let's get you out of here. I'll beat Brando here in the morning and get in with his secretary's key. No one will know. Let's go." She reached to pat him on the back and missed, squarely hitting his butt.

He didn't even notice.

"Oops," she said, apologetically. "Sorry." She laughed at herself.

Chris went ahead while Liza delayed so that they would arrive separately at the car. Minutes later, she joined him at the Lexus. He was leaning on one foot, hand on the car roof.

They had just enjoyed the best time either of them had had for months, but too much to drink. They bumped together at the car door. Touching led to a thank you hug. He held her too long, she probably thought. But it was Chris, her bud.

Liza, concerned, offered to buy him a cup of coffee for the road but he refused, saying he was "fun" instead of saying fine.

"Okay, Chris, put that package in the trunk of this beast. Now, last time. WHERE did you get this car?"

Chris, fully socked by the effects of too much whiskey, laughed. "Might be Sam Johnson's car. Everrrr thin of that?"

Momentarily though, his laughing turned to crying. He quickly turned away to hide his face, but she spotted it. He tried several times to open the car door, as Liza stared in distress, hands on hips.

She then saw real tears running down his face. "What did you say? Johnson's car? That is not at all funny. Hey, Chris, you can't drive. Come with me. You need to lie down and you need to tell me what the hell you're talking about. I'm getting you that coffee, you big dumbbell. I can't believe I was putting you in this death trap. I'm sorry; I wasn't thinking."

He mumbled, "It's not a deaf trap; it's my coffin. I'm dead anyway, Lizzz, so I may as well go now."

Liza didn't understand, except to walk Chris across the great veranda in front of the Peabody, across the street, and into the Marriott Residence Inn where the company provided employees lodging at a reduced rent, including Liza and her roomy, Mary, Mr. Brando's intern. Mary was in California for the week. There would be an extra bed for Chris and no questions asked, for now, at least, and at no cost. The desk clerk was off until morning. Liza without her purse or keys, found and used the master key, a plastic card to open her apartment.

She pushed him onto the bed and stared at him. She wondered about his future. Had Chris ruined his promising career with the Martin nonsense, she wondered. "It is entirely possible knowing you Chris," she said to an unconscious man in the bed.

He opened his eyes. He looked up. "Aren't you going to tuck me in?" he asked.

Liza's face betrayed her heart, heavy with a yearning to comfort him. He was a special person to her because she had discovered him, a future genius reporter. He was that boy reporter at the Congressional Roll Call paper with her. Now, he was becoming a man, she thought, except at that moment Chris was a damn mess and in her hands again, her responsibility. And she loved him.

Liza leaned over and pulled a cover to his chin, careful to avoid his eyes.

He reached out to her impulsively. He pulled her to him and kissed her. He loved her very much.

She gave just a little resistance. She might have thought she'd regret it, but, if so, it was likely her final thought before they committed to making love for the first time.

Their passionate desire was a great surprise to both of them. When he sensed that she wanted him too, he straddled her willing body as he rolled her over, him on top.

Chris hesitated. This was his friend Liza. He assessed her willingness, eased his grip on her. No, she was not moving away. Liza's eagerness aroused him more. He only continued to encourage the moment because she had indeed committed herself. He felt her desire was sincere.

She received Chris on top of her.

* * *

Afterward, she made no effort to initiate more lovemaking. Liza was having second thoughts. She looked confused, not unhappy. She smiled at him.

He, at least, was sure they had not made a mistake, that she was happy to be intimate with him then.

The sex began to sober up Chris. He had never felt such sexual intensity before, in his limited experience. And it must have been intense for both of them. Liza had given in, likely an impulse or deliberately thinking she'd please him. Then, it had transformed to more than that.

After sex, side by side, they stared in silence at the ceiling—just a couple of old pals from The Hill, the Maryland Inquirer, then this?

Neither expected something so good.

Their heart rhythms soon slowed. They became profoundly aware of the silence that engulfed them. What to say? Who first?

They rustled the bed sheet that covered them. Each turned on their pillow, facing the other. They spoke at the same time. He said, "So, how are you doing?" She said, "You okay?" They laughed guardedly, at the ridiculous questions. Liza was more subdued.

They fell asleep in each other's arms. Content for the time being.

Chapter 60: Fool's Confession

At the first morning light, Chris was already awake, feeling amorous. He stroked her hair. From her edge of the bed, Liza pushed him back. With just a hint of rejection, Chris supposed she wanted to tell him their lovemaking was a mistake. He fidgeted with the corner of a pillowcase and looked downtrodden.

She finally came out with it, "Chris, you know how I feel about you. You are my dear friend. The best friend somebody could have."

Chris thought, *Oh boy, I don't think I want to hear this.*

Liza insisted. "I don't think we should continue with what we did. There is someone I've been seeing so maybe this is not a good time."

Without hesitation, Chris responded, barely audible. "I know. The one you mentioned. Me, too. I've been seeing someone." But, Liza meant much more to him than Amy did.

Liza said with a matronly tone, "But, it is quite natural, Chris, especially for a male, they say, and....."

Chris stopped listening. He sensed that she was trying to distance herself. His heart slowed down and he felt an ache in his chest. He felt alone and tried to hide tears welling up. With Liza pulling back, he remembered again the horrible situation that brought him to her at the resort—his messed-up investigation.

Desperate to block out the pain, he tried to rekindle her affections, "Screw this talk Liza, come here."

But she said no. Rebuffed for another go at sex, he slowly sank emotionally back into the nearly broken man he was when he drove there the previous day.

He fell silent for several minutes as he sat up to think. Maybe she was right about the sex, he figured, but he still needed her support. He thought she might understand it if he opened up completely. He had shared his love with her. He hoped she too felt a stronger commitment. He had to take that chance. He foolishly rationalized that now there would be less risk if he tried to gain her sympathy and thus it was reasonable to share his struggle with her again. He took a shot.

"Look, I need to tell you something. You are better off, Liza, with no friendship at all with me. I'm finished. My career. My big start in D.C. Maybe my life. I just wanted to get that impossibly great story for myself. It was mine."

"Chris, what are you talking about? Make sense. Are you in serious trouble? You have not been yourself since you got here."

To soften what he was about to confess, he started gently, "I was sure I was the one to report the story the right way. I tried and I tried. I tried everything and it got ugly."

He confessed it all, his weeks of stumbling and bumbling to rescue the Johnny Martin murder story for himself. He hoped she would understand that he had to compromise his personal and journalism principles and ethics for the bigger goal of reporting the story and getting the truth to the public. It was his obligation.

He told Liza again about his meeting with Vickie although she already had some knowledge of it.

Liza watched; remained calm.

Her silence was a false signal for him to continue.

He told her of the pot-smoking session with Knife and his gang at what was left of Martin's once lovely Charmington Village. He detailed the pounding he and Dickie got from bouncers at the Tickle My Pickle fiasco with Madinoff and about his stripper friend Denise whom he knew from his hometown.

Still, no reaction; but a cold stare from Liza.

He tried to explain his masquerading as a Redskin luxury box server, losing his press badge to Sam Johnson at FedEx Field and running for his life, only to be saved by a Denny's waitress he knew at the game who inadvertently shielded him from security.

Liza let out a heavy sigh with "Humph."

Finally, he shared with Liza the frightening tale of death threats on his newsroom phone from Johnson. "The car is Johnson's, too. He thinks he bribed me. He thinks that will keep me quiet and not write about him. I didn't take it as a bribe. He tricked me by taking my car from my apartment building and giving it to a bogus mechanic who said the Lexus was the only loaner he had. The car is registered to Johnson. I took it with my Visa card."

Liza sat upright, clutching a sheet over her. She howled like a wounded animal. She suddenly took on a look of being personally violated.

"Liza, you don't understand. I …"

She turned and shot an enraged look of disgust at Chris.

"I stopped driving it, Liza, but I had to drive it one more time and that was to come here. I needed a friend. I don't know why. I just got in the car and drove here to see you. I had to see you."

He had revealed his total predicament for the very first time to anyone. It was a kind of catharsis leaving his nerves numb with a sting of an electric shock. What he didn't say was that he was sorry for anything. He would face his situation like a man. That much was clear to Chris. He still hoped she would understand, but he was asking too much.

Liza just looked at him while standing, clutching a sheet to cover herself to her head. Her troubled face conveyed shock that such a friend, whom she had adored, was now just a stupid fool, who had stumbled far beyond simple anxiety of missing the big story. Had Chris made more simple mistakes, perhaps it would have been easy for her to relate to Chris's misadventures in journalism. He was just a small-town boy with a talent. But, he became a very stupid man.

Chris looked up at Liza and saw in her expression a loss of trust. Every quality she had ever admired about him—his professional purity and his innocence—were dashed. All of it. She looked utterly dismayed.

She swung herself quickly out of bed. With one hand on the sheet wrapped around her, the other hand on her cheek, mouth wide open in shock, Liza exploded, "How could you be so reckless, so stupidly reckless? This makes me sick. I can't bear to listen further." But she did.

He said, "Each time I thought I had a good angle, Liza, I somehow got more corrupted by the foolish, dogged clandestine investigation. I rationalized that I was doing it for the public, to get the truth told."

Her emotions welled up and she blasted him, "Chris, you take the cake. Listen, you are not using me anymore for help on this. Don't worry about that. But you have gone way past dangerous. They are going to kill you, man. The only way they don't is that the truth somehow gets published real soon and the creeps are sent to jail where maybe, and that's just a maybe, they can't hurt you from there. But they are smarter than you are. This is not your game. They will hire some hitman. I've seen it happen in New York. You are dead, you fool! YOU ARE DEAD!"

He had nothing, no reply.

She continued, “And no wonder you’re scared. Oh yes, you are. I see it now. I saw it last night at the hotel, too. By trying to do this by yourself you have gotten nothing on these guys because you are too green and naïve. What did you think? You could magically become Mike Wallace? You got absolutely nothing. I wish I could hate you for doing this to yourself. I … I… I wish I could hate you for sleeping together. … Ah, damn. I can’t think. Man, they have everything on you. What are you trying to achieve? What will you do to get them? And let me tell you, my stupid friend, it better be something good, or you are dead ...DEAD!”

She went for the bathroom then pivoted. She marched back over to the bed raising her left hand above him, aiming to slap him as hard as she could. But she stopped short, turned and ran into the bathroom, shaking a fist above her. She slammed the door behind her. Chris laid back on the pillow with hands behind his head.

Liza soon exited the bathroom fully dressed in a professional gray suit. “Put something on, Chris,” she demanded angrily. This was a bitter end to his visit, maybe his relationship with a wonderful friend whom he loved.

Early in their friendship, Chris learned to enjoy Liza’s mood swings, take them in stride, part of her volatile Latin temperament, he thought. It was futile to try to talk to her. And this Liza mood swing was an earthquake, one he deserved.

But he also felt fulfilled. Even throughout Liza’s rage, he felt they were both better off after what happened between them that night and she would get over the hysterics sooner or later. He imagined, *I’ll quit my job and hide out in Glasgow for a while. Maybe we can still be together after that.*

Tongue in cheek, he hummed the saucy Carlos Santana/Rob Thomas colossal 1999 hit “Smooth” about a fickle Latin lover, as he slipped on his briefs. He mumbled incoherently the refrain, “Give me your heart, make it real, or just forget about it.”

It didn’t work. Liza remained cold. “Very funny. I’m not amused.”

But, Chris was buoyed by getting even that response, with her anger toned-down.

He was nearly dressed when Liza finished putting on her makeup, ready for work. She ignored him and walked out of the motel room without saying a word.

He just sat and watched, hoping for another mood change. He could almost time it coming.

Just before the door shut, she looked back, her teary eyes oozing pity for her Chris. The change had come. She slowly walked back into the room. When their eyes met, she reached out and kissed him on the forehead ever so lightly.

He could hardly feel the kiss but loved it, nonetheless. “You have to promise me to be careful, Chris,” she said, again, with her striking dark eyes looking deep into his soul.

He felt safe again.

Chris put on his shoes and didn’t need to watch her leave. What viral young male could possibly make sense of such a friendship at such a moment? So, he began humming the Santana tune again to himself and left. Maybe she’d be okay with what they did.

Climbing back into the Lexus didn’t seem so threatening for the time being.

Chapter 61: Liza, the Snitch

Friday, August 24

After leaving Chris in her apartment, Liza dialed Steve Mothershart's number immediately on her cell phone. It was 9 a.m., his usual arrival time at the Inquirer. She was hoping to make her call before she heard from Chris again. She didn't necessarily want to see Chris for a while, but she definitely wanted to help him if she could.

She couldn't stand for Chris to be in danger.

Liza decided to confide in Steve, her former editor who once gave her a job, wonderful journalism experience, and, by covering the story of Port America development, an inadvertent 'in' with the execs there.

"Steve, it's Liza. We need to talk. It's about Chris. He's okay, but he told me some things that I think you should know. Only you can protect him from getting very hurt, Steve, no one else."

"Protect him," he said, half laughing. "I wish I needed the kind of protection he doesn't need. The world is going to be that young man's oyster. We can talk though, Liza. How are you doing down there in fun city anyway?"

She cut off his questions with, "I'll tell you later, Steve. If you don't help him, he won't even be able to eat an oyster or even recognize one. Can I come up there today? You can bring Benny, too. It's really important, but please don't say anything about this conversation to anyone else until you hear what I found out what Chris is doing. Don't worry. I think we can get him out of a jam."

"What kind of jam, Liza? I can't let you leave it at that. He's important to us."

"OK then, can I come now? I'll say I'm sick here at my job this morning, okay?"

"Fine, but don't jeopardize your job, young lady. Chris can probably take care of himself."

"Not this time."

She drove up to Rhodesville fast in a nasty thunderstorm ahead of a fall hurricane churning up the coast. She had heard his editors say many times that Chris was their project, their future star, and she hoped they would be on Chris's side, despite what he had done to disobey Michele and all the blunders that compromised him as a reporter.

The drive to Rhodesville was laborious. She used the time to think about what happened last night. She began to feel differently about the old Chris. She considered his new courage, his bold adventures, his willingness to take risks for his craft, and she was indeed quite impressed.

She reflected on her anger. Her previous maternal feelings to protect Chris were in the past. She recalled that as Chris had confessed his self-inflicted dilemma, she also admired him for never quitting, for standing up against the bad guys.

Liza gripped the steering wheel tightly. She smiled despite the very poor visibility and the dangerous drive. Sheets of heavy rain pounded the windshield. Friday rush hour traffic was at a crawl.

She laughed a little out loud as she remembered how her anger and admiration at the same time changed their friendship in her mind, even before she let him pull her into the bed with him. Chris had grown up during his eight months at the paper. She was proud of him for becoming such a man. She was ready to help protect him and, yes, see him again soon.

* * *

Benny Bradley met Liza in the Inquirer's parking garage.

"Hey, Benny, why the garage? This isn't Watergate tips I've got here, ya know," Liza said with her arms out wide, palms up. "How you doin'? And thanks for coming. But why here?"

"No, not the garage. Steve thought we'd be more comfortable using his bigger car, going out for a bite together. He's over there," said Bradley, as they moved toward Mothershart's roomy, silver Toyota Camry, with the motor already running. Steve sat behind the wheel with his hand on his chin studying Liza's body language for hints of the trouble she talked about. Even in a full-length raincoat, her marching gait revealed her determination.

As Liza slipped into the white leather passenger seat, Steve said to her, "Yeah, hope things are good down there in fun city and..," quickly stopping to realize he was repeating the same small talk he spoke on the phone. He added, "We thought you might want to talk over an early lunch at the Si Porto Rico. It's your favorite, right?" he asked.

“Hey, that’s nice. Better than that Don Quantos dump where Chris lives. But, are you sure you got the time” asked Liza.

“For you, Liza, all the time in the world,” said Benny, always the charmer. (Friday morning was past deadlines.) They all laughed, most at Benny, and they climbed into the car with Steve for the five-block drive to the café.

Liza got right to it. “Hey, guys. Chris has been investigating the Martin murder on his own.”

Benny said, “I knew something was up with that boy.”

Liza told them of Chris’s recent events that he confessed to her over drinks. They listened without interrupting her for the 25-minute drive in the rain to the restaurant.

As they sprinted into the Puerto Rican eatery their umbrellas blew inside out in the gale. Meanwhile, Benny and Steve were likely mulling over separately how to react to Liza, what to say first. The two editors always discussed crises together privately. This was a doozy. They had to be upset over Liza’s account about Chris, but each of them would internalize their disappointment and shock over Chris so they could find a way to focus on finding a way to help.

Chapter 62: Hump Hurt

The following Friday, August 31, late afternoon

Benny Bradley asked Chris to remain at the paper late past the usual Friday short workday.

"We are holding a late story meeting over sandwiches because we need to rework some things, need to make some changes for next week," Benny said.

Chris thought, Odd, *Michele is still on vacation. They wouldn't make serious changes in a meeting without her.* Chris had not ventured out of the newsroom for a week for fear of his life. He had been secretly sleeping on an old couch in the company warehouse.

He wondered, *I'm being let go. God, Johnson got to Chuck Bear. To Steve. Or even worse, Michele. Did they find out about the Lexus? The theft of Madinoff's files? The pot smoking with Knife and his gang of hoodlums?* Chris was now even scared of his bosses, scared for his job. *What will I do if I'm fired from my first job?* he thought as he walked on eggs into the conference room for what he thought would be the last time. He glanced at the monster clock.

5:58 p.m.

Typical of a Friday, no reporters were left in the newsroom when Benny had summoned Chris to the conference room. *They're going to fire me for sure. Do it now to save me the embarrassment at least.*

But maybe not. He glanced across the conference room table full of many of the staff. It didn't appear to be just about him. The usual reporters and editors were missing from a typical meeting of the business and real estate desk.

But there was Liza, sitting next to Steve Mothershart.

"What are you doing here," he asked. She didn't answer, preferring to look at Steve for a moment.

Chris spotted other surprises. There was Dickie Randim in his yellow cap. Statuesque Martha Read sat squarely across from Dickie, who was sitting next to Knife Garcia. Then there was old, wrinkled former crime reporter Harry Blalock. There was also a stern-faced middle age black man, who was clean shaven and wearing a pinstriped gray business suit. He looked vaguely familiar, but Chris couldn't place the man.

Steve was sitting in his customary seat at mid-table, Benny at the end. No Michele, no Lloyd and thank God, thought Chris, no Chuck Bear.

Chris whispered to himself, "Ah oh. This is not about changes in the newsroom, at all.

Steve began, "Chris, Liza told us what you've been up to and that certainly explains a lot about... well about what you've been up to for the last month or two."

Liza turned to Chris. "Chris, I had to tell them because I know you're going to get hurt doing what you're doing. You are just trying to get the story, but you are not getting much accomplished by yourself except putting yourself at risk acting like some clumsy private investigator. I'm sorry; I had to…"

Chris shrugged and gave Liza a small, approving smile. What else could he do? He had missed her all week. Besides, she was right, far more than right. He'd gone too far investigating with no help.

"Okay, let's get on with the meeting. I'm okay with whatever you have in mind," Chris said with a strong voice, stronger than anyone at the table would have expected from the boy who walked into the newsroom like a child about nine months ago.

He noticed that Liza looked at him with admiration and kindness. And then he saw other faces at the table that were not scornful, as he would have expected, but compassionate and friendly.

Steve reasserted his control, "Liza told me and Benny that you've been getting into some tight spots trying to find out what happened to Boss Martin and his building. I thought I'd get a few folks here to help figure out what we could do, without anyone in management knowing about this, except for Mrs. Read who learned of the meeting and asked to come. Is that right Martha? And let me acknowledge proper protocol and ask your permission to proceed."

Martha Read nodded her approval. (She had heard about the meeting from Carrie who said it was to be a strategy session to deal with Dickie and that he was about to get arrested again for Martin's murder.) Read flashed an almost imperceptible quick glance to Randim. She said, "Okay Steve. I'm mum on this. Please go ahead."

Steve continued, "I hope you can appreciate that we are behind you, Chris, even though we don't approve of your methods. You were wrong to defy us.

"However, Benny and I think you're on to something and we want to help. We have also been noticing some real gaps in the staff reporting of the Martin murder."

Chris burst out laughing and quickly stopped, putting his right hand to cover his mouth and making circles in the air with his left hand open as if to say 'go ahead, sorry.'

Steve ignored the outburst and continued, "Actually, there are serious things lacking in all the media reports on this. We are going to let your behavior go, as long as you agree to work with us, play it straight from now on."

Chris clarified, "You want to help me now, but Michele took me off it and kept me off it. Isn't that still a problem?"

Benny, with a disgusted groan, stretched his arms, cracked his knuckles, and said sarcastically, "Oh, yeah, that was a smart move by the paper. We had it handed to us on a platter and Chris was plugged into the story. Unbelievable." He tossed his arms up to face level in despair. "Like Steve said, there are some gaps, what? Four months of them? But no need to be cocky, Chris. This is a new page."

"Well," Steve said to the group, "Benny got a bit wound up over that. Yes, that part is over. Let's go on. We want to go through what you knew, step by step, Chris. I am presuming you aren't exactly ready to run to Newsweek with a cover story yet?"

Chris replied, "No, Steve, I just couldn't let this go unreported. I have a pretty good idea who's involved. Are you sure you want me to show my hand in front of all these people?"

Steve explained, "Everybody here can contribute to tying up some loose ends. Follow my lead, please. You don't have to tell all tonight. The loose ends need tying first and maybe we can get to the point where you can write your story. I'll try to make our bosses go along," said Steve with a glance to Read, who gave an agreeable nodding of her head.

He continued, "Michele did the right thing, then. This is now. I think I can make it happen." he laughed, clearly confidently.

Everyone laughed a bit but refocused their attention quickly on Steve.

"Steve, that would be great," said Chris, nodding gratefully.

Steve responded, "I think you all know each other, except Colonel Hurt. Let me introduce Colonel Humphrey Hurt. He is the Chief Operating Officer for Johnny Martin's company. Is that correct Colonel?"

"Please call me Hump. Everybody does, unfortunately," he said with a smile.

Liza, snickered, unnoticed, but mumbled loud enough to be heard by Benny and Chris, "Hump Hurt? You got to be kidding" She glanced at Chris. She was rewarded with another half-smile and familiar slumped shoulder shrug from Chris.

Steve continued, "Hump and I actually go back to a Q&A I wrote about his outstanding career what two, three years ago? The firm you began was purchased by Martin, after your Army days?"

"It was more like four years ago, Steve. I can't believe you still remembered me."

Liza added, "Steve forgets nothing."

"My firm was in high-quality building materials," Hump Hurt continued. "It was time for Johnny Martin's JDR to go that route. I presented a plan to him that would increase revenues in the long run. It took me a year to convince him. His newest buildings were getting too complex for slipshod construction, in my opinion, and I took a chance to confront him with a better alternative and he agreed. He was a strong-minded man and I doubt if I would admit to all this if he were here, God bless his soul. And, thank you for your kind words, Steve."

Steve said, "When I heard your name associated with Martin, I remembered it was part of our profile series on black executives of King's County. But, I must be honest, though, the name rang a bell but I had to go online to find my piece on you. Hump, this is our publisher, Martha Read; Liza is a former reporter here and still a friend of the staff, Mr. Randim is …"

"I know Dickie and of course Mr. Garcia. Nice to see you, Juan."

"And, then you've met Benny and you know Chris from our previous discussion. Again, let's get started." Steve launched into the inquiry. "Chris talked with you in one of his reports from the scene of the building collapse, I think, but you didn't have much to say."

Not waiting for a response from Hurt, Steve turned to Chris to answer, "Is that right, Chris?"

"Yeah," said Chris, "Colonel, you seemed to be stunned, well, for sure more than stunned, happy to get out alive, maybe uninjured and didn't want to say much, but you did admit you were with JDR. I remember the exhaustion that showed on your face and the smoke residue on your shirt. Your pants were ripped at the knee and you were wearing red socks, with no shoes on."

"That is remarkable, young man," Hurt said. "Yeah, that's exactly right. I had taken my shoes off to cool my feet at my desk just before it happened."

Steve smiled with, "That's our boy."

Chris said, "But, Mr. Hump, I mean Col...."

"Call me Hump."

Liza snickered again, this time shielding her face with her hands as she looked down at her lap.

Chris asked, "Sir, you have not been available since then for comment, right? Have you talked with any reporters, ours or anybody else?"

"After it happened, I disconnected my phone and left for our vacation home in Rehoboth Beach. My secretary was the only person who knew where my wife and I were. My wife was really scared. So was I. Unlike her, though, I had some theories."

Steve responded, "Oh, you did? Why didn't you want to help find Martin's murderer or who blew up your office?"

Hurt changed his tone of voice, getting more formal. "Mr. Mothershart, I'd rather not say right now. Maybe I can tell you privately."

"Fair enough. Call me, Steve. We don't want to make you uncomfortable, Hump."

"Richard," said Steve, always preferring not to call Randim by Dickie, "I want to thank you for coming. I know you were not willing to talk about this at first, but..."

Dickie interrupted, "Steve, it's not that. It's ... it's ... well, it's..."

"Oh, come on, Richard," Martha interjected, mid-sentence. "This is important. Stop thinking of yourself for once. Be a man."

If anyone at the table hadn't been paying attention up to that point, they surely were then. Martha Read sounded supremely pissed off and a bit embarrassed to be mucking it up with editorial over a story that clearly involved, of all things, her former, though, short-lived lover, the sneaky Dickie Randim.

Steve pulled the emotions that were flying in the room back to reason with a chuckle. "Well, I can't say I disagree with Martha. This is quite important, Richard."

Steve then thought of a way to shift away from Mrs. Read's awkward lecture, by asking Randim point blank, "Why don't you tell us your opinion of the guilt or innocence of Vickie Martin? Did she kill her husband?"

"Definitely not," Dickie said quickly.

Read used a civil tone in her next response to Dickie, "How do you know, Richard? She's due to be sentenced on Monday morning and my money is on guilty."

Dickie replied quickly, "I agree with Knife, that is, Juan, who told the police that Vickie was not trained on how to use a gun. That gun was just for show. She kept it in her car. Hey, she is a beautiful woman, she works in the hotel late at night and the parking lot was pitch black."

Steve said, "Her prints were on the gun. Fresh enough to be the killer, according to Sheriff Standard."

Dickie spoke quickly, "I don't know how that happened. I'm telling you, Knife here, I mean Garcia, told the judge it was an execution style shooting, expert shots. He was the one who showed her how to use the gun. But she never did use it again, ever. Not once, I think. She could not have made those shots. Right, Knife?"

"Dats right Dickie. She couldn't do it." Garcia was nearly in tears, but continued nevertheless. "Dickie, I sorry I told the cops you musta did it. But I know that couldn't be true. You just mad at Mr. Martin for hurting Vickie dat night."

Dickie replied, "We've been over that; it's not helping."

Steve retook the lead, "Thank you, Juan. Yes, we got that from the court testimony, but let's clarify. Richard, we need to put all the cards on the table, no matter how embarrassing. You had a special relationship with Mrs. Martin that night, we all know that." He glanced at Col. Hurt, who shrugged and shook his head discouragingly. "Well almost everyone. So, Richard, when was the last time you saw Johnny Martin alive?"

Dickie flared up, "Look, man. I told you before. I had nothing to do with killing Boss Martin, see."

"No, no, no. I'm sorry," Steve clarified, "Richard. I phrased that all wrong; it must have sounded like a police interrogation. Let me rephrase. How do you think he got killed and ended up in that explosion? No one seems to have seen him on Sunday, the day between his Saturday evening meeting at the Radisson and the explosion that Monday when his body was discovered in his truck there. You must have some theory because you were at the hotel the night of the meeting. Witnesses placed you there arguing with Martin or something? And, you certainly don't want your girlfriend to be convicted of a crime she didn't commit. Right?"

Dickie nodded in agreement. "I'm sorry."

"So, tell us what you think happened, just your theory maybe."

"Well Steve, it is a bit fuzzy."

"Try."

"I got drunk with Vickie after Johnny roughed her up in a hotel elevator and his men pounded on me. It was terrible. I didn't even know he was there. It was some kind of 'neutral location,' right Hump? And he had his father Vincent staying there too. Johnny surprised Vickie and me together as the elevator opened on the wrong floor. Man, I'll say."

"Go on," Steve said.

"I was just back from vacation. I missed her real bad. It was like everybody was there at the hotel for different reasons, coincidently. I had no intention of confronting Johnny. I was there for the grand opening of the hotel. Everybody knew that who saw me—everybody except Johnny and those men in his meeting.

"Badly," Chris muttered.

"What? Oh. Badly. Okay, I missed her badly. Do you have to be so damn smart, kid? Well, Vickie told me Johnny's dad, Vincent, was there earlier, but I didn't think..."

Col. Hurt jumped in, "That was something entirely different, just a coincidence as you guessed. He met with Johnny; I was with them and brought Mr. Martini to the hotel for some R and R."

Dickie asked defensively, "What? I didn't see Martin's father there."

Steve interrupted, "Excuse me, Richard. Hump, what was that all about, if I may ask?" he said, always acting the diplomat.

"It came out in the trial to help Mrs. Martin, I think. Vincent Martini never liked the way we ran our business. It was his once, you know. He just came to our office to meet Johnny to talk some strategy that day of the tragedy. They argued. Then Johnny invited his Papa to come with him to the Radisson and stay there, live like a king that weekend; all expenses paid; you know. I set him up in the best suite. That's all."

That did not seem right to Steve. Humphrey had emphasized in the 2002 Q&A that Mr. Vincent Martini never spoke with Johnny about the business.

Steve leaned forward with intent. "Okay, Richard, who killed Martin?"

"I've got some ideas but I really don't know," Randim responded.

Benny Bradley chimed in. "God damn it, Steve, this is not going anywhere. He's hiding something. Randim, you need to be more honest for once in your miserable life. Don't you want Vickie Martin off the hook? Or don't you care about that either," he asked.

To the surprise of everyone, except Steve, the conference door flew open and the heavy frame of Mr. Bernard Madinoff entered the meeting without knocking, escorted by a cleaning lady. He said, "Sorry I'm late, Steve. I thought it was at your old building in Gaithersburg. Guess I ain't been in the news lately, not that I'm complaining or nothin'."

Earlier in the week, Lloyd had told Steve he cleared Madinoff from his list of suspected murderers. He was sure that Madinoff was not one of Martin's enemies, at least not any more, and there were no links to the murder at BOM. Furthermore, there were still dozens of scars on his face and arms everyone in the room could see, from glass shards in the FUC'M tower explosion. Clearly, Madinoff hadn't expected the tower bombing.

Steve addressed the group, "I invited Mr. Madinoff," he said redirecting the conversation to the new guest, "How've you been since we covered that deal you made in Annapolis? And thanks for coming."

"Fine. Just fine," Madinoff said as if he just smelled a skunk.

Col. Hurt was shocked see Madinoff, whom he considered a predatory lender. He shifted uneasily in his seat and averted his eyes, looking down hands folded at his lap.

Dickie smiled uncomfortably, too, and nodded a weak hello. Fear showed on his face.

Steve cleared the air, "Everybody, this is Bernard Madinoff, of Best Opportunity Mortgage. He lost his office and, I understand, almost lost his life in the explosion at the First Union tower. Isn't that right, Mr. Madinoff?"

"That's right, Mr. Mothershart. Nearly scared the livin' daylights outta my bones, for sure. Came runnin' out of that place like a coon in a hen house, yes sir, I did. Pert near burned my damned ass off. Pardon me, ladies."

Col. Hurt shook his head and whispered to Chris on his right, "Oh well, what are you going to do with the guy?" He loathed Madinoff, but had too much class to show it.

Steve persisted, "Yes, well, I asked Mr. Madinoff here because of his association with Johnny Martin's JDR Company in the tower. We talked this over. His company is one of the leading lenders for JDR homes. The housing market has crashed, as we all know. I told Mr. Madinoff that we have reported correctly I think that all the law enforcement agencies, the county sheriff Mr. Standard, Homeland Security, and even the FBI, though we still don't get that, have questioned all of Mr. Martin's business associates for leads. There has been no legal action against Mr. Madinoff and his BOM company at this point. I called Mr. Madinoff to discuss this mystery. He doesn't know why we are meeting this evening yet. In fact, I suppose you thought we were doing a one-on-one interview on you, Bernie, right?"

Madinoff nodded in agreement, looking suspicious.

Steve continued, "We think the wrong person is being accused of murdering Mr. Martin and our young reporter Christopher Gilley has been getting his neck in some pretty sticky spots."

"I do know that. You're a lucky fella, Mr. Gilley," said Madinoff. He leaned back in his chair and gave out the same menacing laugh Chris heard at the strip club.

Chris held his head in his hands and ran his fingers through his hair roughly, as he rested his elbows on the table. He kept his head down and hoped Madinoff wouldn't go on about Chris and his ill-advised trip into the retail erogenous zone.

Steve probed, "It seems some of us in this room know or fear some of the truth, but won't say what they are thinking." Steve then looked at Dickie.

Madinoff chimed in, "If you mean Dickie, sure, he knows too much for sure. That handsome dude right there is a tricky one. Dickie, did you tell 'em you bin helpin' Boss nail me and Johnson? Hope he paid you good. You got nothin' from my operation because there was nothin' to get."

Dickie pleaded, "Bernie, you know as well as I do Johnson is no good. Johnny needed some leverage on him. Johnson profiled young black couples, took their money, and tricked them with bad loans. You should know. You're not exactly a saint when it comes to bad loans."

"Wait a damn minute, boy. I didn't come here to get insulted and lumped in with that racist pig Johnson," said Madinoff as he rose from his seat and took two steps toward the door. He pointed back at Dickie and said, "Yes, my firm targeted black churches to find clients. We deliberately made friends with the pastors, yes. Church life is big with black folk. Sure, we took advantage of that because we could sell to them church-goin' people. We are smart. We offered good loans to black folks who were all excited up about King's County and saw our ads, heard their preacher talk about us. Man, oh man. I run a legitimate business, you sorry ass. I can't help it if people can't keep up with the times, I ..."

Steve jumped to his feet and remarked, "I'm sorry. Please sit down and stay Mr. Madinoff. I am very sorry, sir. I didn't expect Richard to be so assertive. Out of character, I'd say. So, let me ask this. [He looked at Dickie.] What's this about you working for Boss Martin, Randim? Did we know that Benny?"

Benny opened his mouth, but Dickie jumped in, "We only met once or twice and Johnny said he liked my newspaper reporting. He asked me to look up some records of Johnson's and Bernie's mortgage deals. I passed on a lot of what I found about profiling blacks to Trichina too. Didn't she tell you? Man, sometimes you don't know who your friends really are."

He never gave Trichina anything on Johnson.

Liza shifted awkwardly and turned her head away from the table to avoid laughing.

"Go on," said Steve. "I, for one, am curious. You're snooping for Mr. Martin and dating Mrs. Martin? I don't want to know if he was paying you," said Steve.

Benny Bradley made a mental note to ask Chuck Bear to fire Randim.

"No, no," Dickie replied, looking around the room.

Liza and Chris were smiling, watching Dickie twist in the wind.

Dickie said, "When I met Vickie, they were separated, … [He looked around; found no sympathy.] … for years. When she found out I was digging stuff up for Johnny, she didn't object. She hated Johnson, too."

He lied. As far as Dickie knew, no one ever told Vickie.

Steve, boring in on Randim, "Seems you, Johnny, Vickie were all afraid of this Sam Johnson." He turned to Martha Read for clarity, "What do you think, Martha? You said Richard confided in you, wanted protection? Why?"

"I think he did, yes. Dickie told me that Johnson found out he was spying on him for Johnny Martin," responded Martha and looked down, stopped talking.

Steve was still listening for more.

Her head cocked back like she was about to say something she'd maybe regret, and then just added, "That's all I know."

Steve turned again to Dickie, "Richard, were you in danger?"

"It was Johnny Martin, Steve," Dickie responded. "He was getting very annoyed with Johnson and I helped him get evidence of Johnson violating federal civil rights statutes, big time. Yeah, I got scared. I didn't know things were getting so ugly. I just wanted to keep helping because Vickie wanted me to. Like I said, she hated Johnson too. And, I'm sorry I involved you, Martha. I really am."

Again, he was lying. Vickie never knew about Dickie helping Johnny until Dickie confessed to her at her jail cell.

Chris and Liza exchanged glances. They were surprised by Dickie's sudden boldness and his caring for others, even while he sat in a trap like a rat.

Martha replied, "That's okay, Richard. That's in the past. I'm glad this is getting out in the open so nobody gets hurt and the paper gets the story. We *are* getting the story, aren't we Steve? Benny?"

Benny said cautiously, "I'd say we're getting something, but I don't know if that something is newsworthy yet."

"I've stayed silent long enough," interjected Hurt. "Can't stand this. The missing piece here and why everybody is afraid of Johnson is that he was getting blackmailed by my boss. Yes, it's true. He didn't think I knew but I did. He's dead now and it doesn't matter if I say so. Johnny was blackmailing Johnson and would have done the same to this fellow too if he could. [Hurt flicked his thumb disrespectfully at Madinoff.] I hate to say that. It was because Johnson is such a bastard, hates us blacks, and Hispanics, Asians and everybody else who isn't lily white, for all I know. He was becoming very dangerous. He hated Johnny for blackmailing him. They used to work together you know. But if he didn't pay up every month ..."

"How much," Steve interrupted.

"50," Hurt responded.

Steve asked, "50 what? Thousand?"

Hurt was quick to answer. "Yeah, 50 grand, every month. He had that much on Johnson, thanks to Dickie here."

Bradley scribbled: *Fire Randim!*

"Were you in that meeting, Hump?" asked Steve, "when Johnson and his men came to meet with Martin at the Radisson, the weekend when Martin disappeared?"

Col. Hurt said boisterously, "Hell, no. Johnny wouldn't let me come within a mile of that racist pig. He thought, quite correctly, that I'd get too upset with Johnson and things would get out of hand. I am a peaceful man but it was prudent not to attend. As it turned out, things did get out of hand and I wish I'd been there. Johnny might still be alive. The whole thing was stupid, not good business at all."

Madinoff said to Steve while avoiding eye contact with Hurt for fear of another argument, "According to rumors in our field, Sam Johnson was going broke, not that anyone is sorry for that. And he couldn't keep paying Johnny. My understanding is that Johnson was the one demanding the meeting."

"You knew about these payments," asked Steve, with a hint of incredulity in his voice.

Madinoff answered quickly, "Lately, yeah, yer boy Dickie told me when I caught him spyin' on me. I stayed plum clear away from Johnson ever since I fired him from my company nine years ago. I knew he was a bigot, the worst kind. Right, Colonel?" He glanced at Hurt.

Madinoff's biases were in his strip clubs, gambling, and heavy drinking with his golf cronies, not racial. In his business, he had refused to buy into Johnson's racist attitudes and had voted him out of BOM.

Hurt responded forcefully, oddly teaming up with Madinoff, "I didn't even know about the payments until Juan told me just recently. But you are right Mr. Madinoff. Sam Johnson ruined a lot of families, many black families that I know personally in King's County and beyond. Johnny was mad at Johnson for giving fraudulent loans to our employees, even some of our execs at first, but mostly vulnerable people living a dream, cutting finances close to get their homes.

"Steve, Madinoff is right. These are good, church-going, upstanding citizens. We could help some of them keep their houses, thanks to Johnny. He was always good to his employees.

"His only protection that night was Knife Garcia here. Johnny told me before I left that he'd make Knife bug the room and listen in. Then, he sent me home. Maybe that's how Knife heard Dickie confront Johnny [Garcia nodded because it was true. He hadn't been in the conference room, but listening in the next room.] That was when Dickie busted into the room and threatened Johnny for hitting Mrs. Martin in the elevator. Dickie, I'm sorry to say, you're more than harmless. You're spineless. Knife said you simply passed out right there. Isn't that right Garcia?"

Knife agreed. "I heard from the other room. I came in to help get Dickie out of there, man. He was stone drunk out of hez mind, man. I think he went to Mrs. Martin's car. Yes, she said dat."

"Mr. Garcia," Steve pressed. "If you were listening then, what happened then, with the meeting of Johnny and Johnson and his managers at the Radisson that night? What happened? I think that's important to know."

Benny, again sarcastically. "Would seem likely, I'd say," as he pushed away from the table.

"No, no," said Garcia. "I don't go back after dat. Mrs. Martin told me to stay with Dickie and get him to de hospital, but I just get him to lay down some. She then went up to Mr. Martin meeting I think, not sure, very upset. I told her I had to get goin' cause my girlfriend, she come pick me up at the front lobby, you know ..."

Garcia suddenly looked around scared, perhaps realizing he was rambling and sounded defensive in front of the nice people at the newspaper. He flashed a look of guilty shame. Garcia shut up, glanced at his hands, and then snuck a quick second look at all the puzzled faces around him.

Steve said, "Don't stop now, sir. Where were you when you heard Randim threaten Mr. Martin?"

"Oh, God, not that again. I didn't do anything," said Dickie, sounding frustrated.

"Shut up, Richard. You're not helping," said Martha, raising her voice.

But Garcia was done talking.

Col. Hurt picked up the pace, "Johnny told me to set Garcia up in the next room before I scrammed. It's another conference room, separated by sliding panels. You know the type they install in hotels. After that, I left. Johnny's orders. I'm too black for that meeting, he said. I was on my way to my house in Bowie before Johnson and his thugs even arrived."

Steve, instinctively honed in, "So it was you who set up the mike Garcia listened to?" He had no idea where his question might lead, even if there *was* a mike or a bug." But, the question was to be central to the mystery. As was often the case, Steve's fishing question had struck gold.

Colonel Hurt lowered his voice. "Yeah, little transmitter stuck under the tabletop, a receiver with headset and a little recorder in the closet in the next room behind the thin paneled wall. That was all."

Hurt's faint, quick uttering of the word 'recorder' did not escape some ears at the table.

Benny leaned over discreetly to whisper to Chris who sat on his right. "What the hell did he just say?"

Chris mouthed the word 'recorder,' using his hand to hide his lips from the others.

Steve surveyed the room in a flash to see who heard the word and concluded that not everyone did. He saw lots of placid expressions prevailing.

Benny, Chris, and Liza looked sheepish. Old crime reporter Blalock was about to burst and was shifting from side to side in his chair. Martha Read, Madinoff and Dickie either didn't hear what Humphrey just said or hadn't registered the significance of the word 'recorder.'

Humphrey's brown face paled, evidently remembering, perhaps for the first time, that the eavesdropping of the conference that night might have involved a live recording of the meeting. He took on a ghostly expression and slipped out of his chair and headed to the door without the slightest hint of thanks or goodbye to anyone, including no eye contact with Steve who was watching him carefully now. "Gotta, ah …gotta go now," he said.

Steve, fully composed, delayed him, "Colonel, will you be available Monday at your phone? It's been reconnected, hasn't it? Could you stay just a minute longer?"

"No, no. I mean yes, the phone, yes …," Hurt sat again, but in the last chair by the door holding his raincoat.

"Good, Thank you. Just a minute first, Hurt." Thinking fast, Steve efficiently adjourned the gathering.

After a short pause, Steve feigned a fit of anger. He shouted, "Damn it, Richard, you should have known better than to get involved in all this. Don't you ever consider the reputations of the rest of us? Or the paper? We need to have a talk right now, young man. Damn! Working behind our back for Martin, keeping vital details of the story from your editor. You should be ashamed."

Steve Mothershart rarely cursed or raised his voice. Those familiar with him, like Chris, knew he was faking. Steve wasn't interested in reprimanding Dickie Randim as much as setting him up as a willing contributor, out of guilt, if Dickie had any more background to help complete the story.

The reporters in the room also realized at that moment that Steve likely had outlined that story in his mind—the story he would make sure to be Chris's.

With no further delay, Steve dismissed everyone. "I think we are keeping Mrs. Read too late." He gave Read a discrete wink and she acknowledged with a nod in agreement. She turned and left without a word.

Steve said, "Thanks for coming in Mr. Madinoff. I think it was kind of you to attend and you were very helpful and on such a stormy night too.

"Liza, please have a careful drive back to Port America, okay? I can hear the rain pounding on the roof again. It is a long drive ahead of you. Chris will call you tomorrow about all this.

Lightning flashed through the building with a deafening thunderclap as Chris and Liza's eyes met.

"Wow," Steve said with a duck of his head. Then continued, "Folks, let's keep quiet about what you heard here tonight in this room, okay? And, we will pick this up on Monday," Steve had no intention to let the Inquirer rest on things for the next three days. He exchanged glances with Chris and Benny while patting his hands down in mid-air to tell them to stay.

He then turned to Garcia. "And, Juan, in just a few minutes Richard and Chris will need to talk with you. It's really important. You can be a great help, sir." Being nice to Garcia was critical at that juncture. Steve figured to keep him from bolting, noting the fear on Garcia's face. "We will be just a few minutes. Wait at my desk, Juan, please. It's right next to the business desk coffee pot; help yourself."

Madinoff left, waving goodbye dismissively as if he'd just put up with a room full of fools.

Once he was out of the conference room and disappearing fast, Chris watched him and said, "Whew. The big man is obviously uninterested in any outcome and glad to be rid of us newspaper snoops."

Only Steve, Benny, Chris and Dickie stayed at the table with Colonel Hurt.

As soon as the door closed behind those who left—Madinoff, Garcia, Liza Lopez, and Martha Read—Humphrey Hurt let out a noticeably vocal sigh and said in a suddenly well-composed voice, "Oh my God. Gentlemen, I am so very sorry. I completely forgot about the recorder. It must have been Johnny's back up to the microphone under the table, listening device, or whatever."

He paused to collect himself. "I was well on my way out of the hotel that evening, rid of any thoughts of Johnson and the meeting. We were in Rehoboth for two whole weeks. I guess I put the whole stupid meeting out of my mind completely. I am so sorry. This is the first time I remembered so much detail, honest."

Steve wasn't convinced. Hurt didn't have to add 'honest,' in his opinion. His performance was suspect to Steve and the others. Was everything else he said a lie? Steve responded, "That's okay, colonel. Please tell us. It's important. Is there a recorder and maybe a recording of that meeting, if only a faint one?"

"I remember a tiny recorder being there. That's all. It was one of those tiny digital jobs, but I don't know if it was working. I got it from Dickie."

Bradley gave Dickie another killer look, let out a disgusted, "Goddamn," and scribbled another note.

Col. Hurt explained, "I told Garcia to put it on the shelf in the corner closet in the next adjacent room to Johnny's meeting. Housekeeping kept supplies there I think. But, gentlemen, I don't think Garcia understood what I was giving him. He probably didn't turn it on. I don't know. I do remember that Garcia was already terribly nervous about Johnny. I remember Johnny asking him to just listen and not to shoot anyone. I was nervous, too, that night because things were crazy, with his angry father Vincent coming, then Johnny discovering Dickie and his wife in the elevator making out—I saw all that too—then knowing there would almost surely be a confrontation with Johnson, who, as it turns out, was losing money fast. It was hell being around Johnny that night. His nerves were tight as a drum when I left. I just remember that I wanted to get the hell out of there.

“Furthermore, I was relieved when Johnny told me that he wanted Knife to stay, to listen in case there was a fight. He wanted Knife to come into the room to protect him if there was trouble. I do remember that, just as Mr. Garcia said.”

Hurt’s military stoicism couldn’t mask a sheepish look that Steve alone detected. Hump talked way too much about it, Steve thought. Hurt was hiding something and covering his butt. While Steve was pondering what to say to Hurt, the colonel spoke again, right on cue, Steve thought.

Hurt stood up and announced firmly, “I do need to go now gentlemen. Should we tell the police what we learned tonight, or wait for your story? You’ll run something tomorrow? You don’t need to include me, right?” Hurt asked.

Steve quickly responded. “Hump, this story has been going on for so long, and nothing I heard tonight can help Mrs. Martin, or help the police nail down the murderer. For all I know, she did it. But, to answer you about the cops, I say not yet. We don’t have enough for them, nor a kernel of a news story. What do you say, guys?”

The three newspaper men spoke at once reluctantly but their words stumbled over each other. saying ‘no,’ ‘of course not’ ‘nah.’ They shook their heads dismissively, almost comically. They sensed Steve was on to something.

“No, I don’t think we have a story and probably wasted everyone’s time. Thanks for coming in Hump.” Steve stood up, walked him to the door and they shook hands. “Take a few copies of our weekend business magazine there on my desk Hump. Lots about the community you deal in. If you want any past copies of the paper, wait there and I’ll be out soon to dig them up for you. Good night.”

As the conference door closed behind Col. Hurt, Benny spoke first. “God damn it, Randim. How stupid are you? You gave a recorder to Martin for his meeting and didn’t tell us? Didn’t tell Chris, Fayme, Lloyd, Martha, anybody? Are you just that fuckin’ lame, boy? We are a team here, if you ever noticed.”

“Of course not,” said Dickie.

Benny was furious and asked, “Of course you’re not stupid? Or, of course, you didn’t give them a recorder? Or of course, you didn’t know this was a team?”

“Give him a chance, Benny” Steve said.

"I didn't give Johnny my recorder for his meeting," said Dickie. "I gave Martin's secretary my old recorder a long time ago if that's the one when my Daddy bought me a new Yamaha Pocketrak. She was a good source for me."

Steve wanted to get Bennie back on track by handing him the reins, thus tapping into Benny's reliably responsible side. "Benny, what should we do now?" he asked, knowing the answer already.

"I'd say we have to get into that closet at the hotel before Hurt does and he's got a head start," said Benny, unless he is reading the Inquirer Business magazine. Nice thinking, Steve. Oh, no I can see in the window he is gone."

"I agree we need to get it certainly if it is still up there on the closet shelf," said Steve. "But first, I need to apologize to Richard for bawling you out in front of our guests. I couldn't think of any better way to distract everyone after the colonel remembered there might be a recording. I needed to delay him and clear the room quickly to get to the matter of the recording if there is one. So, I am sorry for that."

"That's okay," Dickie said. "This meeting I have to say was a very good idea, though it was hard for me. I'll try to cooperate as much as I can. I'm the one who should be apologizing."

"Okay then, if you do want to amend your mistakes, please do two things for me. I know you will," said Steve. "First, and I mean very first, try to get that recorder quickly. I think you have the fastest car on the planet for getting to that hotel pronto, that Porsche. And, second, get a hold of Vickie Martin's attorney right away. Tell him you've got to visit her first thing in the morning. He'll allow that if you say you have further evidence to share. But call him from your car so you don't waste time.

"Now, get Garcia and the both of you get into that Porsche of yours and race to the Radisson before Colonel Hurt gets there. Garcia knows where it was hidden. The roads are likely terrible in this storm. You've got positraction or whatever they call it?"

Dickie smiled, "Oh yeah. Hugs the road like its flypaper,"

Chris laughed, "Oh sure. Does the bullshit ever stop with you?"

Steve ignored the exchange and insisted, "Find that recorder, if it exists. Please don't get distracted by anything, Richard. I am counting on you."

Dickie ran from the room, gathering Knife. They soon hit 95 mph on the D.C. Beltway toward the Radisson, clearing a swath of water on the road like a speedboat. And, for once, Dickie was not lying. The Porsche hugged the Beltway as if it was indeed on flypaper.

* * *

Steve asked Chris to start writing his story, revealing everything he knew with at least two sources about Sam Johnson. "Madinoff and Hurt just provided plenty of substantial facts, for example, Chris." He also asked Chris to call Hurt with some extraneous but ostensibly pertinent questions." Tell him to meet you in the morning Monday at the hotel to go over the layout of the Martin meeting with Johnson on May 12. Maybe that will divert him from going to the hotel tonight, but I doubt it."

Trying to control Hurt was risky. They couldn't trust him, a close confidant of the late Boss Martin.

Chris was happy to stay at the newspaper writing until the monster clock struck 2 a.m. He wrote several good leads connecting Johnson to the crimes, even one if Vickie was guilty. It wasn't necessary to outline his story or write anything further down the pages after those leads. He knew the story. It would just flow, as long as he had a few lead paragraphs down first.

He spent the remainder of the time organizing notes in his secret files on the story and sketching a mental plan to hide out from Johnson permanently.

Steve also needed Dickie's loyalty, shaky as that seemed to him. So, he assigned Dickie's worst critic, Benny Bradley, to stay in touch with Dickie concerning his visit with Vickie in jail.

Steve then wanted Chris, Dickie and Juan to meet Steve and Benny at the hotel at noon the next day, Saturday, normally not a workday at the paper. No one objected.

* * *

At 10:09 p.m., Dickie and Garcia barely did beat Hurt to the hotel. At the second-floor conference room level, Dickie stood guard at the elevator while Garcia returned to the conference room closet, where he had eavesdropped on Martin's meeting with Johnson way back in May. They figured that the chances of finding the recorder still there were slim.

Moments later, Hurt got off the elevator, as they had anticipated. Garcia and Randim ducked down the stairway unseen after they checked the conference room shelves.

They had not found a recorder.

Chapter 64: Man Up, Dickie

Saturday, 8 a.m. Sept. 1

Despite the early hour, Dickie visited Vickie at the federal jail in the morning as he was told.

"What recorder? I didn't know that," Vickie said. Thinking fast, she added, "Mr. Dundeili will be here any minute, Dickie. Go to my condo. There is a hotel master key in my red handbag in the bathroom if mother hasn't moved it. Then at the Radisson, use the master key. Someone in housekeeping could have brought the recorder to the front desk or the Lost and Found. The Lost and Found box is in a cage inside the last storage door in the back of the gym. You will need the hotel key to access it."

"Hotel key?" Reddy Dundeili said arriving unnoticed by Vickie and Dickie talking, or Garcia, who was playing a video game on his smartphone instead of standing guard as Dickie had instructed.

Dundeili continued. "Why the hell should he need a hotel key? Hasn't this fellow gotten you in enough trouble already, Victoria? Randim, you letch, can't you leave the poor girl alone?"

Dickie exploded into a rage, surprising Vickie, even himself. He knocked Dundeili down with one solid right to the jaw. Forgetting all about sharing any new evidence as planned, Dickie stood over him and threatened, "Get her out of jail, you goddamn parasite. She didn't do it! Do you hear me? You can stop sucking her tits for cash now, you Goddamn slacker excuse for an attorney! That train has left the station."

Vickie loved it. A whole new Dickie.

* * *

Tuesday, Sept. 4, U.S. District Court. 11 a.m.

The jury returned its verdict to Judge Scarley after only one hour of deliberation.

He directed the accused to stand as he read the verdict.

"Mrs. Martin, a jury of your peers has found you guilty of the murder of John Martini, your husband. Do you have anything to tell the court before I sentence you?"

Vickie stood erect and proud in her conservative skirt suit and without shedding a tear, said clearly and unemotionally, "Your honor, I think the jury has done what they think is right, according to the evidence presented."

There was a long pause before she continued, "I have been framed, your honor. New evidence will show that I am truly innocent. My little girl lost her father and I lost my husband. The killer will be found, because I am innocent, your honor."

"Mr. Dundeili, do you or your client have new evidence? If so, it is a little late," said the judge.

Dundeili shrugged and began to speak, but Vickie interrupted. "May I ask a question, your honor, a legal question, because my attorney seems to be lost?"

Dundeili tried to motion for her to sit, forcing a heavy hand on her shoulder, but she abruptly pushed his hand away.

"Of course, my dear, … er, that is, Mrs. Martin."

"If after the trial, someone confesses to my husband's murder or new evidence proves I didn't kill him, would that change the jury's decision?" she asked.

"It might change the verdict; that is true," the judge said. "Although the jury is finished with this case. Has someone confessed?"

"Not yet. But, there is lots of new evidence, Your Honor. Please [She lilted her eyelids and pouted just a bit.]."

"Sentencing is hereby delayed two weeks," ruled the judge, obviously sympathetic to the possibility. He too had known and secretly admired Peeps for years for her pleasant personality. "In the meantime, you will be confined to federal prison in Washington until then, or until this phantom evidence, if any, appears from the heavens. Good day. Court's adjourned."

Chapter 65: Play it Again

While the jury pronounced Vickie guilty of Johnny 'Boss' Martin's murder, Dickie and Knife were arriving at the Radisson, 10 miles to the west, with her hotel master key. Yet, they had no plan or hope for a reversal of the verdict. But thanks to a call from Vickie at the jail to the hotel ahead of them, they did have the blessing of hotel manager James Strait, a Peeps supporter, to search for new evidence to get Vickie off.

Strait was pleased to have heard from her.

Hotel manager Strait told Dickie and Garcia, "Ask the housekeeping crew first, then come back to me if anyone prevents you from doing what you have to do" Strait suggested.

The daytime housekeeping crew was little help but suggested to the strangers that management always instructed them to take any lost items to the front desk.

At the front desk, hostess Marlenna Diaz, plastered smile and all, directed them to manager Strait's office, circle complete.

Dickie was angry and got James Strait to walk them back to the front desk, where nice Marlenna finally decided to direct them to the gym where the Lost and Found was located.

Dickie said, "What's this, the fuckin' CIA? You folks know me for God's sake. Why all the games? This is important to help Mrs. Martin get off." The hotel personnel indeed knew Dickie Randim, but had no reason to trust him.

Shuffling through the pile of unclaimed smelly bathing suits, coats, pants and jockstraps, they finally reached the bottom of two large, stinking barrels in the gym closet. No recorder.

They gave up the search in the Lost and Found and, remembering Vickie's instructions, headed instead to Vicki's office. Their key opened the door to her dusty office, clearly unused for weeks.

There it was.

On top of her desk blotter was a little, bronze digital recorder. "That's it, Juan," Dickie was ecstatic. "That was mine; the one I gave to Johnny's cute assistant."

Attached to the little device was a Post-It note: *Miss Peeps, maintenance found this by the AC vent between conf. rooms. Is yours?* It was signed *Angelo, the night cleaning foreman.*

* * *

Within the hour, Steve and Benny arrived at the hotel and entered the second-floor conference room —the very conference room where Martin's fateful meeting had taken place the night the hotel opened.

Chris then arrived and took a seat at the table unwittingly in the same chair Johnson sat in.

Knife entered, snickering.

Dickie was the last to arrive and said slyly, "Well, guys, I guess you want to know if we found something on the recorder. Well ..." he reached into his jeans and whipped out the recorder. "This be whatcha lookin' far, gentlemen."

"My God, Randim, be careful with that. This is no time for theatrics," bellowed Bradley, "Garcia called; said you found it. Sit your ass down."

Steve just stared at Dickie. "We want to do this at the scene of the crime, so to speak."

"And so Randim, you didn't lose the thing on your way up here in the elevator?" Benny slipped in under his breath.

The biggest smile anyone there had seen on Richard Randim face spread from ear to ear. "It's all here, fellows, I think," as he placed the recorder on the table in front of him. "We played a little. It's clear. Voices are distinct. Just listen to this clip I cued up."

They heard Samuel Johnson's voice: *"Don't even think about touching this woman, Brick. She's going to be our killer. Let's get Martin out of here. Go get Slim."*

Chris let out a cry of joy, "We've got him, Benny."

Dickie shouted, "Well yeah. But didn't you hear? They framed Vickie."

Steve, "Maybe. Let's hear it from the top, Richard."

Dickie played the tape from the beginning:

"Here take this, Juan. Johnny wants you to put it in the room next to you. Okay?"

"That's Colonel Hurt. I remember that," said Garcia.

"What did you do with it?" asked Steve.

Garcia did not answer.

Steve set the stage, "Here goes, guys. Stop it a moment. We are here to re-enact, rethink what happened here more than four months ago. Remember, Chris, every word of what we will hear happened in this room, at this very table, I think," Steve said, pen and pad in hand.

Dickie pressed play on the small, handheld machine again. They could hear Martin greet Johnson:

"Close the door behind your guys, Sam."

Then, Johnson asked Martin if he knew his two employees, and said their names, Brick and Verdi. The listeners could hear chairs pulled up to the table across the hardwood.

Johnson thanked Martin tersely for sandwiches on the table but declined the offer: *"We're not here to eat, Johnny. We are here to talk. We are here to make you stop fleecing me for fifty bills each month. We can't do it anymore. Business is bad, even if you give the feds those records your man Randim stole."*

"You are going to make me do what? Think again," Martin said. "And Dickie stole nothing, Sam, and you know it. He just put facts together from records your so-called lending company filed with the county and state. Yes, the FBI would be quite interested in your choice of rates and terms for new black families in King's County."

Later, on the tape, after more threatening talk, there was a crashing sound. Garcia said, "That's Dickie." He's busting the door open and threatening Mr. Martin for hurting Vickie. They heard Johnson say: *"Right on cue. Here's your boy, Johnny."*

After so many words, there was a thud, likely Dickie collapsing to the floor.

"Just like Vickie said," Dickie said. "I can't remember any of that. Vickie said security pulled me out."

Bradley, "Yeah, yeah, yeah, so you said. We're not interested in what happened to you, Randim."

They kept listening. They heard Johnson insisting that he could no longer pay Martin. He suggested swapping high-priced commercial properties he owned in Greenbelt near the D.C. beltway for undeveloped farmland. Chris figured that was farmer Claggett's land.

Martin replied: *"I'm no damn fool. You'll keep paying until your bled clean, Johnson, or until you offer better terms to my home buyers, black or white. You hate blacks, always have since 'Nam and since GW. You're a racist pig, man. You need to change before you are exposed and I'm ready, pal."*

Johnson was enraged: *"You, of all people, a hack builder, son of a dumb guinea immigrant whose only way to make a living in a big market like Chicago by fucking a rich lawyer's daughter. Suddenly, you're a saint. St. John Martini himself, passing judgment on whether I'm nice to niggahs who come to me on their own free will to buy one of your shanty shacks."*

The four listening to the recording then heard Martin scream at the top of his lungs: *"Fuck you, Sam. I'm gonna set you straight, you fuckin' bastard. Somebody shoulda done this a long time ag...."*

They heard his chair move. They heard him gasp and lose his breath as he said, *"Oh my God, ah ..."*

The listeners sensed that Martin had moved very quickly in the room, by the sound of his voice becoming louder as Johnson grunted and chairs fell. There the obvious sounds of a scuffle. After a moment, someone said: *"He's out cold."* After another moment: *"He looks dead."*

Johnson's voice shifted to across the room: *"He's not dead, Verdi. He can't be. Hardly touched the bastard."*

The other voice said: *"I seen you do worse with one punch, Sam. Remember that time we was..."*

"Shut up, Verdi. Someone is coming. You guys, get him into the closet there. Maybe he won't wake up until they're gone. Somebody probably heard us yellin' and stuff."

There was knocking at the door. The listeners heard Vickie enter the room, obviously upset: *"Where's Johnny?"*

Either Brick or Verdi, the listeners couldn't tell, responded: *"He went home."*

"You're lying because Johnny's pick up is still on the parking lot." She demanded to know where he was because she needed them to leave: *"We have a lot of guests in the hotel tonight and I don't want any more trouble."*

"Oh, you do, do ya?"

"I know who you are and I know Johnny doesn't like doing business with you. I don't approve either," Vickie demanded.

"Oh, you do know me, do ya," Johnson's voice was threatening.

Chris, Benny, Steve, Dickie and Juan were all amazed by what Vickie did next, a surprise that had not come out in depositions or at the trial. She said in a tough tone: *"Okay, start steppin' gentlemen. Step, step, step before I shoot your balls off."* She had pulled a gun.

They heard Johnson laugh and say: *"You stupid broad. What ya gonna do with that?"* The others laughed.

The four listening to the recording heard a fist hit flesh.

Vickie yelled, *"Ouch,"* and then Johnson's voice trailed off after apparently hitting her hard, *"Give me that."*

"That hurt. You coulda broken my wrist," she cried, as Johnson or someone had relieved Vickie of the pistol.

The listeners could hear the gun slide on the wooden floor and tap against something, likely a table leg.

"Leave it, men. Leave the gun right where it is. She's not going to hurt anybody, shoot anybody's balls off." They all laughed, cracking several sexual jokes at her expense, with Brick inviting her: *"How 'bout a little horizontal dance on Johnny's table?"*

Johnson told Brick to behave: *"Hey, show some respect, would ya? Mrs. Martin, we were trying to reason with your husband about some money. And he said he needed some time. He went off with some people. I'm sure he will be back soon with a proposal to compromise. Meanwhile, maybe we can come to an understanding before he returns. You say you know about us?"*

"You didn't have to hit me."

"Ma'am, yes, I did. Sorry. You pointed a gun at me, remember? I AM sorry. Please sit down. Let's have a drink. We have a bar in this room. Johnny said for us to help ourselves. Perhaps we can do business too if you are a partner and his wife." His tone was threatening, though his words were friendly.

Chris pictured Frank Nitti again.

She said, *"Sure, a drink. Okay. I'll wait for Johnny."*

Later, Vickie would say to Johnson and the others that she was scared for Johnny.

Steve said her play for a drink was gutsy, "I think she was playing along for her personal safety at that point, while hoping Johnny would return soon. Maybe she'd have that drink, wait for Johnny, make sure Dickie didn't come back and maybe figure out what she could do to solve their impasse on the money Johnson mentioned." It was a lot for Steve to presume.

The Inquirer group listened for five, painfully long minutes of what seemed to be meaningless conversation between Johnson and a cautious Vickie Martin, seemingly playing along. Then, not a word was heard from Vickie, just mumbling among the three men.

Dickie offered, "Maybe I can explain. Vickie has told me that she woke up on the floor in that room, with security shaking her and those guys gone about midnight."

"Rohypnol," whispered Steve.

"What? What's dat," asked Garcia.

"The date rape drug," said Dickie. "Puts the mind into outer space within minutes. Some sensations stay awake. Steve, do you think they..."

"Don't know, Dickie," Steve answered.

Dickie stared back. Filled with compassion, Steve had referred to him as Dickie for the first time ever.

Finally, they heard Johnson again, the recorder was still playing: *"Don't even think about touching this woman, Brick. She's going to be our killer. Let's get Martin out of here. Go get Slim."*

"What for? Slim's just watching the car outside."

"We need his help moving Martin. As I said, if Martin dies, she can be our killer. If not, he is not dead, just passed out, maybe he will be dead soon. In any case, see if he is reviving. Get Johnny Martin out of here. Do as I say, go get Slim to help."

Vickie did not talk again, nor did anyone mention her on the recording again. The recording came to the stop at the end of the digital file folder in the machine.

Dickie asked, "But how did they get Martin's body to the tower in his pickup without being seen?"

Steve said, "Well, we don't know that. But we do have enough to get Vickie Martin off, Dickie." He smiled at Randim.

Steve said assembling at the hotel gave them "all the color and feel of the events, how it happened that night. He said, "This is more than enough for Chris's story. Here, Benny, let's make a copy of this recording. After running our story tomorrow, take the recorder to the cops." Steve looked to Chris who was giving him a knowing, gratified look, thinking,

His story, YES, Chris mulled over.

Steve recaptured his attention, "Chris, make some calls to try to confirm the people on the tape, get Vickie's take on it.

“And, Dickie, I want you to make a personal visit to your girlfriend. Do not use a cell phone of your own to talk with her, but have her talk with Chris on my cell phone for quotes. Here.” Steve handed Dickie his cell phone. “I’ll depend on Benny to get any of my calls. Benny and I are going to be joined at the hip for the next few days.”

“So, what else is new, boss?” Bradley said sarcastically, with an appreciative smile.

Steve continued, “Chris, write your draft, revise it after we see the police to tell them we are going to publish. When they arrest Johnson, I hope they do, we’ll publish the story only then, okay? Sorry for all the trouble you’ve seen. Don’t do anything like this again, or you are fired, here?”

“Thanks. But, I’m not out of the woods. Johnson will want my ass dead.”

“Pack your things and stay with me a while in D.C.,” Steve said.

Chris declined the invitation but thanked him nevertheless. He had another hiding place in mind to sleep. “May I borrow your cell phone a minute, Benny?” he asked (still could not afford his own) and took it into another room.

* * *

Liza returned Chris’s call to his number at the paper while he was en route to the Inquirer.

His heart skipped a beat when he settled in at his desk, seeing the phone in-coming message light on at his desk phone with a message. He exhaled when he heard Liza’s voice.

“I can’t wait to see you with all the news, stupid you.”

Chapter 66: Nailed

As soon as the sheriff was briefed on Monday by Steve Mothershart and Chris Gilley, and listened to the recording, he thanked them for coming. He then called the "G-men," a phrase he loved to use for the FBI. The federal boys gave the sheriff their okay to arrest Johnson, Brick Wall, Harrison Verdi, and another Johnson employee named Tom "Slimboy" Hope, or as the boys at the Largo firehouse called the skinny kid, "Slim Hope."

Lender Arrested for Martin Murder; "Peeps" Released
Boss Recorded His Own Demise
by Christopher Gilley, staff reporter

LOWEVILLE, Md., September 7—Two days after sentencing for the murder of husband John Martin was postponed, Victoria Martin has been released on surveillance. Police have now linked new evidence of the same murder to suspects Sam Johnson, CEO of Lifetime Deal Financing, Corp. (LDF), and three co-conspirators.

In the latest in many bizarre twists in the Martin murder case, police have obtained a digital recording that Mr. Martin scheduled a meeting at Johnson's request to settle a long-running dispute between the two men.

A confession by LDF employee Thomas Hope has also shifted the case. Hope admitted helping Johnson and two other LDF employees remove Martin's body in a hotel laundry cart the night of a meeting at the Radisson Hotel on May 12, the last time any friends or acquaintances saw Martin alive.

Although Mrs. Martin was convicted by jury trial of John Martin's murder on Aug. 30, she is still on the hotel payroll as a concierge, where she is known as Peeps, a childhood name from her maiden name, Victoria Peoples.

"I never thought Vickie did it. No one at my hotel did," said Radisson Hotel manager James Strait, who once hired Mrs. Martin on John Martin's recommendation.

In Mrs. Martin's trial, her .22 caliber pistol with her fingerprints was identified as the murder weapon. Also, witnesses placed her at the murder scene and described violent quarrels that night between the defendant and her husband.

King County Sheriff Barney Standard is now convinced, however, of Johnson's guilt, he said.

Just before arraignment today, Thomas Hope told the Inquirer, "When we took Mr. Martin out of the hotel, Sam told us about framing Vickie Martin with the murder."

Hope said Johnson left Hope in the hotel lobby and parking lot while Johnson and two other LDF employees met with Martin. Hope said Johnson later called for him on his cell phone. "He said there had been an accident and he needed my help. They stopped me in the hallway and said 'we need you to find a laundry cart in housekeeping. It was late he said and we could take one. I didn't ask why, so I did find one."

The Inquirer managed only a few minutes to interview Hope at the Loweville Police Barracks before he was locked up. Attorneys then advised Johnson and the other two men, as well as Hope, not to comment further.

Meanwhile, Mrs. Martin spoke from her home in College Park, "As I've said all along, I'm greatly disturbed by the death of our little girl's father and even though Johnny and I found that we could not bear to live together anymore as a couple, we were good parents. He didn't deserve to be hurt in any way. It is tragic."

She refused to comment on Johnson and his arrest. Mr. Martin, known in the trade as Johnny 'Boss' Martin, had been acquainted with Mr. Johnson for years, dating back to George Washington University Law School, where Martin earned a law degree.

Sam Johnson's real name is James Samuel "Pinky" White. He changed it in 1980 to honor Andrew Johnson, president of the Confederacy after he served five and a half years in the U.S. Army before he was dishonorably discharged. Pinky was a childhood nickname.

Chapter 67: Chris, Who Did It?

May 2008

By coincidence, the Johnson murder trial began on Monday the 12th of May, exactly one year after he and his thugs met with Johnny "Boss" Martin at the Radisson Hotel.

Chris covered it.

On the final day of the trial, May 14 at 4:35 p.m., he sat on the courthouse steps in Loweville with his laptop to file his story via email, as he did the previous May 14. His nightmarish first venture into investigative reporting was a closed chapter, as he looked forward. As would be expected by his editors and friends at the paper, Chris just focused on the current story, completed it efficiently, and hit 'send' from email to his editor with no thought of last year.

Benny wrote back before Chris closed the laptop, ordering him to report to the Inquirer's editorial board room the "second you get here." Chris asked why, waited 10 minutes, and with no reply motored back in his old sputtering Mazda. Some things just don't seem to change in his line of work.

Back at the paper, Chris entered the board room cautiously with Benny's words "the second you get here" ringing in his head. The modest size room was swelling with his colleagues.

Everyone applauded. A few cheered as he entered the room.

All the principal "investigators" on the big story, besides Chris, were standing in the back—Benny, Steve, Lloyd, Trichina, Fayme, even Michele. Melissa's gang was seated along the table as well as special guests, ex-reporters Liza and Dickie. Most of the staff, editorial and advertising alike, wanted to attend to learn more about the crime story of the century for the Inquirer. Everyone knew such an investigation would not likely happen there again in another 100 years. The room was to hold only 12, according to the fire marshal. That day there were 27 squeezed in, standing room only.

They were all there, at Michele's calling, to hear what Chris learned at the trial.

Steve, standing proudly, arms folded in the far corner, said, "Okay, Chris, let's have it. Spill your guts, man. How did they do it? Magic? The old saw-Boss-Martin-in-half trick" Or what?"

This was typical. Steve began the usually serious meetings in that room with a welcomed light dose of humor.

Chris, from the end of the table, standing where everyone could see and hear him, began, "It's a doozy, folks. You couldn't make this stuff up. First, all three accomplices tried to cop a plea, tried to rat on their boss. It was a circus. A transparent circus of snitchers and clowns, in my opinion.

"Only Slim Hope, 'Slimboy' that is, got a decent plea bargain. He told the whole story to the police, as you may know, and then in court, corroborated later by the Sheriff. Johnson's principle strong arms, Brick and Verdi, testified separately, that is, each with the other out of the room, and confirmed the key facts too.

"Here goes: On the night of the meeting at the Radisson with Martin, Johnson and his colleagues saw Johnny fall unconscious by hitting his head on a piece of furniture, or even by Johnson's glancing blow to Martin's face. I think that is the thud we heard on the digital recorder.

"So, after they drugged Vickie Martin—I think you all heard about the date rape pill in the drink— Slim found a big, rolling laundry cart he had removed from the sub-basement and made his way to the service elevator. They dumped Martin into the cart, covered him with towels and left with Victoria Martin's gun wrapped in a handkerchief with her fingerprints on it. She was there with it earlier pointing it at Johnson who wrestled it away. I think most of you also knew that.

"They had Martin's truck keys which they found in his pocket. It was a perfect frame of Vickie."

Dickie groaned sighing, drawing several glances his way.

Chris continued, "Brick and Verdi put Martin in the back of his pickup truck, covered with a heavy canvas sail, and drove to the woods, far behind Perrywood Elementary School. Hope said he saw them pull Martin, still unconscious, from under a canvas cover, drag him to an old tree where they propped up the body and plugged him with two bullets from his ex's gun. Slim could not tell in the darkness which man pulled the trigger of Vickie's gun. Maybe both because there were a few seconds between the shots. It was held with a handkerchief as they plugged Martin in the eye and chest. The bullet missed the heart.

"Slim drove Johnson's car and he and Sam followed the others in Johnny's pickup to a warehouse behind the Largo Volunteer Fire House where Slim thought Johnson's group kept hidden explosives. It was Johnson's history you might know to play with bombs. Hope let them into the warehouse with a key from the firehouse. Johnson was a supporter of the fire department."

Chris paused and took in the crowd, "Ever wonder how the Largo Fire Department got to the Loweville explosions at the FUC&M tower before any other officials? The answer is simple: Slim Hope told me. He is a lifer with that fire department.

"Johnson, Hope said, paid two men every month at the firehouse to watch over his special warehouse on Route 20.

"That night they loaded Martin's pickup with explosives from the warehouse after shooting Johnny. They sent Hope back to the Radisson with Vickie's gun in an old rag, which he threw into the dumpster there. That was the end of Slim Hope's involvement, he claims.

"Martin's keys got Johnson's men into the FUC&M tower basement garage. They laid him on the seat and set a timer for the bombs to go off at twelve o'clock, Verdi testified.

"Johnson's plan was to blow up Martin's office just above his garage parking space, with all his records. Martin reportedly held the files on hundreds of lawsuits against Johnson, according to a mole Johnson had working there. Can't tell you who that was. Do you know, Dickie?"

Dickie coughed, and said "No," with a smirk.

"Where'd they get all the explosives, Chris? Tell them," Benny insisted.

Chris said, "From his days as an Army ordnance officer, Johnson and his cronies conspired to steal them. They would slip explosives away from Fort Meade under papers that were falsified by an insider at the Army base, likely one of Brick's cronies."

Michele was not convinced. "Bombs stolen from the Army caused Martin's dream building to crumble to the ground? Just dynamite? They must have had a lot more than a few sticks in a pickup truck to do such a job, Chris," she pressed.

"You are right as usual, Michele," Chris said carefully, still intimidated by the by-the-book managing editor. "Stick with me," he continued, eyes fixed on Michele, the smartest of a roomful of skeptics. "Here's how Michele. When they parked the truck with Martin's body and the dynamite, they didn't realize that Martin's parking space where they put it was right next to the main propane tank outside and that the gas lines came into the garage over that parking space and connected right up, throughout the entire tower.

"Even Johnson's boys testified that they were all amazed that the entire building collapsed. It was not their intention, evidently, though Johnson did not admit to anything. He sat with a sadistic smile throughout the day. He did say under oath—not that that mattered for him—that it was Martin's fault for the whole building blowing up because of its shoddy construction.

"Johnson was some piece of scumbag work. The prosecution revealed that Johnson's acts against blacks also included paying minors to use some of his explosives to bomb unoccupied new and as-yet unoccupied houses located near black families. It worked to discourage black contractors from working on the houses used as models in Southern Maryland.

"He had accumulated an arsenal of highly explosive devices by May 2007. He was an out of control, freaky bigot from hell. Really more than the throwback racist, we thought. He was insane.

"The trial revealed the weak link in Johnson's plan and the utter stupidity of his co-conspirators. Verdi admitted that Johnson asked his men in the early hours of Sunday morning to rig the timing of the explosives at the FUC'M garage on Johnny's pickup truck to blast away at 12 o'clock midnight Sunday. No one would be in the building, theoretically. In their haste and maybe in fear of being seen, or even lack of illumination, the men mistakenly set the timer on the bomb to go off at 12 p.m. instead of 12 a.m., Verdi said."

He heard Michele say quietly, "Oh my God," as her eyes flared open wide.

Chris said, "We all know, the explosions occurred at noon on Monday, 12 p.m. instead of Sunday night, slash Monday morning, at 12 a.m. Can you imagine such a mistake? I can because I've been watching these guys.

"That's how the firetrucks arrived so soon. I think Slim Hope had the Largo fire truck boys on their way just before midnight Sunday because he expected the bomb to be set and explode at midnight. Hope said, 'It was to look like Martin's murder.' Then, when it didn't go off, they hung around waiting for the call for an explosion after midnight, he testified. They must have waited all night, maybe they hid behind a school, office complex, or even at the Loweville Courthouse. Who knows, just my guess. They were seen at 5:00 a.m. at Pickin's Truck Stop, five miles from Loweville having breakfast, three fire trucks parked there, right in plain sight. Stupid, huh?

"And then, the next day just after noon they were there first at the bombing having waited nearby all morning. I saw them. Didn't you Dickie?"

"Not sure," said Dickie, scratching his short blonde head of hair.

"And no one could explain why until now," Chris said.

Chris shifted gears and continued at a faster pace, excited to share:

"The FBI was already onto Johnson, tipped off by vengeful King's County residents, even before Martin was found dead. Or maybe by Madinoff, right Dickie?

"That's why Vickie's trial was expedited, to get to the bigger case, in the FBI's minds, the federal civil rights violations by Johnson and possibly Madinoff.

"Yes, Johnson and his boys were as surprised as anyone that the entire building collapsed. Johnson's security man and co-conspirator Brick "Face" Wall said they all had a good laugh over it because Martin had a reputation of shoddy construction practices. Pathetic? You bet." Chris leaned back against the wall and folded his arms to get the reactions of his colleagues, some of whom made their shock evident in their faces, jaws down, eyes flaring or scratching their heads. Chris enjoyed seeing them wondering.

Steve took control of the meeting, directing discussion to looming deadlines on Thursday. "Benny, Friday's paper should be a special edition covering the legend of the First Union Credit & Mortgage tower, sort of the rise and fall of the notorious Johnny 'Boss' Martin, a legend in his own mind, maybe."

Chuckling filled the room.

Steve continued, "Dickie, if it's okay with Michele, I'd like to have you come back on contract this week to help us nail down this story for the Friday edition. [Michele nodded her approval.] They're still not exactly pleased with you upstairs, so I can't hire you back. But your inside knowledge will be invaluable, I bet, especially for Chris's centerpiece on finalizing the murder and tower collapse details. We can pay you a daily rate if that is agreeable. [Steve didn't wait for Dickie to respond, but continued.] I also see a bio side story on Martin, and…."

Trichina Brown interrupted enthusiastically, "I think a piece on the King's County black community reaction to the arrest of Sam Johnson would fit," she suggested.

"You got it, Sheena," Steve said lifting a finger slightly off the table toward her.

Lloyd Sollem suggested that Fayme get reactions from other, perhaps more prominent or reputable builders than Martin and reactions from lenders to the shady practices of Martin, Johnson, and Madinoff. He'd work with her on it, Lloyd said because he knew most of the builders in the state. Steve nodded with ever so slightly raised eyebrows when Lloyd looked toward his favored Fayme.

Several other suggestions in quick, enthusiastic order were enough for the entire front page and business section of the newspaper. It was a sharp departure from the normally sluggish Tuesday story sessions at the Inquirer.

Steve Mothershart uncharacteristically stood up to adjourn the meeting, ignoring superiors Michele and Lloyd for the moment. Steve hated long meetings. "Well, ladies and gentlemen, this is indeed a special kind of day," he said. He was wound up, ready to gloat over their success, their plans for Friday's edition, and get to work.

But instead, Dickie jumped to his feet, too, to redirect attention from Steve to himself. "It's really special for me, Steve. I mean, this day, if I may?" said Dickie, now with his head of marvelous blond locks grown back some and shaking from side to side as he excitedly looked into all the faces present, "Today marks one and a half years since I met Vickie."

Not willing to relinquish the floor so easily, Steve sat down again and retorted, "Hey, Dickie, that hook up with Vickie nearly ended both you and Chris. Are you sure this is a good anniversary?" he asked. "And who celebrates a year and a half, anyway?"

"We do. And yes, sir. It did cost me my job at the Inquirer. I get that. No hard feelings by the way. But the amazing thing was that Vickie actually said yes." Dickie looked for reactions but everyone was silent, even Steve, who was too stunned to speak.

Dickie said he wanted to settle down. Without a peep from anyone, he continued as if they had agreed that his day was the better one, better than the paper's day. "Yes, that's right. Vickie and I are getting married. She said yes today. You all are invited to the wedding. "Chris? Best man?"

Chris shrugged his shoulders and half-heartedly offered an affirmative nod. "Well, okay. Why not?"

"Awesome, Chris," Dickie said, clapping his hands together as he sat down.

Chris, eager to cover himself if people noticed his repulsive shrug at Dickie's invitation, offered a compliment, "Dickie, let me say for everyone's sake, that your cooperation, although I'm sure, knowing you, was a real chore at first—turned out to be great. I think everyone appreciates what you did. And we appreciate that it was you who did it. Thank you, Dickie."

Applause all around.

Dickie blushed. "I don't think I could have kept being so damned selfish, you guys." He started to stand and stopped halfway. Instead, he leaned forward and put his hands open on the table facing Chris. "But, wait a minute. We got off track. Have we forgotten why we are here. It is for—who said it? —the rest of the story,' right?" Dickie asked, looking at Chris who had taken a seat.

"Paul Harvey," know-it-all Benny volunteered, conservative columnist, radio guy. Nevermind.

"Who?" asked young Trichina and Fayme, their response in unison.

"Forget it. Before your time," Benny snapped.

Dickie continued to stare at Chris and inquired, "Seriously, there is still something I don't understand, Chris. Something that might be important, which you left out."

"Yeah, what's that Dickie?" Chris said with a knowing, cocky smile.

Dickie stood upright and pleaded to Chris with palms up, "If they didn't kill Johnny in the tower bombing, and they didn't kill Johnny at the hotel with Vickie's gun, and we know Vickie didn't kill him, and, of course, I didn't kill him, then who did kill Johnny Martin?"

Chris smiled as he sat upright, paused for emphasis, "This is the craziest part," he began. "You all know by now that the coroner dug up Martin after the new evidence from our little digital recorder."

Steve and Dickie nodded, while Benny looked skyward, waving his hands up then brought them down flat on the table. He smiled proudly at his boy wonder and said, "Well? You're killing us, no pun inte … well, never mind. Say who, for God's sake. Who killed Martin?"

Chris paused again for emphasis, then smiled broadly and answered, "He was probably dead of stress, most likely, before he hit the floor," Chris said, "when Johnson tried to punch him. Even that was probably a glancing punch said the coroner examiner. There was no bruise on Johnny's face at all. We heard him fall, which was the effect of his heart attack, I think, from the recording we listened to when we were assembled at the hotel. It must have been when he grew angry and lunged at Johnson. Remember? We all heard him gasp and mutter, 'Oh God, ah' It seems that the events that day and evening were just too much for even tough Boss Martin's heart to bear.

"So, Dickie, Benny, friends and esteemed colleagues, the answer to who killed Johnny 'Boss' Martin is …. Drum roll if you please? [He paused again and smiled.] The answer is no one. No one killed Johnny 'Boss' Martin.

"The coroner now says Martin died instantly when his heart literally exploded—a massive heart attack."

Chapter 68: Quiet Riot

Legal and penal systems are not adequate sometimes to tie crimes neatly to proper punishment. But then again, human nature may offer poetic justice when least expected.

* * *

Nov. 11, 2008, Veteran's Day
Kingston Federal Penitentiary, central Florida.

Pinky took a long drag on his Marlboro. He was leaning against one of four mildew-stained gray walls of the penitentiary's recreation yard. His tall frame, clothed in prison blue, blended in with the sea of identical prison uniforms dispersed in small groups across the expansive yard of clay. There was no grass. The only green life not yet trampled were scrawny weeds in crevices around the bases of the 20-foot stone gray walls.

The groups of inmates were engaged in mundane conversation, but always more alive and more active than the guards would prefer.

On that overcast and humid November afternoon, the heat was unbearable, even in the shade. The humid air was laden with dust scuffled up from heavy boots.

James Samuel "Pinky" White Johnson, though, was more than willing to stand the blazing sun. In King's County, he had been convicted only of manslaughter in the death of the handful of immigrant janitors who died in the FUC&M office tower, some 934 miles to the north, and for complicity in the destruction of public property. No murder rap.

It was the latest in a string of consecutive humid days, but Johnson was still his old cocky self. He was again called Pinky, his boyhood moniker, inside the prison walls to knowing inmates, those who read the northern papers about Samuel Johnson, aka, Samuel "Pinky" White. He was teased for a short while, then embraced it as an honor and leery inmates backed off.

In prison, people seem to know everything. Inmates can be persuaded to tell what they know. Pinky's story of his bizarre crime was known all over the penitentiary, and Pinky captured his share of admirers. He even had the audacity to brag to the whites that he'd killed "that no-good bastard" Johnny Martin, fucked Martin's gorgeous wife, and gotten away with it.

Though he'd done neither, the story had legs among angry men desperate for excitement.

On that sweltering day, the compound was especially vibrant with activity—inmates dealing cigs for sniffs and pops of limited drugs from the guards, or sex with hot, young male inmates controlled by the gangs.

Most of the inmates were lifers. At Kingston, each of the convicts, the real convicts, and the inmates serving shorter sentences for lighter raps, had something going on, even if it was just hanging with their own gang.

Pinky had a game too.

He took another long drag and sneered as he watched six brothers playing a high-altitude game of full court hoops at high speed on the blacktop court, despite the Florida heat and humidity. Their bare black backs glistening with sweat as they talked trash and laughed, mocking and threatening each other on every other play.

Pinky also noticed one smaller black inmate he'd not seen before, hanging out just off the court. The smaller black's chore that day appeared to be to retrieve the ball when it bounced off the 'court' and to bring cups of water to thirsty players from a galvanized bucket shielded from the sun with plywood. The young man looked familiar to Pinky while he silently cursed looking at the small man's milk chocolate skin tone. He wasn't as black as the others. But Pinky's pall of hatred prevented him from placing where he'd seen the young man previously.

Of course, no one in that place yet knew the depths of Pinky's racial hatred.

Blacks there were strangers to Pinky. He made a habit of avoiding personal contact with them even in prison.

He watched the basketball game in disbelief, *Them dumb niggah sons a bitches actually enjoyin' themselves in this hell,* he thought, shaking his head while he crushed the Marlboro butt against the concrete.

Why the small black man was sporting a tattoo of Jesus on his forearm, Pinky wondered. Pinky resented him for it. He watched as the smaller, lighter-skinned inmate with the Jesus tattoo retrieved the ball again and again. *That boy don't know nothin' about Jesus. Bet just a cover, keep from getting beat up.*

But, of course, Pinky White couldn't be too bothered. He had better things to do. He was playing his own game.

* * *

Several months earlier, when the correction officers brought him into Kingston, Pinky was not his buoyant, confident self. He was entering a maximum-security prison, with an 80 percent black inmate population. Parole was not possible for 10 years.

Mostly it was the humiliation of having been caught that bothered Pinky, paying a price for his sins for the first time in his 63 years.

But his attitude began to change when the institution assigned a little balding white fellow as his cellmate.

Figures. They give me a spic, Pinky thought. The upside for Pinky was that the little Latino man was someone he could manipulate. For a while, he did. The little man disliked his big, nasty cellmate, but was a good actor. He kept himself safe in prison by helping Pinky learn which men were in prison for the long term, which men were about to be released, and which men were the most dangerous convicts who were not in solitary confinement.

Pinky also discovered that most of the highly ranked guards were "good ol' white boys," as he referred to them.

And in time, Sam "Pinky" White (Johnson) adjusted to life behind bars. In a place like Kingston, a man quickly finds out what one most misses. For Pinky, he missed the rush of the deal, the deceit, the vengeance he measured on minorities in the cesspool of his career lending money on unfair terms.

After a time in prison, Pinky managed to get his fair share of visitors—mostly they were his real estate and mortgage cronies.

Pinky had thought his dealings were done for good when he got to prison. But he was still clever. It took him no time at all to find out that in Florida at the bedrock depths of the housing decline, there still were plenty of cheap homes and plenty of guys out there -- families of inmates -- eager to get suckered into home loans. And, prisoner Pinky still had some scratch. Samuel Pinky Johnson had opened a Swiss account just before his desperate meeting with Johnny Martin at the Radisson, just in case something went wrong with the threats and ultimatums he planned to dish out.

In Florida, some of Pinky's buddies, who weren't involved in the Martin crimes, set up businesses in the town near the prison. He even befriended the owner of a small bank, who was impressed with the hefty accounts Pinky's men deposited there, money from Pinky's European stash.

It didn't take long for Pinky to hatch new schemes using guards and visitors alike through his fast-growing little bank in the suburbs. Obscure realtors attached to Pinky's new outfit like deer ticks on campers in the woods.

While thugs and rapists in the compound dealt in homemade drugs from ordinary cleansers and stolen meds from the infirmary, or sex with new, 'young bitches,' Pinky and his Floridian gang were busy setting up a real scam. They gave unfair terms on shantytown shacks for the wives, mothers, and girlfriends of inmates who were awaiting release, short timers identified by Pinky's scared little cellmate.

He found houses for family members of the short timers, while giving a generous cut for a cooperative correctional officer who smuggled paperwork to Pinky, and transited checks from unsuspecting wives and mothers to Pinky's secret accountant at the little bank-that-could in town.

By the time a family would get wise to Pinky's unfair terms for a dumpy house, their loved one was released from Kingston and unable to hurt Pinky. It was a smooth and perfect scheme.

* * *

All was working perfectly for Pinky and his outside associates, until that sweltering day in the yard when Pinky was leaning on the prison wall watching and leering at the black inmates on the basketball court.

That day would always be known as the day of the quiet riot.

He thought no one was watching when he left his secure spot against the prison wall and swaggered past the medical building toward the nearby admin building, which also happened to be considerably closer to the blacktop basketball court.

He couldn't help but admire four bulked-up white inmates, one holding a second basketball while standing at the edge of the court closest to him.

They were staring down the black players. Pinky was intrigued.

At first, the brothers played on and ignored the whites. Then the whites began taunting the black players, threatening to break into their game. They wanted to play too. They accused the blacks of hogging the court too long.

For a moment, caught up in watching. Pinky forgot what he was supposed to be doing. He'd lost concentration on his deal.

His deal that day was to walk to his usual drop point near where he was standing and wait for his dirty guard and a possible message from his clandestine financing gang. He was enjoying the racial tension building on the court and the possibilities of a scrape between the two groups of players. *This is gonna be good,* he thought.

But business was business. He tried to regain focus. He waited for his drop, a home contract smuggled in by the dirty guard. Pinky had bought him off weeks ago.

Pinky caught himself laughing as the players hurled obscenities. He stepped back into an alcove to avoid attention. He was then hidden from everyone except the one guard who stood atop the tower at the far end of the compound. He was otherwise shielded by a 12-foot high stone wall and a chain-link fence that separated the infirmary from the admin building and the warden's third floor office. Its lone window protected the warden from the ugliness of the prison, and instead offered him a scenic view over Suwannee River and the idyllic sunsets to the west, where he enjoyed his evening cocktail every day.

Pinky waited in the alcove, the drop point, and enjoyed a brief moment in the shade. He felt a merciful stiff breeze cut across the yard.

He spotted his man.

The pasty, white face of his bagman, Officer Dan Guiltiason, approached on his regular rounds of the compound. He signaled Pinky. "Good afternoon, Sam. Lovely day, ain't it?" A sinister grin showed beneath his mirrored shades, which hung crookedly from his wide ears. The guard acted the part of a mean Southern boss man. He wore an undersized and unstarched brown shirt that clung to his middle, the buttons turned sideways ready to pop off from the stretched shirt pulling on them.

"It certainly is, Dan. Are you fine today?" he asked. It was another signal.

"Yes, I am fine today," said the guard, confirming that he had on him a contract signed by the wife of a soon-to-be-released con. The document stuck to his bare chest by a sweaty prison shirt. "And Sam?"

"Yes."

"Those books you wanted through the prison library exchange are in. I'll set them out for you. Come by before chow, but you better hurry. There's a big storm coming in and you don't want to get those books wet."

Whenever Pinky's outside men scored a contract from an unsuspecting family member, the corrections officer picked it up at the little bank wearing civilian clothes. He'd notify Pinky after leaving the paperwork for him to sign in a pre-designated book on the prison library bookshelves. Pinky used lesser experienced guards who worked long hours for low pay and were easily bought off.

As Officer Dan turned to leave, he reached out for a handshake. Pinky palmed $200 into the overweight officer's hot, sweaty hand. The exchange, though, was difficult. Pinky nearly dropped the cash as a basketball flew in between the two men. It was the white players' ball that had been kicked away from the court by the biggest of the black players.

The guard walked away calmly with his reward.

"Get cher motha fuckin asses outta here," the big sweaty black man yelled to the white players, far louder than necessary, it seemed to Pinky, who was again distracted by the small black man with the Jesus tattoo.

"You Mr. Johnson, right?" The small man asked as he retrieved the ball.

How the hell does this niggah know my name, Pinky thought. "Yeah, that's right. I'm Mr. Johnson. What of it? I don't know you."

"Everybody know your name, Mr. Samuel Johnson," he laughed.

"You best get back to the game before they kill each other," Pinky, shaken a bit, ordered the young man to get away from him.

The small man tossed the ball back and sprinted to the game again.

By now, the black and white players were shoving each other on the court for territorial rights. The fight drew a commotion across the yard as more whites and blacks took sides and pounded on each other.

Pinky, watching the melee, let his guard down for a second. He didn't see three thick, bruising black inmates slipping along the wall toward him, as if undercover by the high volume of shouts and screams.

When the three reached the small alcove, they blocked in Pinky. Their faces wore menacing expressions, their shaved heads slick with perspiration. All three big men were sleeve-tattooed from neck to hands.

Suddenly, without warning, a flash of lightning filled the yard along with an explosive crack of thunder.

The men filling the yard cheered. Then, they resumed fighting with more intensity.

The three bruisers closed in on Pinky.

"You remember da heat, don't cha cracker boy?" said the biggest one to Pinky. He had only one arm, which was covered by tattoos. His left arm was missing. And his right arm, the size of an average man's thigh, displayed the word "Nam" across an American flag on his forearm. The three, in their late 50's, hung with the prison gang known and appreciated unanimously as "The Boyz," black Vietnam War veterans, a network of black vets in U.S. prisons.

Stunned, Pinky replied, "What? Yes, hot, ah, yeah."

"Like the heat in 'Nam, right? Course, you do 'member the smell, cracker boy, dat stinkin' firefight smell? Boys dyin' next to ya? You 'member that, don't cha boy?"

Johnson froze. All three wore the identical 'Nam tattoo. Pinky's mind flashed back on scared black soldiers in sweaty fatigues. The soldiers in his memory image weren't in combat. Instead, they were on the U.S. Saigon base where he'd trucked in munitions from his ship dockside.

The one-arm man replied to Pinky, "Course not scum boy. Oh, I forgot. You were not fightin' gooks, cracker. Your in-country time be taken up trying to kill black boys, you own side black boys, mother fucker! That little boom-boom party you scum boys laid down on our rec house in 'Nam. I know you 'member that, boy." He stopped talking as the three stared at the now-petrified Pinky.

The one-armed man continued, "Yeah, dat's right. Last smell I 'membered in 'Nam was dynamite smell. Didn't know we just outside there, did ja? I gots a Purple Heart for this," he said as he clutched his stump. "You was fuckin wit us brothers. Mess us up pretty good."

The prison yard roared with sounds of violent fighting on and off the basketball court.

The two other bruisers closed in on Pinky, almost nose to nose. One said, "You wastin' time, Josh, do it."

One-armed Josh just stood his ground three feet from Pinky, eyeball to eyeball. "Nah, dis boy needs ta get somein' special. What's bin comin' to 'im long time. Yessah, long time comin.' We just couldn't believe they brought you in here scumbag, Mr. Samuel Whitey-boy Johnson. Seems just right, don't it boys."

"Ah huh."

"Ah huh."

"My posse and me gonna thank ya, Lt. White for our Purple Heart discharges. But ya know we didn't really want to leave 'Nam, fighting for our side, see. It was a better gig for us black folk than back in the hood, man. You be part of that too, I do believe.'"

Johnson finally spoke, "Look, I don't know what you fellas are talking about. Maybe you should back up before I get the guards. Do yourselves a favor," he said. He sounded as if the guards worked for him.

"Hey, boys, he want the guards," they laughed in unison, standing stock still. As the fight on the basketball court escalated between the whites and blacks, the three brutes boxed in Pinky like a clam in a shell.

Pinky couldn't find any guards if he wanted to. Officer Guiltiason was long gone. The only tower with a view of the medical corner was mysteriously empty. *Damn, they're changing guards*, Pinky thought. Oddly, only a few guards were on the compound, and they were standing by, letting the men fight it out … It was noisy, but sort of fake fighting almost, Pinky sensed, too late.

If only he could stall the three brutes. That would delay his beating, he thought. Guards would be back. Pinky had only one chance to escape harm. He had to get entangled in the race rioting. The pushing and shoving was getting closer and then was just behind the three men who were bent on kicking Pinky's ass.

"Hey," Pinky screamed as he pointed to the 'Nam tattoo on the man's arm on his right, left of the one-armed man. You guys are vets. Me, too," he said as if he hadn't been listening. "I think we can settle this peaceful like if we could just ..."

He made his move.

With all the strength he could muster, he threw his left fist past the one-armed man's good right arm, hitting him squarely on his jaw, knocking the big man back. Pinky kicked him hard in the groin. The one-armed man groaned as he bent over. Pinky grabbed his sweaty, shaven head and shoved it down, into the legs of another of the brutish inmates, who was reaching to grab Pinky.

Pinky could see his plan unfolding before him—an opening between the blockading attackers, only for a second. Pinky took a step towards the rioters and freed himself of the bruisers. He had escaped.

But meanwhile, another man ran straight at him. It was the water boy/man with the Jesus tattoo, holding a 6-inch blade hidden low to his side.

Pinky felt the sharp steel cut deep into his abdomen. Then another thrust. The third one seemed to puncture Pinky's abdomen quicker. In again, and again. The small man twisted the knife up toward Pinky's heart. As he gasped, Pinky fell, writhing in pain. One of the heavy thugs held him down as the so-called riot continued to camouflage the killing right in the prison yard. The rioting men, blacks and some whites surrounded the stabbed man.

"This is for Mr. Johnny Martin, you bastard. You gonna pay, you fuckin' murderer," said the attacker, gritting his teeth.

With the knife still deep in him, Pinky managed to grunt. "Same as you, niggah boy."

"No, not me. I don't give a flyin' fuck. Already killed two your men, Johnson. What they gonna do to me? Now, die you fuckin' bastard. This is for killin' Mr. Johnny Martin, and hurtin' Miss Vickie."

He disappeared into the commotion, leaving the knife stuck firmly atop Pinky's bloody torso, a bloody surgical glove still gripping a homemade wooden handle of the knife.

Across the east end of the yard, the chaos, which was later called a riot in the Gainesville media, dissipated as quickly as it began. It was as if someone fired a gun or rang a bell for 'all clear.' But there had been no such cease fire order. Action ceased instantaneously with Pinky's demise.

Prisoners marshaled themselves obediently into lines, two-deep, and paraded toward the admin building.

The heavens then opened with deafening rain and thunder. Lightning struck the razor wire atop the west prison wall with a loud, sizzling sound as wires split, dangling against wet stone.

A guard finally arrived at the north tower. He watched the inmates break into a run toward the admin gate and out of the storm, leaving just one man down. At the sound of the alarm, medics ran toward the injured man.

Inmate Samuel White, called Pinky in the big house, was dead.

The large pool of warm blood from his lifeless body stained the clay in the shape of a scorpion after he was dragged off. It remained there for too long, frightening some inmates. For more than a year, storms failed to wash away the scorpion. Inmates stayed clear of it.

The following spring, a thick clump of deadly nightshade, the highly poisonous cousin of the tomato plant, grew from the blood-stained clay. The large serrated leaves were lush and beautiful.

Inmates assigned to gardening staked the tall, dark green foliage, telling guards that tomato plants had sprouted from Pinky's blood.

That summer, as the first, telltale, pure white flower trumpets of the deadly nightshade bloomed, the plants disappeared, likely pulled up from the ground, dried and stored by another gang perhaps bent on rubbing out an adversary with its poison.

The only suspect in the killing was cleared by investigators for lack of evidence. That suspect was Jerome Jackson, the light-skinned African-American with the Jesus tattoo and who was said to be helping with the hoops game the day of the quiet riot.

The only possible motive that could be linked to the killing was that Jerome, who, like White, hailed from King's County, Md.

He was in jail for killing a drug dealer in a place called Charmington Village.

Federal investigators told the Kingston warden, as he sipped his evening brandy enjoying the Suwannee River sunset, that the murder weapon was clean of any prints.

"Damnedest thing, though, warden," said the chief investigator, though the warden was no longer listening after his second brandy, "the only identifying mark on the weapon, sir, was the word 'Knife' carved into the wooden handle."

#

After being fired from the Maryland Inquirer, **Richard "Dickie" Randim** collaborated with his bride Vickie Randim in restructuring Johnny Martin's JDR Builders, Inc. The new business strategy was building upscale designer office complexes. She renamed Johnny Martin's Jobs Done Right company to Just Dream Right, with the motto of 'Stylish and Sustainable.'

Years later, Gigi Martin, Mrs. Randim's 22-year-old daughter, became president and chief executive officer after getting her architecture degree.

Dickie Randim proved to be a public relations genius by promoting his construction company nationwide. He often mused about his playboy past, hawking up sexual cravings of attractive women, pleasing them, and stroking his male ego. He could still charm females for new accounts. But in Vicky, there was no better woman for Dickie to please. He stayed faithful. They had no additional children, for Mr. Randim was sterile.

Thomas "Slim" Hope, who turned state's evidence against his part-time, wealthy employer Samuel Johnson, served five years of a 12-year sentence as an accessory to attempted murder. He was not accused in the bombing of the First Union Credit & Mortgage tower because his companions corroborated his claim that he returned to the Largo Fire Hall while they transported Martin's dead body, in Martin's pick-up truck, to the tower.

Friends had said Slim Hope always had a nose for quick money. He but found contentment working at Airport Car Wash at Thurgood Marshall Baltimore-Washington International Airport. He is still a volunteer fireman, at the fire hall next to his favorite eatery, Bob's Dairy Queen, on Camp Meade Road in Linthicum, near BWI. He and his live-in girlfriend Barbara, an aviation engineer at Northrop Grumman, are raising their six children in the conservative Baltimore suburb.

Juan Garcia spent a decade trying to distance himself from his nickname 'Knife.' In fact, after a fishing trip in Florida with Dickie and Chris a few months after Samuel Johnson's trial, the unique knife with his signature, hand-carved name 'Knife,' was lost, he said. Each of the three had a different story to tell about how Knife lost his knife. Was it a fishing mishap? A snorkeling accident? Or, was it a gift to a friend?

Garcia studied hard for two years to finally complete a GED. Five years later, with financial assistance from Richard and Victoria Randim, he earned a business degree in transportation management from the Robert D. Smith School of Business at College Park Maryland. He manages JDR's Turnkey Office Systems, LLC, which set up business systems in buildings built and sold by the company.

At the insistence of her ex-boyfriend, **Amy Steinholder** became a regular at the Southern Maryland Alcoholics Anonymous where she met her husband, brain surgeon Brandies Tyson Dyson IV. After his patient, Sheriff Barney Standard died when the surgeon botched removal of a small tumor, at the Sea Vista Hospital in Prince Frederick, Dr. Dyson retired at age 37 and became a prominent historian of the region with his best seller on his ancestors, *The Day Dyson Met Tyson, a St. Clements Love Story*. Steinholder and the surgeon now live over a seafood raw bar they own and operate on the first floor of their dockside home in the resort town of Solomon's Island.

Knife Garcia's best friend, **Jerome Jackson,** was paroled from Kingston Penitentiary in Florida after serving 12 years of a life sentence for killing a drug dealer, who in truth, had tried to kill him and take over his neighborhood of foreclosed houses in Charmington Village.

It was also a secret well kept by Garcia and Randim that Jackson, armed with a long-range telescopic rifle, also shot and killed both Brick Wall and Harrison Verdi, as the two were escorted by armed guards out of the Loweville Courthouse. The rifle slugs were found in a mountain of rubble from the destroyed FUC&M Tower. It was rumored that Jackson escaped capture by running through creek beds to his car that was parked next to a church on Route 20, where he zipped to the D.C. Beltway and bought a round of beers to celebrate at the Congressional Lounge at the Radisson Hotel in Largo. That part of the rumor has been corroborated by witnesses at the Lounge that day.

Christopher Gilley, now in his 30's, can be found in his office morning, noon and evenings at the new streamlined offices of the Baltimore Star-Herald. He enjoys a career there as a highly successful reporter and editor, secured after his Pulitzer Prize winning series exposing the insider methods used by the nation's 10 least-known predatory lenders to target and rip off minority home buyers. He no longer needs to watch Nick at Nite to escape from being a poor, lonely boy who once chased criminals.

Tribune Co. president Alex Chadwick flew into Baltimore on New Year's Eve from his office in Chicago to honor the astonishing transformation of the once proud, old Baltimore Star-Herald. Reporters, editors and management gathered in the newsroom for a modest late afternoon party. Chadwick, 74, told the gathering, "Before you all run out all over town to make damn fools of yourselves reveling in the new year, I want to propose a toast to the fifth year of the brilliant marketing strategic plan conceived by marketing director Liza Leah Gilley [huge applause], … and don't forget managed by the best executive editor on earth, our own Christopher Gilley.

"Thanks to Chris, we now have local news slants in editions of 22 neighborhood regions of the city, in addition to the best of the stories each week in our six statewide editions, each of those uniquely tailored for readership. It's a digital miracle. *And,* we're making money again!

Thanks to everyone, and especially to Chris and Liza Gilley. Happy New Year, everyone."

Liza stood up on a stool to get seen by the staff. She said, "Just a minute, Mr. Chadwick. Chris and I thought you'd be up to something like that." We brought our kids to set the record straight. This is a team effort."

She picked up 3-year-old Michele Gilley and stood her on a desk holding a notebook. Chris lifted their 4-year old son Esteban to stand with his little sister. The two read acknowledgments for everyone on the staff and each's contributions to the year's success. They read clearly and without mispronunciations--the latest Gilley kids in grandad Gilley's tradition of being literate at an early age.

Namesakes Michele LaProbe and Steve Mothershart in the back led the applause after the kids finished reading. She whispered, "Sky's the limit for those kids."

Steve whispered back, “Unless they take a joy ride in a Porsche convertible to see some building explode.”

Michele smiled and hugged him.

#

Author's Note

This story is set in fictional King's County, Maryland. The characters are fictional and any possible resemblance to living or deceased persons would be coincidental.

Made in the USA
Middletown, DE
12 October 2022

12504218R00208